AF483151

AMERICAN MUSE: STARLITE PULP NOVELLAS, VOL. 1

PULP DONE RIGHT.

FEATURING:

BRIAN TOWNSLEY ✦ ALEX SLUSAR ✦
JEAN-PAUL L. GARNIER ✦ MANNY TORRES

For information, contact : editor@starlitepulp.com
Site : www.starlitepulp.com
Instagram : @starlite_pulp
Youtube channel : youtube.com/@starlitepulp

Book and Cover design by Tristan and BT
Executive Editor : Brian Townsley
Associate Editor : Jake Naturman

ISBN: 979-8-218-50313-0

first edition: October 2024

PRAISE FOR AMERICAN MUSE :

"When I was a kid, I bought most of my books at flea markets, anthologies like *Alfred Hitchcock Presents...,* but sometimes I'd find a book that included two novels by the same author, a Signet Double Mystery. Treasures! In American Muse, Starlite Pulp has rekindled my early joy of reading fiction by marrying one of my favorite forms (the novella) with four vastly different, accomplished writers of genre fiction. Whether it's the soaring prose of Brian Townsley's *Days of Bone, Nights of Ash,* with passages that read like a virtuoso's guitar solo or the Elmore Leonard rope-a-dope prose of Manny Torres's *The Idiot Caper.* In Alex Slusar's *The Hot Streak,* a stranger comes to town in the form of an old cowboy movie star, while in Jean-Paul L. Garnier's *Black Trail Line,* it's man versus nature in an opening scene that'll make you want to stay safely indoors. Gripping, smart, and thrilling – these are the kinds of electrifying stories that made me fall in love with reading in the first place. Buy a copy. Hell, buy two."

-John McNally, author of *The Pinned Butterfly* (writing as Johnny Mack) *&*
The Book of Ralph

"A dark lens on the American dream, but be careful: these four propulsive, razor-sharp tales will cut to the bone. I couldn't stop reading, and now I want more."

-Daniel Pyne, author of *Twentynine Palms, Catalina Eddy & Vital Lies*

"Sentence by sentence, this is some of the best old-fashioned storytelling I've read in ages."

-Charles Ardai, author of *Death Comes Too Late,* Edgar *&* Shamus award winner, and editor for Hard Case Crime

"American Muse is a collection of new pulp fiction shot through with attitude and steeped in sweat~Americana past and present, through a glass darkly. In Brian Townsley's *Days of Bone, Nights of Ash*, he provides a fresh take on the old west with three eccentric noir heroes taken into the heart of darkness that beats under the wide, blue western sky, meting out justice with wry humor and deadly force. In Alex Slusar's *The Hot Streak,* we're handed A mid-century western noir that reeks of fear and stale cigarette smoke, where the road back to Hollywood is soaked in blood and strewn with poker chips.

In Jean-Paul L. Garnier's *Black Line Trail,* he delivers a grim survival story told in a unique voice that taps into rich veins of American literature, conjuring echoes of Bierce and Hemingway. And finally, Manny Torres brings us *The Idiot Caper,* A gritty and visceral tour through Atlanta's sprawling labyrinth of subterranean personae, where 'kill or be killed' trumps 'live and let live.'"

~Nevada McPherson, author of the Eucalyptus Lane novels *Poser, Cracker,* and *Baller*

"At a time where we seem to be witnessing the death-throes of our empire, where many are escaping into phones only to exasperate the march towards mediocrity, rest assured there will be pillars like Starlite Pulp to uphold and preserve the bygone style of storytelling that could have only happened—and still be happening—in this strange and desperate country. In *American Muse: Starlite Novellas Vol. 1*, Brian Townsley and Jean-Paul L. Garnier offer us two brutal, beautiful, and idiosyncratic tales of tested men versus the lawless desert, seething with existential pain and expired glory. From there, Alex Slusar picks up the pace, racing through the sands of the American southwest to gamble with the hazy tiers of Hollywood deception, until Manny Torres cuts a sharp right to Atlanta's timeless dead-end hustle, orchestrated by the calamity of addicts spitting whip-smart dialogue that would make Tarantino jump out his seat."

~Gabriel Hart, author of *On High at Red Tide*, and editor at *Beyond the Last Estate*

AMERICAN MUSE: STARLITE PULP NOVELLAS, VOL. 1

DAYS OF BONE, NIGHTS OF ASH

(PART 1)

BY BRIAN TOWNSLEY

"God is indeed dead. He died of self-horror when He saw the creature He had made in His own image."

-Irving Layton

1.

October, 1864

The nearly weeklong storm that brought with it rain and lightning and hurricane gusts has subsided and in its absence is birthed something both fortuitous and chaotic, some pinhole in the habit of normalcy. The boy stands against the dawn and looks for all the world to be made of mud. Neither of the fellow soldiers beside him stand to peer on the clear day, one that smells of moss and jasmine and feces. There is a hole now in the prison wall, a crack really, large enough for the boy to slip through, he reckons. He kicks each of the men beside him, both of whom are heavy now in death. He spits on each of them, for everything they have done to him these many months and everything they did not, though his mouth is dry and thus the action is more theoretical than actual. The old soldier in the corner, his beard matted like an island tribal shaman, looks at the boy without expression. The mudchild takes three quick steps and lunges to swipe the man's hat, a gray wide-brim, pinchfront hide that he slaps against the filthridden thigh of his woolen pants and smashes it atop his own dome. He puts his finger to his lips and locks eyes with the man, and all of the absence to be seen there.

He is not cuffed, has never been, any of them, and so slides his thin frame through the split wall tightly and into the night and is gone in an instant, wearing only the pair of muddy fatigue pants and the gray hat, and Asa becomes a part of the seamless dark and with it is lost from Tennessee and the misbegotten war there, forever.

2.

August, 1870: Abilene, Texas

Asa, now 20, leaned with his back to the bar and peered out at the happenings, an empty whiskey glass in his right hand. Crow sat next to him in silence, drunk again.

"Watch this here," Asa said, and heeled the tribesman's stool.

Crow raised his head, which seemed an effort, and looked to where the young man pointed. An argument was afoot at a gaming table in the parlor. There were four men seated and one now standing, drawing the attention in the saloon like a lightning rod. The outlier was shouting nearly indecipherable vulgarities in a Scotsman's English, clearly deep in his cups, and was pointing at one of the seated men in particular. His voice was deep and throaty and made the whole place small. The room itself and each within it seemed to inhale, as if some scene had been writ and none here contained within them the authority to challenge it.

The wild Scotsman continued his bellowing, turning a complete circle at one point, so encompassing his outrage at the cheat before him, or so the charges would indicate. Two of the men at the table slid their chairs in reverse to stand and back away from the moment. The two remaining men at the table stayed seated. The tables around them had begun to empty as well, men and women alike backing into whatever empty space had been afforded, whatever lostness could be found. The piano playing from the southern corner of the facility had gone quiet.

Asa fingered the handle of his Colt revolver in its holster but did not pull it, eyes focused on the ugly poetry before them. Crow looked on with bleary eyes and a smirk touched the corners of his lips. The bartender shouted something from behind them but it was lost in the moment, unheard by most and unheeded by all and the first shot came not from the man accused but the man who sat beside him, a deafening blast that missed the standing Scotsman entirely but took off the top half of the head of a whore behind him, vandalizing the wallpaper with a thousand splinters of crimson and brain matter and skull shards. She slid down the wall and then the wainscoating gracefully, her one remaining eye wide open as in expectation to the rest of the proceedings.

The Scotsman attempted to pull his gun but it caught on the edge of the leather holster and so his first shot went into the floor and the second man shot again into the wall this time and finally the accused himself shot and hit the Scotsman in the belly. The man doubled over and unleashed a barbaric cry of torment and finally cleared his own holster and fired back and the accused man took a bullet in the chest and his chin fell to his breastbone and then slammed on the table, dead as every corpse in every graveyard. The Scotsman went to a knee then, and shouted something unintelligible and tried to stand by using the gun barrel to push off but fell instead and lay on the floor, moaning. The smell of gunsmoke and an extended, living silence carried the next long moment.

The second man, seeming to add up the pieces of the scene—he had murdered a woman, his friend was dead, the Scotsman dying—stood and bolted for the door. Before he was halfway, a crowd had closed around him and his gun taken and he was carried from the saloon by a posse of men. He looked at Asa as he passed and his eyes held in them the panic of the hunted.

Asa and Crow walked down the steps and unhitched their horses and one other mare from the post and saddled up, riding the animals at a walk from town. As they did, Asa spoke:

"Now, did that man get anything he wanted? He felt cheated. Did he get the hand back? He did not. Did he get his money back? He *did not.* Did he get his respect back? Certainly not. Now nobody cares. Did he get his revenge? Well," Asa said, and spat a wad of tobacco juice into the mud. "I ask you, Crow, what good is a spot of revenge if ye ain't around to enjoy it? The accused man is dead and that Scotsman is dead and that other man is no doubt hanging from the rafters in the stables as we remove ourselves from this godforsaken township." He shook his head at the absurdity of it. Crow showed no sign of listening, but Asa knew better. "And all because the Scotsman couldn't keep control of his emotions—Scots are weak people in that regard, Crow, and best to remember it. They are always going on about some disrespect or outrage and it don't add up to nothing in the end but hurtful feelings and death."

"Aint you got some Scot in you?" Crow asked, grinning.

Asa smirked at that but otherwise ignored the comment and took a pull of the bottle of corn whiskey he had taken in the melee and handed it over to Crow. "And that is also why you must always put your drinks on a tab. When a shooting or ruckus or fire or somesuch misfortune arises, ye get out without paying whatever debt ye may have amassed." He smiled at this, and put his hand out to reach for the bottle in return.

Crow listened intently though he had heard most of it before. He let Asa whitesplain as he would, because Asa was a talker sometimes, but also because he was very good at it. And besides, Crow had little he wanted to express. Really, what was there to say in a world where men died over nothing at all?

A figure darted from the woods on their right and leapt silently atop the trailing third horse in a single motion as had been done hundreds of times previous.

"Mattie," Asa declared, and tipped his hat though he did not look in her direction. Crow turned and smiled widely at the girl in the dark, content to have the murder together again.

***

They rode west from Abilene and on the third day walked a muddy road into an assemblage of humble buildings with a sign posted that declared New Oslo in red paint coupled with a wooden cross taller than a man.

Asa halted his horse, whose name was Harrison, in the mud and his two companions did the same. He scrunched his eyes and forehead and looked about at the woodframe structures, some finished, many not, and all new enough to carry with them nary a scar of weather or season. There seemed nobody about.

"Big damn cross," Crow said.

Mattie snorted at this though neither man knew the meaning behind it. She wore black markings around her eyes and down the slope of her nose, with a fan of red mixed in, a mixture of grease and a clay from berries and other assorted sources, and a hat made of raccoon fur. Asa took her in, this wildling with curly chestnut hair cascading from the rim of her hat, as unkempt and unruly as the rest of her.

"Well," Asa said, in response to Crow, "at least they lettin' folks know where they stand," and chucked his horse, whose hooves were suctioned from the mud with a splat.

Asa and Crow sat the beasts while Mattie stood in the stirrups atop her own, leaning forward in the saddle and stretching her legs. They all watched a carriage battle through the muck slowly and then rattle to a stop two storefronts from them. A woman in a long black dress halted the two horses and stepped down from the bench seat. Asa did a doubletake and saw it was a woman indeed in a long black dress, but her head wore something that looked more akin to torture than fashion. It was a metal cage with horizontal bars, black in color, and fastened in the rear with a lock. Two more people stepped from the open carriage door, another young woman in a similar arrangement of severe dress and head gear, and finally a young girl, the only one whose head was uncaged. The little one looked furtively at the three of them, her gaze lingering for a moment on Mattie, then skipped forward and followed the other women quickly into a store. Asa looked and saw it to be a Mercantile and thus he and Crow walked that way and entered as well. Mattie stayed behind, content outside holding the reins.

The store was one that carried everything within it, from tallow and wax and ammunition to candy and dish sets. The shopkeeper was a long, thin, balding man, with cheeks that caved inwards and eyes that bore no welcome. The women had picked up a small package wrapped in paper and were paying as the two men entered. They shuttled past the men, none raising her eyes in consort, the small locks at their necks clinking upon their fastenings, and left as quickly as they had arrived. Asa saw that the cages had small spikes near the mouth area of each.

When he heard the doorbell chime behind him, Asa said to the shopkeep, "we'll take two pigtails of tobaccy and whatever jerky ye got."

The man nodded, seeming unable to keep his eyes off of Crow, who looked on at the accoutrements about him impassively.

"Big feller with you?" he asked, jutting his pointed chin in Crow's direction. He began reaching into a glass jar filled with tobacco knots.

"Why," Asa said, and smiled at the man, "yes, he is. The little wildling outside is with me as well. The holy trinity, as such."

At that, the man looked out the front window and saw the painted young lady atop a horse. He then looked at the three of them, disapproval etched like agony across his visage.

"So hey," Asa said, "what variation of slaughtered plains animal are ye offering up in jerky, and, the curiosity here is palpable, I'm afraid, *what in bible and sword* were those women wearing atop they heads?"

"You got a strange way of talking, and I don't like it," the shopkeep said, in a short, clipped tone.

Asa smiled at that. "Ye don't like the way I talk," Asa said, enunciating each syllable as he approached the counter, "but women walk amongst your town with cages upon they heads, and that's fit as a fiddle," he said, "is that about right? Have I got that?"

"Them women have displeased the father, so they git what they git." He pointed at Asa, who was now across the counter from him, "that's between man and wife and God, and aint none the wiser. But you folks, no, the likes of yall need to pass right on through. Father aint gonna be none too happy with the looks of you." There was a hand movement to this, and then, as an afterthought: "And it's buffalo. The jerky."

Asa plucked the twists and meat from the counter and pocketed them in his jacket, then looked at Crow and outside to Mattie, whose attention was somewhere down the main road. He nodded, slowly. "Yes, sir," he said, "buffalo it is. I do like me some buffalo." He smirked widely at the shopkeep. He dropped a coin on the counter—he had yet to ask a price—and turned to leave. Crow was before him and was holding the door open as Asa turned back and said, "as a God-fearing man myself, I am curious as to this 'father' in reference, one in the same as the Lord himself, as if He were here in this very town, this...*New Oslo*," he added with a flourish.

"Father is down at the church. Ask him," the man said, and looked down and busied himself with something unseen as if to will away this motley trio.

"The church," Asa said, grinning. "Aaaand that would be," he said, pointing in one direction, then the other.

The man nodded down the street in the direction Mattie was facing, never looking up.

"Ahhhh," Asa said, raising his voice, "and thus the truth is known, *and this is the thing you are to do to them to sanctify them for acting as priests to me*," his voice was a near shout by the end of it, and he pointed at the shopkeep and said, "Exodus 29:1 and we do thank ye," and he brought his hands together now as if in prayer, "for such kind stewardship, and may the heads of your family be put on pikes and their eye sockets sewn open to peer upon your deeds." Asa walked through the door and Crow let it close and the door chimed and the shopkeep stood in his place, unsure then or now of what had just occurred.

Asa and Crow mounted their horses and the three of them rode in the direction the man pointed. "Anybody know what day of the week it is?" Asa asked, when Crow had cut three pieces of the tobacco loose and each were stewing it in their gobs. Mattie spat forth a large brown lob of juice and shook her head. Crow looked forward, neither answering or acknowledging the question, working his jaws over. "Well, dangit," Asa finally said.

***

That evening the three of them camped about a mile from town, tending a small fire and eating hardtack and whatever edible meat they could find from a rabbit that Mattie and Crow had caught. Mattie kept the fur from the skinning, as was her wont, and none of them slept well, a common occurrence, and so one of them keeping watch was never an issue.

They rode back into New Oslo with the winter sun at near its apex and headed directly for the Church, which proved to be a mostly finished building near the western edge of town. A white picket fence outlined the property and it had space for a bell in the tower but none had been erected yet and so gave off the impression of an empty head.

The three of them hitched their horses and walked through the picketed gate and to the church steps in their normal order. Asa walked first with purpose, Crow and Mattie well behind and next to one another. The church doors were open and so they entered the place of worship without invitation or ceremony. It held several rows of wooden pews and a small stage with a lectern and a large, raw wooden cross hung against the back wall. There was still a portion of the back corner of the building unfinished, holding only support beams at present, and so one could walk from the stage to the corner and directly outside, onto the grass and mud to peer into the endless sky under the unmerciful and watchful eye of the almighty himself.

Asa saw the same girl from the day prior, her head still unadorned, who was readying something or other for the pews and she looked at him furtively and then at the two behind him, focusing again on Mattie.

"Well," the group heard before seeing from where it had come, "I see we have some visitors." It was a booming voice, a preacher's voice, as Asa recognized its type immediately. A tall man walked from a small side room near the front stage and held his hands out towards the visitors as a gesture of welcome, though he did not come close enough to shake hands.

"It is always a blessed day when our township is able to welcome new believers into the fold," he said, smiling, though his eyes seemed without mirth to Asa.

Asa grinned back and nodded, tipped his hat, and looked about the room. The preacher looked at Crow and Mattie, and his features slid into something bordering on disgust before reordering themselves so quickly it may not have been there to begin with.

"In the house of the Lord, son, we ask that his flock take off their hats," he said.

"Yeah," Asa said, "about that. If it's all the same to ye—and even if it aint—I'll be keeping mine on. Them two, well, ye got to ask them yer damn self." He tilted his thumb towards his companions, in case anyone was unclear. "And, uhhhh, as for the 'son' you managed to throw in there, only one man had the right to refer to me in that manner, and that was my daddy." He pointed at the preacher, "he was a preacher too, by the by, and he is also very dead, so I'll be asking ye to avoid that particular nomenclature."

"Just a figure of speech, I can assure you," the preacher said, and his words carried in them the hint of an accent. Dutch, perhaps, or one of those variations. "So, to what does New Oslo owe the pleasure of your company?" He asked.

"Well," Asa said, "we're just passing through and found ourselves facing a...challenge of the conscience, one might say."

"Need the Lord to hear your troubles, now, do you?"

Asa half-smiled at this and took his hat off and smashed it against his thigh where a cloud of trail dust exploded as if conjured there from nothing. "Lord knows my troubles all too well, preacher man," Asa said, after some time, and rehatted himself.

"Then what troubles you, son?" Then, realizing his error, amended it, "I mean, young man."

The young girl had shuffled off from the conversation, but had stayed in the corner, hoping to be overlooked. Crow took a seat in one of the pews, while Mattie leaned against its end, arms crossed.

"You got a sheriff in this town? I aint seen him." Asa said.

"In time," the preacher said.

"That's interesting," Asa said.

"We intend to build this town from the Lord's word and towards His will," the preacher said, gesticulating upwards as he said it.

"Well," Asa looked up at the mostly finished wood beams above in the ceiling, as if searching for some words that may be found there. "I've studied the good book more times than I care to recall—was forced to, mind ye—by my father, and I can scarcely recall a time when Jesus done tole his flock that puttin' folks heads in cages was copacetic." He pointed a finger at the preacher here, "Now I aint claiming that I know the book like ye do—I might, it just depends, but I'd sure appreciate some learnin' on why all these women in town got cages on they heads."

The preacher looked at the tribesman sitting in the pew, obviously annoyed, and then at Asa. "That would be between them and their husbands and the eyes of the Lord," the preacher said, irritated. "And I don't see how it is any of your business, how we conduct things in our town."

Asa smiled in return, a large, genuine, toothy grin that made him look even younger than his twenty years. "Yessir," he said, and repeated it. "Ye may just be right there. Maybe we aint got no business mindin' others." He looked back at Crow and Mattie, and asked: "Am I out of my territory, here?"

Both of them looked back at Asa and said nothing. Mattie picked at her teeth; Crow did not acknowledge the question. Asa swung his head back to the preacher, winking at the girl in the corner as he did, and said: "Well, as ye can tell by my compadres reaction, they'd like an answer as well." He put his hand on the butt of his pistol, casually.

The preacher looked at Asa and then at his hand atop the gunbutt, and it was clear now that a small sort of rage had taken root, some small fire seeking fuel. It was writ in the man's eyes, the sharpening of his expression, and his tone when he said: "We defer to God's will here in this township, and the women here have displeased their husbands, a woman's place is *to serve*, and will unto them be given lessons upon which not you, or anyone else who comes into this place of worship, shall have any providence over."

Asa nodded at that, calmly, and replied: "ain't that just a fancy preacher way of sayin' it aint our business? And maybe you right. I see that side of it, I do. And we may, just may, ride on out of here with nary a concern if it wasn't for ye workin' blaspheme on the good book. I ain't a believer, me, but I believe in free will, and ain't nothin' lower to one Asa Jebediah Hiram Townes than using the lord's word, nevertheless what I think on it, for one's own manipulation." Asa had warmed to the moment, and his voice carried to the rafters towards the end of his lament, his last word becoming much longer than its given five syllables. He looked over to the girl, still hiding in plain sight in the corner, and said: "hey sweetie, do Asa a big favor and go get them women with the cages on they heads, would ya?" He saw the girl's trepidation and nodded towards Mattie. "She'll go with ye," he said, and smiled warmly.

The preacher raised a hand towards the child and said sternly, "Lucinda, you will do no such thing lest you risk the wrath yourself! You upset me and you upset the Lord as well!"

"Ahhh, hosrsehit," Asa said as he pulled his gun and shot the preacher, a through and through just beneath the right shoulder that was meant more as message than any real intent to injure. It was anything but a fatal shot. He heard the girl cry out and Mattie had taken her by the hand then and he saw them hurry out the front doors.

The preacher had taken a knee and his longish hair had become unkempt and hung over his face like drapery and held his left hand to the wound which was streaming blood down his right arm, creating rivulets that dripped onto the plank wooden floor.

"You can't!" the man said, his voice booming despite the pain.

"I can't? I can't what?," Asa said, and looked around. "I just did, preacherman." Asa said, grinning. "Ye ain't hurt much." Asa walked to the man and sat on the nearest pew. The man had spittle hanging from his mouth and did not look at Asa. Crow walked behind the preacher and kept eyes on the front doors.

Asa looked up at the cross and leaned back in the seat. "Yall know what always bothered me," he asked. "The whole 'flock' thing in the good book. 'Cause that's what these folks are—sheep. Right? And maybe rightfully so. But ye, knowing the message, and knowing this power ye got," and he nodded here to the pulpit, "y'all use it to afflict the downtrodden." He shook his head. "Ye know the lord's will? Shit, man, ye don't know any more about the lord's will than what the fuck yer wife wants. But ya pretend, don't ye?" Asa ran the barrel of the gun across the man's face, a still warm, metallic caress that he brought down the man's cheek and finally under his chin, raising the man's head with very little pressure. The two men locked eyes.

"The Lord will—" he started.

Asa moved the barrel to the tip of the man's nose and said, "I ain't worried about the lord, preacherman. When a man seen what I seen, it ain't possible to worry about it no more. But ye wouldn't know nothing about that now, would ye? Where's the key for them cages?"

The man said nothing.

Asa nodded to Crow who stood behind the preacher and he bent down and grabbed ahold of the man's head and neck and began to lift him when the preacher held out his hands wide in a show of surrender, and pointed to the pulpit. Crow threw him into the nearest pew.

The huge tribesman turned and walked to the pulpit, returning with a key on a leather strap, as well as a US Marshal's badge. He handed both to Asa, who looked at each in its time, turning the badge over with genuine interest, then slipping it in his vest.

Asa looked upon the preacher and saw there a pleading in the man's eyes that had not been there before. Something desperate and small. "Hear my words, fraud. I'mma come back this way about springtime, and if ye are still preaching the word of the lord in this here church, I'mma burn this fucker down and ye in it."

The preacher began to sob, his body wracking painfully, though he was loathe to show it. "This turnin' out to be a fine day, ain't it, Crow?" Asa asked.

Crow grinned, deep dimples cratering his cheeks, and he nodded to the door. Asa turned and saw Mattie had the girl and near a score of women with her, all besides the girl ornamented with the metal headwear, some vestigial procession of the damned. Behind them, he saw through the open doors, was a passel of men and boys, maybe ten overall, most with rifles, some young enough that shaving was still some years off.

***

Asa approached the open double doors of the church with the key in one hand and his Colt pistol in the other. When the women had been herded inside and the men had gathered on the steps before the doors, Asa fired his pistol into the ceiling, the echo of it a thing of its own. The winter sun made shadows of the men on the steps.

"This man here is a fraud, and we have been sent to disabuse any notion otherwise!" Asa bellowed, and pointed to the preacher, whom Crow held tightly by the neck. "Now, I will not ask how yall were persuaded to"—and he motioned here to the women—"well, put them torture things on yer women's heads, but ain't no way yall got that learnin' from the good book. Him or ye. It don't make no damn sense to—"

A man began to wail. Asa believed it unintelligible and then realized that it was simply a language he had no hold of, and waited for the man. He was, from what Asa could discern, imploring the men of the town—as to what said message may contain, he knew not, but did not judge it aggressive in nature.

He nodded to Crow, and turned with the key in his hand and began unburdening the women of their headwear, cumbersome and heavy as the cages proved to be. He did this deliberately, making sure the townsmen saw the task at hand. No violence, no trickery. He saw the men having a discussion from the corner of his eye, now three or four discussing in the same language filled with vowels that seemed outsiders to his experience. He continued his work, and it was not without difficulty, as the cages stuck in the women's hair at times and some were near bald on top from the rubbing of it on the crown of their heads. He looked about and noticed that Crow was watching the men impassively but with a rifle at the ready and that he did not see Mattie or the preacher.

The women, as they were freed of their burden, ran in turn to their husbands or families, while others waited for a daughter to be uncaged as well. Asa watched it all and felt no small sense of confusion. He felt right in freeing them—but, why were they so happy to reunite when it was these men who did nothing to stop the act in the first place? He knew not, but figuring human beings out made no damn sense anyways so far as he could figure it.

***

The townspeople had emptied the church, some quickly with their heads down, others with a nod of thanks towards the outsiders, when Asa heard the unmistakable sound of flesh being bludgeoned. Be it cattle or elk or buffalo or man himself, the sound is a similar one. He and Crow sat on a pew and looked at one another and Crow smirked.

The two men walked to the doorframe, one whose door had not yet been set, that lay on the left wall of the main room and there saw Mattie hacking at the neck of the preacher, who now wore one of the cages himself. Asa had two thoughts near simultaneously: I do not recognize that massive knife, and *must've displeased the lord*, Asa found himself thinking, while he bore witness the removal of the caged head from the rest of his body. Mattie had plunged her own knife to the hilt in the man's chest earlier, the handle standing obscenely erect given the lifeless husk that lay prostrate on the floor. Her arms were streaked and flecked with crimson and she picked the head up with both hands by the top of the cage and stared at it, bringing it close. She held it, and looked at it, his visage inches from her own, then she screamed at the head, a guttural howl that was feral in its roots and wore no pretension as cloak. His eyes remained open and peered back impassively, whatever fire and brimstone once held there extinguished like daylight dissolving into the coming darkness.

"*And to the dust we shall return*," Asa said, more to himself than the others. He knew that Mattie's story was one akin to his own, that the abuse that had been reaped upon each of them knew few boundaries and was impossible to uproot and so you lived with it, drowning in it, until this life beat it out of you or you simply inhaled all of it and exhaled it back into the world. A beheading wasn't his way, but he thought it an interesting touch nonetheless.

They left the town of New Oslo deep into the night, with no idea as to whether they were seen as savior or demon, and left the caged head of the preacher on a pike to cast judgment upon those who would cross its unseen borders.

They rode west, always west. Californy was the goal, and they would arrive when they did but did not hurry in their approach. Last Asa checked, it wasn't going anywhere, and what waited for them would not lose resolve given time. They rode the night down and watched the sun rise in the east amid angry hues of orange and red, and they rode their horses through pygmy forests of saplings and cacti alike as if every variation of life were welcome in this land.

Asa remembered the marshal star in his vest pocket and so removed it and turned it over in his fingers and wondered at its origin. He saw Mattie look at it in confusion and nodded towards Crow and meant to speak in way of explanation when Crow said: "think the preacher was a lawman?"

"Hell no," Asa responded. He turned the star over again and said simply: "He didn't have no sand. Marshal's in these parts, they got to have some sand. Can't have it no other way." He passed the badge back to Mattie, who deftly snagged it singlehandedly.

"Tell ye what though," Asa said, "I put that on my vest, and it'll fool about 98% of folks."

"Who's the other 2%," Mattie asked, her voice hoarse from lack of use. She would go days without speaking at times, so Asa smirked back at her.

"Other sheriff's, I reckon," he answered. All three of them found humor in that, and laughed each in their own way. By noon they found an abandoned structure that had once had fire set to it. The small barn had burned mostly to the ground and the wooden pen was nearly fenceless but the main structure was in the best shape. Flames had blackened some of the interior and only half of the roof remained intact but it would serve. Crow tended the horses while Asa looked for a well and Mattie headed to the nearest rise with her spyglass.

3.

Home is an amorphous concept, and one that each man has individual to his heart alone and thus the three of them settled into a sedentary life for the next week. The gutted home served as shelter and Asa figured it time to take a short break from their westward journey, and the constancy of saddle life. They took turns finding game, although Mattie volunteered most days. At night, Asa slept within the walls of the opened dwelling while Mattie and Crow slept outside beneath the stars, at once together and fully apart.

It was near middle of the third day when two men rode towards the dwelling, the dust clouds announcing their arrival well before the actuality. Asa believed Mattie to be hunting but really had no idea where she might be. He sat smoking on a bench atop the porch and watched them approach. He couldn't see Crow but knew him to be close by. Asa stood and leaned on one of the posts that held up the tin roof over the porch and waited.

The two men rode up with purpose, straight-backed and serious in manner. As if courage a thing that could be simply willed. Asa smiled widely as they reared their horses. They did not dismount and instead turned their nags and straightened, facing Asa. The two men were not fighters; Asa recognized that from a distance. Being an experienced soldier by 12 and a POW by 14 and then riding the plains all the years since had taught him in ways he didn't fully recognize—and one of those was how to spot dangerous people. And these men weren't. Farmers, Asa guessed.

The first man, a tall thin figure who wore a shapeless hat and spoke with an English accent pointed a finger and said: "You can't stay here."

Asa smiled, amiably, removed the cigarillo and exhaled. "And good day to ye two souls, as well. My name is Asa. To whom do I owe the pleasure?"

The other man, who was opposite in appearance to the other, bearded and round and wearing a top hat, accent all piney backwoods, said: "Ye cain't stay here."

"Does the pair of you know any other words?" Asa said, and smiled. "My friends and I are—" the two men stopped and immediately looked around in a panic, as if the thought of others had not occurred to them, "—not staying here but another day or two. We've been riding for some time now, and figured the place looked abandoned."

The taller man was still looking around, and the short one said: "Well, it ain't."

"I see," Asa said. "So," he motioned with one hand towards the dwelling, "someone lives in an abandoned, soot-blackened, no-roof house?"

"That's Jeb's place," the skinny man said.

"Ahhhhh," Asa exclaimed. "A brother in arms if only in name—my first middle name is Jebediah," he said.

"Jeb wouldn't want ye here," the short man in the top hat said.

"And...where is Jeb, may I ask?"

"He went on a buffalo hunt, some months back," the short man said.

"And...was his home in this shape when he left?"

The two men looked at each other. One of the horses whinnied. "Some injuns came and burned it," the short one said.

"Like that one?" Asa said, and pointed to Crow, who had been sitting for some time now in the ruins of the barn, partially obscured by the burned stubs of a retainer wall. The two men started then, and one made a sort of high-pitched whine while the other was having trouble controlling his horse in his panic.

"What in the all-out hell?" tophat said. "Ye cain't just—"

Asa hopped off the porch and pulled his vest back to reveal the badge pinned to his shirt, smiling as he approached the men. "My name is Asa Townes, and I am a duly sworn federal marshal normally up in Kansas territory, and that there is Crow, a tracker who is travelling with me. We are searching for a mean bastard of an outlaw by the name of Solomon Westlake, though he often goes by the name of The Undertaker."

The two men were in rapt attention and Asa decided the tale was simply too much fun so continued: "He is wanted for killing whole families, and he often removes the heads of his victims and throws them at his adversaries," Asa lied. "A difficult task, I can assure ye, as heads are quite a bit heavier than they may seem, but it is a calling card, nonetheless."

Both men sat in their saddles, openmouthed. Finally the skinny man blurted: "Well, now, Marshal Townes, we didn't know." He looked at the short man and nodded, saying: "Now, I'm sure Jeb wouldn't be too bothered by knowing a lawman holed up here on the hunt."

"Well, shit, I think he'd be honored," the short man agreed.

"Now, we'll only be here for a couple more days, for I fear the trail grows cold—but he has been known to travel west—what is the nearest town in that direction?" Asa asked.

"Well, marshal, that'd be Red Rock Canyon, about a day's ride," the short man said.

"And, who runs that particular township?" Asa asked. "I reckon I'll need to coordinate with him."

The two men looked at each other. "Well, ain't no man, marshal. It's Miss Duvernay, she's kinda the mayor. I mean, she runs things. And, uhh, runs the whorehouse too."

"Well, I appreciate fine frontiersman such as yourselves coming out here and looking over Jeb's property for him. We'll be on our way soon enough, and I'll be sure to mention ye in Red Rock Canyon," he said, and wore a shit-eating grin that could have sold matches to a burning man.

"Happy to help, sheriff. Anything you want us to do?" the skinny man asked, in his accent.

"Just mind your families, and tell others of The Undertaker. With a man like him, it takes a village to keep safe," Asa said, and winked at the men.

"Yessir," top hat said.

"We will do that," the tall man said, and with that they turned their horses, and each with one nervous glance at Crow, began to ride away.

Asa turned back to the porch, whistling, and Crow shook his head in amusement at Asa and his many words that now combined with a badge found in the property of a dead preacher may prove to be an omen indeed in such lawless lands.

The rest of the week passed with no small measure of peace, though the afternoons were hot and nights cold, as if winter had hold on only half of the day. On the morning of the 7th day squatting, the three of them packed their horses and headed west, and left the remainder of Jeb's shack for good.

***

They rode through foothills and arroyos dotted with cholla and yucca cacti and forests of sparse pines and birch trees with knotted white trunks and stretches with no flora to speak of, as if the earth herself were afflicted with bald patches. They found a man dead by the remains of a fire, an old man who had no obvious injury but whose skin had tightened and blued in places and so the trio buried him with rocks and Crow took his rifle and Mattie his boots, so small were his feet, and Asa a blue and black blanket of Indian design. There was a half bottle of whiskey so Crow and Asa drank that in turns. The man's saddle was in no better shape than him and whatever horse it once adorned was long gone. They stayed in his camp that night and would finish the journey to Red Rock Canyon in the morning.

Crow had dozed off and Asa was in and out of sleep when Mattie kicked him.

He sat up and reached for his Colt immediately, then looked at Mattie who held wide eyes and a single vertical finger over her lips, while she nodded to the east. He looked in that direction and raised his Colt. The fire was only embers at this point, and they heard a branch breaking and then the footfalls of a horse. A man walked into the sparse firelight with his hands up, the reins to his trailing horse in his right hand.

"Hello there," the man said, amiably. "I pose no threat." The man wore a dark suit with a derby hat. He was clean shaven. That was about all that could be seen in the moonlight.

Mattie pointed her rifle at him as if he had not spoken. Asa said: "better ways of meetin' folks than walking in on a dead fire, mister."

"Yessir," the man said, slowly. "I am headed in the way of Red Rock Canyon, and smelled the fire." He reached to his jacket slowly, and pulled it back to reveal a badge. "I am Jonas Jenkins, of the Pinkerton Detective Agency. I, uhhhh, apologize for interfering on your evening," he said, and looked earnest while doing it.

"A Pinkerton man," Asa said. Both he and Mattie kept their guns raised.

"Yes. I have been deployed here in the service of hunting a fugitive, with my starting point in Red Rock Canyon. In fact, I hear that the agency may be sending reinforcements as well. Problem is, the train was run aground some ways back, a track issue, it appears, and I have no knowledge of the territory. If you assist me, I can pay you."

Asa nodded at this. Normally, an offer for pay to go someplace they were already going would be automatic. He looked at Mattie, then at Crow, whom he recognized as pretending to sleep but with his hand on his skinning knife, and then back to the detective. Asa smiled amiably as if about to speak and shot the man then, twice in the gut before he fell, then stood to put a third slug into the man's forehead while the detective lay on the ground and gurgled, blood bubbles popping as they rose from his lips. The horse whinnied and trotted away slowly.

"I will not abide a Pinkerton man," Asa said, simply, and walked off into the night. In the darkness, he said, "Mattie, go get that horse. We'll need her."

It was mid-morning when the three of them, with two $20 bills and with an unmarked 4th horse now in tow, arrived at a crest that overlooked Red Rock Canyon. There were pieces recognizable even from here—a large circus tent, assemblages of buildings and wood structure along two main streets. They were also about two inches high from this distance. Some other properties scattered about the valley like dice. The crest they found themselves on, however, held no easy trail down its face and even the switchbacks looked treacherous.

"Well, shit," Asa said. "Guess we'll get there about supper time."

Crow was wearing the Pinkerton man's derby now, as it had proved near impossible to find a hat big enough so large was the dome of the tribesman but Jenkins the Northern squarehead had proved his equal and so he had tried it on, as astonished as the rest of the crew when it fit, and had taken to it. He wore it low on his head and Asa knew already he would probably sleep with the damn thing.

The road forward proved as difficult as expected and seemed they were headed in any direction but west most of the time but eventually all things find their way, and this was no exception. The sun was well into the west but not yet beginning to set as the four horses and their three riders broke the town boundary.

4.

The three of them entered the town from the east at a trot, covered in trail dust and furs and more resembled ancient beasts than any citizenry of modernity and its charms. "Well, damn," Asa said. "Enough mud to drown most folks."

Crow, who mostly ignored Asa's remarks, nodded and said, "aint dried up yet."

The town was small but bustling, and featured every manner of horse and ass and covered wagon and those open to the sky and men and women of lilly white skin and solid black skin and every tone in between. There were squaws and black children and Mexican caballeros and while most spoke some manner of English, each spoke it with an accent peculiar to their knowledge and background alone. The thing they all shared, however, was mud.

"Notice something, Crow?"

"Reckon I do," Mattie said. Both men looked at her then and waited. Asa was expecting 'mud' as the answer.

"Not a soul here lookin' at us," she said, and jutted her chin at the happenings about. "That last town, you'da thunk we were green and nine feet tall. And we weren't even the ones in cages." She spit at that.

"Well, heavens to Betsy, Mattie girl, ye may be right," Asa said, looking about at all of the people completely ignoring them. They rode their mounts at a walk about the two main streets in the town in ten minutes, the shoed hooves of the horses sucking and splatting in the mud, avoiding the wheel ruts, taking it in—the storefronts, the sheriff's office, the two churches, the mercantile's and haberdashery and stables and barber shops and hotels alike.

"I'm gonna get checked in to one of these here hotels. The Continental, I think. You two want rooms, or you open-skying it?" Asa asked, knowing he should ask, and knowing the answer before he asked it.

"No hotel," the two of them said in unison. Asa nodded.

"Well. Follow me around til I'm settled in then, so we know where to meet up."

An hour later, Asa took in dinner at the hotel and sat by himself. Despite his outwardly verbose manner, he was not one that required company, and so the lack of it did not bother him. He was aware that his trio was an unusual one, but knew also that fashioning his own desires and standards about his company would fit as a noose might. And so he sat alone and devoured the steak and biscuits and gravy as if eating were a new experience entire. When he finished, he walked up to his room and lay on the bed.

His room was on the third story—which in and of itself was a rarity in most towns he had passed through—and had a window that looked down onto the main drag that fronted the Continental Hotel. It was also accessible should he need to leave quickly, as he figured he would be able to slide down the roof tiles to a balcony below his room, which he could easily swing over and into the street and to the stables and Harrison there inside of thirty seconds. Not that he imagined having to do that. He stood and stretched and looked out the window, deep in thought, and caught two scenes, one immediately following the other: first, across the street on the roof of a building, he saw a husky white man stand up, naked as a new baby, his erect phallus in front of him like a divining rod, and a second thereafter saw him lean down and help a lady up, her large black breasts exposed to the sun, though her dress reordered as she stood and so he saw nothing below that. She leaned her head against the man's chest, and for a moment they embraced, before shouting on the street caught their attention as much as Asa's. He leaned out the window and saw the source of the shouting—two men were creating a scene on the street, and as a herd knows to keep from the injured or the old, people instinctively moved away to create room for the foolishness of these two men. It was dusk then, and the sun like a child ignoring his bedtime instructions, and thus some fading light remained in the west.

One man was very large and white and hatless and mostly bald, the other a Mexican who spoke clipped English, though it was clear from any speech whatever that he was well in his cups. Asa didn't get that feeling from the bald man. He saw a man in a black hat with a badge leaning on a nearby porch. He held a cigar between his lips, and while his hand rested on his gunbutt, he did nothing to influence the scene in front of him. The street became unnaturally quiet, and women were shepherding children, their own and others, from the spectacle. The Mexican was hurling insults at the bald man, in both English and Spanish, in quick succession, and Asa knew some of the phrases while others went unrecognized—although the bald man seemed able to converse in either, though he did not shout, so his words went unheard by Asa. The Mexican pulled his gun at one point, and while Asa assumed that would be a point of no return, the bald man did not pull in response, nor did the lawman. Both simply watched, as the Mexican insulted the bald man, and slurred at women on the streets, and waved the weapon about like it were as harmless as a spoon and it was when the Mexican stumbled in a muddy wheel rut that the lawman reacted, taking three steps, far more quickly than Asa would have expected, and smashed his gunbutt on the back of the head of the Mexican. Just like that, the scene had concluded, although Asa reckoned the exhalation from the crowd was as much relief as disappointment for having missed out on unnecessary death, as American in these parts as the railroad and the fur trade.

He hatted himself and walked down the stairs and into the town.

He parted the double doors of the downstairs saloon and before him the town as a whole. There were boys on ladders lighting gas lamps along the storefronts. Asa saw the sheriff's office across the street to the west and headed there along the plank board walkways before crossing the muddy thoroughfare. One of the deputies was sitting outside and shot him a glance but said nothing and Asa walked through the open door. There were four desks though three were empty and seated at the fourth was the man Asa had seen outside and who had smashed his gunbutt on the Mexican's head. He was small and wiry and Asa saw in him intelligence and curiosity immediately. His mustache was a majestic beast of its own accord and was threaded through with silver, and, as his black hat hung from a peg behind him, his dark hair outfitted with some gray as well.

"Help you with something, son?" He asked, in a friendly tone.

"I'd appreciate you not calling me son, sir, my name is Asa" Asa answered, then continued: "I was watching from my hotel room there, and saw what ye did to that Mexican fella, and—"

"Where you staying at?" the sheriff asked.

"The Continental. Way up on the third. Anyways," and the sheriff nodded here in confirmation, "I just wanted ye to know, I been in a lot of towns, and seen a lot of war n bloodshed n shootouts n hangings and the like, and I's impressed with how ye handled that."

The sheriff said nothing for some time. Maybe he was surprised. Maybe he was thinking, or sizing up the young man. Maybe he was insulted. Asa couldn't tell.

Finally, he said, "well, that Messican's name is Ignacio, but everyone here calls him Nacho, and he's a good fella, and a darn good smithy, despite outward appearances. About once a month, around that, he gets in his cups. Sometimes, he pulls his gun—you saw that—but he aint the type to shoot it. Never has. So, I saw Nacho doin' his particulars, and just figgered I'd wait."

"How'd ye know the big, bald guy wasn't gonna shoot him?" Asa asked.

"Well," he said. And looked at the ceiling. For long enough that Asa wondered if he'd forgotten the question through. "I didn't. And that's a good question. That bald man, he aint from around here—lotsa stories there, on that man, and he likely could have, all things being equal. But I didn't sense it in him," the sheriff said. He nodded towards one of the three cells against the wall.

Asa looked that way and saw the Mexican, lying on a cot, hat low over his face. "He'll be there a while, I reckon," Asa said.

"Damn right," the sheriff said, and chuckled. "About a day. He'll sleep it off. Then I'll lecture him about how he can't swing his gun about whether he plans to use it or not and he'll apologize, and he'll go back to being a good citizen, and blacksmith to boot, then, in about another month or two..."

"He'll be back here," Asa said.

"Yessir, son. He will." Then he pointed and said, "sorry. Asa. It's Asa, yeah."

Asa nodded, barely recalling that he had given his name.

"That's biblical, aint it?" he asked.

"Yessir. Asa was the third King of Judah. He was a good king, as them folks go," Asa said.

The sheriff nodded. "You a bible man, Asa?"

"No sir."

"Interesting," he said. "Imagine your daddy named you, yeah?"

"He did."

"And he a man of god?"

"He was."

"And you not."

"Nope."

The sheriff looked at Asa a long time then. Asa glared back.

"Well," the sheriff said. "It is peculiar how folks name they kids, aint it?" He rapped the desk then, twice. "It's a bit like ascribing your own expectations and feelings on them that aint even had a say yet."

"Reckon so," Asa said, and yes, he did think that. He looked briefly towards the wall opposite and stopped, his gaze settling on a rifle hung on the wall. "That's a Henry rifle," he said.

The sheriff looked in that direction, then back at Asa. "It is," he said.

"Mind if I take a look?" Asa asked. He stood, and began that way before an answer.

"Not atall," the sheriff answered.

Asa didn't so much as walk to the wall as glide there, as he didn't recall the journey. His head filled with reckonings and embarrassments and violence and fear and lying in mud holding the rifle itself tighter than he had held anything, before or since. He reached and removed it from its hooks and felt it in his hands. He held it and looked down its barrel and in him something yet again reached for some foothold from the lostness it represented.

"I see you're familiar with the Henry," the sheriff said.

"It was my weapon in the war, sir," and was surprised he had referred to the sheriff that way.

"Indeed," he said. "That one there has felled many a man, I do not say with pride."

"I killed 'em on both sides," Asa said, without provocation. "The Union tried to burn us out and trap us and get us in crossfires and bury us with sheer numbers. Shot plenty of them boys in blue, stabbed near as many. Then they put us in camps and my own in butternut did near the same to me. I's but fourteen at the time. Killed them too. Towards the end, there wasn't no difference."

The sheriff said nothing to this, and Asa wondered if he had spoken it aloud at all.

Asa cleared his throat then, and looked down at the weapon again. "Aint held one since," he said, sounding normal to himself again, and put it back on its hooks.

"Well. Point is you made it out, son—Asa," the sheriff said.

"So hey, I wanted to talk to ye about my party," Asa said.

"You got a party comin' through I don't know about?" The sheriff asked, amused.

"I ride with two others," Asa said, and sat back in the chair. Tilted his hat back, which made him look younger than he was. "One is an injun, he is my partner, my friend. But he don't stay in town. Won't," he amended. "And we got a girl with us—anyways, they gon' be staying outside of town, but I just wanted to let ye know that, if and when yall deputies find some injun and a white girl camping near town—"

"These two together, now?" the sheriff asked.

Asa laughed at that, an unexpected occasion in an unexpected place. He was embarrassed when he realized it, and looked at the sheriff, who seemed nonplussed.

"Nooooo, sir. I mean. He's *old*. Maybe fifty. And she's—damn, I doubt she's...hell, I don't know. It never came up. But one time, when we was sleeping by the fire in south Texas, north of Laredo, shit—anyways, Crow, his hand dropped over her as she slept? *Whoooo* boy! Crow had a knife to his neck so fast it weren't funny. I sat up laughing, and Crow didn't know what to do. Anyways, Crow says she's a two-spirit. So, that just is what it is. She's the best hunter in the group though," Asa said, and sat back as if he had said it all and there could be no questions.

"I see," the sheriff said, nodding. "So...what may I ask is a *two-spirit?*"

Asa rolled his eyes slightly at this. "Look, Crow *speaks* English—when he wants to—but that don't mean I know everything coming out of his gob. All I know is, she ain't quite like us. And that suits me fine. She hunts like nothing the lord ever seen. Sometimes I think she's part coon hound."

The sheriff smiled at this. "You Mississippi?"

Asa looked at him, stricken. "I was a Tennessee volunteer, sir, my brothers the same, and don't got a lick of Mississippi mud in me."

"Apologies," the sheriff said, raising a hand. "But here you are."

"Here I am. And aint going back," Asa said.

The sheriff nodded. "Got a question for you. Why you use 'ye' as opposed to 'you'—that's standard out here now. Or at least getting that way."

"It's how I was taught at home."

"Well," the sheriff said. "You always do what you were taught?" he asked, with a smirk.

"Sure don't," Asa said.

"Well, I appreciate you coming to see me, Asa." He reached back and hatted himself. "Now I've got to walk the town a bit, do the rounds, since you can see Nacho there is going nowhere anytime soon."

"Yessir," Asa said. "And, in what direction is Ms. Duvernay, may I ask?"

***

Asa stood in front of the circus tent. It was huge and red and white and he could scarcely imagine the amount of cloth and sewing it must have taken to fit the damn thing. There was light from within, and the whole of it looked like some felled balloon that had crashed into the earth and would not deflate.

The light had faded and it was full dark. The stars had begun their nightly show, and inside the tent Asa could hear something going on, though he was unable to discern the particulars. He parted one of the curtains and its innards contained perhaps ten rows of chairs and benches separated by a middle aisle and lanterns placed thereabouts and towards the front a stage that gave voice to what he had heard and upon it a group of actors involved in their craft. He let the cloth close behind him and stood and watched.

It was only when the actors had completed their practice and were amongst themselves discussing lines and cues onstage that the sheriff entered the tent.

Asa saw him first, and the small man had something that Asa did admire. He seemed to carry within him some benevolent energy that people liked yet he knew firsthand that the man was quick and violent when necessary. The sheriff milled with some of the folks in the tent and then spotted Asa and walked over. He pulled two hand-rolled cigarillos from his vest pocket and offered Asa one.

"Much obliged," Asa said.

"So, what'd ya think of the traveling group?" the sheriff asked, and lit both smokes, removing the glass cover on a lantern.

"Interesting," Asa said, in earnest.

The sheriff looked at him, then nodded.

"I mean, we just come in off the road, sleeping under the stars and whatnot, and these folks here bringing culture to the hinterlands."

"Yup," the sheriff agreed. "Some Shakespore or something or other."

"Shakespeare," Asa said, and nodded. "I still ain't found Ms. Duvernay, just been watchin' these folks go about their skills."

"It's something, ain't it?" the sheriff asked. "I admire folks like these; they go from town-to-town actin' out stories and rehearsing for a buncha drunk cowboys and laborers and the ladyfolk, well, they seem to enjoy it quite a bit. It seems brave, to me. Crossing these parts in a wagon for a bunch of people they ain't never seen and trying to entertain 'em while putting their own lives on the line to get there." He nodded at this in confirmation.

"Ain't thought about it like that before," Asa said. He puffed on the cigarillo, and exhaled towards the tent ceiling. "I'll bring Crow and Mattie to see it when it shows—when is that?"

"Opens tomorrow night," the sheriff said, not looking at Asa but instead the actors as they stood on stage talking out a scene. Asa then noticed, as both he and the sheriff had been preoccupied, that a lady in a crimson ruffled dress was standing next to them, not saying a word, partially hiding behind the sheriff. She had brown hair in ringlets and green eyes and was certainly pretty, but more than that, Asa noticed how calm she was. She was the kind of calm that made men act out, or talk too much. He knew the type, but admired it nonetheless. She made eye contact with Asa, put her finger over her lips in a conspiratorial way, then looked him over and came to some decision, whatever it was Asa had no idea, and then kicked the sheriff lightly behind the knee, making him briefly lose his balance. He caught himself and said, "Damn, RJ, hi to you too," and looked sheepishly at Asa.

5.

RJ, Asa would learn, was RJ Duvernay, de facto mayor of Red Rock Canyon, madam, entrepreneur, owner of about a third of the town, and general belle of the ball. After introductions, RJ snaked her arm through Asa's elbow and walked the township with him, first about the tent and its contents, then into the town proper, pointing out things both relevant and mundane. It took Asa about thirty seconds to realize he was smitten, though she was older than him by a decade, he figured, and he imagined she was just being polite. The evening concluded with her walking him to the doors of The Continental and taking his hand and him promising to bring himself and his friends to the show tomorrow. She kissed her fingers and placed the tips on his forehead and turned and walked into the night.

When Asa was in his room, he felt full of energy and light on his feet and as awake as he could remember. He snapped his fingers, and suddenly felt like dancing, and it was that individual thought alone that made him put his hat on and head downstairs. *Damn fool*, Asa thought, *couple hours with the lady and you're ready to go dance in the damn acting troupe*, and he walked to the bar on the ground level. He had no idea the time, besides simply *late*, and saw that it was empty besides the barman.

"Got any books?" Asa asked.

"Books?" the man asked back. "How about we start with a drink," he said.

"Give me a bottle, a glass, and any damn book ye can acquisition in this establishment," Asa said. "And do not bring a damn bible unless the damn bible is the only book on the premises." He dropped coins onto the marble.

The barman looked at him with a furrowed brow but went about his business. He delivered the bottle and the glass and disappeared in back and when he returned, he had in his hand a leather-bound tome. He slapped it on the counter and said, "that's what we got in the way of books. It's from two years ago."

Asa glanced down at the book, *The Standard Dictionary of Facts* and grinned at the man. "I do thank ye," he said. The book was a fascinating bit of definition, platitudes, drawings, and general information. There were sections on every notion possible, from history to literature to geography and travel to politics and science, among others. Asa drank, and flipped the pages, stopping here and there, until the Natural History section, upon which information was given for various animals, critters, reptiles, sea creatures, and the like. He read on the alligator with fascination, having never seen one, and compared his own knowledge to the printed word on the opossum and fox and bison, but it was the manatee that drew his attention. There was a picture of one in comparison to a man, and the information that they were known as the sea cow, and grew to between ten and thirteen feet in length. They were found in South Africa and some of the America's, it claimed. Asa looked at the bottle, half-dead now. He had only seen the ocean once, in the war. It had been gorgeous and terrifying. Neverending. Dark. He had not seen it since. He lamented not visiting the gulf while in Texas, though he doubted he could have seen a manatee. But imagined it nonetheless. The book claimed that their anterior limbs were flat and not adapted for walking, hence they did not go on shore. He closed the book, and looked at the spine of it again, as if in appreciation. He decided he needed to have the book, and did not see the barman anywhere, and so retired to his room and woke some four hours later, with no recollection whatever of the process of getting to his room, though he did remember much of the magical manatee.

He and Harrison rode out to a blinding sun and the outcropping at which he knew he would find Crow and Mattie, to check in all things that needed attention. It was an excellent spot, all things considered, flat and with a small cave should cover be necessary, with enough space for sleeping and a fire, and clear view both above and below them. It was a smart decision to camp there, which is how Asa also knew to meet them in that location. Experience being the ultimate teacher. Mattie was already gone, no surprise there, out hunting, and Crow sat under a blanket, sharpening two knives, one the length of his thumb, the other the length of his thigh. The remains of a fire in a small circle of rocks held ash and the remains of a small spit.

"How is Asa?" Crow asked, his hands never stopping their rhythmic motion with the knives.

"I got something to show ye," Asa said.

Crow raised his eyebrows, his mouth turtling in doubt.

Asa pulled *The Standard Dictionary of Facts* from his saddlebag and could barely contain his excitement, flipping the pages to show the tribesman, his friend, these new forms of creatures in other lands and under the sea. They were both stricken with the detailed illustration of the manatee/man comparison, and Crow held the book out with both hands and stared.

"We must find one," he said, earnestly.

Asa grinned at this, and it was shortly thereafter that Mattie returned, with the morning's haul of corpses in her bag. She nodded at Asa, not one for ceremony, and began to spill the small animals for skinning when Asa showed her the book, and even Crow stood and they all looked then through the flipped pages, and then in awe at the sea cow and its relation to man. Mattie bore a strange expression of disgust and curiosity, as if the manatee itself may simply spring from the pages, then and there.

After Crow went back to his blade duties and Mattie her skinning, Asa said: "I want ye to come into town tonight. There is a...show, a play, happening. Can leave after, if ye like, but ye should see this. Meet me at the hotel. I figure we'll head out maybe sometime tomorrow or the day after. Back into the sticks."

Crow and Mattie looked at one another and something there Asa didn't know but Crow nodded and thus it was set. He knew they didn't want to go back into town, but he also knew that 'the sticks' was their nomenclature for the road, the road west to Californy and whatever there offered that here did not. So, Asa was in his way demanding, but offering as well.

"How ye learn 'bout this show?" Mattie asked, working on the last of the small game.

"RJ told me all about it," Asa said.

Crow and Mattie both looked at him then, for explanation.

"Sorry, RJ is Ms. Duvernay's first name, err, initials, I guess," Asa said.

"She purty?" Mattie asked. "I bet she is," she said, grinning. She wore smudged black paint on both cheeks which raised as she grinned.

"I mean," Asa said, "sure, she's a fine-looking lady."

Crow and Mattie burst out laughing at this, looking at one another and Crow pointed at Mattie. Some message there lost to Asa, though that was not uncommon. This lasted for some time, and Asa had turned beet-red and so uncomfortable he was thinking of leaving. He paced for a moment, then turned around in a circle entire, unsure of any action but movement. Crow and Mattie, sensing their friend's discomfort, toned it down some.

"I don't see what that's got to—" Asa said.

"You are a romantic," Crow said.

"Wha—?" Asa said, mouth agape. "I am very much inured to the—"

"It is so wrapped up in you, you cannot see it. It is a part of the binding that makes you. A wolf can only be a wolf," Crow said, his face grinning playfully.

It was then they heard the footfalls, small rocks cascading down the trail, obviously a horse, and more than one at that.

Crow grabbed the large knife and Mattie her rifle and Asa brought his hand to his holster.

Two horses slowly made their way down the dried wash, now mostly shale and pebbles, riders atop each. The first tipped his hat, then the second. They were dressed in three-piece suits and derby hats, much like Crow's, and one was mustached, the other plain. They sat their horses and looked at the three of them.

"My name is Williamson, and this is my partner, at least for this journey, McMasters." Each of them tipped their hat, again. "We are from the Pinkerton Detective Agency and are headed to Red Rock Canyon."

Crow nodded, pointed at Asa, and said, "he is a romantic."

The two men looked pleasantly confused, and Asa said, looking at Crow, "call me that one more time," and he pulled his Colt and shot both of the men. One, McMasters, was hit center mass and fell immediately and was dead before he landed because his neck broke with an audible snap when he fell from his horse but he did not react. Williamson, however, seemed stuck in the moment, atop his horse, shot in the neck, and holding it, as if he could just plug the wound and go on about his day. He looked at Asa, but did not reach out. Just held the wound, and, at one point, even attempted to turn his horse, but the horse turned sideways and the man leaned against the large rock next to him and soon was still. Asa walked to each of them and shot them again, at close range, and said once, loudly, "*I will not abide a Pinkerton man,*" and set to putting the two men atop each other. They took what was for the taking and left the rest, and morning or no, set fire to the corpses. "Reckon you two don't sleep here tonight," was all Asa said.

Horses were becoming an issue, as they now had six for the three of them, so Asa decided before they left town, he would sell two, and keep one for insurance.

***

Crow and Mattie met Asa that evening at The Continental, and they each looked as if they may have even bathed in a creek to ready for it. Asa was almost proud. Mattie had still blackened her eyes, but left the coon hat in Asa's room. He was unclear why, but Asa felt this to be a day upon which other days would be shaped by. He smashed his black pinchfront hat low over his forehead and nodded in the direction of the festivities.

They left the horses at the stables and walked to the tent, which had already begun to fill. It seemed most of the town was headed in the same way so they weren't leading or following but more being herded in a single direction. It occurred to Asa that with this much of the town at a single event, this would definitely be the time to search through hotel rooms or hold up a store, or whatever mayhem some children of god would put themselves upto. The bank was long closed, so there was that.

The performance was one that featured scenes from a sampling of Shakespearian plays, and Asa recognized many of them—*The Tempest, Twelfth Night, Titus Andronicus,* and *A Midsummer Night's Dream* he was certain of—there were a couple others that he couldn't place, and another he had no idea the origin of. Crow seemed to enjoy himself, smirking many times at some of the comedic turns, though Asa caught him asleep at one point as well, derby hat low over his eyes. Mattie, for her part, was a different tale entire. From about the middle of the first scene on, she was sitting on the edge of her seat, caught in a panoply of emotions—fear, surprise, laughter, wonder. Asa had never seen her so animated, and ruminated upon whether she had ever seen a show such as this.

When it was done, Crow jarred himself awake with a grin and Mattie stood and clapped, and whistled loud enough to deafen someone. They went to one of the nearby bar's after—The Paris Saloon, by its sign—and the fact that Mattie was going to choose to be inside and at a bar was evidence enough of her feelings for the theater. This was a rarity indeed. They took a small table and drank beer, although Asa got a bottle of whiskey for the table as well. Asa was about to chide Crow for sleeping during the performance when the sheriff and RJ walked to the table.

The sheriff tipped his hat at Crow and Mattie, and said, "this the company you been ramblin' on about?"

"Indeed," Asa said. He tipped his beer in the sheriff's direction.

"What'd you folks think of the show?" RJ asked, seeming very much the de facto mayor of the town at that moment.

Asa was about to open his mouth, to expound on his knowledge of Shakespeare, to carry on with careful wordplay as was his way, to ruminate and deflect and qualify, when Mattie opined: "It was amazing! I only heard about these before, aint never seen one."

RJ looked down at Mattie and they touched hands, an intimacy so against anything Asa knew of her he had to consider that there may indeed be some form of lunacy that was catching in this town, and RJ said, "well, that is just about the best thing I've heard today. You must be Mattie. Asa told me about you last night." With that, she winked at Asa. Which was perplexing. Now the whole table was looking at him and here they hadn't done anything! She had kissed her finger and touched his forehead! He knew he was getting red, he could feel it. *This is ridiculous*, he thought.

"Yes," Crow said, and nodded. "Asa was telling us of his romantic feelings for you."

"I—!" Asa started, and stood, then looked at RJ and then at Crow and pointed and exclaimed some mumblings that nobody at the table could discern, before looking at everybody at the table once more and sitting again.

"I do believe that yall are making me the butt of the joke of the evening, some good hearty laughter to be had by all at my expense, well—enjoy it," Asa said, and grabbed the bottle of whiskey and took a long pull. And it was true; all four of them were laughing, or smiling, or pretending not to. The sheriff looked at him with sympathetic eyes, attempting to hide his humor at Asa's embarrassment.

"Sheriff, we're headed west soon," Asa said, attempting to move the conversation somewhere, anywhere, else. "Californy."

"Well," the sheriff said. "Okay then. You may run across a calvary unit. They were here last week. It is run by a Captain Miller, and if he aint the biggest fool in the state, I aint met him. But he is headed into some pretty rough Apache territory, and wouldn't hear no word otherwise. He's a man that aint got both oars in the water, ask me. See's this as some type of holy war, or somesuch idiocy. He's got an injun with him, too, a scout, and sometime marshal. Rye something or other. Smart man, from what I can tell, but his patience was running thin when he was here."

"An Indian marshal?" Asa asked, his brow furrowed. Crow looked interested as well.

The sheriff thought about it and pushed his hat back on his head. Took a sip of his beer. "Well, I don't know if he is a duly-sworn, badge on the vest kind of deal, but I know marshal's hire him to do work for them in the territories all the time. They give him the jobs they don't want—or are hesitant to do, is another way to put it."

Asa nodded at this. Crow said nothing. Mattie and RJ had begun their own conversation, RJ leaning down and speaking closely and giggling.

"If you run into 'em, tell him he's a damn fool. If they're still alive," he said.

RJ, now removed from her private conversation with Mattie, smacked the sheriff on the arm. "Don't talk like that," she said. "Although that man was something of a blowhard, wasn't he? Expected some kind of big to do, too. He brings in this unit of men, half of 'em looked younger than Asa here, and he damn near expected bugles and a parade just for being here," and she waved her hand, dismissively. She smiled at Asa, then. "Be sure to say goodbye before you go," she said.

"Yes'm," he answered.

The sheriff and RJ turned, and RJ began talking to another table. Asa couldn't fathom the amount of socializing one would have to do to be a mayor. It seemed inconceivable. The sheriff turned back around, as if remembering something, and said: "hey, I meant to ask. We have some Pinkerton men coming into town. Some type of train robbers who stole a whole payroll for a mining company or somesuch. I aint heard much of it. But they want to start here, and we been telegrammed, but they aint come. You folks haven't seen any lost Pinkerton boys around, not knowing the North Star from their own armpits, have you?"

Crow looked impassive. Mattie looked at Asa. Asa looked at the sheriff and said, "I'll tell you what, sheriff. I do not abide a Pinkerton man. They aint nothin' but misguided tools and hired thugs for rich men always looking out for the big man and not the little one. And based in Chicago, to boot. Doesn't help." He took a pull of whiskey and shook his head.

"I reckon that's the war talkin," the sheriff said.

Asa just looked at him, a small nod barely evident. "But what that does mean, sheriff, is that if and when I see these men who have I have no desire to socialize or consort with, I will recognize them."

"But you aint seen any yet," the sheriff said, more statement than question.

"No, we have not, and I, personally, am glad for it."

The sheriff tipped his hat, and turned back, catching up with RJ, who had moved to another table.

Crow got exceptionally drunk that night with the remainder of the bottle of whiskey and while Mattie slept near a small and dying fire, he sat atop his horse and talked in riddles and abstract thoughts. He smashed his words together thus what came from it was a sort of tangential philosophy, some slurred poetry given the night. Asa leaned on a tree and listened. Crow spoke of the starless dark and its meanings, a gray-hearted man from his tribe who was exiled due to his obsessions, of how this land was death, of how unwanted knowledge was both a blessing and a stone bruise to the soul, of how death frolicked in the epiphany of life, and of snakes that turn to humans and vice versa. He did not speak these things to Asa; he was far too drunk to be addressing anyone. He simply spoke aloud, and Asa bore witness the words, some small burden of proof met that they existed anywhere at all. At one point, Crow began to fall off his horse, as if in slow motion, and Asa caught him and laid the large man, with no small effort, on the ground as deftly as he was able. He tethered Crow's horse and found a blanket rolled behind the saddle and lay against a tree. He did not return to the hotel that night.

***

Asa woke first to his surprise, the sun just over the ridgeline east, and started the fire and then the coffee at which point Mattie woke and they shared the first steaming tin cup of the morning. Crow sat up sometime later and looked disjointed and unaware and brown leaves hung in his long hair like ornaments and he simply stared at the morning sun, unspeaking, for some time.

They all agreed to leave in early afternoon should Crow be functional enough, and they agreed again to meet at the stables, since they would be selling horses as well as riding their own.

Crow and Mattie were perplexed as they sat their horses outside the stable at the proposed time. Asa was not there. His horse, Harrison, was. They hadn't spoken to the stablemaster, a thin black man, as that was Asa's job, the talking portion of anything requiring other actual humans, but they could see Harrison well enough, the big bay's large head looking in their direction at times. It was not like Asa to be late.

"Do you think—" Mattie started, until they both saw Asa amble into the thoroughfare. He was attempting to right his boot on his left foot which had been put on hastily and he stopped then, pulling the boot off entirely and dropping from it a stone the size of a grape and rebooting himself. He continued his walk, and looked spent and in a hurry all at once. He saw the two of them and raised his hat in their direction, and they both noticed the many pieces of blonde straw that clung to his short hair.

He reached them and Crow wore a toothy grin Asa almost never saw, and Crow said, "awful sweaty for walking from your room."

Asa pointed at him and said, "Shut it."

"Is that a bruise on your neck?" Mattie asked. "Where'd that come from, we just saw you this morning."

Asa looked at Crow, not Mattie, and glared. As if to say, *don't, old buddy. Just don't.*

Crow grinned and said nothing, turning his horse. Mattie said, "it's just a question."

Asa walked into the stables and when he returned the horses were sold and he was atop Harrison and trailing a black mare, the best of the Pinkerton horses as he saw them, and with that they trotted from Red Rock Canyon into the west, the sun shining brightly above, turning the waterlogged muddy hoof prints and wagon tracks into blinding craters guiding their departure.

6.

They rode west navigating the bluffs and crests as they found them, the flora changing from lowland scrub to rocky pines and cacti, and the three travelers spoke little. At sometime past noon, as the sun had begun its slow descent west, the three of them ran across a gruesome scene. A passel of dead and skinned buffalo lay about like so much detritus. Their tongues had been removed and their furs as well, though the meat glistened in the sunlight and the buzzing of thousands of flies was nearly deafening near an individual carcass. The crew slowed their horses to a walk and looked about but saw nothing besides the aimlessness of man and his lusts. There was one human body as well, hidden partially beneath a buffalo. He may have once been a Mexican, with brown skin and black hair, and his face forever wore a look of surprise. His eye sockets had been picked clean and bore no witness to anything this world had left to offer. His boots had been taken, he had no weapons, and his hat was gone. An empty vessel sent into the void. These were new kills, within a day or two, and the group saw three members of what they assumed to be a pack of wolves waiting just inside the treeline, waiting for the men to pass. They had in all likelihood been sharing a small piece of the bounty when they smelled the small group riding the breeze.

They camped that night near a creek that ran north-south, Asa reading parts of *The Standard Dictionary of Facts* out loud for both Crow and Mattie, both of whom were curious at the amount of diverse and abstract knowledge the book contained within it. Between the book learning and the shooting stars careening about the night sky, the evening proved entertainment enough.

The next day was overcast and humid, with intermittent gusts of wind that came and went as was their wont. It was midafternoon when the travelers came upon a dwelling, a small home of solid log construction and so Asa halted the group and went up on the porch. He passed a single mule, nearly emaciated with its ribs evident as piano keys, in a ramshackle corral at an angle to the left of the house. He knew that even a small group riding up to a dwelling without a greeting, whether friendly or hostile, was unusual in these parts, and often meant its owner was either away or worse. He knocked on the door, and hearing nothing, he swung the door open. The scene inside took him a minute to disassemble. He motioned with his hand to Crow and Mattie to join him, and soon they had fallen in behind him. They stood together, each taking in the scene in their own way.

The room held five corpses. Four of them were obviously children. Asa, Mattie, and Crow walked about the room, each holding a kerchief or piece of their clothing over their mouth and nose. The smell was nauseating, but made bearable by the fact that these had not been very recent deaths.

"Mattie, take a look around the property, make sure we aint missing anything," Asa said. "Crow, do me a favor and figure this out as best ye able. I'm gonna tend to the other rooms."

They each attended their duties as Asa checked the one bedroom and tiny kitchen and found nothing of note, besides a small cast iron pan that could be useful. There was little in the way of food. An empty bottle of laudanum lay sideways on the counter. He found a man's faded red shirt near a sewing needle and buttons on a small desk. Mattie returned and nodded, meaning nothing of note in her own way.

Crow had been kneeling and looking carefully to the bodies, then ambled to a window and opened the wooden panels. He walked to the other two window frames and did the same. Flies buzzed about the room. Finally, Crow spoke: "I believe the woman had had enough. None of the children seem to have moved, none bear evidence of a fight. I think she shot each of them, in turn, then shot herself." The woman, if she could be called such in her state, sat in a chair. A large shotgun lay on the floor near her feet. Crow pointed to the ceiling, and the dried brain matter in small clumps there and long, individual chestnut hairs hung from the wooden beams, swaying in the slight breeze with the windows open. "Man probably left, went on a hunt or to a town or for work, didn't come back," he said. It was Crow who spoke it into the world but all three of them had already thought it.

"Reckon she loaded 'em full of laudanum, herself as well, and used the twelve-gauge there," Asa said, and shrugged.

Mattie scrunched her face into something resembling revulsion and Asa nodded, and exhaled. "Who wants to burn, and who wants to clean?" Asa asked.

"I'll clean," Mattie said, disgust etched on her face like a tattoo.

Mattie found a mostly full pail of old, cloudy water but water it was and used what she could and Asa and Crow dragged the bodies by the feet out of the house. There were two girls and two boys altogether, the youngest in a makeshift crib. The male baby, a toehead by the caked evidence, between the gruesome gunshot and the passing of time had become difficult if not near impossible to separate from his sleeping area and so Asa took the whole thing, blanket and all, out to burn.

7.

It was dark by the time the house was rid of the hair and caked blood, if not the dried remnants, and the bodies burned in a nearby field. Asa sat on the porch with a blanket from inside the house, while Crow and Mattie found lodging in the nearby trees. Dinner had been jerky and some hard tack, and there was no fire this night. The horses and the donkey were fed as some oats and grain had been found in a burlap sack, and all of them resting in the crumbling corral.

Asa had dozed off, still leaning on the porch bench, his leatherbound book beside him, when he heard the tread of horses approaching. He had been drooling on the blanket and wiped his mouth and stood. Felt for his Colt. The moon was near full and so he saw the five horses and the accompanying dust clouds approaching in the given light. Because of the direction of their approach, the corral was partially hidden by the side of the small house.

He hatted himself and pulled the Colt from his holster, then leaned on the post nearest the steps.

The five men rode in a trot, and were halted and sat as one man spoke. Asa couldn't see him perfectly in the moonlight, but enough to see that he had a large dark mustache and a high-crowned dark hat. His voice was higher than he imagined but also held in it that which expected to be obeyed. "We'll be bedding here tonight, stranger, so best you find somewheres else."

"How ye know about this place?" Asa asked.

"Well shit, this is Ned's place," the man said.

"Who the fuck is Ned?" Asa asked.

"He done went into the mountains a time ago," the man said. "Searching for gold or so he said." Then the man seemed aware of the fact that he was answering questions from a man who was outnumbered and who he did not know, and seemed to reorder things a moment. "Need you to go," he said.

"I take it that was Ned's family in there?"

Two of the men laughed at that.

"That funny?" Asa asked.

"Mister," the speaker said, "I'm done answering questions. But I'm in a good mood. So, I'll give you a count to five to get off that damn porch and on your way. You don't, that's on you."

Asa pulled back his jacket and there the US Marshal badge on his vest, shining brightly in the moonlight.

Two of the men made slight audible noises, and one adjusted his hat. The silence changed in tone, from one of expectation to one of discomfort. Like a simple shift in the wind when a predator is near.

"You knew there were dead children in this house?" Asa asked.

Nobody answered that one.

"I'mma start counting, lawman or not," the man said. "One," a few of them began reaching for their pistols, "two," Asa heard one of the guns being cocked, "Thr—" and it was then that Mattie hopped upon the man's horse, just behind the saddle, quickly, effortlessly in the dark, and had Crow's large knife to his neck, her other hand wrapped around the man's forehead as his large hat fell to the ground. She had already drawn blood as she held it there, and the man's eyes widened sharply.

One of the other men spoke: "So you got one girl?" He raised his pistol and a loud rifle shot came from the treeline. The man slid off his horse and did not move. In fact, no one moved. Two of the horses whinnied, and one man had to keep his from turning, but no one said a thing.

Asa walked down the stairs. "Yeah, we got one girl. She's a helluva girl though. And got us a shooter too," Asa said, and smiled, his teeth white in the moonlight. "Mattie, put a little pressure there," he said. And she did.

"WAIT!" the man said, his neck slicked in crimson to his collar. "I can see when we're beat." He tried to turn his neck to his men but could not, so his wide eyes rolled in their sockets.

"Drop ye guns, boys" Asa said.

One of the men grunted at this, he looked either Mexican or Indian, difficult to tell in the moonlight, and shook his head.

"Drop 'em or your dude here gets to see what life looks like without a head," Asa said. Another loud rifle shot rang in the darkness as Crow put a bullet near the feet of the man's horse, which shifted its shod hooves and had to be held from turning.

"Ye can keep the knives," Asa said. "If yall good enough to get up on us and kill us all with knives, we damn well deserve it. But I aint having ye halfwits come back 'cause yer angry or drunk and taking shots at us. Aint happening."

The men dropped their pistols, then their rifles.

Asa noticed then that Mattie had not really let up with the knife and the man's neck was now just a red sheet of blood to his collar. "Mattie, ease up," he said. And she did. Slightly.

"Can we, uhhhh, take his horse?" the man asked, pointing at the dead man's mount, face still unmoving with the thigh-sized knife at his throat.

"We seem to be in the habit of collecting horses, at this point, so yeah, ye can take her," Asa said. "Not him though." Asa pointed at the dead man on the ground.

Once the men rode off, the remainder of the night was a restless one. Asa had collected six pistols of various makes and qualities, and three rifles, one of which was a fine German model with a scope. The dead man's hat and clothes were not worth the effort, and his boots were worse than any in Asa's crew wore. He did find a pair of brass knuckles with spikes on the fingers in the man's pocket, and so took those. The morning came too quickly and with it the singing of the blackbirds before even the sun had broken the eastern skyline.

It was on the third day of travel from the suicide house, as they had begun to refer to it, that they saw from some distance the camp of what Asa assumed to be the cavalry unit. It may not have been, of course—but he was sure it was. The tents were numerous and uniform in color and set about like a practiced unit.

The previous days had been spent on the trail of a very large bull elk that Crow and Mattie had been following but little had come of it. It stood as tall as Crow at the shoulder and had one massive eight-point antler while most of the other had broken off, a natural occurrence with the coming of winter. Crow had come to calling it a spirit elk because every time they saw it writ large and plain as day it had disappeared immediately thereafter. Asa found the whole thing amusing, and did not discount Crow's thinking on the matter, but looked at it another way: sometimes nature won. Period. He had given the brass knuckles to Mattie, as once she had seen the item and placed it upon her hand and felt the weight of it, she could not stop playing with it and it seemed as though she wanted it though she did not ask. So Asa gave it to her, though he felt no small sense of despair for the man she would inevitably use it on.

That afternoon they rode into the cavalry camp. Two soldiers came out to meet them as they approached, but Asa sent his regards from Red Rock Canyon and simply asked if they could eat with the camp. They would sleep on their own.

Sometime later they were introduced to Captain Miller, as well as his assistant, a Sergeant Wrenhorst, and their scout, the Indian, Rye Lonehand. Asa recognized the scout's name from the sheriff mentioning it. They were all under a large crème-colored tent and the captain was looking at large maps set across a table, though it was clear that Rye was disputing what was on the page.

"You cannot enter this way," Rye said. "It is a death trap."

"We WILL enter this way and we'll show the savages a thing or two when it comes," Miller said in return. Rye turned his head and looked at the travelers, Crow in particular, some combination of resentment and absurdity etched across his visage. He was a large man, nearly as tall as Crow, with about the widest set of shoulders Asa had ever seen on a man. At least an ax-handle across. He wore a pinch-front black hat in a similar style to Asa's, and had intelligent, green eyes and straight black hair halfway down his back. He wore a look both contemplative and formidable.

Miller, on the other hand, was a smaller white man in full cavalry regalia and a clean shave. He did not speak, he barked. And it was clear he expected those barks to be heard and received.

"Captain," Asa said, "I'm Asa Townes, and these are my companions, Crow and Mattie. We just come from Red Rock Canyon."

The captain looked the three of them over quickly, then said: "I know the town. Didn't care for it much. Have any war experience, Mr. Townes? Don't look like you do, too damn young. Well, we're qu—"

"I was in the war of the states for three years, sir," Asa said. "Paid my dues, I can assure you."

"Well," the captain said. "Then I expect you understand that we are at a crux at the moment."

"Sir?" Asa asked.

"This Indian guide we have says different than our own intelligence—intelligence it took quite a bit of money to acquire, I might add," the captain said, and looked at Rye.

"So," Asa began, "yall looking at a question of faith here, sir. I have no doubt that this man here," he motioned at Rye, "believes he has the correct information. Ye have been told differently. And yet, the decision is on ye alone."

"That's the cut of it, isn't it?" the captain said.

"And how is it ye see to making these decisions, Captain Miller?" Asa asked, his face open and receptive.

"I trust in the good Lord's will, son. Thine will shall be done."

Asa let that one go.

"The heathen has been set upon this land as a distraction and a barometer," he said, "a barometer of our faith and our steadfast qualities, and I will not have another heathen—even a redeemed one at that—telling a white man the way of things."

"Then the way is set, captain," Asa said, and slapped the man on the shoulder in solidarity. He turned and rolled his eyes at Crow. Rye saw the gesture as well and smirked.

"Wrenhorst!" the captain declared, "let the camp know we leave at dawn."

The three travelers and Rye Lonehand walked their horses to a tent that sold libations and there tied their horses and took up stools under the given cover. They ordered a bottle of whiskey and received it and four glasses.

"You going with them tomorrow?" Asa asked Rye.

Rye shook his head. "When the moon is high tonight, I will head east. The captain will say it is desertion, but his route is madness. I will not be an accomplice to suicide."

Asa smiled at that. "You speak pretty well for an injun," he said.

Crow said, "he is part white." Asa and Mattie both looked at Rye.

Rye looked at Crow and slapped him on the shoulder. "Half Irish," Rye said. "Half Pawnee."

"You look Pawnee, then," Asa said.

Rye nodded. "Yes, and my Irish family never let me forget it," he said, but there was no bitterness there. Just a fact. "Where you all headed?" he asked.

"Californy," Mattie answered. They all looked at her. They had almost forgotten she was there, but that was easy with how little she was and how little she spoke. She wore black face paint down both cheeks with a vertical red line on each.

Rye nodded at the news. "They say it is good country, once you get past the deserts," he said. "Something there for you?"

"Yeah," Asa said. "Got some property set aside, family stuff. Found out after the war."

No one said anything. They drank and took in their surroundings—mostly the men in uniform at card tables.

"Most of them are gonna die tomorrow," Asa said and motioned with his thumb at the men in cavalry navy.

Rye shook his head at that. "Nope," he said. "It won't be tomorrow. It will be the day after or even more likely the day after that. And they will be so far into Apache territory, among the canyons and bluffs, there will be escape. Tomorrow is the road that gets them there."

"Shit, I'd go east too," Asa said.

"Are you a marshal?" Crow asked Rye.

Rye smiled at the question. "No," he said. "They aint gonna make no red man a marshal," he said, and looked at the other tribesman. "But they hire me to do all the work they don't want to do. And I do alright with that."

Crow nodded at this, satisfied.

"We're headed west," Asa said. "Anything to know?"

Rye looked at the small glass of whiskey in front of him and did not answer. The din of conversation from the card tables was all around them. "Not for some days," he finally said. "You will head into Arizona territory before too long—lots of red rock and bluffs. If I were you, I'd be more concerned about water than people."

Before they set for camp, Asa bought jerky and biscuits along with a bottle of whiskey and an extra six bladders, and took as much water as they would carry, most of it on the extra horse and ass that they now rode with, each of them a declaration and witness to the route that had gotten them there. The extra animals themselves harbingers of loss. The group made a small fire among a cluster of cottonwoods and settled in beneath the darkness.

8.

There are more things lost to ash in a life than remembered, regardless of the intent of memory. The trivial, the mundane, and the exceptional are tossed about until recall gets the last laugh: so it is with travels, as with life itself. It was nearly a week later among difficult mountain terrain when Crow noticed something that caught his eye atop a crest and so the travelers went out of their way, for it was both more efficient and an easier path to avoid the bluff altogether and continue west, but the unusual held sway for a traveler, and so they followed that particular impulse.

They reached the crest and sat their horses. The view was one that seemed to span a swath of land larger than one's own imaginings. It brought humility and with it a sense of how much was left unfinished. A large river snaked the canyons below, the crashing whitewater still evident from this distance, but even in this presence the shadow of death was evident.

In front of the view, blocking it in some ways, stood a makeshift gallows that had been constructed, and upon it the four men they had run off from the Suicide House. Each of them swayed according to one's own physics and nary a one of them carried on him a shred of clothing. As naked as in the womb. The man whose neck Mattie had nearly cut in half was now missing his eyes as well, and the injury she had given him was fully evident beneath the noose. One of the men had been scalped, and a stubborn crow perched on the man's shoulder and pecked at the offerings on top of his head, looking intermittently at the travelers while dining.

None in the party said anything, though they sat there for some time, each in thoughts unique to them alone. The sun had begun to set in the west, and that is what Asa had come to think of them as doing: chasing the sunset. It didn't matter when, but he knew at some point they would reach a part of their journey where there simply was land no more, where the chase would be incomplete, the sunset never reached. The shores of the black and impenetrable Pacific would see to it, and erase whatever footprints had led this mad dance of the soul forever west, though it was not this day.

Asa looked again at the dead as they swung lightly in the breeze, free now to travel whatever journeys await the damned, and turned his horse to find a place to set camp.

THE HOT STREAK

BY ALEX SLUSAR

I

Ward McCoy gunned the white Cord 810 Phaeton over hot cracked Arizona asphalt, snaking the automotive beast along the highway coursing by the Gila River. He'd practically flown it down from Wickenburg, and as the sun fell away behind the short peaks along the western horizon, he steered off the highway and into the town of Sentinel just as it slipped under a purple shroud of night.

It wasn't easy driving. The Cord juddered underfoot and the suspension felt chancy on the right front wheel. Not surprising for a car nearly twenty years old which he'd ridden hard around the state over the last two weeks, but Ward figured he'd get a tune-up later, when he made the rest of the money. When he got the cash into Del Pascoe's hands.

When he was in the clear.

One more win could make that happen. The Silver Bell would have that win. It had to.

The Silver Bell was a square, squat building of pinkish adobe at the far end of town, on a desert flat at the base of a short and scrubby mountain. Above its ramada entrance orange neon was twisted into its name and white neon tubes formed the shape of a bell which flashed one way and another so it looked like it was ring-ding-dinging.

The dark and dusty parking lot swelled with cars. Ward found a spot and eased the Cord's broad nose into it. He adjusted his white Stetson and his bolo tie. He tugged at the right sleeve of his sport coat and gently felt along the inner stitching. He checked that the trunk of the car was locked and ensured that the brown Samsonite briefcase inside was secure. He went under the ramada and into the Silver Bell.

The double doors swung in on a wide foyer of pale adobe. Most of these small-town numbers were dives, Ward knew, but this one had some sheen to it. It was pretty in its way. Wagon wheel chandeliers cast a muted glow on plush red curtains framing the archways. There was a counter in the center of the foyer, and two archways behind it which opened to the play floor. Speakers played a hot jazz lick which mingled oddly with warbling from the darkened cabaret off to the right. Ward smelled cleaning solvent and cigarette smoke. At the counter were a broad and ruddy-faced man in a dark suit and a waif of a girl

with blonde hair in a bouffant.

"Anything to declare?" the man said.

Ward turned over his Colt M1911 .45 automatic pistol. It had pearl grips

with a 24-karat gold horse-head cameo set in the center of the grips and *W.T.M.*

engraved in gold on the slide.

"Swell piece," the man said.

Ward nodded. The girl gave him an orange ticket for the gun. Ward

tipped his Stetson to her and walked onto the play floor.

It was a hive of jangling chrome one-armed bandits devouring nickels fed

by jovial suckers. Rows of shiny tombstones vomited silver coins into steel

troughs and blue plastic cups. Someone laughed phlegmatically over shrill ringing

bells. A bandit arm ratcheted. A string of curses followed.

Ward found the cashier. He slid five hundred in bills through a slit

under barred windows. The girl behind the bars changed them into clinking

chips of red, white and blue and pushed them back through in a plastic tray.

Ward tipped his Stetson, smiled, and asked for the poker tables.

They were in a cavernous back room thick with a veil of acrid, cheap

cigar smoke. Two of the five tables had play and one had an open seat. The

players were men around his age, though they seemed sallower, unkempt and

worn-out. They wore stained hats and chambray work shirts and salt-rimmed

neckerchiefs. They sported long mustaches and unruly beards very unlike his manicured Vandyke. Two of them gnawed on cheroots. They shot him an eye as he approached the free chair and sat down.

"Fellers," Ward said. He settled his chip tray on the worn green felt. "Welcome, sir," the stocky dealer said.

Ward stacked his chips and joined on the deal. The man to his left anteed. Three rounds later Ward folded a pair of eights and the man to his right took the pot. For five hands Ward played tight. On the sixth, he pushed four players out by the turn, drew down on the river, edged the other player out on a high card pair of Ace-Queen to Ace-Jack and collected. He scooted the chips around on the felt. Down the table a player rolled his cheroot from the left side of his mouth to his right and muttered.

"Seen you somewheres."

"Probably," Ward said. It was a rattling, throaty response from where the cords were irreparably bruised. "I get around a fair bit."

The man perched on his left elbow and cocked his finger at Ward. "You're the fellow from the pictures."

***

Jesse Butler sat alone in a booth at the back of the dark and cloistered Silver Bell Cabaret. The booth gave him a full view of the stage, a quick step to the bar, and enough space he could hear himself think. On the table were his essentials— a tumbler of neat Irish whiskey, a half-empty silver cigarette case, a glass ashtray stuffed with broken butts, a tarnished steel zippo lighter engraved with the insignia of the 504th, and a black notebook. He was making notes.

Butler stubbed another cigarette out in the ashtray. Danny Belmonte wailed onstage. Danny pounded at a baby grand and hollered out of a grey sharkskin suit which was too large for him and looked wet and rumpled under the lights. A handful of fools in the front row chortled. Danny wrapped his caterwauling and bowed. The small crowd clapped half-assed and Danny bowed again. He disappeared stage right. The red curtains drew shut.

Butler shook his head. Danny was a syndicate recommendation—Mr. DiNunzio's cousin's half-brother. Danny wanted a stage in Vegas. The syndicate said he had to earn it. They left him with Butler and the Silver Bell for a two-month engagement. It hadn't made a dynamo out of the dud, but Butler had honored the favor. In a week, Danny would be Vegas' problem. He sipped whiskey and made a note. Soon he could go and find a hungry local with some actual talent, maybe a guitar player. Maybe a full band.

Dixon Donnelly took the stage and the mike. The spotlights changed from blue-white to scarlet. Dixon was yammering chiclet teeth, a blonde pompadour, and a stained dickey.

"Wow, folks, what a show, what a show from Danny Belmonte! Wow. What a time. You can't see it, but backstage they're throwing water on those keys, they're so hot!"

Someone said "*Ehhhhh.*" Butler made a note. Dixon needed new material.

"What a show," Dixon said. "Such a pleasure to have you fine folks here tonight in the Silver Bell, the Jewel of the Sonoran. And you're in for a real treat now, folks. It gives me great pleasure to bring you a tantalizing display of sensuality personified by the beautiful, one and only Princess of the Desert, Miss Veronica Venus."

The spectators clapped. Dixon darted out of the spotlight as the curtains parted. The light hit Veronica and held.

She stood with her back to the audience. She wore a red sequined dress with an open back and the spotlight illuminated her creamy skin. Her arms were gloved in white silk and her shoulders were gilded with a thick white feather boa. Her heavy blonde tresses spilled over the boa and swayed along her hourglass shape as the beat kicked in over the speakers— *Whatever Lola Wants*, on record.

This number, Butler thought. It was alright enough, though he preferred her sailor-suit routine. He made a note.

Veronica vamped and swished her hips. The boa swung with them. She exposed a slender leg and ran the feathers along it. She spun to face the audience and pursed her lips to the gawkers. Someone wolf-whistled. The boa flew. She smiled crimson over white porcelain and peeled the gloves off one-and-two. She took her time with the tease.

She'd done it better, Butler thought. It didn't matter to the yokels going ga-ga stageside, but something was off. Probably still sore about last night, he thought. It had been a bad one, maybe the worst one yet. But, he thought, she needed to know he could only take so much whining. She'd been on a tear for weeks about pulling up stakes and making for Los Angeles. Last night she kicked it into high gear. *Come on, Jesse, it's been years, we can make it to Hollywood, you can make it happen, just tell them you're done, baby, I want my shot at the stars, I'm sick of the Bell, I'm sick of the boys, I'm sick of it all.*

He got sick of it then. She'd done a swell job covering the bruise he put on her cheekbone. He looked at his left hand and was briefly thankful he'd ignored her pleas for a ring, too. Rings made marks—crisscrosses, slashes and star punctures. She might've pissed him off, but any mark on that face would be a problem, in more ways than one. Butler sipped whiskey. He made another note.

Veronica turned around and bent over for the room. She wiggled as Flip Suggs shambled up from the bar and crowded Butler's view. Suggs' toothy grin and lacquered duck's-ass haircut wobbled on a pencil neck.

"The hell do you want, Flip?"

"There's a coffin-nose Cord sled in the lot, Mr. Butler."

"So?"

"It's Ward McCoy's."

Butler's eyes widened. "Ward McCoy? *Here?*"

"Nicky checked him in," Suggs said. "I saw the car, and Nicky said he looked familiar, said he turned in a real nice .45 automatic. Fancy piece, swell old sled, and Nicky figured it's Ward McCoy, the cowboy actor, and you should know. He don't look quite like he used to in the pictures, but Nicky said it's him for sure."

"He's on the floor?"

"He's at the hold 'em tables, been playing an hour maybe."

Butler's eyes narrowed to slits and he stood up. "Flip, why didn't you tell me right away?"

Suggs stiffened. "Well, I‚"

"The man's been playing for an hour without a proper welcome? You asshole, didn't you ever see *The Guns of Diablo Canyon? High Noon at Cimarron?*"

Suggs' eyes flicked and darted. "I...well, actually, not sure I did."

"Christ, Flip! The man's a legend. How do you miss out on pictures like those?"

"I, uh...I—"

"Is he winning or losing?"

"I didn't see."

Butler glared. Suggs twitched. His bottom lip quivered and he stammered, stopped, and swallowed words. Butler clamped his hand down on Suggs' shoulder right where it met the neck. Flip flinched.

"Flip, you gonna wet yourself in front of everyone? I've got to go make an introduction. This is a real get, understand?"

Suggs wobbled out a nod.

Butler cocked his head at the stage. Veronica was down to red pasties, a gold-fringed red thong and a ruby grin. The fringes shivered over her thighs.

"Bring her over when she's done and changed," he said. "We're going to give Ward McCoy a proper welcome."

Suggs nodded and shuttled off into the dark, headed for backstage. Butler sat back down and downed the whiskey. He fished a cigarette out of the case and lit it. He drew deep on the cigarette and exhaled a cloud.

Showdown at Five Arrows came to mind. He grinned. That was his favorite, no question. He'd seen them all, but that one was the best. He remembered Ward McCoy crouched behind a covered wagon, levering and firing a Winchester repeater at bandits on horseback as they thundered across the mesa toward him, and Ward stood there, steely-eyed, fearless as smoke billowed at the edges of the screen. Jesus, Butler thought. He'd been just a kid when he saw that. He'd faced his own bandits since, and he'd thought of Ward then, too. Butler flicked the lighter open and shut absentmindedly and ran his thumb over the symbol of the 504th. He wondered what he was going to say to a bona-fide legend.

II

"*Showdown at Five Arrows*," one of the players said. "What a show."

"That was the best," another said.

The others smiled and nodded. So did Ward. He'd heard that before. His own preference was for *The Guns of Diablo Canyon*. Watching that one, he'd nearly forgotten it was him on the screen.

The players loosened up. Ward's stack hit seven-hundred-fifty-five. The funny thing to him, as it ever was, was that they didn't seem to mind their losses. As the cards came around, they asked questions about *Stallion River, Long Train to Bisbee*, and *The Riders of Red Rock*.

"Fellows, we keep table talk light here," the dealer said.

"Just a little chit-chat," one of the men said.

The dealer shrugged. "It's house policy."

"Well, amigo, I reckon we can keep friendly without takin' away from the game," Ward said. "I trust you'll keep us in line." He slid the dealer twenty dollars in chips. The dealer slid the chips into his pocket. Ward grinned.

"You'd know the Duke, then?" a player said. "Figure you must."

"Knowed each other from the start," Ward said. He didn't tell them about the falling out, in that bar on Wilshire in 1931. Ward made some crack about *The Big Trail*. Marion knocked him on his ass, called him a coward and a sniveling backbiter. He also didn't tell them when producers were cool on *Stagecoach,* Selznick suggested it could get made with Ward instead of Wayne, but John Ford pulled it, said would be made with Wayne or not at all, and found the money to do it the way he wanted. *Stagecoach* had been big—big for

Hollywood, big for Wayne. It slipped through Ward's fingers. Yes, he knew the Duke.

"What about Tom Mix," another man said. "I always thought he was all that in a ten-gallon."

"Never a finer fellow," Ward said. "I owe it all to Tom." That was true, for Tom showed how a cowboy with skill and the right look could crack into the pictures. Mentored him some when he got his start. But Tom always favored Wayne. After that fight, Tom came down from the Sells-Floto tour, called on Ward, tried to wring out an apology and broker peace. Ward was drunk at the time. Raised all manner of hell about Wayne and even Tom, swung a bottle of Old Fitz around and called the man he idolized a washed-up cur and a circus clown. Tom stood there on the front stoop of Ward's house in Indian Wells and took what he hurled, then turned and walked away. They never spoke again. When Tom rolled his car into a dry wash near Florence, Arizona, in 1940, his wife called to tell him and said it would be better if he stayed away from the funeral. So he did. Spent the day drinking alone, then went and bought the same kind of Cord that Tom had. It was years before he went to Tom's grave and asked for forgiveness and heard nothing back.

Earlier in the week, coming north along State Route 79 from clearing a table in Tucson, he saw the wash where Tom crashed. There was a stone cairn and a plaque and a steel cutting shaped like a horse with its head bowed low which was pockmarked with bullet holes. Ward kept driving, had to make a table in Queen Creek. His throated tightened up thinking about it.

Hold it, he thought. Spare thoughts when there's time to spare. Remember why you're here. Remember what you've got to do.

He looked at the men and smiled. They were still loose and intrigued. He needed to stay cautious, stay alert. Stay in the game. Stick to the plan.

The cards came around. He made two pair, nines and tens, then three kings.

"You're good with them cards, Mr. McCoy," one of the men said.

"Always loved a game," Ward said. "Best thing after a long day on the trail or on a set."

"So, what you doin' here from Hollywood?" another asked.

"Headin' back there. Just come from Wickenburg."

"What's in Wickenburg?"

"Old friends and tables."

"Tables? Ain't much play in Wickenburg."

"True enough, amigo," Ward said. "Reckon I cleaned the last one out."

They chuckled. More out of politeness, Ward thought.

"You got another pitcher comin'?"

"Mayhaps," Ward said. He eyed his fresh cards. Seven of hearts, nine of diamonds. "I'm mostly workin' television these days."

"Television?"

"Did an episode of *Colt .45* last year. Y'all see it?"

The heads around the table shook.

"Well," Ward said. "Doing a new show in a couple weeks, a bounty hunter show."

"You the bounty hunter, then."

"No, it's a guest appearance," Ward said. "I'm playin' an honorable town sheriff."

"Sounds swell," one player said.

Ward smiled and nodded. The town was a passing stop and he wouldn't survive the episode. Swell, sure.

His stack dipped for several hands until he made four jacks and the stack spiked. Two of the players cashed in, leaving with far less than they brought. They got up and shook hands with him. He said it had been a pleasure.

Ward eyed his chips. Two hundred and ten to go, he thought. Smooth so far, arguably too easy. The conversation helped as it always had. It introduced a slight distraction, something to stick in the mind of the other players and the dealer. A few more plays and he'd have what he owed Del Pascoe, maybe a little more. And he'd played well, Ward thought, even with the little advantage. It came down to some skill in the end, even a corner or two got cut. What he needed now was razor-keen attention on the game for the final push. Clinching it was just around the corner. It was time to put the blinders on.

"Mr. McCoy," a man said.

Ward looked over. A man in a cream suit stood behind him. He was about forty, barrel chested and dark-eyed. He sported a black high-and-tight haircut on a square, broad head. Hanging on his arm was a shapely blonde woman in a red sequined dress. She was a shade over twenty going on twenty-five, and though it was probably a dye job her hair was thick and lush in that bombshell way. Her lips were full and red, her shoulders were open and the dress showed she had curves in all the right places. She was built like a Ming vase with two moons colliding above it.

"Howdy," Ward said.

"I'm Jesse Butler. Operator-Manager of the Silver Bell Casino. It's a real honor and a privilege to have you visit our establishment." The man extended a hand like a catcher's mitt.

Ward nodded. He kept his hand on his cards. "Well, thanks, amigo. Nice place you have."

Butler returned his hand to his side. "The Jewel of the Sonoran!" he said. "Finest place for play between Phoenix and Los Angeles."

"Sure is," Ward said.

Butler gestured to the blonde. "Oh, and this is my girl, the one-and-only Veronica Venus, the Princess of the Desert. Our star of the cabaret. Ronnie, honey, this is Ward McCoy, the best cowboy actor ever on the screen."

"A pleasure to meet you, Mr. McCoy," Veronica said. Her voice was nectar and Ward could tell it was affected, but it was pleasant enough. He smiled.

"Very nice to meet you, miss," he said. "That's quite the name."

Veronica started to say something. Butler said "It's a damn sight better than Ella May Mudd, ain't it? She's from Oklahoma, if you can believe it. Not much dancing for Ella May in Pawhuska, but plenty for Veronica Venus in the Silver Bell Cabaret. Ain't that right, Ronnie?"

Ward saw the ruby-lipped smile twitch at the edges. "I chose my stage name for Veronica Lake," she said.

"Excellent choice," Ward said. "I've met your namesake lots of times. I can see the resemblance. Pleased to know you're a talent of the show business yourself."

The girl's blue eyes flashed. "Oh, wow," she said. "That's very sweet of you."

Butler slid her hand from his arm. "I've got to tell you, Mr. McCoy, I'm a real big fan," he said. "Nothing ever made my day like seeing one of your pictures. I mean, *Showdown at Five Arrows*, that was...that was the best."

"Right," Ward said.

"*Long Train to Bisbee*, too. I went to that at least three times."

"Sure."

"Remember when you rode up chasing the train, on Copper? And jumped onto the caboose? That was, well, I never saw anything like it."

"Made that jump in one take. The director wanted more from different angles. Fourth try, I jumped short, missed the train, broke my leg in four places. The bastard used the first take anyway. And there wasn't one Copper. There was three horses, not one."

"Oh. Well, I sure did love it."

"Glad you did," Ward said. He turned back to the game.

"You, uh...you sound like you got a sore throat, Mr. McCoy," Butler said. "Certainly dry around these parts. Get you a drink if you like, on the house."

Ward grimaced. He tapped at the right side of this neck near the Adam's apple. "Another old accident. Horse spooked, threw me and trampled my voice box."

"Oh. I had no idea."

"Happens when you do your own stunt work."

"Right, right," Butler said. "Still, you want a drink? On the house, as I say."

"I don't drink when I play."

"Alright then. Well, anything else you want, Mr. McCoy, you just ask."

"Wouldn't mind continuin' the game, thank you."

Butler nodded and licked his lips. "Well, absolutely. Say no more. We'll, uh, we'll leave you to it, then."

"A pleasure meeting you, Mr. McCoy," Veronica said and smiled.

They started to leave. Ward said "Say, Mr. Butler, you want an autograph? Somethin' you can put up over your bar?"

Butler smiled. "Sure! That'd be right nice of you."

Ward reached into his jacket pocket for a pen and a slim stack of photos. He chose one, laid it out on the green felt beside his cards, scribbled on it and signed and gave it to Butler.

Butler looked at the photo in his hand. The Ward McCoy of twenty-some years ago looked back at him. He wore a fringed shirt, a neckerchief and a white ten-gallon hat. His jet-black hair was slicked and his lantern jaw was clean-shaven on a near-boyish face with sparkling eyes and a mouth curled up slightly into a bright, roguish grin. The man at the table might have had the face once. It was looser now and looked beaten and tired. The sharp eyes in the picture had a weepiness to them and the black hair was streaked with errant grey. The clean and bold visage was now surly faded leather. The man at the table had written in a loopy hand *To Mr. Butler - Keep riding the high trails. Your amigo, Ward McCoy.*

"That's great," Butler said. "That's, that's real nice. 'The high trails.' Thank you."

"Pleasure," Ward said and turned back to the game.

Butler sucked his teeth. He waved the photo limply and looked at Veronica. She looked at Ward. Ward worked the cards and angled for a straight. Butler left. Veronica followed. Ward collected.

***

Butler went to the cabaret bar. A neat whiskey came to him. He set the signed photo on the counter beside the glass. Veronica sashayed up alongside and leaned against the countertop, facing him.

"What the hell was that?" Butler said, sloshing the brown liquid in the glass.

"What was what?"

"Ward McCoy comes into my joint and doesn't want to talk. Can hardly talk, he's so banged up. Just wants to play cards like any one of these bums."

"What did you want to talk to him about? His pictures?"

"Well, not necessarily, but just to…" Butler shrugged. "You don't get it, baby. That guy was…well, maybe not the best, but I *liked* him the best. Everyone likes the Duke, and Roy is Roy, and maybe he didn't sing like Gene Autry or anything, but goddamn, when Ward McCoy threw a punch it sure as hell seemed like he meant it." Butler drank. "Somebody said 'never meet your heroes.' Now I get it."

"You should've told me he was an actor," Veronica said.

"I said there was someone important to meet," Butler said. "The hell does it matter what he does?"

"When you said that, I figured he was just another whoever from the syndicate."

"What difference does it make?"

"Had I known he was an actor, maybe I could have been…more of a hostess."

"Why would you do that? Why would you do more for some shitbird actor than someone in the business? This business is what counts."

"If it meant getting a break, getting to Hollyw‑"

Butler flung the glass hard across the bar. It flew and shattered crystalline bits and amber droplets against the back counter. Someone in the crowd laughed. Veronica inhaled sharply. She turned away and Butler caught her by the wrist. He turned her to face him.

"Baby, what did I tell you?" he said. "Did you forget already?"

"Jesse, you're hurting me."

"You don't know hurt. I said I didn't want to hear about it ever again. I am *this* close to having the syndicate hoof you across the border. You'll be the star attraction in one of those dives where the desperadoes cut strips off of blondes."

"You wouldn't."

"Try me. Say 'Hollywood' one more time."

Veronica looked into his dark eyes. Her lips quivered. He cocked an ear at her, as if to listen. She said nothing. He let go of her arm.

"Goddamn you," Veronica said.

"Oh, He can try," Butler said.

She turned and faced the bar. She saw her reflection in the bar mirror. It was wet and warped by spilt whiskey. "Why'd you have to say anything about Oklahoma?" she said.

"Because you need to remember, baby," Butler said. "Where you came from and who got you out of there."

Veronica stared down at the countertop. She splayed her fingers out on its cool surface.

"Your problem is, you think you're at a crossroads," Butler said. "There's this path of your life, it's like a gravel road, and it reaches all the way back to a shack in Osage County where there's a little dark-haired girl pulling the legs off frogs in the ditch, hoping for a night Daddy would stay in his own bed."

"Stop it," she said.

"Can't stop. That's part of my point," Butler said. "Because that path goes on, and you fill out and get bigger. And then one night the shack burns up and Daddy goes with it. And maybe he had it coming, maybe he did. But did your brothers and sisters?"

"Jesse—"

"Good thing there's a guy in town on a job when it happens. Someone who can get you out of town quickly, just as folk are thinking about picking a sturdy branch to hang you from. Someone who sees how you're filling out, and how, with a little work, you could dance. And can you *ever* dance."

Veronica's bottom lip twitched.

"So, this path takes you a few places before it drops you here. *Plunk.* And after five good years of being someone other than scared, violent little Ella May Mudd, you get this surprising notion. You think either you stay here and dance or you push me to help you make for Los Angeles, where they'll put your name up on the marquee, among the stars. But that's the fatal flaw, baby.

Because there's no crossroad on the path. It only carries you forward. The gravel might turn to gold if you play your cards right along the way. I learned this real hands-on, ten years ago. When the door opens, you jump out of the plane, and you run when you hit the ground. Think you have choices, you die. Stop, you die. Try to go back...well, you can't go back, can you?"

"I wasn't scared."

"What?"

Veronica turned to him slowly. Her eyes were ice-blue slits.

"I was never scared, Jesse," she said.

"My point still stands."

A tear welled up in her right eye and rolled down her porcelain cheek. It smudged the coverup over her bruise. "And just what is your point? I'm supposed to keep dancing until this gets better, is that right? And stick with a man who makes me his...*whore?*"

"The only man that's ever been there for you."

"Sure. Passes me around like *meat.*"

Butler scoffed. "How many times have we been over this? Sometimes the syndicate boys want a favor, and some of the guys you can't say 'No' to. I don't like it any more than you do. It's not my fault you're the hottest tail in the county."

Veronica laughed bitterly.

"Not like you aren't compensated, anyway," he said.

"You keep the money."

"For your own good."

"Go to hell, Jesse."

Butler exhaled. He watched whiskey drip down the back counter mirror. A twinge burned in his gut like a coal.

"It's not like I don't love you," he said. "I do, ever since I first saw you. You know that."

Veronica stared at her reflection in the mirror. Her eyes were flat and faraway.

"I don't know what love is," she said.

Butler picked up the photo of Ward McCoy. He slipped it inside his jacket pocket. He smoothed his jacket out and re-buttoned it. He turned to face Veronica.

"You want something different so badly?" he said. "Maybe you *should* play hostess for McCoy. See what kind of lay a beat-up old cowboy can be. We can be disappointed together."

Butler walked away. He left her tense and shaking at the bar. He made for the foyer. He craved night air and a cigarette. Flip Suggs walked up to him followed by a large, swarthy man in a dark suit.

"Mr. Butler," Suggs said.

"What now, Flip?"

"Pablo's got to tell you about what's going on at one of the tables. It's Ward McCoy."

Butler sighed. "What about Ward McCoy?"

Pablo told him what he'd seen. Butler forgot about the cigarette.

***

Ward took the pot a hair after midnight. He thanked the remaining players for their fine card-play. The one-armed bandits rang all around him as the cashier turned his chips into bills. She counted them out: one thousand, one hundred and thirty-five. Ward pocketed the bills in his jacket, next to the photos, and couldn't help a grin. He tipped his Stetson, turned onto the floor and strode for the foyer. He fingered the orange ticket for the Colt in his pocket.

They stopped him before he reached the counter. Two tall and broad men in dark suits flanked Ward on either side and the one on his right caught his arm in a vice grip. Ward recognized him as the man who'd checked his gun.

"The hell?" Ward said.

"With us, sir," the man said.

They guided Ward into the cabaret. It was nearly empty but for a portly blond man at the bar jabbering his big white teeth at the bartender. They hustled Ward past the bar and behind it where there was a narrow hallway which led off the cabaret. They led him down the hallway to a brown paneled door marked OFFICE and ushered Ward through it.

The room was cold, dim and windowless. The walls were unpainted concrete instead of adobe. Jesse Butler sat behind a battered wooden desk in the center of the room which had a phone and stacks of papers and a stuffed ashtray on it. On the wall behind him was a desert landscape painting and a metal filing cabinet. In front of the desk was a chair.

The man let go of Ward's arm. The door closed behind them. Butler gestured to the chair.

"Sit," Butler said.

"The hell is this?" Ward said.

"We need to talk."

"About what?"

"I think you know what."

Ward frowned. He looked at Butler and back at the men. "I ain't sure what you're talkin' about, amigo. And I have to mosey along," he said. He stood up from the chair.

"Nicky," Butler said.

There was a rustle of cloth behind Ward and something hard and metallic jabbed him deep and sharp between the shoulder blades. He yelped and saw stars. He buckled and pitched down and onto the concrete floor. Hands clamped on at each arm, heaved him up off his knees and sat him back down hard in the chair. The man from the counter went to the desk with Ward's Colt pistol in his hand and gave it to Jesse Butler. The pearl grips and the horsehead cameo gleamed in the dim light of the office.

Ward coughed and grimaced. The chair was cold on his back and the cushioning was worn out. The tender space between his shoulder blades throbbed and he winced.

"Take a moment," Butler said. "Catch your breath."Ward wheezed. He coughed again. "That ain't right," he said.

"Maybe not. But you stay in that chair, or you'll get another."

Butler eased the slide of the Colt back and peered into the chamber. The first round sat unchambered and snug in the magazine. His eyes glided over the engraving, the bluing, the pearl inlays and the polished gold.

"Beautiful," he said. "This is the Army model, no question. I'd know that feel anywhere. You bring this back from the war?"

Ward shifted in the seat. "No," he said.

Butler frowned. "You weren't Army?"

"No."

"Navy?"

"No, I...was with the home effort."

"Hold on. You were stateside?"

Ward nodded.

Butler's eyes narrowed. "Jesus H. Christ. You were a discharge? A fucking 4-F?"

Ward looked at the floor. He winced again.

"How does a 4-F get a piece like this?" Butler said.

"This is your problem, why I'm here? Where I got my gun?"

"No, but I'd like to know."

"It don't matter."

"Maybe it does."

Ward shook his head. "I...the studio got a government contract for recruitment serials, to build the ranks. The gun's a gift for doing that."

"Recruitment serials."

"That's right."

"You made pictures to get recruits."

Ward nodded.

Butler leaned back in his chair. His grip tightened on the Colt. "I remember right before the pictures, they showed a newsreel with the *Arizona* going up. That big black plume," he said. "It made me pretty angry. Then a U.S. Army general appeared. Brown tunic, helmet, all that. He said that good men were needed to stomp out Tojo and Fritz. Didn't occur to me 'til later that it was an actor playing a part. Did you ever do that? Put on the uniform like it was a fucking costume?"

Ward swallowed. "No, no, I...I just talked as myself, is all. Up on a horse."

"Copper One? Two? Three?"

"No, it...another horse."

"What did you say, up on your horse?"

"Oh, I mean, it's been years," Ward said. "Something like, 'I've been in many a tussle. Let's take the fight to them.' Something like that."

Butler ran his tongue over his teeth. "I joined the 504th Parachute Infantry Regiment, 82nd Airborne. North Africa, Sicily, Anzio. A shrapnel wound on the Market Garden jump put me in a field hospital, but I healed up enough in time for the Battle of the Bulge. I'd say I took the fight to them, wouldn't you?"

"You...well, of course," Ward said.

"A lot of guys lost the fight," Butler said. "One thousand in the 504th alone. Guys I grew up with. My brother Johnny, on Omaha Beach. And a lot of others. I wonder how many of them answered your call to the frontlines."

Ward swallowed.

There was a sharp knock at the door. Butler nodded and one of the men opened the door. Ward looked over his shoulder. A slender man in a dark suit walked in with a half-cocked grin and his head bobbing slightly. He held a weathered brown leather duffel bag in one hand and a brown hardshell Samsonite briefcase in the other. Ward had last seen them locked in the trunk of the Cord.

"What have you got?" Butler said.

"You're gonna like what I got," Flip Suggs said.

Ward started up out of the chair again. A set of hands caught his shoulders and pushed him back down into it.

"Sit!" Butler said.

"What the hell are you playing at here?" Ward said.

Butler racked the slide back on the Colt, chambering the round. He flicked the safety off. He trained the Colt dead-center on Ward's chest.

"Mr. McCoy, you're going to sit right there while we sort this out." Butler said.

"You...you can't go rootin' around in my property," Ward said.

"Yes, I can," Butler said. "Flip, show me."

Flip Suggs dropped the duffel on the floor. He lay the briefcase flat on the desk in front of Butler. He snapped open the catches and opened it. Ward winced. Butler looked inside. The stacks of bills were rumpled and bound together with thin elastics.

"Well," Butler said. "Where'd you get the money?"

Ward exhaled thinly. "Been winning."

"Where?"

"Everywhere. I'm on a lucky streak."

Butler eyed Ward. A smirk turned up at the corner of his mouth and he shook his head slightly. "Well, Mr. McCoy, that's why you're here. Because your luck's run out."

Ward tensed up in the chair.

"After our chat earlier, my guys saw you push some players out of the game pretty quick," Butler said. "Pablo kept an eye on you. That's him standing behind you now. Pablo says you also got the players talking a bit. Against policy."

"Fellers always ask questions about the pictures. It don't matter."

"It does if it means they don't notice what you're up to."

"I don't know what the hell you're talkin' about."

Butler flexed his grip on the Colt. "Hold your arms up and out and sit still," he said. "Pablo's gonna check you out."

"You're makin' a mistake," Ward said.

"We'll see. Arms up and out."

Ward held his arms out like a scarecrow. They trembled. He kept his eyes fixed on the Colt. Pablo came from behind him and went to his left arm. Pablo patted it like he was tenderizing meat. Pablo rolled the sleeve back and revealed Ward's square gold Elgin wristwatch and his skin underneath, saw the cloth of the sleeve deform and the lining rumple.

He went to Ward's right arm and rolled the sleeve back. The cloth buckled and went rigid. Pablo followed the stitching of the sleeve to the lining. His fingers probed the lining, found an opening, found a ridge, and held there. Pablo removed a playing card from the sleeve and flicked it onto the desk. Jesse Butler looked down at the ace of clubs.

"Well." Butler said. "There it is. Good work, Pablo."

"Thanks, Mr. Butler," Pablo said and stepped back.

Ward lowered his arms slowly. His eyes went with them and drifted to the floor.

"Pablo noticed when you got a little chit-chat in, you shifted your hands a bit before some really swell plays," Butler said. "So how many hands tonight you won because you snuck a high card in?"

Ward said nothing.

Butler nodded at the briefcase. "How many pots in other places have you won with your little trick?"

Ward said nothing.

"You know that's an old way to cheat? Not even the best one."

Ward said nothing.

"If you want to explain yourself, Mr. McCoy, now's the time."

"Goddamn it," Ward said. "I borrowed money in California for a bet. It went bad and now I owe. Was a time I could square a debt like that, but work don't come like it used to. I had to make it back outside California, and I always played cards."

"You always cheat, too?"

"No," Ward said. "Not always. I just...I needed to make sure. I've got to pay up by the end of the week, two days from now. I've been playin' all over the state, makin' it back. Tonight, what I made, that's the last of the debt."

"How much do you owe?"

"Ten grand," Ward said.

"To who?"

"Fellow named Del Pascoe."

Butler's eyes went dinner-plate wide. Nicky and Pablo shifted in their shoes.

"Of everyone in California you could've borrowed money from," Butler said, "you borrowed from Del the Butcher?"

Ward twitched.

"Unbelievable," Butler said.

"So...so you can understand how bad I need the money," Ward said.

"Understand?" Butler said. "I understand you lost the Butcher's money. I don't understand how that makes it all right to rip me off and rip off the people I work for. On top of who knows how many chumps around Arizona."

"It, it ain't..." Ward stammered. "It ain't all right. But I didn't have a choice."

"Of course you did," Butler said. "You just chose wrong. Jesus, you were so stuck on your fucking game earlier. All because you were busy screwing me."

Ward swallowed. He shifted in the chair.

"Look, Mr. Butler. I'm sorry. I really, truly am. And I...if you just let me square what I owe, I'll get it back for you. I swear it."

Butler's mouth went slack. "You want to saddle *me* with a debt instead?" he said.

"You're a reasonable man," Ward said. "Far more reasonable than Del Pascoe is. All I'm asking for is your help here. I...I need your help."

Butler stood up. He re-trained the gun on Ward. Ward flinched in the chair.

"The Ward McCoy I knew never needed anyone's help," Butler said. "Never asked. Never begged or cowered. Jesus, I used to think you were something."

Ward stared down the dark void of the Colt's barrel. His grip on the armrests tightened. The tunnel before him seemed to widen and he awaited its report, its flashfire, its cracking bright lightning which would snuff out the cell-like room and everything he'd known in the world.

Butler relaxed the Colt's hammer. He set the safety, put the gun on the table, and sat. He took a deep breath in and exhaled slowly. He looked at Ward and rolled his tongue around inside his cheek. He seemed to mull something over. He blinked.

"Here's the thing," Butler said. "There are people who will be very happy to know that Del the Butcher is out ten thousand. In a way, you've done me a favor."

"I..." Ward said. "I don't understand."

"Do you think Del would come for you, if he knew you had his money ready?"

Ward shuddered. "Prob'ly," he said.

"Of course he would. He'd prefer it brought to him, of course, but he'd come for it, if he had no other choice."

"Sure. Sure," Ward said.

Butler stood up. He walked around to the front of the desk and sat back against the edge. "So, Mr. McCoy, what if I were to see that your debt with Del was erased?"

Ward blinked. "You'd do that?"

"In a way, yeah."

"Well...then I'd be in your debt, Mr. Butler."

"Then here's the deal, McCoy. You're a liar, a cheat, and a sniveling fraud. By all rights I should handle you like we usually do cheaters and drop you down a mine shaft. That's where the name of this place comes from, did you know? The old Silver Bell mine, south of town. The desert is littered with old holes and dead cheats. But I have something else in mind. So, I'm going to keep the money you made for Del, and you're going to lie low in town, at my discretion, until I say so. When the time comes, you leave town and you never set foot in this state again."

Ward twitched. "You want me to lie low until you say so?"

Butler nodded. "I'll have someone keep an eye on you."

"You could just give it to me, and let me get it to Del. Then I'll make it back for you. Squared away on all counts, and everyone wins."

"I'm not interested in everyone winning."

"Well, fair," Ward said. "But I did a lot for that money. It ought to be me sets it right."

Butler shook his head. "McCoy, you fleeced it from a number of legitimate state gaming establishments. You're entitled to precisely none of it, nor to what's done with it."

Ward eyed the briefcase. He stroked his chin. "You're...you're not going to give it to Del, then?"

"What I do with it isn't your business. You lay low for the next few days and trust me to see that the debt is no longer your problem. Or you can pick out a spot in the desert for yourself. Your call."

Ward swallowed. There was a dry tension in his throat that wouldn't go away. He looked at the coal-black empty eyes of Jesse Butler. He looked at his Colt on the desk and the briefcase of money near it. He considered the offer. It was less an option than a direction.

Ward nodded.

"Good," Butler said. "I believe you still have your winnings from tonight?"

Ward said nothing. Then he nodded again. He trembled slightly as he reached into his jacket pocket and took out the stack of bills from the Silver Bell. Some of the photo singles came out with the stack. He tossed the bundle onto the desk.

Butler swept the photos aside. He counted the bills. He put them back neatly on the desk and nodded solemnly.

"Flip, you and Pablo take him to the inn," Butler said.

"Sure thing," Flip said.

Pablo took Ward under the arm and yanked. Ward got up.

"What about my gun?" Ward said.

"What about it?"

"You've got the money," Ward said. "But the gun is mine."

Butler put his hand over the Colt. "That's a soldier's gun, McCoy," he said. "You're a cheating liar, a broken-down old wreck. A goddamned disappointment. There's nothing soldier about you."

Ward started to say something. Pablo pulled him toward the door with Flip coming up behind, carrying his duffel. Jesse Butler said something as they hauled Ward out of the office.

"Keep to the high trails, McCoy."

They took Ward to a motel down the road called the Gila Trail Inn. It was two levels of flaking cactus-green brick with white doors. Flip and Pablo rode with him and had him park the Cord under an awning. When he got out of the car and came around, he saw the furled and scratched underside of the trunk where someone had wedged a crowbar in to pop it and reveal his treasure. Suggs grinned and shrugged and held his hand out. Ward handed over the keys to the Cord. Pablo prodded him towards one of the first-floor rooms.

The room was ready for him. Jesse Butler had some kind of standing arrangement. It was musty, spartan and brown. It was decorated with plastic cacti and a watercolor of a cowboy bucking a rodeo bronc. There was one window by the door draped with ratty mauve curtains.

"We'll be outside, and around," Flip said. "All you've gotta do is stay here, pal."

Ward said nothing. They closed the door on him. He dropped his leather duffel beside a bulbous television set with spindly tripod legs. He put his Stetson on the beaten and cracked easy chair in the corner. He sat on the bed, slipped his boots off, and stretched out in his clothes.

The exhaustion and the tension seemed to well up right then. The game, the plays, the backroom conversation with Butler, the sudden impact of his pistol in his back, the sight of it trained on him and ready to end him right there in that cell of a room, the money slipping through his fingers like so much had in his life, the thought of Del Pascoe's blades gleefully paring him away. It set his nerves alight and burned them out at the same time. Ward coughed out something like a sob and slipped away into the merciful dark.

III

Butler woke at six in the morning. He drank a mug of coffee and smoked and looked out the window of his apartment. The place commandeered the top floor of Sentinel's three-story yellow brick post office and overlooked the sparse and quiet main street. Veronica was asleep in his king bed in the bedroom. After Ward McCoy was hauled off to the Gila Trail Inn, Butler left a message with the syndicate in Chicago, then found her asleep at her dressing room station. He'd roused her and she'd gone with him without saying a word, crawled into bed with her back to him and drifted off. Which was fine for the present, he thought. She'd come around eventually. And she wasn't talking about Hollywood.

Chicago called back at six-twenty. He laid it all out: Ward McCoy, Del Pascoe, the debt of ten thousand dollars stolen from their Arizona enterprises, which was now recovered and secure in his office at the Silver Bell. There was a real opportunity here, he suggested. The men in Chicago made approving noises. They saw the opportunity like he saw it. They said they would call back.

Butler grinned and hung up. He finished his coffee and turned the radio on low. Frankie Laine sang about cool water. The street outside was empty and silent. The sunrise lent everything a light sheen of straw-gold.

He figured they wouldn't take long to decide. It was a question of logistics, really. Should it be done? Yes. Could it? Probably. Would they? He thought so. The only thing he didn't know was what they'd say about Ward McCoy. He wondered if he'd allowed some sentimentality into the equation by stashing Ward at the motel. He could have had him taken out to the desert like others before. There was no reason to treat him different—the man had even insulted him on top of it all, with his card stunt and his goddamned photo and his mockery of a service weapon. And yet condemning someone he'd looked up to didn't sit right. Butler scoffed. Maybe he'd been a little soft. Sentimental. Sure. He could make up for it later.

He heard the soft padding of bare feet coming in from the bedroom and turned. Veronica walked into the kitchen wearing a pink satin kimono.

"You're up early," Butler said.

"Got all the sleep I need, I think," Veronica said.

"There's coffee," Butler said and gestured to the stovetop pot.

She murmured something. She picked a chipped mug out of the sink and filled it halfway.

"Were you talking with someone?" she said.

"Chicago."

"Was it important?"

"Maybe," Butler said. "We might have something to celebrate soon."

"Like what?"

"All in due time, baby."

She sipped coffee. She purred. "How would we celebrate?"

Butler grinned and winked. "Ladies' choice. Think of something you'd like."

Veronica licked her lips. "Well, I'm going to lunch with Sylvia today, and then I'll spend the afternoon rehearsing at the studio. That should give me time to come up with something."

"Swell. Remember you're on at seven-thirty and ten-thirty."

"I know."

"Otherwise, it's left to Dixon, and I swear, it's like he's stealing material from Fleer Funnies."

Veronica undid her sash. She let the kimono slide off and drop to the kitchen floor. She carried her mug out of the kitchen and went toward the bathroom. Butler watched her shapely nude body shift and bounce a little with each step as she walked. He heard the shower start up. He chuckled. She was coming around, all right.

The phone rang. He picked up. The syndicate gave him the green light. One caveat: the Silver Bell was off the table. He would have to set it up for the establishment in Yuma. There were more men there, and there'd be even more within three hours. He told them he could do it with one call. They lauded him, even DiNunzio—*Jesse, my boy.*

They said to take Ward McCoy out when it was all done. He winced and said he would. The line clicked off. He felt a pang of regret at the last order. First things first, he thought. He reset the line and found a number he wasn't supposed to know. It was on a nondescript page in his notebook. The operator connected him. The line rang shrill and high-pitched. A high-grade, special line. A man answered.

"Malibu Construction."

"Get me Del Pascoe."

"He's not available."

"Make him available."

"You have any idea how early it is? Call later."

"Oh, I'm so sorry. Is he getting his beauty sleep? Does he have his Pond's Cold Cream and hair rollers on?"

"Who the fuck do you think you are, shitbird?"

"I need to talk to Del about a debt."

"Call later."

"Friend, if he finds out I called and you didn't tell him right away, he's going to take it out on you, and we both know what that'll be like."

The man audibly winced. "Hold on," he said.

The line clicked and whirred. A veneer of static tickled Butler's ear. The line clicked again. There was an annoyed grunt and another man's voice, canyonlike, deep and furrowed.

"This had better be important."

Butler snorted. "Del the Butcher, I presume? All you California pricks sound the same."

Del Pascoe exhaled into the line. "So do you Chicago assholes. Always trying to sound tougher than you really are. What's your problem?"

"My name is Butler. I'm an operator in Arizona."

"Butler. Butler," Pascoe said. "Sort of rings a bell."

"It should, unless you're dumber than I thought."

"Are you trying to annoy me, Butler? Your outfit's so broke it does crank calls?"

"Ward McCoy owes you ten grand," Butler said. "I thought you should know he made it back by ripping off tables all over Arizona, cheating at poker. Except we just caught him red-handed with everything he took, so I guess that means you won't be getting your money. Oops."

There was a slow, reedy breath. "I don't know what you're talking about."

"Yes, you do."

"*You* don't know what you're talking about."

"I'm looking at a briefcase full of cash right now. He nearly put a bow on it for you."

"Put McCoy on."

"It'll be pretty hard for you to talk to a dead man."

"You're lying."

"I don't care to lie to you, Del. You don't have time for it. We caught McCoy, and he sang like a canary before he saddled up for the big rodeo in the sky. Tomorrow morning your ten thousand goes to the Arizona Gaming Commission as evidence in a statewide fraud investigation, then redistributed to its rightful owners: us. Then it will be well and truly gone."

"You little fuck," Del Pascoe said. "Even if I believed you, why would you tell me this?"

"Because you've been a problem for my associates for years, Del. Your little coastal plays put a bug up some asses in Chicago and Vegas. But you knew that already. You've taken out a lot of guys Mr. DiNunzio liked over the years, and now we know a washed-up old cowboy actor lost your money, and it's good for a laugh. The money is at the Four Aces Casino in Yuma, but it won't be there for long. I suppose you can try for it, or you can cut your losses. But I don't care what you do, Del. I just want you to know who fucked you, and to hear you squirm."

"Squirm, shit. I'll get what I'm owed," Pascoe said. "And then I'll come for you, you two-bit bigmouth. You small-time piss-monkey. I'll flay you alive and peel your eyeballs like grapes before I feed you your fuckin' nuts and watch you choke."

"Now who's trying to sound tough?" Butler said. "Best of luck, chuckles."

He hung up the phone. He replayed the conversation in his mind. Now that it was done, he wondered about whether he should have used his name. But Del needed to believe him, and that meant credibility, putting as much truth as possible on the table—a bit of truth to obscure the lies and give the Butcher someone to hate. Hate enough to get angry, hate enough to get stupid. If it made him a target, so be it. He could handle himself if he needed to, and the syndicate would help. And damned if it hadn't been a little fun to poke the bear. He put himself in Del's shoes. He'd be hopping like there was a habañero up his ass.

Butler chuckled. *Who stares down the bandits now*, he thought.

He lit a fresh cigarette. He ran his thumb over the lighter and the emblem of the 504th. He listened to the shower water cascading over Veronica's skin. He started thinking about breakfast.

***

Ward woke to fingers of light coming in through moth-holes in the curtains. The room was hot and the air was stale. He'd sweat clean through his clothes and felt damp and rotten. He grimaced. He threw his jacket on the foot of the bed and removed his billfold from his pants pocket. The orange ticket for his Colt came out stuck to the leather. He tore it up and let it fall to the carpet.

He coughed and made his way to the stifling windowless bathroom. The single bulb above the mirror threw dim, pale light on tile the color of nicotine. He worked the spigot and cupped coolish water into his mouth and over his face.

It loosened his throat some. He let the water run, touched it to his cheeks and forehead. He looked in the mirror at water beading on the worn and weathered face of a ridiculous fool who'd made a goddamned mess out of what was already a catastrophe.

Stupid old man, he thought. In so many ways. Could have kept the game simple and cleared out when he was ahead. Should've slipped the ace back in the deck—he'd managed that every other time. Why forget when it counted the most? Got cocky. Distracted. Soft. Useless. The same reasons he'd lost Del Pascoe's money. Had to make it worse.

Should have kept driving last night, he thought. He could've tried Yuma. But that was a bigger town, and he'd counted on things to be looser and for the money to be less secure in the smaller places. Could have kept on driving, then, and pulled in home for another night in a cold bed. Wake to another morning waiting by the phone for a call bringing another bit part, if it rang at all. Or maybe the doorbell would ring instead, and there'd be Del Pascoe and his crew, carrying everything from stilettos to cheese graters, and he'd explain— well, Del, I know you *said* ten thousand, but here's nine – and hope that Del would understand. Yes, he could hope. And then he'd learn what dying in the Medieval Age was like. Few men got to experience being hung upside down by their big toes and having their pecker sliced off and fed to them.

If he even got that far, he thought. The luck he was running with, had he tried to blitz it home in the night he'd nod off at the wheel. Nose the Cord off the road and plunge into some deep valley to mummify there in a grand white sarcophagus, turn sun-blackened and fossilized, a mystery to be unearthed in fifty years' time.

Ward stared into the mirror and found the rheumy blue-green eyes of a man who knew that everything had gone about as bad for him as it could have with no sign of getting better.

All right, he thought. What are you gonna do, cowpoke?

Wait until my say so, Butler had said. Trust him to clear the debt. How was he going to do that, and how could he be trusted to do it? There was some kind of angle the man had going which Ward couldn't put his finger on. Somehow it meant Butler needed him lying low, hiding out in this room like an outlaw. He felt a sudden chill in his blood. Outlaw, hell—fish in a barrel, more like. Because Butler might aim to keep the money and give him up to Del. That'd see the debt cleared. What then?

Could make a run for it, Ward thought. Sneak past the Silver Bell boys outside and fire up the Cord. Make a break for Mexico. He didn't know anyone in Mexico, but nobody knew him there either. Maybe neither Del or Butler knew anyone across the border. He could find a *rancho* and sign on to work horses. Surely some *hacendado* would have room for another *vaquero*, even a *yanqui*. He could hide among the bunkhouses and barns and the musky scents of horses and cattle. He could rest by the desert campfires, find friends among the hardworking men of the land down in Sonora. Sleep under the stars with a saddle for a pillow under the warmth of a thick Mexican blanket. It could be like the old days, back before the money and the fame which had flooded in before ebbing away. It wouldn't matter that he didn't know where the *ranchos* were, that he barely knew how to ask for a *tortilla*, that he was old and busted-up and hadn't broken a horse in decades, that anyone looking could locate an old jabbering *gringo* inside of five minutes, that he'd have to survive the desert first in order to have any kind of a chance at all.

Ward spat in the running sink. It plopped in a half-full bowl. The drain was plugged with thick dark hairs which wafted like seaweed in the bottom.

"Goddamn it," he said. He turned off the spigot.

He checked his wristwatch. It was eleven-fifteen in the morning. He stripped his rank clothes off and showered under an erratic lukewarm spray. He went to the duffel and donned a fresh white shirt, brown pants and black socks, all laundered the prior morning in Wickenburg. They stuck to his clammy body like bandages.

There was a knock at the door. Three sharp, short raps. Ward froze.

"Mr. McCoy?" a woman said from the other side.

Ward opened the door.

Veronica Venus stood outside his room. She'd traded last night's red dress for a white blouse and thigh-hugging flared orange pants and a thin blue scarf at her neck. She looked at him over the top rim of red cat-eye sunglasses perched halfway down her nose and smiled.

Ward froze. "You?" he said.

"I thought I'd take you to lunch," Veronica said.

Ward was suddenly aware of a gnawing hunger beyond the pit of his gut.

"Did Butler send you?"

"If anyone asks, yes," she said.

Ward stared. He kept his hand on the door.

"You could ask me in," Veronica said.

"It's hot in here," Ward said.

"Come on out, then," she said. "I know somewhere you'll like."

Ward eyed her. He nodded and closed the door. He couldn't figure why she was there. He put on his boots and his jacket and his Stetson and went outside. She was leaning back against a support beam, looking up and out at the high sun. She smiled at him again.

She had a white '53 Buick Skylark soft-top parked next to the Cord. Flip Suggs was inside the Cord reading a Life magazine.

"I'm thinking Trudy's counter, Flip," Veronica said. "Jesse wants Mr. McCoy to experience some hospitality while he's here. I'll have him back in an hour."

"I ought to be going with you," Suggs said.

"Nonsense, darling. He'll be perfectly safe with me."

Suggs' eyes narrowed.

"You're so dedicated, Flip," Veronica said. "I should put in a good word with Jesse for you and see to it that you have a proper night off. Maybe you and I can get up to something."

Suggs' eyes widened. He grinned and his head wobbled.

"An hour," he said.

Veronica blew him a kiss.

They got in the Buick. Ward picked up her scent of clean lavender and pear. It cut through the funk of stale booze and cheap tobacco which clung to his jacket from the Silver Bell. She drove them away from the Gila Trail Inn and down the road to a diner off the highway. She had him wait in the car and came back with sandwiches in wax paper, French fries in paper sleeves and two glass Coke bottles. She steered the Buick onto a side road leading away from Sentinel.

"Why are you doin' this?" Ward said.

"I heard you were still in town. I thought you could use a proper welcome," Veronica said. "You look a tad shaken, Mr. McCoy."

"I had a hard night," he said. "Could maybe use a drink. Steady my nerves."

"There's an idea."

"Where are we goin'?"

"You'll see."

Ward watched the gravel run underneath the car. He scanned the bright tan stretch of silent desert which was dotted with scrubby tufts of sage and tall, looming saguaros. He thought about deep dust-choked underground chambers packed with men who pulled fast moves in the Silver Bell like he had. He saw rattlesnakes slide and weave around their bones.

"This somewhere out of the way?" he said.

"It's worth it," Veronica said. "I promise."

The road curved under the shadow of a small mountain and started to rise. The Buick climbed with it and eased up the grade. Veronica gave the car some gas and purred languidly with the rolling engine until the ascending road plateaued and flattened out.

"Here we are," she said.

They stopped at an overlook with a weathered, sun-dried and pale grey wooden picnic table. She laughed and reached a slender hand into her purse. Something clinked and sloshed. She took out a pint of bonded Kentucky bourbon which was three-quarters full. She held it up proudly and tipped it toward the table.

"Presenting the finest picnic in the Sonoran, hosted by the Princess of the Desert," she said. "Sorry I don't have glasses."

Ward managed a chuckle. Veronica got out of the car carrying the food and the bottle. He followed. She went to the picnic table and laid out the sandwiches and popped the caps on the Cokes.

He went to stand at the edge of the overlook. The azure sky was faintly streaked with pale cloud. Below, Sentinel was a sporadic collection of buildings and poles and wires, small edges and ridges rising faintly against the dry expanse like an outbreak of hives on sunburned flesh. Ward could see the Silver Bell down there, with its neon sign dead and muted in the sunshine. A light, warm breeze out of the desert passed over him. He breathed with it.

"Long time since I was properly out here," Ward said.

"What was that?" Veronica said. She sat at the table with her back against it like it was a chaise-longue and crossed her legs.

"Nothin'," Ward said. "Was a time we'd drive cattle over from Texas for sale. Spent a lot of days and nights under these very skies. We were out on these ranges, guiding the herds. That was before, though."

"Before the pictures?"

"Yeah."

"Is that where you're from? Texas?"

"Tennessee, originally."

Veronica ran her finger delicately along the neck of the bourbon bottle.

"Everyone's from somewhere else," she said.

"Yeah," Ward said.

"Come sit, Mr. McCoy. You said something about steadying your nerves."

Ward turned away from the lookout and went to the table. He sat beside her, doffed his Stetson and set it on its crown beside the open bottle. He took a swig of bourbon. It burned its way down his throat and into his empty stomach like a hot thin ember.

He handed the bottle to Veronica. She smiled. She tipped the mouth of the bottle to her red lips. She drew an easy sip and exhaled.

"That helps a bit, doesn't it?" she said.

"Sure does."

They sat at the bench and ate. There was nothing special about the sandwiches nor the fries but Ward appreciated them. He minded his lunching, careful not to drop anything or drip Coke or bourbon down his shirt.

"You said you had a rotten night," Veronica said.

"Mm-hm."

"So did I."

"Sorry to hear," Ward said. "What was the trouble?"

"The same man behind yours."

Ward stopped mid-bite. He eyed her. He swallowed and washed it down with a bit of Coke. "Who'd that be? God?" he said.

Veronica licked salt and grease off her thumb daintily. "This morning, I overheard Jesse on the phone with his business associates about your situation," she said. "It's how I knew where to find you."

"What situation?"

She told him. About the cards, the cheating, the debt. Jesse confiscating his ill-gotten winnings. Everything he already knew.

Ward balled up crumb-dusted wax paper and pitched it off the table to the edge of the overlook. "All right," he said. "So, you know. What's it matter to you, anyway?"

"I don't know," she said. "I only learned about it."

Ward scoffed and shook his head. "He don't even know you're here," he said. "How d'you think he'll take it, once he finds out you brought me out here?"

"Not well," she said. "But I can handle that."

"Oh, that's dandy. Reckon he'll take it out on me, then. I'm in enough trouble as it is, reckon that'll be what does it for good, abscondin' with his woman."

"We're not so close as you might think."

"He called you his girl."

Veronica laughed. "Do you have a girl?"

"No."

"Suppose that you did. Would you pass her around to any guy you wanted to make a good impression with?"

Ward frowned. "I...is that what he does?"

She glanced away from the table, past the overlook. "'The price of the business we're in.' That was how he explained it, the first time. At first, I thought maybe that was just how it was. But when I finally got to refusing, I learned that there was no saying 'no'. If one of them comes to town, and he sees the show, and he gets the inclination..."

Ward shifted in his seat. He clasped his hands together.

"Not just any guy, mind. Only in the business," Veronica said. "They have some kind of pecking order. Guys under Jesse, like Flip, can only look, and lust in private. But if someone above Jesse wants it..." she snapped her fingers. "Then that's it. And it's only a matter of time before guys like Flip get their shot. Sure, they pay for it. But they pay him, not me."

Ward looked her over. He stroked his chin. "Last night, he said something about people he worked for. I wager he's involved in somethin' big?"

"It's a syndicate from the east. They run most of the gaming interests out here. He met some of the people involved during the war."

"And he...he pimps you out to some of the guys in this...syn-der-kit?"

Veronica bit her bottom lip and glanced away.

"I'm sorry," he said.

"So am I. I'd hoped to forget about all of that for an hour. I mean, here you are, the first decent guy to come to Sentinel for the longest time. A hero, no less. And I have to go and bring up all the problems you and I both have."

Ward shrugged. "I only been a hero on the screen."

"Have we got any other kind?"

Ward said nothing.

"Anyway, that's how it is," she said. "I'm sorry for bringing it all up."

"You got nothin' to be sorry about."

"Neither do you. What if we weren't sorry about things?"

Ward smiled. "I reckon I'd like that."

"So would I, Mr. McCoy."

"It's Ward."

"Ward." She rounded her lips around his name. She sipped bourbon from the bottle and handed it to him. "Can I ask you something?"

"Sure."

"How did you get in the pictures? Why did you?"

Ward drank. The rim of the bottle mouth was still wet and slightly waxy from her lips. He caught a hint of her taste before caramel fire washed it down.

"You know Tom Mix?" he said.

Veronica shook her head.

"I left home when I was fourteen," Ward said. "Ma died when I was seven. Pa was a drunk and I wager he's dead. I worked farms until I could ride and when I could ride, I rode away and never looked back. Went to Texas and cowboyed. Every horseman I ever knew looked to Tom. See, Tom cowboyed a while before he went into the pictures and became a real star. When we came to town on a drive, if we were lucky, there'd be one of Tom's pictures playing. We used to jaw about if we could ever be a star and all that. One day I thought, hell, why not? You ain't ever goin' to find out unless you go to find out. So I went to California, nosed around, and found people. I even found Tom. I guess I had somethin' they liked, because 'fore I knew it I was ridin' and ropin' for the camera."

"Just like that?"

"That's the short of it."

Veronica leaned forward on the table. She propped her head on her hand. "What if someone wanted to be in pictures now, Ward?" she said. "Suppose a girl knew how to dance, knew how to act. How would she get in?"

Ward cocked an eye at her. "You want to get into the pictures?"

"Yes."

"You act?"

"Every day," she said. "I act the loving lady friend, the performer, the hostess. The woman happy to dance for nickels in the middle of nowhere."

Ward sipped bourbon slowly.

"What would it take?" she said.

"Same as always. You audition, make the right connections with studio people."

"Auditions are no trouble," she said. "You would know studio people, wouldn't you?"

"Well, I...I know some, sure."

"So...maybe you'd have some connections."

"Maybe."

"Would you put in a word for me?"

Ward smiled and shook his head. "If I'm alive to do it, sure," he said.

"You might recall, I'm in a bit of a situation right now."

Veronica straightened. She fixed her blue eyes on him over the sunglasses.

"What if you had your money back?" she said.

Ward smiled. "Don't joke with me, girl," he said.

She stared at him. She splayed her fingers out on the picnic table and leaned in.

"Jesse's keeping your money in his office," she said. "Anything important, he keeps in a safe in the wall, behind a painting. That's where he keeps the money I made entertaining his syndicate friends, too. It's at least four grand by now, and I'm owed it."

Ward cocked an eye. He stroked his chin.

"I go onstage twice tonight, at seven-thirty and ten-thirty," Veronica said. "Jesse never misses a show. He has his own booth in the cabaret and runs things from there while I perform. Which leaves his office open and empty. Suppose someone went in there during that time."

"Suppose," Ward said.

"Well, he keeps the combination for the safe in the same little notebook where he keeps everything. I could get him alone in the office after my last performance. All alone, he could be subdued. And he would cough it up." Ward looked her over. He looked for a tell. There was no twitch at the corner of her mouth, no flicker of the eyes. There was no sudden tension or throbbing in the big vein at her slender neck. She was still as an ice sculpture.

"You've thought about this," he said. "You're serious."

Veronica drained her Coke. The last dark dregs vanished behind full red crimson. She pitched the empty bottle over the edge of the overlook where it fell silently into the sandy rocks below.

"I am. What about you, Ward?" she said.

Ward said nothing.

"I left home young too, you know," Veronica said. "We had...we had a darling little farm in Oklahoma, with chickens and cows. My father and my mother were...oh, they were hardworking, decent people. But there was one bad season, a dry season, and who knew what caused it, but there was a fire. Mother, Father, my brothers and sisters, they couldn't get out of the house. I was the only one who escaped."

"My God," Ward said.

Veronica looked out into the desert. "I didn't have anyone else, or anywhere to go. There was only Jesse, and I was young and in love. He was strong, he'd been to war and seen many places. I was entranced. If I'd known what he was involved in, what he would turn out to be, I wouldn't have gone with him."

"I'm sorry," Ward said.

"All I want is another chance at a good life, Ward," Veronica said. "Just another chance. A chance to do something my own way, to make something of myself instead of being at the whim of some brute and his brute people."

"And you wager it's in Hollywood."

"It changed your life, didn't it?"

Ward eyed her. He nodded. He looked past the sunglasses at the ice-blue eyes behind the lenses. He thought about second chances.

"Say we *could* get my money," Ward said. "You'd want a ride."

"You have a beautiful old sled."

"Which one of those boys is sitting in right now with the keys."

"We can get it back."

"How?"

Veronica sighed. "If we could get your car, and your money, would you give me that ride to Hollywood?"

Ward thought about it. He considered whether it was even possible, or whether it was worth it at this point. He thought about what he had to lose – hardly anything, at this point. He thought about what he had to gain – well, that was the question.

"Yeah," he said. "Yes."

Veronica smiled. "Then we should drive back," she said. "Our hour is almost up."

She collected the detritus of their lunch and put it all in the back seat of the Buick. Ward put on his Stetson and went to the car. They drove down the mountain and down the side road, rattling along in the dust and kicking up a fine ochre plume which trailed them. At the motel, she parked next to the Cord. Flip Suggs was still seated inside the car and she waved to him. He nodded back.

"Thank you for lunch," Ward said.

"Thank you for your company."

"I suppose we should figure out how ─"

"Not now," she said. "Can I walk you to your door?"

He nodded. She shut the Buick off. He got out and she went with him. They stopped in front of his door.

"Well," Ward said.

"Aren't you going to ask me in?" Veronica asked.

Ward swallowed. "It's hot in there," he said.

She removed the sunglasses. She looked up at him with icy blue limpid crystals.

"I don't mind if it's hot," she said.

He opened the door. She followed him into the dark heat.

***

Chicago called Butler again. Six men were in place in Yuma, backed up by locals who owed favors. Intelligence from contacts in California suggested that Del Pascoe was gathering a complement to move on Yuma in the night. Butler asked to join up with the boys in Yuma. The syndicate kiboshed it. They let him know they knew who would get the credit when all was said and done.

He hung up pleased. He called the Gila Trail Inn. The manager found Pablo, who had switched out for Flip, who was now back in the Silver Bell watching the play floor. Butler asked Pablo to keep an eye on McCoy into the night. Pablo said that was no problem – McCoy had been occupied by her hospitality most of the day. It made watching the motel room easy.

"*Whose* hospitality?" Butler said.

IV

Ward lay on his back in the bed. He stared up at the mildewed white stucco ceiling. He felt a long and supple warmth beside him. Veronica was face-down in the pillow with her blonde hair fanned out over it, covering her head. She snored gently. He slid away and left the white sheet draped over her nude, lithe body. He went to the window.

Some small piece of him was scratching and clawing, wanting to kick and kick himself again and again. The hell with that, he thought. There was a good chance this was the end of the trail, he thought, and if that were the case there were worse ways of spending it than with a beautiful girl. Even if she was using him. Or was she? Hell if it hadn't been fun though. Nice change of pace from tables of old men and old talk, stupid questions about the pictures and the Duke. The last two weeks felt like years now, and there'd been years of that nonsense on top of them. Something different was good. It was almost empowering. It cleared his mind of trouble.

When she closed the door behind them she said something about being Veronica but being someone else, even when she was on the stage she was always being someone else. He remembered Butler calling her by some backwoods name. Something stirred then in the sweltering room, brought them together and she took him in openly in a warm soft crush of heat. Strange as it was there was something businesslike and inevitable about it, a way to mark the accord reached between them, seal the contract. Their complicity became a tangle in the heat of the room and not without some strain but somehow Ward had managed his part. In the aftermath he felt stunned, in a way—in the saddle, but loose on the reins. Now he stared through the space between the curtains at a near-empty motel parking lot drenched in late afternoon sunlight.

Veronica stirred behind him. The sheets rustled. She rummaged through her purse and a crinkled pack of cigarettes. He heard a match strike and a soft inhale.

"What time is it?" she said.

"Near four," he said.

Veronica sighed. "Just as well."

"Yeah," Ward said.

Veronica exhaled smoke. It billowed up to the ceiling.

"What are you thinking?" she said.

"I'm thinkin' your idea might be my last chance to stay alive."

"Oh?"

"I know what Butler's playing at," Ward said. "He's got ten thousand dollars that's already been paid out. Can't be traced."

Veronica frowned. "You think he wants to keep it for himself?"

"Wouldn't you?"

She blew smoke. She tapped ashes onto the carpet. "Earlier today he said that we, meaning he and I, might have something to celebrate soon."

"There it is," Ward said.

"But he told the syndicate he had your money. Why would he, if he was planning to keep it?"

Ward went to the bed and sat down. "Last night he said he was going to clear my debt," he said. "Maybe he's working out a way to keep it and needs me alive until he can figure it out. Or he's keeping me to give me up to Del the Butcher, strike some kind of deal. Any way I look at it, the odds of making it out of this ain't good."

Veronica took a long drag on the cigarette. She held it out to him.

"Unless," she said.

Ward took it. He drew a mouthful of menthol and smoke. It seared his tongue and made him cough lightly as he exhaled. He handed the cigarette back.

"Unless," he said.

She drew smoke. "Jesse looked up to you once. He told me so."

"That was before he met me."

"You ready to show him what you're really made of?"

Ward smirked. "There's only one way out of this I know for sure," he said. "We get my money, I get the money to California. Square the debt with Del."

"And you'll take me with you?"

"Of course."

"And if Jesse comes after us?"

"We'll be on better footing in California. And Mexico's not so far."

Veronica nodded. She rolled smoke out of her mouth. She stubbed the cigarette out on the bedside table. It scorched the worn lacquer.

"All right, then," she said.

They got ready. Ward showered and shaved and dressed. He packed his duffel while she rinsed off under lukewarm spray. He waited for her in the easy chair.

She came out naked. She toweled off and wrapped herself in the bedsheet, like a Roman toga. She went to her purse and pulled out a thin black bulbous strap and tucked it under her hand where it held the sheet together.

"What are you doin'?" Ward said.

"Getting your car," Veronica said. "Stay there, Ward. Don't move."

She opened the door and ran out with the sheet trailing behind her. Ward heard her shout something frantic outside. He stood up, confused. He heard the patter-patter of hands slapping automotive glass outside and the chunky unlatching of a car door. She was babbling in a high, hurried voice. A masculine rumble answered. Her voice grew closer. A shadow flickered over the open door. He heard her voice, clearer now, as she came closer to the room.

" – and we were in the bed and he just fell and I don't know what happened, if he had a heart attack or what but he, Oh God, he, he –"

A hulking dark shape came in through the open door. Pablo. He entered the room and strode toward the bed with Veronica right behind. Pablo saw Ward standing by the chair and stopped.

Veronica dropped the sheet. The thin black strap in her hand came up slicing the air. It connected with the back left side of Pablo's head just behind his ear and made a *thwock* against his skull. Pablo stumbled and spun, his face pained and angered. She swung again. She hit him on the left temple just above the eyeline. He toppled onto the brown carpet.

"Jesus!" Ward said.

Veronica stood over Pablo, bare and panting. She watched to see if he got up. Pablo was on his side with his eyes rolled up, lids half-closed over the whites. His tongue lolled out and he breathed shallowly over it.

She shut the door. "Get the curtain sashes," she said.

Ward pulled them off the curtains. She had him bind Pablo's feet and tie his hands tightly behind his body. Ward tore long strips from the towels and hog-tied Pablo at the bindings.

Veronica started dressing. "Gag him," she said.

Ward tore a strip and wrapped it in Pablo's mouth as a gag. He kept it loose enough that the big man wouldn't suffocate. He checked him at the neck. Pablo was pale and motionless, but he was alive.

"What was that you hit him with?" Ward asked.

She showed him. It was a leather sap, slender and black and weighted at one flat end.

"Hell," Ward said.

"Check him for a knife or a gun," Veronica said.

There was no knife. Ward found the gun inside a shoulder holster inside Pablo's jacket. A black .38 snub-nosed revolver. He found the keys to the Cord in Pablo's pants pocket and took them for himself. He tossed the gun on the bed.

"Keep that with you," Veronica said. "He'll wake up. Make sure he doesn't get away."

"What are you gonna do?" Ward said. He picked up the gun.

She eyed him. "I'm going to dance," she said. "You come to the Silver Bell before ten-fifteen. Park behind the building. There's a door at the rear. I'll make sure everything is clear, and at ten-fifteen, I'll open that door and let you in."

"All right," Ward said. "And you'll get me into Jesse's office?"

She nodded. She tossed him the sap. He caught it in his free hand.

"You'll hide there. I'll bring him to the office after my show, and when he's not looking, you knock him out like I did Pablo."

"Hold on," Ward said.

"It's the only way we'll get his notebook and the combination."

"I didn't intend to get anyone hurt," Ward said.

Veronica gestured down at Pablo. "Little late for that," she said.

Ward said nothing.

Veronica went to him. "It'll be all right, Ward. It's going to solve everything," she said.

He nodded. He pocketed the sap.

They made sure they had everything. He went with her to the door and she kissed him and smiled. She reminded of the time. He nodded. She kissed him again and went to the Buick.

As she drove away, Ward stood there in the room with his hand on the gun and the late afternoon sunlight seeping in. The high trails of the desert, he thought, seemed very far away.

***

Veronica arrived at the Silver Bell and made for her backstage dressing station. Flip Suggs was waiting for her there. He brought her to Jesse Butler's office and stood her before the desk where Butler sat.

"Baby, baby," Butler said. He crushed a cigarette in the overstuffed tray and leaned forward. "I suppose, on some level, this is my fault. I did say that maybe you should play hostess for McCoy. But I didn't expect you to actually do it, or that you'd lie to me."

"It's not what you think," she said.

Butler scoffed. "I think you found McCoy and took him to lunch and fucked him, is what I think," he said. "What I haven't figured out is why, or how badly I'm going to lose it."

"Jesse—"

He stood up. He flung the ashtray off the desk. It whistled faintly in the air and exploded against the concrete. It blanketed the wall in a star of ashes, glass and bits of nicotine-stained paper. Veronica recoiled. Butler came around the desk and grabbed a fistful of her blonde hair and yanked it back. She wailed and went rigid in his grip.

"Jesse, please," she said. "Please listen, please, please, just listen."

His hand was up to strike. He let go of her hair and stepped back. His eyes were burning coals.

"Talk," he said.

"I...I meant to do what I said, with Sylvia and the studio," Veronica said. "But I saw his car outside the motel. And I thought...it's so silly, Jesse. I was so silly about it. I was thinking about what you said about life being a path and...how you never wanted to hear about going west again. I thought if I talked to someone who knew that life, then I'd know for sure. So, I told Flip you'd asked me to look after him for a bit and make him comfortable, and I took McCoy to lunch. I asked him about...life in the pictures."

Butler faintly trembled. "And?" he said.

"And you were right," she said. Her lip quivered. "God, Jesse, you were so very right. All he talked about was dead cowboys, studio people, guys he knew from the old days. How many times he'd been thrown off those stupid horses. It was all so *boring*. I thought there would be glamour and wonder about the stars, having your name on the marquee. But it was dull. I smiled and listened, played along with it, but it was so dull."

Butler exhaled. He leaned back against the desk.

"I drove him back," she said. "He talked about pretty girls like me in the pictures, and...I suppose it was like a reflex. I wanted him to clam up, for it to be over. And it was just like you said it was. Disappointment. He was two minutes, grunting like a pig and flopping like a fish. But it got him to stop talking. I just lay there a while, and I thought about you and what you said this morning, about having something to celebrate. I thought, that's what I want. To celebrate. With you."

Butler stood up. Butler started laughing.

"So we both got fucked badly by Ward McCoy," he said.

Veronica tensed up.

Butler came forward from the desk. He came up within a foot of Veronica. He cupped her neck and the back of her head in his hand. He gazed into her wet, wide eyes. He nodded.

"All right, baby," he said.

"I'm sorry, Jesse."

"I know."

She reached up. She touched his arm, kissed inside his palm. "I want to do something for you," she said.

"What?"

"I thought tonight might be good for the sailor-suit routine. I know you like it."

Butler grinned. He stroked the nape of her neck. "I do," he said.

Veronica drew in closer. She rested her head on his shoulder. "I want...I want to make everything right," she said.

Butler drew in a deep breath and exhaled slowly. He ran his hand across her shoulders, smoothing out their tension. "All right," he said. "Look, it's a hell of a day."

"I'm sorry. I didn't mean to make it worse."

"It's okay. You've got to get ready to perform. I want to see you happy out there, all right?"

Veronica sniffed. "I will be," she said. "That's all I want."

"All right," Butler said. "I love you."

"I love you."

"I'll see you onstage."

"I know you will."

Veronica let go of him and turned away. She left the office, left him standing there at the desk watching her dab at her cheeks as she sauntered down the hall. She went backstage to her dressing station and sat at the mirror. She regarded the wide, still, luminescent blue eyes where they were frozen and unblinking in the clear glass. For a moment she was somewhere else, briefly away from it all, and had she dared show it, she would have smiled.

***

Pablo came to around seven o'clock. Which was a relief to Ward, in a way. He'd sat in the worn easy chair with the .38 held on the prone man for so long, he was starting to worry about what the blows from the sap might have done inside the man's skull. That Pablo was alive gave Ward some faith in the sap for Jesse Butler. The sashes and towel bindings did the trick, too—years in the saddle hadn't dulled his rope skills none, he thought.

Pablo lay on the floor, trussed up like a hog, mumbling words behind the gag. Ward managed to decode one of them – "*Agua*" – water.

Ward shook his head. Pablo glared and lay his head down on the brown carpet.

The lights of Sentinel had fallen into a deep purple repose when Ward left the hotel room. He closed the door on mumbling, hog-tied Pablo. He carried his duffel to the Cord and drove back up the road.

The lot of the Silver Bell was full again. He edged the Cord around the lot, looking for anyone looking for him. A few people made their way in through the front doors on the hunt for slot machines. None of Jesse Butler's men were out and about. He skirted the building. He drove around to the back.

He found the back door and pulled up beside it. He checked his Elgin in the glow of the headlights off the adobe wall. It was two minutes to ten-fifteen. He pocketed the .38, checked that the sap was in his pocket. He killed the lights and got out. He waited by the door. He looked around nervously.

The door opened. Veronica wore a blue dress with white piping and a white sailor hat. She carried a baggy camel leather purse.

"Quick," she said.

Ward followed her in. They were in a narrow concrete hallway lit by faded halogen and red backstage bulbs. Veronica led him onward. They passed the stage access and she stopped. He could hear muffled music from the cabaret stage. She skipped ahead, looked around to make sure there was nobody else coming down the hallway, then waved him forward and turned the corner.

Ward crept over. He rounded the corner and found her at the door to Jesse Butler's office.

They went inside. She shut the door behind them and shunted the purse at him. "I'm on in fifteen," she said. "You wait here."

Ward looked around the room. He considered vantage points, where it would be best for him to lie in wait. "I'll hide behind the desk," he said.

Veronica looked at it. She nodded.

"You get him here," Ward said.

"I will," she said. She kissed him. She slipped out the door.

Ward looked around the room. One of the walls had ashes and paper smeared on it and bits of glass lay at the foot of the wall. He went to the desk. The photo he'd given Butler was next to a stack of paper. Cigarette burns bored holes in Ward's eyes. Ward scoffed. He looked down beside the desk. His Samsonite briefcase was on the floor. It was empty.

He went to the landscape painting. He touched the edges. The painting moved slightly. He found a latch and pulled the frame toward him. It swung slowly on hinges. He peeked behind it and saw blackened lacquer set into the concrete with a combination dial and a handle. A veneer of locked steel between him and his salvation. He pushed the painting back. It clicked into the latch.

Ward settled down in the space behind the desk and the chair, with his back to the desk. He put his Stetson and her bag down on the floor beside him, near the Samsonite. He checked his wristwatch. Ten-twenty-three. She'd be on by ten-thirty. Jesse hung around the cabaret, she said. He never missed her show.

Ward figured five minutes for her show, and a minute or two for them to come here.

He waited in the cool gloom of the office. He slipped the leather sap out of his pocket and dropped the bag to the floor. The sap was a smooth and alien flatness in his hand. It looked and felt like something that belonged on a saddle but had nothing to do with one. He held it down at his side.

It was strange, Ward thought as the minutes ticked by. Yesterday it seemed that his luck had finally run out. Now all he had to do was rap Butler on the head. He didn't relish the idea of cold cocking the man, even if he was a bastard. Briefly, Ward wondered if it was right and whether this would be worth it. Maybe it wasn't, stealing back what he'd stolen from crooks to pay other crooks. Or maybe it was right but meant doing wrong. He couldn't tell anymore. The whole plan was either a good bit of luck or one more shovel stroke into the hole at his feet.

Ward shook his head. It was the only play left, he thought. A play against a bad egg in podunk Arizona. Better than a date with the Butcher of California, being opened up in unnatural ways. Ward's grip tightened on the sap. Remember what you're here for, he thought. The money. The gun. That's it. Oh, and the girl. He recalled her scent, her smooth touch. He thought he might enjoy having more of that around.

There were sounds through the door from the hallway. Voices and clattering footfalls. Ward crouched behind the desk and the door opened. Jesse Butler chuckled. Veronica giggled.

"Thirty minutes, Flip," Jesse said. Someone in the hallway said "Alright."

Ward peeked over the side of the desk. Veronica led Jesse in. She wore a purple silk robe. She carried the sailor suit and hat in her other hand. Butler chortled as he shut the door behind them.

"Baby, you were the bee's knees up there," he said.

"Oh, Jesse," she said.

"I mean it. That's your best bit, bar none. We ought to make it nightly."

"They'd get tired of it," she said with a smile.

"Never ever, sweet thing."

"Lock the door and get me out of this," Veronica said with her arms out.

Butler locked the deadbolt. It made a loud *click*. He went to her, his hands reaching for the robe closure. He kissed her. She embraced him, turned him around so his back was to the desk. Ward stood up.

Butler chuckled as he fumbled with the knotted satin. Ward crept over. Butler was sucking at Veronica's neck while he moved to undress her. She moved her hands over his back. She looked over Butler's head at Ward as he came up closer. Those ice-blue eyes.

Ward belted Butler across the back of the head with the leather sap. It made a popping sound on the upper half of his skull dead-center. Butler went loose and fell away from Veronica. He dropped to the concrete like a sack of potatoes.

Veronica went to Butler. He lay still on his side. She turned him over onto his back. His eyes were closed and his mouth hung open loosely. Ward could see the shallow rise and fall of his chest.

"Goddamn," Ward said. He pocketed the sap.

"We gotta move quick," Veronica said. She reached into Butler's jacket and took out his black notebook. She flipped through pages.

Ward went to the picture on the wall. He unlatched it and pulled. He unveiled the safe.

"You get it?" Ward whispered.

"No, no...wait." Veronica said. She rested on one of the pages. "Here. Thirty-five."

Ward spun the dial three times and rested it on thirty-five.

"Seven."

Ward spun it twice in the other direction and held on seven.

"Twenty - *WARD!*"

He whirled around. Jesse Butler was up off the floor and charging. Butler plowed into him and Ward felt the sudden hardness of the wall and the safe door against his body. He lost all his air and his Stetson. A fist like a sledgehammer took him in the gut and he pitched over onto the floor, retching.

Veronica made for the door. She scrabbled at the lock just as the door flew open and caught her in the face. She fell to the ground with a whimper. Flip Suggs came in. He saw Veronica on the floor, clutching at her face. He saw Ward lying on the floor with Butler standing over him.

"The hell?" Flip said.

"She brought Mr. McCoy back, Flip," Butler said, panting. His face was twisted in pain and his right hand clutched the back of his head. "He clocked me good, but not good enough. Seems he really, really, really wants to die. Give him what he wants. Then do whatever you like with her."

Suggs pulled a .38 snub-nosed revolver from under his jacket. He trained it on Ward.

There was a *click*. Veronica bolted up from the floor toward Suggs with her arm outstretched and something flashing in her hand. It went in at Suggs' neck and he made a noise like a surprised gurgle.

Veronica pulled back. The black handle of a switchblade stuck out from Suggs' throat. His eyes rolled up and his grip on the revolver faltered. Veronica reached and got the gun in her hands. Suggs' hands went to his neck, where the red poured down the handle like she'd struck oil, drenching the front of his suit. He buckled and staggered and fell to the floor, gulping like a fish, staring glassy-eyed at Ward.

Veronica's eyes were wild. Her left cheekbone was purple. Her busted lip leaked blood over bared teeth. She held the gun on Butler. He looked at her pie-eyed and raised his hands slowly.

"Ronnie, baby," Butler said.

"Shut your goddamned mouth and open the safe, Jesse," she said from a bloodied grimace.

"Sweetlips, think a hot minute. That thing makes an awful lot of noise. You pull that trigger, and the other boys will come down on you like flies to honey."

"And you'll be dead, Jesse. I'll plug you, I swear. I'd do it just for kicks. There's only one way I won't, and that's if you open the safe and give me my money."

Butler eased over to the safe. He stopped in front of it. He shook his head.

"That's what this is about?" he said. "The money you're owed?"

"Mine and Ward's."

"Ward's money was stolen, baby. He stole it from us, all over the state."

"I know. I don't care."

Ward came up on his knees. He wheezed. He found his breath, found his legs. He found the .38 he'd taken from Pablo and pulled it out. Flip Suggs stopped gulping and went still. Ward held onto the desk for balance, stood up and stepped away from the corpse.

Butler glared. "You dumb fuck, McCoy," he said. "I told you I would take care of it."

Ward said nothing.

"Your money is bait for Del Pascoe. He's going to make a play to get it back. But he's going to the wrong place, and he's going to get killed for it. By tomorrow you'd be free and clear. You really going to throw that away now?"

Ward coughed. "Yeah, right," he said. "And you were just gonna let me go? I'm supposed to believe that?"

Butler frowned. "Believe what you like," he said. "You'd have a better chance than you do right now."

"Jesse," Veronica said. "Open the safe and give us our money."

"You still don't get it," Butler said. "Ward's money is stolen. Your money is syndicate money. This is a syndicate joint and I'm just the guy they put in charge. Your money's theirs, always has been. If you take from here, there's nowhere they won't find you."

"I'll take my chances," Veronica said. "Open it. Else I swear."

Butler sighed. He spun the dial three times and stopped on thirty-five. Spun it back twice and stopped on seven. Spun once and stopped on twenty-one.

"Back away when you open it," Veronica said.

Butler sighed again. He opened the safe and stepped away, his hands raised. Ward saw the safe's insides. Stacks of bills bound together rested beside pistols and a wicked-looking commando knife.

"Now, get back in the corner," Veronica said.

"This is the most amateur play I've ever seen, you crazy Okie bitch," Butler said as he backed away.

"Take your opinion to the corner and screw," Veronica said. "Ward, honey, is your money in there?"

Ward eased over toward the safe. The bills he'd turned over to Butler were in there, wrapped.

"Yeah," Ward said.

"And your gun?"

There were three pistols in the safe. Ward recognized one as a Mauser, one as a Walther, and – *there* – his pearl-handled Colt. Ward took it, eased the slide back and checked the magazine. It was loaded and unchambered. He racked the slide, chambered a round and trained the gun on Butler.

"Right here," Ward said.

"Swell. Get your money."

Ward took up the Samsonite case. He took out the bill stacks. He recognized their paper bindings from the places he'd collected - the Santa Clara, the Armadillo, the Brass Tack. He put them back in the briefcase.

"Now get mine," Veronica said.

Ward glanced at the safe and back at her. "How much you say you were owed again?"

"All of it."

Butler chuckled and shook his head.
"You said around four thousand," Ward said.

"I'll take what I'm owed from what you put in the bag, Ward, and we'll split the rest."

"Ronnie, baby," Butler said. "The more you take, the more time the syndicate will take skinning you alive. I wish I was kidding, I really do. They'll probably start with Ward and make you watch."

"I don't think so."

"You know it's true. They'll enjoy it. They won't even kill you when you're begging for it. They'll make old Ward here wish I'd killed him." Veronica's grip tightened on the .38. "Ward. Put the rest in the purse. Now."

Ward swallowed. He picked up her purse. He emptied the safe's contents into the purse. The bills, the guns, and the knife made it a bulky, awkward package.

"I never saw a man make more mistakes than you, McCoy," Butler said.

"Shut up," Veronica said.

Ward cleared the safe. "That's all of it," he said. He stepped away from the wall and gave the purse to Veronica.

Butler dropped his hands. "Ronnie, baby."

"Don't call me that."

Butler shrugged. He shook his head low. "This is how you want to close it out?" he said. "After all we've had? All we've been through?"

"It's the end of the trail," Veronica said.

"If this is really what you want. Can't say it makes me happy."

"I don't care how it makes you feel," Veronica said.

"Don't say that," Butler said. "We shouldn't end on bad terms."

"It's been bad terms a while," she said.

Butler scoffed. He smirked. "I should've seen it a long time ago," he said. "This is how you are, isn't it? You can't leave anything behind without blowing it all up. You're not happy until you've ruined everything for everyone else."

Veronica glared at him.

"Doesn't matter what someone does for you. What they give you. How much they dedicate to you, even if it means some compromise along the way. Even if it's more than you fucking deserve. You just want to see them all burn and you want more, more, more. Whatever you want, whatever's good for little Ella May ₋"

Veronica pulled the trigger. The air cracked in the room and the bullet took Jesse Butler in the left eye. The back of his head blew out in a crimson spray over the concrete wall. His body shuddered, and he looked confused for a moment before his legs gave out and he fell backwards into the wall. A blackened mess of blood and brains smeared out on it as he collapsed in a heap to the floor, his body faintly twitching.

"Jesus God!" Ward said. "Why the hell did you do that, girl?"

"He had it comin' a long time," Veronica said. "Now are we getting out of here or what?"

She went to the door and threw it open. She took a step out. Ward followed. He turned to look down the hallways. Two men in black suits – Nicky and someone else, he wasn't sure who – were walking toward the office with revolvers in their hands.

Ward pulled Veronica back into the office by the arm. She yelped. A fusillade sounded from down the hallway. Bullets whanged and snapped around the door, shattering bits of drywall, throwing chips of concrete. Veronica screamed something unintelligible.

Ward went to the door. He stuck his .45 out and pointed it down the hallway. He fired twice, not really aiming but knowing the men were somewhere there. The gun seemed to explode in his grip, its volcanic force surprising him. He heard a whang and a burst at his feet. Veronica was down there, crouched low. She leaned out the doorway and her .38 blazed. Between her shots one of the men down the hallway moved out from behind a corner to fire. Ward leaned out and fired first. The man's body jolted and dropped.

Nicky shouted something. Veronica stood up, leaned out, fired. She darted into the hallway. She went for the corner down the hall they'd come in from. Before he knew it Ward was out of the doorway following her. A bullet snapped the air in front of him and he turned, saw a shadowy protrusion at the end of the hall. He fired. He heard a yowl in response. Veronica rounded the corner. He went after her, chasing her footfalls and the scents of lavender and expended cordite.

Ward turned the corner. He saw Veronica running for the back door. She stopped and turned to him. He hoofed it passed the stage access. He heard shouting, loud mutters of confusion and urgency coming from the cabaret.

"Hurry up!" she said.

He caught up. They made for the back door. Before they reached it, the door swung out and a man stood in the opening. His black hair was slicked back in a wave and he wore a sharkskin suit which looked baggy and awkward on him. He froze, open-mouthed and unmoving.

Ward brought the Colt up and fired. The .45 round caught the man in the throat. He jerked and spun and his body went slack. He dropped a pack of cigarettes which was wedged in his right hand. He bled out in great gouts and fell dead against the open door, propping it open.

Veronica shouted something but Ward didn't hear it. She kept moving and he moved with her. She went past the dead man and made a sound like a strangled laugh as she ran to the car. Ward stepped over the man's legs, saw his glassy eyes, the involuntary twitches and workings of his open and bloody jaw.

"Come on, come on, come on!" she said.

They got in the Cord. It roared to life and he gunned the engine, spooling up eddies of dust. The car peeled around the back and leapt into the parking lot. They sailed past the cars in the lot. Slot junkies by the front door gawked. They tore into the empty streets of Sentinel, its lights flashing against the big white car as it fled.

Ward expected an explosive response of gunfire behind them. He waited for the snaps and pops of a fusillade to shatter the windows and riddle him with hot lead. But there was only the howl of the engine and the whooping of the girl in the passenger seat.

***

Ward drove west. The lights of Sentinel vanished under the shadow of the mountains. The black strip wound them along the thin seam of the Gila River.

Veronica dropped the empty .38 she'd taken from Flip in the footwell beside the purse full of money. She arched her head back and laughed.

"Oh my God," she said. "Oh my God."

"That man at the back," Ward said. "I didn't see a gun on him."

"Him? That was Danny," Veronica said. "He was playing the cabaret, a limited engagement. He was terrible."

Ward suddenly felt cold. "A musician?"

"Related to someone in the syndicate or something. It doesn't matter."

"But he…"

"It doesn't matter, baby," she said. "We got the money. We got Jesse. And we got out."

"You didn't have to kill him," Ward said.

Veronica's eyes went to slits. "Shut up," she said.

"We had what we needed. We could've got out quietly."

Veronica laughed again. "Jesse would've yelled for his boys, soon as he got the chance. If we'd even made it to the car, he'd be on our tail right now. What I did was better."

"It sicked his men on us."

"And now they're dead, too."

"I'm…shaking."

"That's called a rush, baby. Jesse used to talk about it, from the war. It'll slow down."

"They'll come after us. The syn-der-kit."

"Baby, we didn't leave witnesses."

"Didn't...it didn't have to be like that. We didn't have to kill 'em."

"Oh, what do you care, anyway?" Veronica said. "You killed how many Indians and outlaws in your cowboy pictures, Ward? It's just like that. You're the hero."

Ward swallowed. "It's not like that," he said. "Back then, that weren't real."

She sniffed the crusted blood at her nose and grinned. "You're right," she said. "It's better. I been wanting to do something like that so long," she said. "All of that. Jesse 'n those assholes. I wish we'd had more time. I could'a burned the whole fuckin' place down."

"Don't—"

"What? Don't what, Ward? Don't say something so horrible? What's so horrible about it? I put up with so much from him, from everyone, all that time. You don't know what they did to me."

"You told me."

"You don't even know."

They were quiet for a while. Ward stared at the highway as the broken road pitched and wove in front of the Cord. In the headlights a ribbon of sandblasted tarmac disappeared underneath the wheels, carrying them further and further along. The front wheels juddered a bit, as usual. Ward felt a cold stone in his stomach. Further and further, he thought.

"Ward, you're tired," Veronica said.

"I'm fine."

"You're still shaking," she said. "It's been a hell of a day, baby. You're tired, I know."

"Need to get home," Ward said. "Need to get the money to Del. That'll set things right. You understand? I need to set things right."

Veronica reached over and touched his arm. "I know. But we don't want your nerves shot, baby. I can drive for a spell. There's nobody following us. Nobody looking for us. I can drive. You can rest."

Ward looked at the road ahead. His arm was tense and rigid on the wheel.

"It's okay," she said.

"All right," he said.

Ward slowed the Cord and pulled onto the shoulder where the road bordered a deep gully. He got out. He exhaled. He inhaled the cool desert night. He breathed again and again. When he was ready, he walked around the rear of the Cord to the passenger door.

"You have to watch the steering," Ward said as he opened the door. "The wheel—"

Ward saw the stubby Walther pistol he'd taken from Butler's safe clasped between Veronica's hands. She pointed it at him. She had a glassy, faraway look on her face.

The gun cracked. Ward felt a hot dull searing streak of wind in his chest. The force of it took him back and he went with the energy, his body suddenly loose, sailing backwards into the night and tumbling down the gully by the road. He landed hard and it seemed like everything broke inside. The air went from his lungs and he rolled, a limp shell of meat and bone battered by gravity along the side of the gully before a sage cluster caught him and he came to rest sprawled out on his back. He looked up wide-eyed at an expansive draping void with small winking stars in it and the muted glow of the Cord's lights high up there on the gully ridge. It had been a long time since he'd slept under the desert stars, he thought, just as they and everything else he knew flared and burst like a camera bulb from the good old days.

***

Veronica peered down into the gully. Its deep darkness struck her as a fortunate surprise. The Walther smoked in her hand. Very interesting, she thought. With Jesse it had been so visual—his eye blackened, his head burst, and the sudden tantalizing sight of blood appeared before his body dropped like a puppet with its strings cut. Ward, though? Ward had simply been there one moment and vanished into the black desert night the next. She threw the Walther into the darkness. It clattered somewhere below, down with Ward in the rocks and sand. Veronica drove on. The Gila Mountains loomed to the west. She wove the Cord through Telegraph Pass, taking the curves as quickly as she dared.

She'd tabbed it up during the drive, around the time Ward got squirrelly. What they'd taken from the safe plus Ward's ten in the briefcase made at least eighteen grand. Giving away ten to cover his crazy debt—*where was the benefit in that*, she'd asked herself. They'd gone to all that length, it didn't seem right to let go of what they'd gained. She supposed the inkling of the idea of keeping it all had come to her earlier. Maybe. If she was being honest with herself. She wasn't sure how to feel about that, or whether she needed to feel anything at all.

Eighteen thousand. That was enough to open some doors in Hollywood, she thought. Wherever they were. Whoever was behind them. She'd find a place and make the right connections. Get a new name. 'Veronica' could still work, but 'Venus' was too...lewd. Uncouth. She needed a solid name, something with class. Something simple, stark, and distinguished. Veronica Butler? No. Veronica McCoy? She laughed. No, Ward would have to keep that too, down in the black gully. Bell, though. Veronica Bell. It had a ring to it. She laughed again.

She came through the pass. The hushed glow of Yuma lay out before her. Veronica accelerated the Cord. Yuma wasn't Hollywood, she knew, but it was closer. It was all closer now than it had ever been.

The Cord shuddered. The right front wheel dipped into a deep crack in the road. Something buckled and snapped. The wheel twisted and bit into the shoulder. The Cord swayed and heaved over, its engine roaring as it left the highway, the dark ribbon vanishing and only the pitch black of the void in the headlights. Veronica's gut clenched as gravity released its hold on her. She floated for a moment and screamed as a sudden maelstrom of metal and dust closed in on her and shut the world off.

***

In the early morning, a fruit truck driver en route to Yuma found the Cord off the highway. It was upside-down in a dry wash with a broken, pulpy mass of flesh and blonde hair jammed in the twisted metal underneath. Ward's briefcase flew clear of the trunk and burst against the rocky side of the wash and scattered the flat with bills. Police examined the bills – those that were recovered, since some were pocketed by the truck driver, who personally considered it a 'finders fee' – and the numbers on some of them matched to various casinos across Arizona, including the Silver Bell Casino, where a recent robbery left five men killed. It was noted with some irony that the Silver Bell theft occurred the same night six men attempted a heist of the Four Aces Casino in Yuma, and all six, including noted organized crime associate Delmar "the Butcher" Pascoe, were killed during a subsequent gunfight with casino security personnel and several off-duty Yuma police officers. Local authorities wondered if these two events were indicators of a new trend in crime.

After the Cord and luggage were identified as belonging to the cowboy actor Ward McCoy, a local judicial inquiry concluded that Ward, who'd been seen gaming in various casinos around Arizona, had attracted the attention of a Jane Doe—that she only wore a robe was potential evidence of a manic episode—who hijacked his car, robbed and killed him, dumped him somewhere in the desert, and robbed the Silver Bell before her psychotic recklessness and unfamiliarity with the automobile contributed to an accident. Though it could not be proven it seemed the likeliest event, and Ward McCoy never made an appearance to oppose the verdict.

The following year was blighted by heat and drought until summer flash floods brought the Gila River to record heights. The floodplains washed out the gullies west of Sentinel to the ranchlands outside Yuma and the Gila Mountains. On a hot clear day at the ranch of Diego Aguilar, the old *vaquero* found himself up in the saddle looking down into a sodden washout where a yawning skull and some bones the coyotes left behind lay bleached and flaking half-sunk in mud the color of powdered chocolate. Aguilar uncovered the remains and discovered the tatters of a jacket. Inside the jacket were weathered shreds of photographs too faded and soggy to discern the portrait on them and a gilded Colt .45 automatic pistol.

Aguilar thought of alerting the police. But the sheriff was new and had not been friendly to him or his family, despite – or perhaps because of – their longstanding presence in the area. Aguilar, who had prayed to San Isidro for rain for months, and remembered his grandmother's lessons of the old deities which had overseen these lands for millennia, saw the gift in the unknown dead man who came with the water. The gun he had no use for as a weapon. Cleaned and treated, its sale could purchase new cattle to replace those lost to drought. They would graze in the new vegetation encouraged by the rain.

Aguilar gathered the bones in an empty burlap feed sack. He rode a hidden trail along the base of the Gila Mountains to where a sheltered spring lay. The spring had wept a dark strand during the drought but now it flowed gentle, clear and steady. It was once a gathering place for the Hohokam and their signs of blackened ancient paint adorned a cleft in the rock. With a hand-spade he dug a hole at the base of that cleft. He lowered the sack inside, buried it, gave thanks to God and prayed that He would grant eternal rest to the nameless soul. When he was certain he was alone he whispered an appendix to Tlaloc in gratitude for the benevolent water, and he remembered that those who drowned or who were struck by lightning were granted eternal life and bliss in the paradise of Tlalocan.

When Aguilar was done, he put the Colt in a saddlebag and rode back to his ranch. The man who came with the water slept under the stars of the West forever.

BLACK LINE TRAIL

BY JEAN-PAUL L. GARNIER

There wasn't much left in me, and sleep felt like it was coming on, one more log on the fire. Sparks went up like fireflies sizzling out on their way to the stars. No moon tonight. Stars spinning. Distant owl. Wasn't going to sleep hungry tonight, either.

Smoke lazily followed the dying sparks, blanket unrolled after kicking away a few rocks. Cold took hold of my body like a plague of ghosts and only grew more intense, slinging me back and forth between closing eyes and aggressive awake. Beat being hungry *and* cold though. Lack of pit in the stomach did leave lots of room for chill, more so than before, nothing to distract.

Low clouds blocked stars and pinyon needles snuck across them like black fingers. Counted money in my head. The numbers were bad. Nothing like years ago, but still a better haul than there'd been since the others came around. Counted money like it was sheep and despite the cold, started drifting.

The fire hissed, bringing me back for a moment. When it settles, it sounds no different than the snap of a twig, propping me up on an elbow to check. Sap *Sss'd* its way dripping down, mixing with the lost fat in the ash. Funny how being fed makes the cold worse, something about all that blood in the stomach.

Another log and the orange flames surge up again, but there's no way it'll last the night. Reluctantly got up, listened to the night, heard nothing. Searched around camp and found some stones for the fire. When the cold woke me and nothing but ash remained those would come in handy, something to curl up with. Something to do to keep from thinking about the cold.

Normally there'd be no need for coming this far up the mountain. But all of that changed. At first it was slow, and then a flash flood. Folks that had never even heard of a wash started showing, big knives on belts, looking like they'd put on costumes for a show. And they went out there seeking their fortunes just like everybody else. And they hunted and trapped, but the thing is, few of them knew what they were doing and then the game caught on. Now, those once fertile grounds of the foothills are as empty as those costumes. So up the mountain it was. Sure, some of them knew what they were doing. But the sheer amount of them... wasn't enough for everyone. Got me wondering what the animals thought of cold mountain nights. Were they dreaming of the deserts below, same as me?

Rocks in place and back down to the cold ground. Near me the meager stack of pelts looked like a bundled-up child, it would have to do. No work since they came either. Unless being a barmaid is suitable for a man. Not me. Normally wouldn't get into the supply but what good was selling pelts if they never get off this hill? Pulled a few from the pile and propped up the old head. At first, the fur felt like icicles and then the sweet warm relief, for the neck at least. Tickling like a kitten, reminding me for a second of younger, warmer days. Thick animal musk drifted with me, listening to the crispy pops and taking in the dying glow.

Eventually they'd make it up the mountain too, scare off the rest of the game, what little of it there was. Couldn't figure out where that would put me next, having to move on most likely, or get back down into one of the holes and break dirt so the man could have his gold for wrist watches and other useless trinkets. The hole held no appeal and this was about as far west as one could go before that big terrible ocean. Heading east felt like a defeat in itself. But they'd find their way up here eventually and those fancy new rifles would sound, taking away livelihoods and life with it. A crack like that ringing through the canyons and a great silence would follow. The birds and everything else knew what that sound meant. Like a crack of lightning on a clear day, they all knew to disappear. Fires left unattended burning out copses and reducing the good spots down to a few fought-over and well-known places. No more solitude for a man—where it should only have been the big tent of sky and the snap of traps, each bringing in pay to fill a man's belly.

They brought with them the fashions, too. Pelt hats not in demand anymore, making sales less than before. Yeah, they brought many gifts. Change coming on like an avalanche. And in their wake, lots of us would be left behind like so much alluvium, didn't make for good sleepy dreaming thoughts. But neither did the cold. But at least with the cold it was you versus it, rather than the losing odds of you versus *them*. Nothing that one could say or do to change minds. Sure, burn a few of them new houses out, but there'd be more in their stead, there always were. But for now, the quiet and the stars were mine. And it'd all be bringing in a small wage. Not a fair one, but something.

A scurrying in the brush startled me awake. On my feet in seconds, pistol in hand. All was quiet for a stretching moment then the scurrying started up again. At first, it sounded like men wrestling in the bush, until the noise traveled up into the pinyons. No man could climb that fast. Thought about holstering the pistol till it dawned that whatever was making its mad flight through the branches might be fleeing a man. God help me if they'd made it this far up yet.

Froze in place and scanned the surroundings, gun following my gaze, ready to blast. The cold had only increased, icing over during my short sleep. That cold brings silence with it. And all was silent except for the commotion in the trees. A mad scramble was taking place, some animal drama, but there was nothing to take the mind off of the most dangerous animal that could be silently lurking there. Animals knew better, knew when to run. Sniffing at the air brought no answers and with the fire long extinguished the eyes were almost as useless.

For a moment the silence became complete. Time stopped moving. Cocked the pistol in anticipation. The hammer sounded into the darkness like the single tick of a dying clock. Shrieking followed, animal and vigorous. Fucking or fighting, there was no way to tell. My eyes and barrel followed the sound through the trees, seeing nothing. The dash was rampant, snapping branches, leaves and needles falling to the ground. Pure animal anger and fear rang through the silence. A small war in a dark ocean of peace. The din escalated and there was no way to know how many were involved in the battle. Protecting the young, territory, there was no way of knowing, but anyone who's been between animals ought to know better than to stand their ground amidst that style of violence. Still, it was moving so fast it was impossible to gauge the direction it was coming from. And in the back of my mind, men still hid in the trees waiting for opportunity.

In the dark, the small stack of pelts was barely visible as nothing but a shape, but that shape brought with it the reassurance that no robbery had taken place, yet. Man or animal, the danger was readily apparent, it was only a matter of direction. Hopefully not both. With only six shots and no visibility, had to pray that there were no more than two adversaries and that my aim was true, even though it would basically be shooting blind, if it came to that.

The tussle moved another tree closer. Terrible hissing moved through the silence, fear of death that accompanies all beasts. Bringing the pistol up again to scan the trees, the sound had no visual. Pain. The sound of pain, icy and raw. It was long, drawn out, a sustained chord of agony. Unlikely that a man had made that sound, though had heard a man wail like that before, falling to shatter both legs.

The hissing continued but with less vigor now, clearly there was a victor emerging in the fight. The steam of my breath rose after finally letting it out. This calm was only momentary. One brief moment of silence and the shriek began anew, this time higher up as the animal scrambled for safety further up in the branches. Its adversary made chase and a mad rain of needles showered the ground around me. Another scream froze in the air. A branch snapped, a thud somewhere in front of me, a low growling, the animal had hit the ground near my feet. There was an insane flight through the trees as the growl continued from the grounded one. My attention narrowed on the patch of dirt in front of me. Fear smell permeated the air, from me or it, there was no telling.

Pistol still at the ready, barrel jutting out into the darkness, it found blackness the only target. Boots stayed planted in place rather than risk approaching the guttural sound of mixed fear, anger, and pain. Knew better than to expect reason or the instinct to flee humans. Wounded animals know only one thing.

Rapid scratching in the dust and debris told me that the last resort action had begun. Firing blindly lit up the camp with a single burst of fire. Mad eyes glinted for a moment in the flash of light and it was on me.

The hide of my pants held for a brief moment, up my leg like a tree, and the claws broke through and wet pain lit up my leg like hot coals. Fire everywhere, burning. Went down into the dirt teeth still locked in thigh. Using the butt of the gun like a hammer brought it crashing down, contact with skull, high-pitched roar of suffering. The sound may have come from either of us, pain was blurring senses. Again, the butt came down accompanied by wet crunching. Again. Again. Lost count in the insanity of pain and kept on whacking long after the sound had become merely liquid. Pain lit my vision like lightning. For a moment thought day had come and then the silver flash dissipated, faded before me as my body fell backwards in slow motion.

Deep hot sun burnt my face, nickel taste in mouth. West dust feeling. Blinking awake fiery pain brought alertness quick. The gun was still in my hand and fingers were cramped from holding tight. Back was stiff as a plank, curled over a mound. Pulling it out from under me it was the bounty of pelts, wet and ruined with blood. The blood made me woozy with the realization that it was mine. Rolled over and blackness returned.

Sun was full overhead when consciousness came back. Mouth sour and dry, face now obviously blistered from exposure, reached up and touched it and the hand confirmed. Came into contact with hot blisters. Sitting up last night's scene returned. The spoiled pelts sat next to me collecting flies in the newly dried blood. Two feet from the boot on my wounded leg lie the culprit. The wreck of what had once been a raccoon. A big bugger too. The carnage of its broken skull not dissimilar to that of my leg. The pants were torn wide open, soaked in rust colored blood, revealing the disaster of my leg. Multiple bite wounds merged into one gaping tear, sticky and fly-ridden already. Tried to stand. Couldn't. Best could manage was to roll over, reigniting the wound as it hit the dirt. Now on my stomach, tried to drag myself toward my pack. Fierce white agony brought me back to slumber.

Came to in the same position but with slightly more clarity. My blanket was yards away, the pack just beyond that. The sun said it was approaching evening. Hunger and thirst burned, only overshadowed by the wound. Numbness and fire intermingled and took turns. Using my hands and good leg, dragged and pushed myself toward the felt blanket. It took an hour to cross that endless stretch of dirt and rocks to the bedding. Each pull exciting the bite back into fresh bursts of horrible. Finally reaching it, rolled over onto the back relieving the pressure from the wound and starting a fresh bleed. Lay there wishing that those last few feet to the pack weren't miles away. Couldn't scoot on my back. Would have to roll over and my mind kept saying, can't, can't, can't. But did.

Black was starting around the bite. Bruise and congealing blood calling every animal in the vicinity to scavenge. That wouldn't do. Tore open the pack, which had fortunately been left alone. Doused the wound in precious water, wasting more than intended as the blood thinned and soaked my now dry pants.

The flies buzzed in mad fury as their meal was interrupted by the deluge. Thirst or infection. Another soaking and the pain began anew. Wouldn't be going anywhere tonight and lacked the strength to build a fire. It was going to be a cold night. Colder.

Sleep came in starts and fits and never lasted long. The night passed in a delirium of aching pain and sour half dream. At one point woke to the sound of animal fervor as something dragged away the festering corpse of the raccoon. Its smell was in the air and it was a surprise that nothing had found it sooner. It should have been the last thing on my mind, but if there was a coyote, or whatever it was, there would be more. No surprise they'd go for the easy target first, but me lying there was a close second. Felt for my pistol to make sure it was still there. It was. Kept it in my hand, at the ready. Hoped that the sun would be coming, not tonight.

Another animal joined the feast, yipping at the first. Coyotes for sure. They argued over the carrion, growling and shuffling. Thought to shew them off, or fire at them, but the ammo was running low and they'd both be back until the meal was all but gone. So stayed there lying in silence, praying the moment would pass unnoticed. They danced and fought in their meat lust, all the while ignoring me, at least for now. Fear kept sleep at bay until finally dawn broke and the camp shone in disarray. My pack was strewn about and my panic broke seeing the canteen lying on its side, its contents long since drained into the gravelly sand. That water may as well have been my very own blood. It was gone. One more problem added to the pile. Standing up wasn't going to happen, but sitting up was possible. First things first. The bite had scabbed somewhat but a lot of it still looked fresh, and it was caked with dirt and grime. It hurt like hell. Would have liked to have eaten that son of a bitch had the coyotes not gotten to it first.

Had to deal with the wound before it was too late. Gathered up some sticks and what few branches that could be reached without straining too much. Every movement was excruciating, and the day was already warming up. Built the sticks into a small pyramid and struggled to get the flint from the pack. Didn't matter how much it hurt, had to get that fire going. Leaning over to blow the sparks into flames tore the leg open again and the silence was broken by a howl of my own. The kindling took but this small victory was overshadowed by the sickening pain. The fire wouldn't last long with what little tinder was in reach. Hopefully long enough. Pulled the blade from my belt, fortunately it hadn't been lost in the melee. Stuck it in the small pile of embers and said a prayer that it would be enough to do the job at hand.

Several times the wind threatened to extinguish the flames. Part of me reveled in the welcome coolness of the breeze, another cursed the heavens for making the situation more dire. Threw a few more twigs in a desperate attempt to keep it going and fortunately the wind died down allowing the kindling to catch. Didn't want to pull the knife out too soon and risk losing the precious heat, but the fire wouldn't stay lit forever. Gazing at it, my imagination transformed the pathetic sight into a raging bonfire, complete with food cooking. The vision brought hunger back into sharp focus, only clouded by the pain. It threatened to knock me out cold. Couldn't let it overtake me, not with the blade in the fire, not while sitting in direct sunlight. My face and hands had already begun to peel and soon the exposure would become as dangerous as the leg wound. Trying not to think about it, my gaze wandered into the trees, not close enough to shade but housing birds of many varieties. Perhaps it would be possible to pick one off and have something to eat, but the risk of moving wasn't worth it, and a single missed shot would drive them all away. It would have to wait. Couldn't stay here forever but if things weren't done in the correct order my days would be numbered. Probably already were, but that kind of thinking spells certain death. Wasn't willing to cross that line, yet.

As the last of the flames died down, shrinking down into the ashes and what remained of the glowing embers, it was finally time to pull the knife out. God must have been on my side for once, for the blade glowed red. The sight made me laugh with delight but it was short lived for there was only a moment until what had to come next. Pulling the tear in my pants out of the way and pushing the flat edge of the blade onto the festering bite made me wince at the excruciating burn of the hot metal. It took everything left not to scream. The smell of burning skin made me retch. Had to force myself to apply pressure and leave it in place despite my entire fabric revolting in a lunatic desire to pull it away. When the numbness began and passing out was near, made sure to flip the blade and press the still searing other side back onto the fresh burn. This time there was no holding back, the frantic cry emerged from my throat without volition. Birds took to flight as the sound echoed through the trees. The scream bounced back at me and for a second it seemed that it was the battle cry of someone here to finish the job of doing me in. That was the music in my ears as consciousness faded out once again.

Came to in the beating sun. Couldn't orient myself enough to tell the time. There was no clarity. An eagle flew overhead, so it had been long enough for the birds to return. The knife still lay loose in my hand. The pain had receded, reminding me of what had come before. Braved a look. The leg was a mess but the bleeding had ceased. The wound was cauterized. At least some small thing to be grateful for. It still hurt, sharp and clear, as if the bite was still being delivered. The bloody pelts were still there, but a ways off, dragged by some animal drawn to the putrefying scent. My pack lie where it had been left. Aside from that not much had changed, but my skin felt even more raw than before. It was time to find shade. As much as the prospect of dragging myself out of the sun held no appeal, it was time to do so. Tried to stand. Still couldn't. The attempt brought searing fire to the wounded leg. Tried to take it. Couldn't. Nausea came, fluctuated between the leg and empty stomach until the retching started. Tried to keep as quiet as possible, so as not to alert the critters, but there was no stopping it. Nothing came up. How long had it been since my last drink of water? Since something to eat? One thing at a time. At least the bleeding had stopped. But it still stank of blood. It was getting past the time to move on.

Didn't matter how much it hurt, things would be getting much worse. With the wound now closed dragging wouldn't be as bad, although that's not saying much. Slung the pack on my shoulder and started pulling. The blanket bunched under me and kept the wound from direct contact with the dirt, which at this point was caked all around the bite anyway. The tree line was a good ten feet off. Turned off the care and pushed with the good leg. One push with all of my strength propelled me almost a foot. Ten, maybe eleven, and there'd be sweet relief from the sun. The care had been shut off, but now it was time to turn off the pain as well. Push. Push. Push. Push. It was rotten. The ground beneath me was sharp with rocks, causing further bruise. If it weren't for the blanket the wound would have reopened, no doubt joined by more. Push. Push. It was close, the temperature already felt cooler even though the shade was still a few feet off. Push. The smell of the pines also strengthened, a bouquet of heaven compared to the blood-soaked furs. Push. Push. By God or damnation this wasn't going to beat me. Push. And my strength was nearly gone. The blanket had bunched up and was no longer protecting my leg.

The last bit before relief from the sun was completed with an undignified roll. But sweet freedom from the sun was upon me. The temperature dropped a good ten degrees. Lying there catching my breath, it was obvious this wouldn't do. Told myself it was only a critter bite, to stop being a baby. After all, the wound was closed and the pain lived only in the mind. It could beat me, or there was a way off the mountain and back to my family. Maybe not all the way back to them, but close enough to send word. Thought of the ruined furs. Damn those who had driven me to this altitude. It wouldn't be much of a homecoming and nothing to send them but a letter of woe speared my pride, cutting deeper than that bugger's teeth. She would understand and be kind as always, but she'd also be telling me all about how foolish it was coming all this way in search of a living. Leaving them on their own, states away. There was nothing but dirt to farm back there. The soil itself had left me no choice.

Let myself rest for a few moments. The situation was hardly an improvement. Had to count it as a small victory though. Bad thoughts would only help the mountain beat me. Each step along the way had to be compartmentalized now, else it was just too big to face. At least the sun was out of my face. For now.

Below the trees the ground cover was different, less rocky. And a bed of pinyon needles softened the hard dirt. Most of them were dry and of no use but there was also a newly fallen branch still populated with green needles. They stripped off easily, covering the fingers with sticky sap. Put a few of them in my mouth and cautiously began to chew. The taste was acrid, bitter, piney as all hell. Without water they didn't go down easily, like gagging down sinew. But it was something. Took in as many as the mouth would allow before it felt like chewing on so much dirt. Fouled the mouth but the stomach quit its squawking, ever so slightly. A squirrel scurried by and the mouth-watering it caused eased the bitter film that coated my tongue. It was out of sight in moments, not even a pause to notice me.

The branches above cast wobbling shadows across the blanket of needles, decent kindling at the very least. A yard away spotted a pinecone. Better eating than leaves. Had to turn off as much feeling as possible. Did my best. Rolled the best my body could manage, and at last was within reach. Held the cone in my hand like it was the Holy Grail, held it up to the light and knew it would do little to kill the sharpness of hunger – tried to view it as a small success anyway.

Finding a flat rock had to be viewed as a success as well. Placed the cone on it and pulled out the pistol, smashing its butt down on the cone with all my might. A few pieces splintered off but it proved useless for breaking apart the fibrous wood, that few centimeters between me and the nourishing nuts. There'd be a need of fire for that. My mind reeling in the loop of what needed to be done. Had to push self-pity aside and retrieve the flint from the pack again.

It took near an hour to get the fire going. Despite the needles being mostly dry they were fresh enough to attempt to avoid catching. The branches within reach were all full of fresh sap and once they caught, hissed and popped like fireworks. Placed a few cones near the meager flames and kept a vigilante eye seeing that they didn't burn too much. Took everything in me to stay focused. Despair kept showing me different pictures, but cast those aside as best as possible, staring at the cones trying to relish the relief they'd bring if getting the nuts inside was possible. Burnt my hand retrieving one. It smoked on the ground bringing that sappy smell with it. Brought the butt down again and this time it was accompanied with that beautiful sound of wood snapping and a single nut being set free. It was a start.

It felt like it took hours, probably did, but eventually several pinecones had been freed of their nuts. High fat and nourishing. One of the cones didn't make it and burned up, popping like toy guns. But it was something. The first thing to work out in a while. Eating just enough to stave off the nagging stomach, then the rest squirreled away in my pack, it was now time to make some serious decisions. My camp was below the snowline but a little too far up for creosotes to pepper the landscape. Water, or dressing the wound? Both were imperative. Both urgent. But making my way up the mountain toward the fresh snow would bring me further from safety. The only hope of getting my wound properly treated was at the bottom of that big old hill. Help from the very folks that had driven me to this altitude in the first place. By my reckoning my camp was at four thousand feet, give or take. It would be a horrible trek the other direction. Decided on down. There was water somewhere. Creosote for sure.

Decided to wait until dusk approached. It was almost here anyway. At least the painful movement would combat the cold. And it would warm up further down. Checked the pack and rolled up the bedding. The pine nuts had given me new strength, but not much. With the gear ready to go, the pelts abandoned, checked the gun and ammo, defeated but ready to try and fight for my life. It'd be coming down that mountain with less than on the way up but what choice was there. Took one last look around the camp, the scene of the scuffle, the ashes that remained – there was nothing there for me.

Using a tree at my back, propping against it for support, the rough bark scraped my back through my shirt as my body rose. Tried to focus on the back rather than leg, but it was no use. Finally got to a standing position while continuing to brace myself against the trunk. Would need a walking stick, if not two. But none of the branches in the camp were long enough for a crutch. Thirst still ravaged at me but fortunately the hunger was no longer screaming. First things first, had to keep reminding myself to do things in order, one step at a time, any misstep could prove fatal and that just wouldn't do.

Stood there for a long time contemplating which direction would most likely provide the timber needed. Thought of her standing on that dusty porch, sending me off with a strange mix of disappointment and pride. Her looks always contained more than one layer. Nothing simple about that woman, except perhaps her unwavering love for the boy.

Further into the trees made the most sense, except that it wasn't down. There'd be no going down anyway without a stick, so up it was. Before trying to walk tried to investigate the wound. Certain movements would be worse than others, might as well know which, without the pain telling me. It'd be reminding me all the way, of course, but anything that could be done to limit that was welcome. Ran my hands through the open tear of my pants and found that tender burn on the back of my thigh. The wound was sealed, but deep. A fortunate numbness prevented me from feeling that missing part of muscle, but it warned me that it could be made worse by not knowing if more damage was being done. Continued on down my leg with my hands and found the culprit for why it had been so hard to stand. On the back of my knee, the tender part, the skin was full of deep lacerations, likely from the furious claws that had climbed me in search of their striking point. They were scabbed over now and there was no turning around to see the extent of the damage. Would have to limit bending that leg as much as possible for fear of reopening the un-cauterized cuts. Would make walking a chore but that wasn't news. Least knew now what to try and avoid. It was going to be a long, slow walk.

Favoring my good leg and keeping the other as straight as possible, hobbled into the trees. The air was damper here and a welcome relief from the relentless sun. Saw several fallen pinecones in the underbrush but thought better than to try and lean down to retrieve them. Kneeling was out of the question. One painful, slow step at a time. Eyed every branch overhead and within reach, but none were the required length. Did manage to swipe a few low hanging cones though, putting them into the pack for later. Couldn't pass up any precious little food.

The trees thinned at a clearing and the view opened up to show just how high up the mountain my trip had taken me. The scene was magnificent, massive rocks jutting up through the foliage, sheer rock faces, and beyond, far down, the desert in all of its open expansive glory. The sight brought a mixture of awe and terror. Days ago it would have been nothing but a sight of beauty. Now, it was an adversary to be traversed. The majority of the mount was impassable even in good health. Very few climbable trails snaked their way through the land, the way that had been taken up, and a few others – none an easy trek even on a better day. Still, let myself have a moment to take it all in. If there was no making it off this rock alive there were worse things a man could see as his last sight. From up here one could see the deceptive shimmering heat of the desert below, a stark contrast to the snowy peak above. Mountain ranges extended on both sides of the valley, but none as high as this. The valley itself was a smear of beige and white, peppered with the occasional outcrop of a few hastily constructed buildings and hovels, most too small to discern from this height. Down there, people would be living out their lives, blissfully naïve of the perils of the mountain, but living in its long shadow in the peaceful evenings. Knew that was an overly romantic vision of the truth but everything down there was paradise in contrast to the awful hike before me. Flat ground was a luxury.

Could have stood there taking in the beauty forever but every second without water was bringing me closer to this being my last sight. Would have liked to paint it for my sweetheart, but that was outside of my skill set and fingerpainting in blood wasn't going to make any hearts soar. Tried to burn the view in my mind in hopes that it could be spoken of in better times, safe on flat ground with a full belly and the warmth of love surrounding me. But despite that beauty this was no time for sentimentalism. The birds were enviable, would have given anything to spread out and soar down, unhindered by legs or landscape. They didn't know how lucky they were, coming and going as they pleased, not having to wonder what part of the mountain they would find their meal at, or what was going to come out and eat them—or perhaps they might, if things kept up the way they were. But these weren't thoughts for now, wouldn't even matter soon if the situation didn't improve. Left the vista wishing all that pretty could mean something more than one more way to not get down.

Back into the trees, backtracking that could hardly be afforded. But the moment of peace, with all of its vast beauty, was a welcome break from the perils that all pointed to no hope. A crutch should be all that mattered. But distraction kept coming. Couldn't hold a thought for long. Tried to snap out of it, but more effort brought more cloudiness. Leaning into the pain was the answer. It, and only it, could lead me down. Me and pain would have to become one and work together. Damn that raccoon! Should have been selling his skin in town by now, trading it for a gift for the woman and boy. Maybe it was raccoon justice. They had seen me as the bringer of death and retaliated. They had moved further up the hill fleeing the encroaching men, only to find me up there trapping and taking their lives one by one. Perhaps they had all been a family merely trying to scrape by in a world with less than before. And, finally, it had sacrificed its own life for vengeance, taking us both to death together. But that was ridiculous, a wild fantasy. My head was swimming in trivialities, there was no symbol here. Was losing sight of what was in front of me. Focus, man.

A critter shot through the brush bringing me back to reality. It may have been hunting, but a man wouldn't make for good prey, or possibly would. There were mountain lions here too, my trail would be smelling of blood and fear. Pain, and the urge to run, were palpable. Even took that first step to run, forgetting all about the lame left thigh and knee. My flight began and ended with that first step. Went down immediately, hands and head first, directly into the brush where the animal had scurried. It was unoccupied now, but thoughts of an attack followed my mind. Laying there listening - only silence returned. A lulling silence that threatened to call me to sleep. It was no time to rest, but the gentle lapping was irresistible. The landscape of my mind filled with my child playing in lush grass, woman on the porch calling him in for supper, and advancing animals, unseen to both of them. A train whistle calling through the night. Commotion of men unloading goods, throngs desperate for wares. Dust kicked up in the streets, pistol shot ringing out, shouts, lawmen's eyes staring down the lot. Woman in fear, gathering up our boy, me frozen and useless to protect them.

Awoke in the bush where the fall had deposited me. Leg and head throbbing. Time of day uncertain. Sun beating strong and grateful for the shade across my face, though little comfort with the settling reality so far away from our town, or any for that matter. Pack lay beside me. One of my only commodities that was being dished out like free drinks from a jackpot winner's drunken generosity. Listened for animal sounds. Nothing. Thirst's clock said it had been a while. That meal on legs was long gone, no way in my state that a hunt would have gone well anyway. Rolling onto my back and looking up at the sun through the branches it danced in an army of shadow and light, reminding me of the beauty of the sky and how oppressive it could be when a solid roof was so far off.

Dozed in and out through what was presumably the afternoon. Sleep helped clear the mind somewhat but was fraught with unpleasant dreams. Evening looked like it was coming on. The temperature fell rapidly. Had to get a fire going while there was still light. Fortunately, the brush was scattered with sticks and branches large and small. Gathered what was in reach, not wanting to waste what little was left of my energy. But the brush was no place for a fire, so wrapped my belt around all that tinder and slowly dragged myself to the clearing. Out with the flint and got to work on the dry sticks. It took twice as long as usual but by the time the stars began to poke out, the flames were rising up like the arms of enraptured worshippers. Placed the remaining pinyon cones next to the circle, would have to make work of preparing what was left of them. The lack of food was blurring my senses, causing me to waste time, and that would only grow more dangerous. There was plenty of wood nearby to keep the fire going most of the night. Threw another branch on, grateful for at least that one small favor. Thought to set up a trap but it was unlikely any game would approach so close to the fire. Did it anyway. Just on the outskirts of the ring of light. Maybe luck would be on my side for a change.

Removing the nuts was an arduous chore. But made sure it was the first thing to get done. Ate a few and stored the rest. They brought little relief, but it did dull the ache. The smell of roasting was pleasant and drifted all around me. The smoke was blowing right in my face but didn't want to waste any precious energy moving up wind. The smoke curled around my shoulders and brought thoughts of the family sitting around getting warm in better days. The boy played with blocks in the single room, unaware that wood and food would grow slender through the winter. Wife looking at me, knowing all too well that reality. It was that night we had talked about me heading west in search of fortune or a better place for us. She had brought it up first. Said it with a look that had no choices attached to it. If we lasted through that winter, it would be time to head out in spring, she had said. Bring back what you can because this was no life to live, and the boy would be growing rapidly but wouldn't be a man anytime soon. There was no arguing with her, and she was right anyways.

All the while, lost in thought, had been feeding the fire branch after branch to stave off the cold, absentmindedly. Had planned to move at night but moving was exactly the problem. Threw another branch in and it caught quickly. Staring into the fire can ease a man's soul but it does nothing to ease pain, or loneliness. A pop from the fire brought me back to the ground. The branch that had just caught on one end was long, too long for the fire, and should have been broken up first, if my attention had been in the right place. Then it dawned on me, a spark of recognition. The stick was long enough to serve as a crutch. Had been sitting next to me the whole time. And now it was burning. My hand got burned too when reaching to retrieve it. Quickly rubbed it in the dirt to douse the flames threatening to consume it. And just in time. Only one side was burnt, but not too bad. Even had a crux on one end. Finally something to lean on. Perhaps my luck had turned. Perhaps my trek could begin in earnest now. But sleep was drifting toward me, so clutched the branch like a stuffed animal and prayed for sweet dreams and energy, so my flight from this damned mountain could get started before it was too late for me.

Awoke still clutching the branch and it was sweet relief. It was still there and now there was a chance, perhaps. The morning was still now, and filled with the sounds of birds. Several varieties at least. A thin stream of smoke rose from the few still red embers where my hope had almost burned up, now it was as if a friend had waited up for me. The early rays of the sun felt good on my back, but it was clearly going to be a scorcher. Reached for my pack to eat some nuts and get the foul taste out of my parched mouth when the sound hit me. A rustling at first, a sound of struggle nearby. Instinctually my hand went for the pistol but the sound came in starts and fits, not a sound of threat but one of fear. The trap! It was coming from the trap at the edge of my camp. What luck was shining down on me? In the night it had snared something. My belly groaned.

Crawling over to it brought fresh waves of hurt to my bum leg, but that didn't matter now, overshadowed by the prospect of a meal. And there it was, still alive, but mine. A large grey squirrel had the misfortune of finding my snare and it struggled in a feral way to get free. For a moment, looking down on it, it felt as though we were the same. Both trapped on the mountain, both fiercely struggling with a useless leg. But these flights of thought would do me no good. Pity was something that would have to be reserved for myself.

Grabbing the cord that attached the snare to an old stump, removed it and whipped the whole thing off of the ground, looping the squirrel into an arc and bringing it down on a nearby rock. The gory scene was over in an instant and its thrashing stopped. Would have to get the fire back up for my first proper meal in days. Threw more sticks onto that last dying ember and blew with all my might, which wasn't much, but rekindled the flames. The heat increased as my mouth watered.

Made quick work of skinning and cleaning the beast as best as could be managed. A ramshackle spit finished the job, then laid next to the fire letting the smell of cooking meat intoxicate my senses. Could have fallen back to sleep right there but the possibility of drifting off and letting the meat burn was unacceptable. All of my attention went to the sizzling flesh and it was time to count my blessings. The smell wafted toward my nose and a warm room seeped with the smells of her cooking and the sounds of the boy playing filled my mind. She'd impatiently call that supper was ready and that the boys best be washing up. Her voice stern, and making her wait wouldn't do. The boy scampered up to the washbasin, needing me to lift him up to the step stool to reach the bowl. Even though he'd been shown before he always liked being taught how to do it, an excuse to play with the water, never wanting play time to be over. Even under mother's scrutiny my notion was to indulge him. Lord knew that even small pleasures were lacking in this world, so why not give the boy a moment. She tolerated it in minor annoyance before stomping her foot and calling us to the table.

The meat was hot and gamey, stopping me from devouring it in several rash mouthfuls. So took my time nibbling, probably couldn't keep it down on this stomach anyway, eating like a starved hog. Tried to savor each bite, and even though the meat was low quality and cooked all wrong it was like a meal from heaven. Thanked the creature while shoveling it down and feeling the possibility of life return. The relief was incredible, but would have given anything for some fresh water, or even stale for that matter, to wash it down.

Didn't want anything to interfere with the small win of the moment, so stifled the thought and went about eating as though it was my last meal, and it very well could be. But now my body was surging with a new vigor and for the first time let myself believe that this mountain couldn't beat me, no matter how hard it tried. Would have howled in relief if it wouldn't have been such a waste of energy. She wouldn't have allowed hollering at the dinner table. Sometimes me and the boy would get to singing and she'd frown at us with that look that reminded us that festive attitudes were best left for after supper. We'd argued about that on many a time, and why not just let the boy enjoy his time at the table. But it was her table, so her rules, and if you wanted things a certain way then you be cooking the meals from now on. So we'd try to sit in silence and smirk at each other, not doing a good job of it. Life would be hard for him soon enough, and if it'd be just the two of them for a while, might as well let him know that his father loves him and isn't leaving for good.

That promise rang in my mind as the last of the squirrel left the bone. A full belly felt like a small miracle. Perhaps it always was. But we take these things for granted in better times, but without a doubt they were. It's the little things we overlook. The sound of that boy splashing around. Her half-angry playful smirk as she called us to the table. That we had food on the table at all, no matter how scant it was. The boy probably didn't know the difference, but he could tell something was up, that there was a change coming. He could read that she was tightening up though he probably had no idea why. Someday he'd be faced with the same dilemmas. We'd shield him as long as we could but no one misses hunger when it comes on, and our meals were growing increasingly simple as the rains continued not to fall. Had taught him how to hunt small animals, but that was growing more scarce too, and while it was a fun game for him, he was catching on that it was becoming urgent when his mother would scold him for returning home empty handed. He'd have to become a man fast, and without me there to guide him through the transition. He had my every faith, but he'd have to grow up fast. Something that one doesn't wish on any child. It had been the same for me, and it was gone before that childhood me could even realize what it had meant. My father would drag me along on those hunts and no beatings would be spared when there was no food on the table. Wouldn't let the boy suffer that, but hunger was a beating in and of itself.

The food eased the urgency for water ever so slightly. But it was still my main concern. It was getting too hot to be finding random patches of snow and probably too low on the mountain as well. With any luck there'd be a spring, or a shaded pool hidden in the rocks somewhere. Had to hope.

Decided to wait until evening to start moving, which gave me nothing to do in the meantime. Cleaned the squirrel pelt and packed it away in hopes that it could bring some small trade if and when folks crossed my path. Pulled out the blade and stripped the bark on the crux of my crutch, hoping to make it more comfortable to use. Thought again about the squirrel pelt and decided to use it as a pad on the crutch. Would be worth nothing to trade now, but that was all a dream anyway. Pulling a few long strips of bark, adhered it to the crutch and hoped that it would stay bound. Tested it out and found it to be little comfort, but better than nothing all the same. That left little but thinking until it cooled down, still the heat made my thoughts swim, an unfocused carousel ran through my mind alternating between survival, bitterness, and a minutia of memories. Water was always at the forefront of my mind. Imagined swimming in it, more than a man could ever hope to drink, my tongue getting drier all the time.

The day was wasted in useless revelry until finally evening began to come. It was time to move, for real this time. One by one the stars started showing themselves on the horizon. And the moon would be coming soon as well. Something to light my way. Throwing my pack on and donning the crutch, took one last look at the camp and moved on. It was slow going. While the crutch took the weight off my bad leg and helped with the pain, still couldn't bend my knee and my gait was awkward and clumsy. Was finally on the move. Had to keep reminding myself to go one step at a time, or at least the leg was reminding me, and the pace was frustrating. Not as frustrating as being stuck in camp, but my descent was painfully slow and was making me resent those rocky mountain trails, not least of all the raccoon.

One foot in front of the other, sort of anyway, it was more like one step and then a lame swing of my left leg, bringing it around in an arc to propel it forward. There'd be no speeding down that hill, and no mad flights should a critter come up on me. Had to move my holster to make sure that the hand could get to it in time should such a thing occur.

Had it not been for my predicament it would have been a joyful walk in the moonlight. The trails were beautiful, exactly the kind of rough untouched country a man would want to visit, if in good health. It was naked and free of human signs, a perfect place for game, or peace and solitude. Or both. It was taking me so long to move that there was time to take it all in. In some ways hadn't seen the mountain like this before, always on the move in search of something. But now the pace gave me nothing but time to think about it, to soak it in, had never slowed down to do so before. But there had been no good reason. Wasn't up here for my health, or some pretty picture. Regardless of how beautiful it was, it was still ugly. The ugliest fucking mountain ever seen in my life. It wanted to kill me and sure wouldn't stop trying. Had damn near succeeded already. And then, amidst my hate and sore feelings, a creosote blocked my path. Wasn't nothing to eat but something needed, and needed bad.

Stopped right there and took the bush in my hands. Most common plant in these parts and it'd been hell finding one this high up. But here one was, right in front of me. The smell ignited my senses, antiseptic and clean. Would have preferred the gun powder smell it gave off when rain was coming, but all the same it was magnificent and welcome. Stripped a few branches of the small sticky leaves and vigorously rubbed them in my hands to extract the oils. Once it was as near a paste as possible got sitting as best my leg would let me and rubbed that paste on the bite and scratches on the back of my knee. It stung like hell as it did its work. Could feel it seeping into my wounds, hopefully killing off infection which was sure to have started already. When rubbing it in a foul stench came forth from the wound, mixed with the earthy smell of the plant. It was probably too late, but had to try anyway, had to hope that this would do the trick. The stink made me feel sick all over again, coupled with the fact that it didn't feel too good either. The smell said infection was coming, so could only pray that the creosote wasn't too late. It probably was. Took an old tobacco pouch from my pack and filled it with as many leaves as it could hold. No knowing when there'd be another one in my path, and there was no doubt that there'd be a continuing need as the days moved on, if they moved on.

One agonizing step after the other, made my way down that trail. Occasionally looking back, it showed how little progress was being made, and still not a single drop of water in sight. But nevertheless it was progress. More than had been made in the last several days. Could hardly feel grateful but probably should have, thirst was too great a distractor. Each step was painful too. Each thought bitter. Each memory. Even each beautiful sight. None of them would help in the least to get me off of this damned mountain and back to safety. But that kind of thinking was useless too. A waste of damn energy that could little be afforded. Had to refrain from thoughts that kept coming on like rain on an already cold day. This day was nothing like that, but may as well have been. Nothing was on my side. The cold of the night would be replaced by heat and either way discomfort was a sure thing, further discomfort that is.

Felt like a whiny little bitch giving into the complaints when there was only one worthwhile endeavor, but aside from that climb there was nothing to occupy my mind. Every useless stale moment came back to me, the ones that should have been used better, the ones that seemed bad but were actually paradise next to this. Had thought trying to scrape a living out of that barren soil had been difficult, or leaving the family behind for a spell. This could be a different kind of leaving, and farming never tried to kill me. The look on her face when she stood on the porch watching me leave was a strange mix of sadness, fear, and anger – but also with a tinge of hope. Similar to the hope in her smile when we had shoved off to get there in the first place, all full of promise and talk of better days. But this time the smile was half cooked, that still had hope but not as much as before, kind of smile. Could tell she was trying to hide it, to not make it too difficult for me, at least not harder than leaving already was.

Never worried about dangers, or hard work, or nothing else but taking care of those two, so that walk away from them that day had been as hard to swallow as it gets. Thought so at the time. Now another kind of leaving was on the table, and my head wasn't so good. What look would she be giving now? There'd be no smile on it. Wouldn't do to think these thoughts though. Had to use her like a lighthouse, a beacon, something to move toward instead of wallowing in what needed to be gotten away from. These notions wouldn't speed up the climb even if they distracted me from it.

My foot hit a loose piece of shale and slid out from under me, proving just how distracted my mind really was. It wasn't a hard fall but my legs slid down and my body fell back, and before knowing it, was lying there in the middle of the trail on my back. Small rocks and gravel scattered off down the mountain tinkling as they went until they disappeared from sight. It was a close one. My pack could have disappeared down that trail, or my crutch, or worse yet, myself.

The idea of slowing the pace was as unappealing as any. Risking a worse fall or running out of time. Wasn't much of a choice, not really a choice at all. So stayed put to catch my breath while trying to purge the attitude that distracted me in the first place. The moon came down making everything look blue and ominous. How easy it would be to give up and give in to sleep. Probably would have to if it weren't for a shard of rock digging into my back, adding insult to the fall.

Using the crutch as a lever, propped myself back up regaining footing on the loose gravel. It was a small triumph just getting up. One that exhausted me. Scanning the trail, it looked like it'd be more of the same going forward. On top of the injury the soles of my boots were wearing thin, not much left in the way of traction. Looking to the left and right there was no alternative but to continue down through the death trap crumbling trail. Typically would have sidestepped through parts like this but even with the crutch it'd be putting too much weight on the bad leg. Certain there would be another fall, opted to get down on my butt and scoot a ways until the ground became more solid. It would be slow, and it wouldn't do my pants any good, but there was no other safe way to descend. Progress was going to be painful, slower than it already was.

Scooted along and thought of water. For better or worse it overtook my thoughts, washing away woman and child in an imaginary deluge of rainfall, lakes, rivers, streams, waterfalls, all the water that was possible. Then other liquids came: cups of coffee, milk, tea, whiskey, wine, beer – anything one could drink wandered across my mind, each coming into focus, teasing how good they would feel spilling across a parched tongue and into a growling belly.

Morning was coming and on the steep incline it wasn't looking like there'd be a good place to make camp. No choice but to get up and carry on. The first rays of the sun came out making a spectacle of themselves, thrashing through the bush and low junipers and manzanitas. Junipers! And filled with berries too! And something about the light on the manzanitas was drawing my attention. Cautiously moved in for a closer look. They were shining in a peculiar way. It was moisture catching the light. Dew from the cold night. Dew! It wasn't much but it was water. Desperately, hungrily, and as fast as possible in fear that it would evaporate, leaf after leaf went into my mouth, licking off the precious moisture. It wasn't enough to sate thirst by any means, but it soothed the dryness in my mouth, delicious and welcome. Spent the next fifteen minutes or so taking in what little moisture possible until the dew was gone in the morning sun. The thirst wasn't even close to gone but it did take the edge off, somewhat. It was better than nothing, and if nothing else it had lifted my spirits slightly. And while the juniper didn't make for great eating, it was food. Pulled a small sack out of my pack and went to getting as many of the berries as I could carry, popping them into my mouth one by one while harvesting. They were bitter and waxy, with barely any flesh before teeth would hit seed. But again, it was something. They left a bitter taste in the mouth with nothing to wash them down with, but it was food. And now my pack had enough berries and nuts to last at least a day and a half. Unfortunately, the manzanitas were devoid of fruit. Would have given a finger for a juicy bite of fresh apple. For a moment caught myself staring at the beautiful red grain of their wood, perfect for carving, but there'd be no time for such frivolities.

It was as good a place to stop and rest as any. My clothes clung to my body with sweat and grime. Must have smelled like the devil rolled in shit. Hands were caked in dirt as well, now mixed with the sticky pulp of the berries. There was no flat place to lie down but the shrub did provide some shade, it would have to do. Used the crutch to try and clear away the rocks and got down on my knees igniting a fresh wave of pain. Scuttled into the bush, hoping it wasn't home to snakes or scorpions and did my best to prop myself up to reapply some of the creosote to my wounds. Mixing the leaves with some spit, tried to make a paste that would adhere to the scrapes and bite, and pulling what was left of my pant leg aside my worst fears were confirmed. While ugly as hell, the bite had sealed up somewhat, but the tears on the back of the knee were a festering mess. Twisting my leg, which hurt like hell, could see a black line beginning to form and branch out from the cut. The black line of death. It only sprouted about an inch out from the incision but no doubt it would be growing. Seen that kind of thing before, and untreated it was sure to be fatal. Treatment was nowhere near. Frantically applied more of the creosote but feared that it would do nothing but deal with the superficial aspects of the damage. Now, it wasn't just the doom of the mountain, but a race against the black line, and there wasn't nowhere to race to. Prayers were the only medicine available. Anything for a stream to bathe in, or better yet a hot bath, hot meal, and a tall whiskey. Every style of comfort ran through my mind. Even things hadn't thought about since being a young man. The comforts of women flooded me, bed after bed, a soft touch, quiet words, a cool hand easing my forehead. The one before the wife, all those big dreams, simpler times. When work was easy enough to come by, before it all crashed and we all went barreling west. Money went further in those days and there was no boy to feed. Could rip it up at the saloon without worry, even lose a few card games without worrying that there'd be no roof over my head tomorrow. Could stay up drinking anything that pleased me. Could bathe whenever, for a few coins. Hot water even. Change of clothes waiting for me.

Water came rushing down the mountain flooding the trail and bringing rocks and debris with it. The deluge hit my body and knocked me clear out from under the bushes. It submerged me for a moment, then came up gasping for breath and there wasn't no water, just me, like a dried fish lying right where sleep had come, same junipers, same bush. Sleep must have come upon me quick because my hands were still sticky with creosote and juniper, looking around no snare had been set. Nothing good waiting for me. Nothing. Sweat was clinging to me all over, and the mountain was still there looming, a giant beast without mercy. The place held no sympathy for men, it just was, huge and towering, ancient and brutal, jutting up into the sky like it always had been, since the beginning of time. A man was no more than an insect in its presence. If only for flat ground beneath my feet. If only my snare had been set and a meal awaited my awakening. No such comfort in my meager camp. A dusty bedroll and a few juniper berries were the best it was going to get. Hastily mashed up some more creosote leaves and reapplied the paste to my thigh and knee. The black line creeped up another inch or two like a dead tree branch scratching at the moon. And the wound still stank. A dead calf rotting in the sun behind the farm came to mind. It had escaped a nearby ranch in the heat of summer, probably in search of locoweed, and perished as it had wandered aimlessly away from the herd. Carrion birds had already found their way and were coming upon it for a closer look, could see that its eyes had already been eaten out and now swarmed with flies, an empty gaze up to an empty sky, nothing now but a feast for vermin.

The telltale ooo-hoo of quail brought me back. Several of them were scratching around under the brush, ripe for a snare that wasn't there. Froze in place watching them go about their business practically unaware of me. Could almost reach out and touch them, almost. Thought about shooting one, but that would be overkill and at this range would probably shred the meat into inedible dirt-caked chunks. Was no good at knife throwing either. Considered doing it anyway but the loss of my knife wasn't worth the poor odds that it would meet its target. Could wait for their approach and hope to get one with my hand, but they were clever little buggers and wouldn't allow capture so easily. Hurriedly set up the trap, it was too late but all that could be done to remove my feelings of ineptitude. Scooted away from the trap and scared the birds off with the noise. Hopefully they'd be back. Tried to be as quiet as possible and sat upright at the ready with the crutch in hand like a spear. Not much of a hunting pose, and bound to be ineffectual, but what else was there to do. Hours passed in the standstill until my arm got sore from holding the branch overhead.

Was just about to give up and put the branch aside when the scratching started up again. They were yards away from me and circling aimlessly, pecking at the dirt. With no way to lure them in, aimed my stick and held my breath. When it lined up just right let it fly, but it clattered to the ground missing its target and startling off the birds for good. At least it was still within reach, but there'd be no meal for now. Could try to wait it out and let the snare do its work but this place was starting to fill with bad memories and failure. They wouldn't be back, not after a commotion like that, they were cautious creatures, and there was something to be learned from that, but it was too late. Pulled together my meager camp and suffered to stand up and get going.

The silver lining was that my body was rested up as could be hoped for. At least lethargy wouldn't be fighting me too. Wouldn't call it vigor but there was a little strength on my side. The scabs cracked upon standing. An ugly reminder that brought fresh sick to my stomach. There was no doing anything about that except hoping that the infection would bleed out. Flies buzzed around my leg, swatted at them with my free hand. Hopefully movement would deter them. So, without much hope started off back down the trail. Evening was only just approaching and sweat came down into my eyes as the exertion made itself present. That rested feeling went away as quickly as it had come and the self-pity came along with it, a couple of old buddies to keep me company and let me know all about the awful passage of time. Got me pining for flat ground and a better, longer sleep.

Our bed had been nothing but a sack stuffed with hay and old corn husks, would have traded the leg for a lie down in it now. Thinking of that kind of comfort made my mouth water. She would fill the basin and fluff the pillows, bring out one of her quilts, light the lamp and generally get everything ready for us. On cold nights the boy would insist on sleeping with us, said our bed was more comfortable, didn't want to admit about fearing the dark, and she would never let me give him any flak for it. Said that a boy needed time with those things and that a man's anger only slows the process down. She ran the house with an iron fist and there was no talking back with her. Didn't matter if there had been a mood for lovemaking, the boy came first. The bed was hardly enough for three and my body would usually end up on the edge while he slept in the middle, curled around her. It was hard to sleep on those nights, laying there looking at the small oil skin window. But it may as well have been a king's palace of comfort. The things we take for granted when we aren't considering their absence. To think that the boy had annoyed me in those moments brought a sad little laugh along with it. In the morning he'd be doing his best to act like a big man again and wanting to go out hunting to show mama that he had no fear. When he graduated from the slingshot he'd begged me to make him, it was a big day for him. His first .22. He slung it over his shoulder like a soldier and marched around the yard with such a proud look on his face. You'd think he was returning from a battle all victorious. His mother chided me for giving it to him,

him being so young and all, but it was a skill he'd be needing to learn sooner or later. Taught him how to be safe with it too, but guns had always made her uncomfortable, even though she accepted them as a fact of life. She wasn't a bad shot either.

On the day he took down his first rabbit, he cheered when the shot met its target. The boy was glowing like the sun until he went to retrieve the cottontail. When he came up on the kill and saw the mess that is death for the first time he burst into tears. Not long ago he'd been feeding them kitchen scrap, almost thinking of them as pets. Then, looking down on that little critter he couldn't believe what he'd done. Suppose every first kill went like that. Mine had been a small bird minding its own business in a tree. Had reacted much the same way. That had been so long ago had forgotten it until looking at the boy's tear-streaked face. He cried all the way through the skinning and butchering, not so thrilled about learning the ways of the knife as he had been with the gun. He kept that up for a while then tried to straighten up when he heard my demand that he bring the meat to his mother. He did his best to hold it in and deliver the animal to her waiting in the kitchen, stretching out his small arm to hand it over. She praised him for the catch, for bringing home dinner, and it was plain to see that he was filled with a strange mix of pride and horror.

When that stew hit the table his demeanor changed again, the gore of the kill had left him and he felt like the man of the house. We let him have his moment. He'd have to get used to it at some point, and the way things had been going with the farm we'd be needing some help with the daily things. His tears forgotten, he swelled at his first contribution and when she patted him on the head and called him a man his face lit up. He grew a taste for it after that and always looked to his mother for praise when he brought home a squirrel or other small game. He'd be needing these skills when my day came and there'd be no one to take care of things, so my heart swelled with pride too.

Hopefully he was taking care of his mama now. Hopefully hadn't left them too soon, not that there had been a choice. When those rains stopped things just kept getting worse. Crops failed several seasons in a row. Game was becoming scarce everywhere along with the drought. And coupled with the rains not coming, town was starting to overflow with newcomers, much in the same way that had happened here. Wave after wave of folks came from the east, all seeking better lives and fortunes, but few finding anything of the sort. Much like when rabbit populations explode, but there was no equivalent of the coyote to keep the growth in check. When town got crowded things got worse, more fighting in the saloon, thieving – hunger will do the worst things to a man's morals, if he ever had any to begin with. These weren't lessons that the boy should be learning so young, but what can you do when things're right in one's face. The worse things got the more trouble showed on her face, the less she smiled. Without her even saying it, it was becoming obvious that something would have to be done, and it wasn't going to happen there if the skies didn't open up and pour soon.

At this point on the mountain the trail flattened out a good deal and started moving sideways across the rock faces. The going was so much easier than trying to navigate the incline. At the same time, it was frustrating to not be making as much progress downwards. But as far as the body and legs were concerned it was sweet relief. Stopped in the shade of a pinyon to sit on the rocks and rest and gather up a few more pinecones. The hard granite around most of the trail wouldn't make for a good place to sleep but it was a mighty fine perch to sit and soak in the view. The deserts below still felt distant, but that much closer. A partial moon lit up that majestic valley and could almost imagine it was the sea in front of me. Though no one would be sailing those sands, they'd come on foot, on horseback, or wagon—any way they could, to keep coming west, for a promise that no one was quite sure who'd made to them. The desert was empty now, dotted with some firelight in the burgeoning towns, but my mind's eye filled it with great swarms of newcomers crossing the sands in search of fortunes, or like me, just ways to get by. How many of them would? Hope is a weird drug, but one's got to hold onto something. Even when someone else's hope is squashing yours—it was so easy to blame those who had driven me up the hill for the things the raccoon had done to my leg, but it really hadn't been them that did it. How far back the line of cause does one go to place blame? Up here, all thirsty and dead tired, there was only me and my shoulders to place it on. The bitterness in my mind wasn't no good as fuel anyway, it wouldn't get me walking and it sure as hell wasn't going to help me survive, but it kept finding its way into my determination. If the mountain beat me then so too would they have beat me. They'd never know it, or have a reason to care. They'd be worried about troubles of their own, which were probably plentiful, but that all seemed so removed looking down below at all of that desert, so far away. Could probably see for a hundred miles from up here, and all that empty land that wasn't doing nothing for anyone's dream and hopes. Had made that crossing myself, marveling at the mountains on all sides, thinking that one of them might hold something for me that the farm couldn't bring. Thank God the woman and the boy had been spared the journey. If they were going to be hungry and beaten down it might as well be from the scant comforts of that one room home. Still, there was something about the beauty that kept my desperation at bay – it might be a cruel world but it sure was full of some otherworldly majesty. A masterpiece painted by an artist that had walked away from its creation.

My tongue felt like boot leather. My prayers for a stream, even a trickle, had gone unanswered. Said one anyway. It had come to this. Pulled out the canteen, shaking it again to hear that it was bone dry, and undid my fly with the other hand. It felt like defiling the vessel, but aimed as best as possible, trying to avoid getting it on my hands and pissed out what little liquid that was left in me into the nozzle. Wanted to get it over with as soon as possible, so lifted it straight to my lips and holding my nose took it all down in three long draughts. It was warm and anything but refreshing, but it was liquid. Quickly popped a few juniper berries in my mouth to kill the taste, and their acrid flavor mixed poorly and made me retch. Took everything in me not to flash and lose it once and for all, but somehow managed. It was humiliating, but it was better than nothing. There wouldn't be much more time with nothing to drink, so stuffed my pride and tried to be grateful that my mouth was slightly less dry than before. It hadn't even been much, but it was all there was to be had. So much one takes for granted 'til it's gone.

The boy had delighted in being taught how to pump water from the well. He'd watched me dig for weeks and when that first jet of water sprang forth he had swelled in delight. Said it was like magic. Looking back on how easy it flowed it may as well have been. Saved us a lot of time too, not having to walk back and forth to the creek at all hours of the day and night. Planned on building an outhouse too. All of the modern conveniences right at our home. After digging the well, wasn't really looking forward to starting to dig again, but the boy was excited to help and stood there with the oversized shovel in his small hand, beaming. He wouldn't be much help but he sure was excited at the prospect of doing adult work. It was plain to see he aimed to impress his ma, and she cooed over him with every new development. Was happy about the well too, and our arrangement with the neighbors to share it in exchange for fresh eggs. Raising chickens wasn't for me, but the neighbors had a sizeable hen house and a few roosters. They never failed to wake me up at the crack of dawn, and if it wasn't for the eggs, might have taken a shot or two at them on many of those mornings. Things had been working out pretty good for a while, until they weren't. Such simpler times, and my heart yearned for them, but those were before the rains had stopped falling.

My breath finally caught, it was time to march on, no matter how foul the taste in my mouth. No matter how nasty it was, it did make me feel a little better. My legs creaked when it came time to stand up, the left full of nothing but dull ache. Moving it made things worse and bending it was still out of the question. It was a shame to move on from such a beautiful spot, but didn't feel like dying here.

Two lizards crossed my path chasing each other and tried to stab at them with the crutch but missed and lost my balance. Landed right on my ass feeling stupid for having tried. They hardly would have been a meal anyway. Would have given a toe for something proper to eat, and drink. Her homemade biscuits, one of them chickens, some jerky, anything. Sat there for way too long imagining all of those wonderful things to feast on, lost in a sensual revelry of every dish ever shoveled into my mouth without thought of how fortunate it was to have anything to eat at all. All that fantasy wouldn't do me a bit of good. She would have told me to quit fussing and get off of my ass. Yes, ma'am.

The sun was starting to come up and it painted the desert and mountains in vibrant pastels, rich and stunning. It was glorious, an incredible sight – how could anybody be down while looking at that? As rich and lovely as it was it also meant it would be warming up quick. This was no place for sleep and my shame ran deep for dallying for so long. Had no idea how far until the trail opened up again and would provide some shelter, or at least some shade. Could be minutes or hours, hopefully not the latter. With each step the temperature rose and the hotter it got the more it slowed me down. Tried to motivate myself to speed up by running through a song in my head but it was distracting and my feet would slip if not looking at the ground for sure footing. It looked like there were trees up ahead but it was hard to tell how far away. One minute they'd seem near, the next far away. Looking to my left the spectacular view was still there, ever present, but that beauty meant nothing if my foot slid off the path and dropped me down that incline. It was nearly straight down, and far down at that. My body inched closer to the rock face to my right, but it still brought bouts of vertigo. Watched as a pebble that had been knocked loose found its way over the edge and toppled down. Never heard it hit the bottom. As the trail steepened my walk became more of a stumble, making me wish there was a second crutch, or someone to hold onto. My balance was unsure but there was no choice but to proceed. Considered crawling but there was no way the knee would allow it. Tried to only focus on the ground beneath my feet. It was increasingly becoming littered with broken stone and pebbles, slowing me down further. Sweat was pouring down my face, moisture my body could ill afford to lose.

Proceeded like that, staring at the ground, until finally my feet hit dirt again and the trail widened out, only then daring to glance in front of me. The trees were up ahead, not too far off now. The sun was directly overhead, suggesting that the walk had taken all of the morning.

She'd come out and holler from the porch that lunch was ready. The boy would drop his shovel and come running. He would be exhausted from the work and secretly complain about the callouses growing on his hands, but the way he looked at her told of a pride growing in him that he could do his share of the work around the house. Didn't have the heart to tell him that this was the easy part of life and that it'd just be getting harder as things went on. He wasn't old enough to register that the looks on our faces were growing weary, or that our meals were becoming simpler by the day. He thought that it was fun that at night we'd sit around the fire and sing a song, never realizing that it was because we couldn't afford candles anymore. We'd made a decision to try and shield him from the way things were going, but soon he'd be catching on that times were changing. We spoke less and less during the nights, letting it go unsaid what we both knew. If the rains didn't come soon then there'd be no choice but for me to set out in search of something to turn our luck around. Other folks in the town were feeling the same pressures. The neighbors were bringing less and less eggs and when the rooster failed to wake me up one morning we knew that they'd had no choice but to start eating them one by one. We hadn't had meat in a while and the porridge was getting so old that even the boy was commenting on it. Every time he did, she would give me a stern look that said it was on me to do something about it. With no way to make the rains come it meant only one thing.

Delerium was setting in. Found a place in the shade and began to make camp. Between no sleep, no water, and hardly any food, my body was in bad shape and my mind was wandering. Rolled out my blanket and plopped down, making sure the crutch was at arm's length. Ate a few nuts and berries to calm the fury in my stomach, they were running low and wouldn't last the day. The mouth was desperately dry which made it hard to chew and even harder to swallow. Pulled out the canteen and tried to position it to save what little liquid was left in my body, but nothing would come. Tossed the canteen back into my pack and wanted to cry. But nothing would come out that way either. My forehead was burning up and the worst of my fears were confirmed when my hand met the hot flesh of my face and it was clear that fever was setting in, or heat exhaustion, or both. Waves of panic and drowsiness overlapped, pushing me in every direction possible. My vision was slightly blurred and couldn't hold onto a thought for very long. Reached for the canteen again, only to remember that it was long empty. My beard had grown out but couldn't remember when, and my face felt foreign when touched. Couldn't do anything but lay down with my pack as a pillow and let my thoughts swirl through the trees above.

Went about searching the area to check if yesterday's traps had been fruitful. One of them had gone off but they were all empty, crushing my hopes of a bountiful day. The boy was still digging. The wife stirred porridge over a small fire while rains fell in the distance, clouds moving away the whole time, always away. Could see the storm heading toward one of the new settlements as buildings rose there as fast as newcomers could arrive. Their herds of cattle and goats trampled the land beneath them and the sound matched the thunder in the sky. Looking at her she pointed in the opposite direction and shook her head. A bell was ringing somewhere far off. Plants withered and died right before our eyes. Saw a man digging where the boy had stood a moment ago, glistening with sweat with a furious look on his face. His mother was old and wearing the black of mourning, bonnet covering her head. The atmosphere was somber and the fire had grown small and smokey. She watched the pot of porridge spill into the dirt and spoil. They quietly went back into the one room house, and following them, found them sitting around the table, heads bowed in prayer. They paid me no mind, didn't notice me at all. Tried to call out to them but no sound would come. The scene froze in black and white. They were like wax figures sitting there, somber and unmoving. The sun set and rose within minutes, flashing like distant lightning. Rains came and brought the colors back with it, but the two figures remained like statues and didn't flinch. Time stood still inside the house but rushed by like a flock of birds outside. She was old and bitter looking now and the man's features resembled my own, but something was off. Outside, the town grew at a fantastic rate. The old homesteads were razed, replaced with larger, two-story buildings, banks, a barber, all the trappings of a modern town. Darkness spread about the town and in the distance gunshots sounded. Still, the two figures remained unmoved. A tree that we had planted the day we started building loomed tall over me and pointed to the sky like an outstretched finger pointing at heaven. It began to topple and fell toward me and the house. Ducking out of the way just in time it crashed through the roof with a terrible clatter. A pile of rubble and ruin crumbled with time becoming nothing but a trash heap within moments. Soon replaced with a barn being raised by a group of dour strangers wearing fashions unknown to me. They looked strange and mean.

The stars shone crystal clear above, but it took a minute to bring them into focus. My eyelids were partially crusted shut with sleep. It made a crispy sound as it flaked off in my fingers. Even though the night was young it was freezing cold. But touching my face let me know that it wasn't the night that was cold. It was warm to the touch and there was no telling if it was from fever or sunburn or both. Either way it was accompanied by great discomfort. The back was so stiff it was difficult to sit up.

Something rustled in the tree above me and the altercation with the raccoon ran through my mind in rapid streaks. It didn't sound like the movements of a mammal, though. The sound was more deliberate. A swoosh of wings broke the night. Death was descending in the form of a giant raven. It came down with mighty flapping, blotting out the stars for a moment. It wrapped me up in its massive wings like a blanket, holding tight until the pressure felt as if it would crush me. But there was no bird. There was nothing around me at all, just my pack lying scattered and open beside me. The stars were as they were, and it was silent all around. The last of my nuts and berries had fallen from the pack, but the nuts were gone, probably squirreled away by some rodent. A few juniper berries lay strewn about the surrounding dirt. Picked them up and ate them one by one, but it wasn't enough to make any difference. Was desperate for some kind of relief but it wasn't coming. Gathered the fallen items from my pack and put them back inside, leaving out the forgotten tobacco pouch. In this state there'd be no hiking out of here this night, and as bad an idea as leaving in daylight was, my body felt too sick to be moving anytime soon. Rounded up what kindling was in arms reach and used one of the last precious matches from the tobacco bag to get the fire going. Any more sleep felt unlikely, too. My head was swimming and a dull ache permeated my bum leg.

The fire crackled with the not-quite dry sticks. They had caught but were resisting the flames. Pulled a handful of drier looking pine needles and coaxed the fire into action. It was a small victory at best. With nothing else to occupy me, took the tobacco and rolled a smoke. Lit it with a twig from the fire and inhaled the lush smoke as if it were the long drink of water my mouth was desperate for. Of course, it did nothing to sate this feeling, but putting something in me was a welcoming feeling, a feeling of calm that hadn't been around for a while. Sat smoking in the dark silence, straining to hear anything, something to fill the night, any kind of company. The moment was filled with aloneness. Exhaling a large cloud of smoke could have sworn it was rain clouds coming to wash away my troubles, but it drifted away, gracefully heading up to the stars. It didn't take me with it. Stared at the cigar in my hand and for a moment it looked like a steaming sandwich. Took everything in me to reason my way out of taking a bite. A fog surrounded me, blanketing everything, but it couldn't be coming from the cigar, and couldn't believe that it was actually the weather either.

Setting the cigar down on a stone by the fire, knew that it was time to check on the wound again. Before looking, made a paste out of the last of the creosote leaves. Fearful of what was under there, there was no choice but to roll up the pant leg. In places it had stuck to the wounds and peeled off in small painful rips. It must have taken hours to get it up over my knee and expose the wound. In the firelight the wounds looked dark and mostly scabbed over except for the fresh blood from the newly opened scratches, which oozed slowly out and down my calf. It was difficult to see in the dim light, so threw on a few more twigs and fanned them with my hands. When it flared up for a moment my worst fears were confirmed. The black line, which had started out only protruding an inch from the wound, now snaked around from behind my knee and was making its way up my thigh. It brought panic with it. It had gotten into my blood and it might as well have been a gunshot moving in slow motion. It didn't leave me much in the way of choices. Again plunged my blade into the embers of the fire, but this time not to cauterize the mostly sealed wounds. My hand revolted at what it needed to do and refused to move. My stomach retched, but there was nothing to come up. Sat quivering in fear at what needed to be done and it took a sheer act of will to grab the knife from the fire and plunge the tip into the apex of the black line. Worms squirmed beneath my flesh as the hot blade sank into the blackness. A scream broke the silence of the night and it took a while to realize that it was mine. At first some of the blood turned to steam and upon removing the knife dark blood seeped out slowly letting off a foul odor. My vision darkened like the blood.

Don't think the blackout lasted long because upon coming to, the still hot knife remained in my hand. The blood was still wet on my thigh but had begun to congeal. Puncturing the infection was a desperate move but what other recourse was left to me? It was going to be a long night. Fortunately, the fire was still going, and retrieved my cigar, relit it in the same fashion as before. It was the only comfort to be found here, and was big enough to soothe me through the next half an hour. Barely a comfort but something to cling to nonetheless. She had always criticized me when she saw me smoking, and in my mind she chastised me, taking away a small bit of the relief that it brought. But she wasn't here now, and in a way, it was good that she couldn't see me in this sorry state. But her voice persisted in the back of my mind and she wasn't pleased. She listed every foolish mistake that had led me to this situation, again and again. She brought up what it would do to the boy, as if it was a secret and didn't already occupy my thoughts. Couldn't take it anymore when her tears came. Her soft wailing sounded like a breeze in the trees. Told her to quiet down and went back to smoking, but she didn't stop. Stared at the leg for a long time and could only hope that the infection was leaving with all of that thick blood. If only for some hot water and a fresh bandage to dress it with. Pulling the pant leg back down was going to be agony, but it couldn't be put off forever.

Cut a strip off of the blanket to try and fashion a bandage but the wool was filthy, stank, and was too coarse to be putting anywhere near the wounds, neither the fresh ones or the already infected ones. Only managed to have less blanket and less energy to expend. The fresh pain wasn't going to let me sleep. Would have given anything to lay my head down and try not to focus on its throbbing, but it was now past obvious that there'd be no rest for me, ever, a doctor, or a place to clean the worsening injuries. With a new determination, gathered up my things and stuffed them back into the pack, leaving the useless makeshift bandage behind. A nearby tree suffering root rot gave me a glimmer of hope. Approached the low branches and broke one off with what little strength was left in me. It snapped fairly easily but almost knocked me to the ground when it came free. Tested it out and it was too short to be a second crutch, perhaps it could serve as a cane, in a bind. Taking a closer look at the branches, identified one that was a better length and tried again. It broke off with one big crack and this time it did send me to the ground. It smarted when my body hit, but my goal had been achieved and this one was going to be long enough for the job. Used it to prop myself back up and retrieved the other one. With both it took the pressure off my leg but it also made the pack precarious to keep on my back. That was the least of my worries and it could be abandoned if absolutely necessary. The fire was still going but there was no time to waste in dealing with it. It wasn't safe to leave it burning but neither was staying put. Kicked a bit of dirt onto it as best could manage and sauntered away, hoping it wouldn't catch the trees if the wind kicked up.

Hobbling on the crutches was slow going but it was slightly easier than trying to manage with just one. The new one had no crux, so it was uncomfortable at best, but instead of cursing it, tried to remind myself that it could save my life. So, one swing of the feet at a time made my slow progress descending.

This part of the trail was gratefully flatter and covered with less gravel and debris, although several times lost footing and nearly toppled down. But with every step managed to get more acclimated to the style of locomotion. As a boy, had once attempted to fashion stilts out of some lumber my old man had left sitting around the house. He'd been furious to find that it had been appropriated for something so frivolous, but that hadn't bothered me as playthings were in short supply and wanted to see the world from a higher vantage. Had climbed on up, and once getting my balance had managed to stride halfway across the yard before falling and breaking my wrist. My initial yell, and subsequent bout of crying had brought my mother out of the house to tend to me. But when my father found out he was doubly pissed. First for my infraction of stealing the timber, and for the fall on top of the theft. He gave me a solid beating even before attempting to set the wrist. When he stormed off to get drunk at the local tavern my mother had attempted to fashion a cast out of things lying around the house, but it was makeshift and didn't quite do the job. There'd been no going to the doctor, for in those days there hadn't been one in our small budding village. She gave me a shot of whiskey to dull the pain, my first ever drink. It wouldn't be my last. If only for a pull from the bottle now. Had to stop myself from thinking about liquids, it would drive me mad and kept threatening to steal my focus. Crutches forward, then feet, that was all that mattered. Made a little song up to try and keep rhythm but didn't have the strength to sing it out loud. Something to break the silence would have been nice, but would have to make do with the sound of my feet dragging through the dirt.

The going was as easy as it was going to get and with any luck the trail would remain tame. My swimming mind could not put together what it had looked like on the way up, or even if it was the same trail. Usually prided myself on paying attention to such things but the fever had erased the trek up the mountain. Dreaded having to pass another thin strip of rocky ledge as the crutches would be no help if the trail thinned out too much. Did my best to try and refrain from such thoughts and focus on one footfall at a time, but my mind reeled with dangers real and imagined. At least the sun wasn't beating down on me and making the heat worse. My face was already peeling and blistered, and combined with the fever never let up from feeling hot and uncomfortable. Again, tried to focus on the steps but my mind scattered.

One time when the boy was sick, had watched the woman soothe him with fresh compress after compress, never leaving his side while he suffered. Would have sold my soul for that soothing touch right now. He had cried through most of the night but she never left his side or let up, gently singing the boy back into calm and reassurance. If only for that gentle tone now, or if only the words of that song could come back to me and deliver something hopeful and tranquil.

They would not come, nor ever, if my frustratingly slow pace was not maintained. Trying to speed things up by swinging the crutches out further was only risking another fall and not worth the miniscule difference in speed. It was difficult to pay attention to maintaining the correct pace, so again my song rode through my mind like a war drum keeping the marching troops in line. With each step my fatigue grew worse and was threatening to halt my progress altogether. Fought against it with every fiber of my being. And there was little fight left in me. Only the pain of my wounds kept me semi-alert. An odd and unnatural comfort in the midst of my descent. The rhythm brought to mind a hymn from the small church the next town over that she would frequently drag me to. It wasn't for me, but now, thinking of all those people in makeshift pews brought to mind how alone my journey was, and how easy it had been to be amongst them, even as my wish to be elsewhere caused me to take the sense of community for granted. The hymn was little comfort, so my mind revisited the somber march, a near funeral dirge accompanied my grim procession. It was hard to keep the rhythm and to keep my feet and the crutches swinging forward. Thinking of each small step as a victory kept me in check. The mountain might beat me but nothing could win against me in the battle of the next small step to be taken. And until the sun began to rise one foot followed the other in a steady downward pace, covering more ground in those hours than perhaps in the last few days of my flight. And as the sunlight ignited the trail into vibrant colors the heat came but went unnoticed in the steamy warm already there from the fever. Resolved not to attempt rest and continue on as long as my body could hold out, to get down that damned mountain at all costs, no matter how much fatigue or fever tried to overtake me. That mountain may want to take everything left to me, but it would have to reckon with the fact that there was nothing left to take except my love for the woman and the boy, and that love was as impenetrable as stone. Was up there for them in the first place, and it was for them that my painful flight had to succeed. It was going to take more than death to interfere with my resolve in that, and even if my leg was going to be lost, that mountain had found a worthy adversary. Pain was nothing. My lack of clarity was nothing next to my determination to reunite with them and provide, at all costs, what nature had tried to steal from us. This country had promised me an honest living and nothing, no matter what, could interfere with my resolve to have just that. One foot in front of the other, one crutch swing before that, that was the mantra that would guide me past the agony, past everything having gone wrong, past any animal or man that tried to stand in my way. This mountain might be stronger than any man, but had never let a man best me and wasn't about to start now, man or mountain it didn't matter because there had been a promise, and a man is nothing but his word. Mine had never been soiled and wasn't about to let it be now, all because of some damned raccoon whose skin would have been being sold by now.

My last haul, my last sale, the clerk had desperately low balled me, said it was inevitable with the flooding of the market by the newcomers. Said the fur trade itself was crashing and waning in popularity. The same clerk who had said this was the one who had guaranteed returns not so long ago, and had put in a special request for certain pelts. Trusted him as little as he was willing to pay out, and both were decreasing fast. It was hard to believe his excuses on account of the animals becoming scarce. One would think that the prices would be going up with these problems, but everything was always changing, and it should've come as no surprise that they'd be getting worse. There was no luck in life, only what it was willing to shell out, and one had to make do with that. It was senseless to talk about what one deserved when the world flowed and moved by an unseen force that man could never even wish to understand, let alone control. But we fought and we fought like hell, because what else was a man supposed to do but take care of his own and try not to get down about it. The woman had said as much when asking me to go out and find something to bring good fortune back, and my approach had always been honest, but every real man knew that intention didn't mean shit in the face of it all. Still, her words were a strength and she was strong, never denying the realities that we faced, no matter how bad things got. All we could do was try to shield the boy from it all as long as nature and God would allow it. Let the boy have a childhood before being forced into being a man. Hadn't really had that luxury myself but it was all the more reason to try and provide it for him. The longer we could keep him blissfully naïve of the hardship the better, but would put my money on it that he had learned by now, what with having to be the man of the house already, and not even ten yet. That'd only get worse if his old man didn't make it back. Wasn't about to disappear on them and walk out the same as my old man had. It was lucky for me and had spared further beatings, but we'd done everything in our power to spare the boy a fate like that. Had worked pretty good too, until the rains stopped and began the chain of messed up events that led me up this mountain to begin with. Thoughts of the boy overrode the ache in my legs and despite the agony, picked up the pace as much as possible. He didn't need no mountain killing his old man. Would have been the same as being walked out on, and he'd been promised that'd never go down.

What was left of my clothes clung to my body damply. Tried to pay it no mind and keep that rhythm. Each step was harder than the last, but judging by the heat the elevation had dropped drastically, perhaps some progress after all. Wanted to yell the boy's name in defiance. Dogged determination drove me on. The pain had grown into a numbness, good or bad luck there was no saying, but it was an excuse to pick up the pace. The sun was full up and beating on me, but there'd been worse beatings and none of them had ever stopped me in my tracks.

A foreign sound splashed through my reflections. Something uncertain yet welcoming, coaxing me on, into what, there was no telling. My senses couldn't be trusted anymore. Had seen mirages before, down in the desert, a messed-up trick, but had never heard of anybody hearing one. Whatever it was it could well be my mind playing tricks on me again, couldn't trust myself wandering off into distraction, had to keep that steady pace. One step then the next.

Many wide boulders surrounded the path along with a lot of smaller rocks on the ground, making for more difficult going. It was hard to gain footing for the crutches as the ground cover wasn't nearly as solid as before. This forced slowing down brought with it frustration, something that could be ill afforded. The song was no use, for there was no rhythm to finding places to step. Stopping to look forward, the trail had become less defined and dispersed. Rocks scattered out before me for as far as could been seen, stretching at least all the way to the next bend. The tree cover was getting thick too, and the shade was a welcome change, but in my confused mind it made direction harder to figure. Told myself not to look back for fear that direction would be lost altogether and might end up backtracking accidentally. The alluring sound grew in intensity and volume. It was coming from somewhere nearby, if it was real at all. It was cooler here in the trees but my face still felt like it was on fire and sweat was still pouring out of me. My exhaustion kept nagging at me to lay down, but there'd be no comfort on the rocks and there was the fear that once the body went down it wouldn't be getting back up again. The boy had splashed playfully when the well first yielded water. On his face was a recognition of magic, a true sense of wonder, seeing that water, cool and clean, spring right up from the earth. He wanted to know everything about how it worked, but there was only so much to be told, it was outside of my expertise. Knew how to dig one but that was about it. And he was unsatisfied with my explanation but soon forgot about that and went back to fooling around. That had been a happy day. Even his mother stopped telling him what to do and let him have his fun. He would have swam had it been more than a bucket full. There was no way of knowing at the time that that'd be drying up too. But for a moment there, we were self-sufficient and happy. It meant not having to schlep buckets for several miles a day, a chore we all shared and none particularly looked forward to. Found that while lost in thought my legs had stopped moving and was just standing there staring into the trees. Couldn't say for how long either. Was displeased with myself for losing track and taking a break, no matter how much had been in need of one. Did my best to get my head on straight and get back to moving forward. Slung the crutches forward, my armpits raw, and when my boots lifted there was a splash. It was no delusion, my foot had been immersed in mud. Couldn't believe it at first and reckoned that my mind was back to playing tricks on me. But looking down my eyes confirmed what my ears had heard, and they hadn't been lying. Below me was mud for sure, and leading into the muddy patch was a small stream, barely a trickle, maybe an inch wide. But it was flowing with clear, clean looking water. A prayer answered.

After lowering myself slowly, trying not to fall on the slippery rocks, set my crutches down and plunged my hand down into the rivulet. It wasn't deep enough to submerge my hand but it was water all right, not my senses deceiving me. Greedily scooped handful after handful into my mouth and drank 'till my stomach revolted and sicked up. But that didn't stop me from continuing to gorge myself. Placed my burning forehead down into it, it was like the woman's touch, almost lulling me to sleep. When the initial glee wore off and my fill had been drunk, a semi-clarity began to return. It was a moment of ecstasy but my troubles were hardly over. Taking the canteen from my pack, which fortunately hadn't been abandoned, filled it to the brim hardly believing my good fortune. It was enough water for two more days, if there was even that much time left to me. Now it was time to address my wounds, finally having the opportunity to get them cleaned up. Tore the rip wide open to have access to the wounds without having to hike up or remove the pant leg again. As it tore places that had stuck to the scabs ripped off bringing the shock of nauseating pain. The spot where my knife had entered the infection was still bleeding, and to my horror the black line had snaked its way up from the puncture and past my belt line. Lifting up my shirt to check the damage, found that it had worked its way up past my waist and was now finding its way up my torso several inches from my hip and climbing up my side. Rinsing my knife off in the water, no time for fire, used the blade to cut a horizontal slash where the line stopped. Dark, thick blood came forth and there was no resisting howling in pain. The sound echoed back at me and only then realized that it had been out loud. Used the canteen to splash water on the fresh cut and the blood ran down my side as it thinned. Before refilling the canteen used what was left to clean all of the wounds, which were long past infected. The pus diluted and made me sick. Seeing it rinsed away was a small relief. The water stung where it made contact with the festering cuts, and ignoring it as best as possible, doused the wounds over and over, hoping to wash away the infection. Nearly conked out on the third pass but forced myself to remain as alert as possible and clean them out thoroughly. Couldn't say how long it took, but the process was excruciating and several times, nearly lost consciousness. Again filled the canteen and drank as much as possible, knowing that the small excuse of a creek could be the last water on the trail. My pant leg hung loose in tatters but there was nothing to be done about that.

The fresh pain of the new cut had woken me up to some degree, so it was now or never to get off of this cursed rock. Leaving the stream after so many days of thirst seemed insane, but no amount of drinking was going to cure my infection or get me back home. Standing back up was difficult, further made challenging by the slippery mud on my boots, but one crutch at a time finally managed to get up and start my limping going again. If it weren't for the downward movement of the stream might have lost direction, was grateful for something pointing my way out of this place. Even though the wounds were slightly cleaner now it didn't stop them from slowing my trek, as one painful movement after another brought me forward along the path.

Soon the trees opened up and revealed the path getting wider, and better yet, the bottom of the mountain was nearing. But the trail also looked rough up ahead. And despite the brief surge of relief the water had brought, fatigue was setting in pretty hard. It'd been a while since any proper sleep and that deadly black line was still on the creep, who knows what it was doing to me. But none of that mattered, the town, or that sorry excuse for one, was finally in reach. It'd be filled with unfriendly newcomers, and that brought no joy, but with any luck a doctor would be around. He'd probably be wanting my leg, and the last of my money. Weren't many choices up ahead, but more than up here. Wished that the mountain had never come to my attention, what with its promises of bounty. Someone had probably pulled a profit but it sure as hell hadn't been me. We'd had such high hopes before circumstance had forced me to head out, we never would have had the boy had we known. But she wanted him so bad and no man in his right mind says no to a woman that good. But if she'd known, it would have been a different song and dance, not sure we would have tried to settle down at all. Not that we regretted the boy, that'd never be the case, but we would have waited for better times, if they ever came. They had, but hadn't lasted long, not long at all. Not long enough. She'd chide the hell out of me if anything like that ever came out of my mouth around her. Could hear her now, mad as hell, and nearly responded with an excuse before realizing that she was near a hundred miles away, if not more. She'd be telling me that the boy was more of a man than me and to quit with the self-pity, get your ass up and be a man, and if it couldn't be done for myself that it better damn well be done for her. Again, had to stop from talking to her out loud. Would have given anything to see that face even if it was busy yelling at me, but she was there in my mind refusing to let me go yellow, chiding me every time giving up felt like a good idea. And it sure did seem like a good idea, that searing pain in my leg, all hungry and moving slow. Pushed on anyway despite my body's frequent and persistent protests.

My heart was beating hard and could have sworn that every drop of water had been sweat out already. Was soaking wet and it sure wasn't from the stream that was far enough back there by now for me to have dried off. But all the while that desert was getting closer and the mountain behind me higher. Could hardly believe that in my state that that much of the trail had been covered already. How long it had taken wouldn't come to mind. Was it weeks or days, it was all a blur. Crutch out, foot next. Tried to remember the marching song but it was gone with the other memories. Tried to think up a new one too, but nothing would come. Nothing came out at all. Longed to sit back down in the shade, but knew too well that there'd be no getting up again.

Had burst through that door, so eager to surprise her that had forgotten to wipe off my boots, and she wasn't too pleased with that, but when she'd seen what was in tow, you would have thought it was Christmas morning. Our first goat. Things had been looking up and for a long while we had talked adding livestock to the farm. It was another mouth to feed but it would return, and we talked about it being the first of many. The boy thought of her as a pet and best friend, laughing in delight whenever we let him play with her. It hadn't lasted long when the droughts came and she died shortly after the crops began to fail. Didn't do well for our spirits, a bad omen really, and explaining it all to the boy had been hell. That was around the time she'd told me to move on and get it figured out.

The good times were over but we'd clung to hope and had faith in my ability to make it right, somehow. For my first few months out further west it looked like our luck might turn, too. But then they came and everything changed again. Now was hoping to run into them, to anyone, even if that'd be letting down my pride and asking for the help that was getting past due. How long had it been since seeing anyone? Spoke out loud to hear if my voice still worked and her name came to my lips but without any sound accompanying the word. Kept saying it though, for something in me told me that there was risk of forgetting. All this time lost in thought and the trail wasn't looking familiar anymore. The trees were giving way to boulders again, and sand, lots of sand. Couldn't remember if that was a good sign or not. Looked up at the sun, didn't know east from west, just that it was still scorching hot. Everything was all mixed up and had to remind myself what the point of the walk was. But it still wasn't clear. Nothing was. When the town finally came up would be selling my spoils and heading back to them, with a lighter pack this time. Fine coon skins too. What was the fetching price? Had it changed since last time? If there was enough, would try to get her something pretty, and the boy a gift too, something nice for them upon returning home. They'd be happy to see me but she'd probably give me some flack for taking so long. How long had it been? Bet the boy was all grown up by now, probably a few inches taller, at least. Wonder how things had gone at the farm, if things turned around. Without me being there it was one less mouth to feed, so that was something. People around there would be looking out for each other as long as not too many people came, making strangers out of everyone. She was probably exchanging some fresh cold clean water for eggs now, getting ready to make a supper for the boy. And he'd be all proud having brought home meat from the day's hunt. With all that money from the pelts it'd be like we were rich for a spell, and we could expand the farm, perhaps more livestock, or maybe even a horse. The boy would love that. Would teach him how to ride and he'd get the chance to see the world when he grows up. Always wanted that for him. He'd be so happy. And we could feel good about ourselves too, having raised the boy right and good and him going off into the world to be a man and do his thing, maybe raise a boy of his own. We'd be sad to see him go, but what parent isn't proud on that day. The woman would cry, probably would shed a few tears myself if no one was looking. No use a boy like that staying around his folks forever when there were fortunes to be made out there. It'd be a proud moment for sure. And he'd come around to see us as we got old, and bring his family along with him. The wife would beam like the sun with the little ones around.

The ground started leveling off and it was starting to cool down with the evening coming on. Leaned up against a massive granite boulder to take a draught from the canteen. Water wasn't cool anymore, but it soothed my dry throat. Was looking forward to something stronger to celebrate my return to town. Put the canteen back in the pack and it came smashing down that there'd be no celebrating. There was next to nothing in my pack save what had been there on my way up the mountain. Started to take a step, forgetting all about the crutch and nearly tumbled down on my face. Everything about the leg came back to me, killing my mood. Steadied myself against the boulder and tried again, this time with the crutches. The going was painful, each step a flame through my body. But each step was oce closer to them, and home. Not too far in the distance smoke rose from cooking fires and my mouth watered thinking about a hot cooked meal. Beans and meat, perhaps a pint to wash it down. Could eat damn near anything. Rattlesnake stew, hell, anything would be welcome. Bring on the second helping, this man could eat a house. Rabbit, carrots—the thought of food drove me wild, reminding me how long it had been since eating proper.

My mind was drifting and had to force myself to stare at the columns of smoke, use them like a compass, a beacon. Stopping to look at the leg was a mistake and made me wonder how it'd been possible to walk on in it at all. Also made the mistake of lifting my shirt to find that the evil black line had made its way past my side and was headed up my chest. No use looking at that, so yanked it back down and kept trudging along as best as possible. For a minute didn't think it was possible to make it as the smoke didn't seem to be getting any closer, and considered firing off a round into the sky to call attention. But most wouldn't be running toward gunfire and it wasn't exactly the friendliest hello.

Distance had a way of being deceptive in the desert, so as the first stars started winking themselves into existence pushed myself onward toward the smoke and hope of help. There had to be a kind soul up there somewhere. Reminded myself that not all men were bad, even amongst the newcomers there had to be at least one that would care and know what to do with a man in my state. A Christian act of charity, or a trade for my weapon, anything, someone would take pity and come forth. Wasn't like most men to leave another there bleeding out. Or was it? How long had it been since seeing another face, or a kind one? Goodwill was a thing, but so was bad, it's often just a matter of knowing the difference. She was a good judge of that and she'd probably been teaching the boy in the way of kindness. Saw a bird overhead but this time it was no raven bringing bad omens, it was a hawk diving into the brush, also searching for an evening meal. It silently swooped down in majestic flight and disappeared into the brush. Something would die but something greater would live, and wasn't that just the way of things. Nature had no use in bowing to the wills of men. Men probably didn't either. Each set out to make his way and some found it. It was arrogant to find cruelty in this arrangement no matter how much we tended to go looking for it. Above, the milky way began to show and spill its way across the sky and the mountain against it looked beautiful and cathedrallike. It was a place of old, honest beauty and it got me thinking about all of the ugly that drove me up there in the first place. The same ugly was headed to right now, but now it was even more beautiful than the mountain, the best possible sight, nearly. The irony wasn't lost on me and there'd be a need of making some new friends momentarily. They'd never showed me much in the way of kindness but they were my only hope, and for the first time their faces would be a welcome sight, a prayer answered, men that would earn my love in no time.

My breath was getting short and the sweating was worse than ever. A foul taste permeated my mouth accompanied by the horrible dryness. Every step toward them felt like the last my leg could handle, but had made it down that mountain, so what could a few hundred more steps cause? The trail had opened up into a makeshift road and the going should have been easier than ever. But it felt like trudging through thick sludge even though it was dry as a bone. Told myself, one step at a time, and it seemed like those words were the only ones my mind could conjure, had conjured, for days. She was pushing me on, riding me not to stop, like a horse being driven past its breaking point with the lash of the whip. She said, if you can't do it for yourself then do it for me. Wasn't the first time she'd used that one and it was obvious she meant business.

Could smell the smoke from those fires as they got closer. It made me ravenous with the thought that there could be proper food cooking on one of them. The boy was particularly fond of watching the rabbits he took down spinning on the spit, the lean meat sizzling while the flames licked at it. He always insisted on getting a leg once it was done and he'd hold it up proudly showing off to his mother. And she'd pat him on the head letting him know he was a good boy and that yes, she was proud. Things had been that simple for a while. Doubted there was any scene like that up ahead, the new towns popping up were no place for children. But everyone out there had once been children until whatever moment, whatever line had been crossed to turn them into men. For some it came too early, and could only pray the boy would be spared those realities for a least a little while. Me leaving could have done it. Hunger could do it. No matter how hard we'd tried to shield him from the harshness of the frontier life, it was what it was, and the boy wasn't stupid. His curious mind was always figuring things out, often one step ahead of us. This time of night she might be reading him a story, and he'd be asking when his father would be coming back if there was mention of anything that might remind him of me. And she'd have no answer.

The protest from my legs kept growing stronger. Even this close couldn't help but think of giving up and laying down. Sleep was calling and it sounded sweet. The prickly old hay and husk bed sounded like heaven, her smell next to me, that beautiful hair wrapped around the pillow, the boy softly snoring in the corner across the room. When first light shone it'd be time to get to attending to the chores and he'd protest, so we'd let him have a little bit more time in dreamland before putting him to work, just a little bit more. The sun coming up over the farm was always a beautiful sight until it illuminated the state of our crops and how bad things were getting. Nature's beauty can easily fool a man into thinking that it isn't against him every step of the way, that everything out there could spell defeat if not handled properly, and even then everything could still go wrong. For all of our trying and mastery, nature had a way of beating folks down, it moved along without us if it wanted to, didn't really need us at all, and the best we could do was to try and stretch out our way against its immensity. So let the boy sleep. Those realities would come crashing down sooner or later and there'd be no shielding anyone from that. One got hard or dropped off, and for as hard as it had made me, couldn't feel nothing but being soft now as everything in me screamed out to be left alone and rest right there wherever my body fell. But my feet kept moving and those crutches kept swinging, and every step was bringing those fires into clearer view. Some were surrounded by tents, others by men sleeping in the open under the stars. A few had figures milling around them, either staring at the fire, cooking, drinking, or just making conversation. Somewhere in the distance a few notes from a harmonica floated through the air. All the signs of life were there up ahead, not quite a proper town yet, but some day would be – filled with folks who faced the same troubles, whether or not they'd brought some of those troubles with them and they spilled over onto others. There would always be someone who had been there first and others arriving late and changing things when they came. This place would be no different than any other, no different from the one left behind in search of something better. The wheel of change would keep rolling no matter who did what, there was just no stopping it, and most of us would get lost in the spokes.

If the men around the fire had noticed me, none made any move to let it show. Would have called out to warn of my arrival if there had been any voice left in me. One more step. One more step, kept telling myself that's all it would take but the road just seemed to go on forever. My crutch slipped when it hit a small patch of mud and my legs went out from under me and sent me crashing to the ground. From down there the sky looked wonderous, big and open, inviting me in with the lure of peaceful calm. The mountain loomed there larger than in my memory. There was no strength left to get back up and sleeping right there sounded like the sweetest thing in all of the world. Tried not to give in to the temptation, was too close to fail, but they still hadn't seen me coming. Using the crutch like an oar, pushed my body forward one agonizing inch at a time. It was like trying to move a stubborn mule, and every push set the leg on fire. The camps could have been a hundred miles away but something made me keep on pushing through the dirt. Pushed and pushed past there being nothing left, and whenever that mysterious reserve ran out it left me but a few feet from one of the fires. Laying on the dirt, flat on my back and staring at the fire upside down, it could have been the majesty of the sun or fires of hell. Several of the men stood up and approached. Their boots crunching on the gravel was too loud, but somehow sounded far away. Could do nothing but lie there looking up until their faces came into view, gazing down at me with strange looks on their faces.

"This one looks to be in rough shape. Where do you think he dragged himself in from?"

Couldn't hear the response but it sounded like babbling water. Let out a groan but no words would come.

"Best run over to town and see if there's a doctor to be fetched. Go on, go, quick."

The man who had spoken kneeled down and put his face close to mine, close enough to smell his strong breath and desert sweat.

"You hold on, feller. He went to fetch the doc, he'll be coming round."

His words were friendly but the foreign voice, hearing a voice at all after all this time, didn't seem right. Another man came to stand next to him and they were sullen and silent for a minute.

"Think this one's a goner? He don't look so good."

"Hang in there, buddy, it won't be long."

"Give him a drink to bring him round."

Sharp whiskey met my lips and made me cough and spatter, but it brought some little bit of strength with its fire. Thought of her and the boy waving goodbye from the porch.

Finally, the words came. "Tell Abigail..."

"What did he say?"

"Couldn't quite make it out. The man's dead."

THE IDIOT CAPER

BY MANNY TORRES

"No human being could ever have the rights of mobility than merchandise has."
Roberto Saviano

"When you clean up a city, you destroy it."
Charles Bukowski

"He's just a whitey that come out the wrong color."
Shane Stevens

Author's Note:

This novella is dedicated to Shane Stevens, whose novels *Rat Pack* and *Go Down Dead* were a huge influence on this story.

Part of this book appears in my new novel *A Simmering Dissonance,* which ties both stories into the same timeline.

1

MIDNIGHT VULTURES

Dead Johnny was there, wide awake, but then again it was his car. He called it his 'Caddy', but it was really a faded brown Olds Ninety-Eight Regency Sedan. Used to belong to his older brother until he got locked up and Dead Johnny inherited it. About the only thing any family member ever left him.

In the fading jade light of predawn, circling the radius of the lot, he was wide awake. Hollowed windows from empty tenements gazed down at them. High fences around a residential complex meant to keep people inside. It made everything seem distant, farther apart than it was.

Inside the Olds it was hard to tell who was left alive and who wasn't. Flames had come onboard in disarray, like he'd been worked over. Brett too. Pike had his neck brace and cane.

This was no way to work.

The Olds had a nuanced squeak about it. Shocks or worn breaks. The springs in the bench seat in the back? The squeal of antiquity. The car circled, gravel crackling under its wheels. Fish in a barrel, the saying went. Dead Johnny figured circling would keep them from locking down on them and finishing them off. Light poured in through the bullet holes in the doors. The webbed windshield. Smoke emitted from the punctured engine.

He thought he felt something in his foot, but he didn't want to look down at it. Lips clenched too hard to speak. Who else got hit?

You could just ask.

Nobody spoke. Things had to remain silent because there were eyes everywhere. Guns everywhere, aimed at them.

Everyone pressed low in their seats, tucked inside the car, afraid of the next bullet that would zipper in from nowhere. Dead Johnny thought of how it all started a day or two ago. The Korean girl's face came to mind immediately, bright and cartoonish like *manhwa*.

He'd been driving past the pizzeria in East Side when he saw Miha leaning against the brightly painted brick wall. The large cat mural looked over her shoulders, a galaxy of comets and stars bursting from its eyes over a background fading from purple to blue to pink. Kind of like Miha's hair, which started turquoise on top then faded to purple and ended in pink. She dressed all black, wearing rose-tinted sunglasses. One of her sneakers was pink, the other green. Her supply bag was slung over her shoulder.

Dead Johnny stopped the car at the corner of Glenwood and Gresham. She pretended not to see him.

"Hey," he rolled down the window. He called out several times before she looked.

"Let's go over here." She signaled him to round the corner. "Looks like you're tryna buy drugs from me."

"I mean, that's why I'm here." Dead Johnny gave her a confused look. He swerved the car into Gresham and parked on the corner. She rounded the other side of the wall and stood beneath an R. Land *Loss Cat* mural. He slammed the car door and crossed while she toyed with her phone.

"You got percs?" he said. "My anniversary is coming up…"

"Not on me," Miha said. "*Sorrrreeee.*"

"Shit. You got nugs?" He was dressed like a biker pirate, dusty leather pants, boots, and bandana wrapped around his skull.

She slipped him a baggy filled with three marijuana trees. He inspected the contents. Stuck his nose in, inhaled.

"Some new shit s'pose to be hitting soon," Miha said, looking around. "I can let you know when it drops."

"What, California shit? *New Jersey* shit?"

"Nah, this some other type of shit." Miha leaned and covered her mouth to whisper. *"Crystal."*

"In Atlanta?" he said. "Who's dropping that?"

"Shh, it's mad DL right now. Some dude was seen walking around with a briefcase of it. At least that's what they say."

"White dude?"

"One of the hipsters from the neighborhood. You know, Man Bun?" Miha said.

"I used to sell to him. When I used to sell. He's slinging meth?"

She shrugged. "He was seen tryna ditch the stash, fo' sho."

"You gonna get some?" Dead Johnny said.

"I don't fuck with that. That case belongs to Purple Rain and his peeps are after it. Shit's gonna hit the street before you know it, though. Don't matter who slinging it. Both sides fynna fight for it."

"Who?"

"Hoodies and Skulls," she said. "They hunting for it. Prolly traded several hands by now. Shit's supposed to give off blue smoke when you light it."

"How do you know?" he said.

"S'what I heard from some meth angels," she said. "Call 'em that 'cause they always got a meth vapor halo."

Dead Johnny sighed.

"Purple Rain gonna move it in," she said.

"Skulls gonna sling it," Dead Johnny nodded his head knowingly.

She was back at her phone.

"Whatever," she said. "I don't know nothing. I'm just an East Side corner girl."

"You said Man Bun was carrying it?"

Miha shrugged. "They say."

"You didn't actually see him with it?"

"Nah. You know that homeless dude, Santa Claus? He supposably saw Man Bun tryna sell it off, but nobody wants it 'cause it's Purple's property."

"He's gonna get killed before he tries to sell it back to Purple."

"Prolly," Miha said. She finished texting and tucked her phone in her pocket. "I'm heading to Six Flags with my friend Shauna. One last chance before the weather gets cold. Are we done with this transaction?"

"Yeah," he said.

"You owe me $65."

He handed her cash. She counted it and smiled.

"*K? Bye!*"

Now in the present, inside the circling car, dodging bullets.

No briefcase.

No way out. Retrospectively, it was easier to gather a few idiots to search for a missing case of drugs. Even easier was getting many guns pointed at you.

2

BUDDHIST ANARCHISTS

Brunch at the Thai Temple meant tourists, along with noisy redneck bikers at full volume, lined up to get soup, noodles, boba tea and fried desserts. Tents lined the river running the length of the park to the parking lot. Inside the sparkling, gilded temple, monks meditated. Their peace shattered whenever the bikers revved up coming and going.

Dead Johnny arrived first. Brett was late, but Flames was here, and he'd brought Chuck with him. They walked under the trees alongside a panorama of food kiosks. An aroma of blazing woks, scorched ginger, chili peppers and seared meat drifted over the promenade.

"We better grab a seat," Chuck said, moving slowly with his cane.

"Not hungry," Dead Johnny said, thin black cigar protruding from under his waxed mustache. "Those motherfuckers are late. They your friends?"

"I know them from the East Side," Chuck said.

"They always this tardy?"

"They can be assholes. Sorry."

"Hey, I'm here on time." Flames raised his hand. He spoke with a slight New Jersey accent so everything he said had a rough edge. He looked spaced out, mentally checked out. *Elevated.* He was in his black western-cut shirt with red and orange flames burning at the shoulders, down to his ribcage.

After waiting in line for food, Dead Johnny bought curry for Chuck; noodles, a fruit drink and sticky rice dessert.

By the time Brett showed up, they were seated at a rickety picnic table eating. With his short, stylish hair and model good looks he affected a young Clint Eastwood.

The crowds thickened quickly. Late summer sun in full effect. Dead Johnny wore a bowler derby to cover up his bald head and the fading pentagram tattoo on top.

"Traffic was shit," Brett said. "Sorry I'm late."

They looked at him from their steaming bowls, mouths full, and nodded.

"Who else is coming?" Brett said. He wore a checkered cowboy shirt and tight cuffed jeans. Black Timberland work boots. Chrome aviator sunglasses. A group of young Asian girls walked past and caught his long, hard stare.

"Got one more coming," Dead Johnny said.

Brett inspected his face, trying to make sense of Johnny wearing black eyeliner and nail polish. And a fake eyelash flipped up on his right eyelid.

"You gonna eat?" Chuck asked Brett. There was a little bit of green curry at the corner of his mouth. "Better get it now. Natives are ravenous today. Shit's tasty AF."

"Nah, I'm good." Brett said, lighting a cigarette. "I never eat."

"No smoking on sacred grounds," Dead Johnny told him.

"What?"

"You're polluting the hallowed air. Respect it."

"Well, they got incense lit," Brett said. "And you're smoking a Clove, so I don't know what the fuck you're talking about."

"My clove ain't lit, my man," Dead Johnny said. "It's an accessory."

With a mouthful of spring roll, Flames laughed.

Brett leaned in. "Now, I know *you*, *DJ*, but you two guys I haven't met before."

"Don't call me *DJ*," Dead Johnny said. "That's what they called me when I worked the line. Call me Johnny, call me Dead. Call me *Dead Johnny*. But never *DJ*."

Brett shrugged. He put the unlit cigarette behind his ear. "Who's the other guy coming?"

"Pike," Chuck said. He wiped his mouth and stared out at the lake. "His mom's dropping him off."

"We used to work for Freebird," Flames said shifting a finger between him and Chuck.

"Uh huh," Brett said. "Wait, you said Pike the Samoan?"

"Yup," Chuck said.

"Oh." Brett looked down, as if trying to hide his face.

"You the guy who threw him down those stairs?"

"Oops," Flames said. "*Awkward.*"

"Wasn't me, it was my buddy, Nolin," Brett said. "Let me ask you, *Dead Johnny*, if you knew this about me and the shit that went down between us, why would you ask me to do a job with the Samoan?"

"That's news to me," Dead Johnny said. "Blame it on mixed messages. Happens all the time in this business."

"This was the best I could do on short notice," Chuck said.

"You did good, buddy," Dead Johnny said.

"What's the job?" Brett said. "A&R? Who's driving getaway?"

"I'm always the driver."

"Then, why am I here?"

"Group effort," Dead Johnny told them. "We just need to find this guy."

"Hit job?" said Flames, washing down his food with an orange fruit drink.

"We're not going to kill him," Dead Johnny said. "This is more like search and retrieve. Where's the last guy?" He looked past Brett to a tall, dark Polynesian limping toward the picnic table. He wore a beige neck brace around his neck. From a distance he waved at Dead Johnny. Nodded at Chuck and Flames.

"You must be desperate to use this guy," Brett said.

"I don't really know him," said Dead Johnny. "They told me *he* was desperate. Chuck brokered all this. Like he said, you're all the best we could get on short notice."

"I'm an all-purpose, *maintenance* man," Brett bragged. "A courier. *Collector.* I can handle the action, whatever it is, wherever it takes me."

"You're the backup 'action man', then." Dead Johnny said.

"I've been at this a long time. How's he 'main action' and I'm secondary?"

"Because we can throw the Samoan into the fire if it comes to that," Dead Johnny said. "You're worth more and have higher standing in this business."

"Huh?" Flames said. "What the fuck does that make me?"

"If I die," Dead Johnny told him. "You take the wheel."

"Fellas." Pike stood over them, leaning on his cane.

"Great, now we have two cripples in the crew," Brett said.

Pike gave him a shitty, unwelcoming look. Like he'd stepped on dog shit and immediately smelled it.

"Don't call my man Chuck a cripple," Dead Johnny said.

"*I'm* not a cripple," Pike said. "*This* motherfucker threw me down the stairs of my shop. Him and that other asshole."

Brett looked up at him. "You took off running. We told you to stop."

"You threw a cue ball at me, asshole."

Brett stood up. Their chests touched.

"Should've paid your loan on time," Brett said.

"Why do you think I'm taking this job?" Pike said.

"Ladies, when you're done, please make some room for Pike at the table," Dead Johnny said.

Brett and Pike sat at opposite ends from each other.

"Go ahead and fisticuff your differences right here and now," said Dead Johnny. "Lay 'em all out. Because when we're on the street, won't be any of this bullshit. Got me?"

Brett looked at Pike, begrudged.

"Sure, I'm crippled," Chuck said, licking his fingers. "I'm only here to broker the job, though. You boys are the ones going into the field, not me. I get to sleep well tonight."

Chuck was the hub wheel. Friend of a friend of a friend. The nucleus. He ate sticky rice and smiled. They smirked at him. Then they introduced themselves. Brett and Pike had nothing further to say to one another.

"I just need guys who can shake a gun in somebody's face," Dead Johnny said. "We're after a guy carrying stolen property. Probably unarmed but he's trying to sell it to the highest bidder."

Pike said, "It is a hit job."

"More like search and rescue," said Flames.

Dead Johnny corrected him. "Search and *retrieve,* man. This walking man bun took a small silver briefcase that doesn't belong to him."

"Purple Rain's merchandise," Chuck added.

Pike looked shaken at the mention of the *Purple One.*

"Contents are rumored to be worth a lot," Dead Johnny said.

"This sounds sketchy," Brett said. "What if he's protected?"

"That's why there's four of us."

"We can't bump with them boys. This is a job for mercs, not a bunch of knockaround losers."

"Thought you were an all-purpose man?" Dead Johnny said.

"Those hoodie clowns are small time," Flames said. "Dime a dozen. We can take 'em if we have to."

"We're not fighting with anybody, goddamn it," Dead Johnny said. "We're just going to find this guy before he ditches the case. He's been floating around the city looking for the highest bidder. At least that's what Miha told me."

"And what happens if we take it from him?" Brett said.

"Collect the reward," Dead Johnny said. "And if nothing else, get us in good with the man who'll be taking over the city."

Flames shook his head. "Purple's not going to give a shit about four white guys looking to work for him."

"I ain't white," Pike said.

"This might get hot," Brett said. "We got an advance coming or something?"

"Whatever reward we get, we'll split evenly after Chuck's 20%."

Brett angered. "He's not even on the job!"

"He brought you guys in," Dead Johnny explained. "If you don't want it, let me know now. But, can I trust that we can work together? Can we pull this off without hissy fits? Might be easier than you think. Find the man bun, retrieve the case. If we gotta flex, we flex. Flex and dash. That's the name of this operation."

"What are you driving?" Brett said.

"The Caddy," Dead Johnny said. "It's inconspicuous. If we come off like base heads looking for a stone, no one will bat an eye when we creep up in the Olds."

"What's in the case?" Flames said.

"What do you think?" Brett said. "It's either drugs, money or the sacred foreskin of Jesus."

Dead Johnny arched his brows and nodded.

"We getting pieces for this?" Pike said.

Dead Johnny looked at him with one eye.

"Tomorrow," he said.

3

FUNTIME

"Is this your idea of a good time?" Pyre said. Chubby white woman, full gothic regalia, and pancake makeup. Black eyeliner, lipstick, and nails. Ceramic fangs that sprung whenever she smiled. Trinkets and silver jewelry draped over her plundering neckline. Her eyes outlined and winged. Short devil horns poking through her wig.

"Yes," Dead Johnny said. "Yes, it is."

"We're just driving around. We've been driving around for two hours."

"Ain't you ever heard of cruising for a good time? What do you think we're doing right now?"

"Thought you said we'd find a party," Pyre said.

"Still looking."

"Thought you said you had *all* the invites?"

"Can't find them if you don't look," he said.

"This is supposed to be a fun anniversary."

He was all steamed up: bowler, goggles, jacket with tails, capris pants and high-top Converse sneakers. Iggy Pop blasting on the car radio.

"All dressed up and nowhere to go," Pyre said.

"We're here, aren't we?" Dead Johnny said. "Be glad your heart still beats and there is blood flowing through you that you may walk and walk and talk and balk."

"You got any bop pills?

"Nope," he said. He reached inside his jacket pocket and withdrew a long cigarette holder. With one hand on the wheel, he reached into his breast pocket and withdrew an impressive joint rolled to a sharp point. He held the cigarette holder between his thighs and loaded the joint into it. "*Try this.*"

"Uh uh," Pyre said. "I don't want that."

"You're saying my shit is skunked?"

"I don't want that," she said.

"Well shit," Dead Johnny said. "Fuck it. I'll smoke it by myself."

"Are you going to pick up Melissa?" Pyre said.

"*Measles?*" He chuckled. "Nah. This is our night."

"But she always comes along for the ride."

"Oh, I know. She shows up covered in cat hair and complains more than you do."

"She's my best friend!" Pyre said. "Practically my sister."

"Maybe I should drop you off at her place and you girls can take the bus."

"Johnny! Come on!"

"No, really," Dead Johnny said. "I'll drop you off at the taco place."

Pyre scoffed and sat back hard, crossing her arms.

"This is our night," he said. "You always want to bring her so she can deflect our arguments."

"Maybe we shouldn't argue so much," she said.

"Don't say the dumb shit you're always saying and maybe we won't."

"*You're such a Sagittarian!*"

"Yes," he said. "According to my birthdate, yes, I am. That has nothing to do with our anniversary celebration."

"Well, if you don't go pick up Melissa, then I don't want to go."

"Oh?" he said and smiled.

East Side was lit tonight. People loitered outside dingy bars and nightclubs. Punks in leather, rough cowboy punks in leather vests, long hair drifting under their hats. Twerking black girls and their gangsta boyfriends flipping fake money at them like they were making a rap video.

They'd made this scene before. Places like this were two or three to the block, all of them trailing cigarette smoke and drug miasma out into the sidewalk.

"Kind of tired," Dead Johnny said. "This shit is played out."

People saw them drive past and waved. He waved back, flipped them off, or saluted.

"Maybe I'm getting too old for this shit," he said.

"You're 34," Pyre said.

They reached the light and stopped. He lowered the window and spit on the street.

He turned and looked at her.

"Get out," he said.

Pyre sighed. "Hell no. "Why? What the fuck is wrong with you?"

"Just get out. The night is dead. *We're dead.*"

"But, wh—"

He leaned over her lap and popped the door open.

"You know some of these people," he said. "Somebody will give you a ride home."

"But I wanted to keep riding around with you."

"Untrue, madam. All you do is yell and complain. Your love sits in me like a nestled gall stone. Maybe one day you'll have your own car, and you can ride around mindlessly like a ghoul in the night. Right now, I need my sleep and my sanity."

She climbed out and stood on the corner flipping him off as he drove off.

He changed the music to something black. Something with soul. Shuggie Otis. Sharon Jones & the Dap-Kings.

He returned to his empty apartment. Much emptier since his father's passing several months ago. He relaxed in the cluttered living room that smelled of old pot smoke and wood polish. He sat on a leather chair that belonged to his dad and loaded his gun.

4

NIGHTCLUBBING

Brett got back to his apartment around midnight, opened a beer, pulled out the glass bowl from his pocket, lit it and stretched out on the sofa. Falling into a stoned sleep while watching TV seemed an ideal way to beat onset insomnia. But the cooking shows would make him hungry, and he'd wind up walking to Cookout for regrettable greasy takeout.

Serial killer docs depressed him. Late night cartoons were aimed at adults and not as fun as he remembered them from Saturday mornings of his youth. So, he fidgeted. That was what it was. He had the *fidgets*. The alcohol could not erase him craving pills, no matter how hammered he got. Several pulls at the crackling bowl didn't give him the jolt he was looking for. He'd been up twenty hours. Drinking for eight of them. Even lunch at the Buddhist temple hadn't instilled discipline nor sobriety.

Why wasn't he sleepy? *Why didn't Baron ask me to come work for him in Florida?*

(Why can't you show up to work on time?)

Brett sucked his teeth at the voice in his head. More often it was Baron's condescending echo than his own.

He checked his phone. His real phone, not the burner. Five text messages to five different women unanswered. He stuck the phone in his pocket and then it rang. He sat up and placed the pipe on top of some magazines on the coffee table. He cracked his neck, left, right, then pulled the phone out and stared at it.

"Da fuck?"

He hesitated then answered it to his immediate regret.

"Cowboy, what is up, my brother?"

"Hey!" Cowboy's voice reminded him of Wolfman Jack, gravelly and growly. "Where are you, motherfucker?"

Brett looked at his watch, scratched his head.

Am I late again?

"I just got in for the night," Brett said. "I'm at my place. Where are you?"

"You just leave work? 'Cause I was just there and you weren't around. Buncha new faces. They weren't sure who I was asking for. You going by aliases again?"

"What? Uh, no."

"I was at The Iron Boot, and then 667," Cowboy said.

"Haven't worked there since Baron sold the place."

"He what?"

"He's in Florida now."

"Okay," Cowboy said. "Well, whatever. Good for him. I'm glad I reached you."

"Why didn't you call me earlier?" Brett said.

"I wanted to surprise you. *Surprise,* motherfucker! Wanna meet up?"

"Now? I mean, I got a thing tomorrow afternoon, but we can meet tonight."

"How's U4EaH sound?"

Like there will be lots of chemicals coursing through me for the next 48 hours...

"Right now?" Brett said.

"Fuck yeah, man." Cowboy said. "I'm wide awake. Zooming through the A as we speak."

"You on something?"

"Nah, man. Clean and sober!"

So why U4EaH?

"I'll meet you down there," Brett said.

"Check," said Cowboy said. "See you soon."

The bar crowd peaked around this time of the night, but it was starting to taper out. They found a booth with a broken overhead lightbulb and hid in the shadows. Jukebox rotated everything from West End Motel, to Mastodon, to Run the Jewels.

"My brother," Cowboy said. He was ten years older than Brett but looked more like 100. Dark, and wrinkled like an old leather satchel, the same dusty black cowboy shirt, black vest, and black leather pants he'd always worn which had all faded to a dark brown. "You good? You sobering up?"

"What's this bullshit about you being clean?" Brett said.

"Weeeeellll, I had to say something to get you out, no?"

"Or you could have called earlier in the day and made plans."

"I was sleeping," Cowboy laughed. "Listen, is this still the hotspot?"

"This and Club Cocaine on the East Strip," Brett said.

"Nice. How's the coke?"

"Fuck." Brett rolled his eyes.

"Nah, man. For me. For *me*. Point me towards the snow, why don't you?"

"It's loaded with fent," Brett said. "You don't want any of that shit. There's a moratorium on all that shit these days."

"Let's check our options, then."

And so it went, and in fifteen minutes they were trading handshake drugs with one of the bartenders.

"I noticed the only thing that's changed here are some of the faces," Cowboy said.

"Every five minutes, this city gets a reset," Brett said. "Every time a white woman walks toward a yoga studio, the rent goes up."

There were two glasses of whiskey between them, hardly touched.

"I'm in limbo at the moment," Brett said, feeling the pills kick in. He wasn't sure what they were or the dosage. Didn't matter. He was a pro. The lights thinned and turned saucer-like. Everything else shined like blurry Christmas lights. "I don't think about the habit. I work through it."

"I stay busy too." Cowboy's eyes sunk and turned black. His demonic demeanor was standard for the course. "Whatever keeps my mind off it. Whatever diverts me so I don't go nuts. What kind of work you doing?"

Brett watched as Cowboy slowly transmogrified into a dark apparition. His face wasn't melting. More like it turned to a mahogany demon. "I was doing collections for Baron until he left for Florida. I've had to scramble and hustle for work. Been doing some bartending. Bouncing. Mostly for rent."

Cowboy's nails began to grow and curl like demon claws. His hands looked like they'd been dipped in boiling tar, sticky, melted, drooping. His ears grew pointy and hairy under his hat.

"Going west," Cowboy said. "Couple of jobs out there. AR stuff."

"That's low-key. Low-grade, low-risk."

Their images distorted and twirled. Sitting only two feet from each other, but the room became elastic.

"Vegas, Phoenix, L.A." Cowboy said. "You want in?"

Brett forgot what they were talking about. Suddenly their words floated like comic strip speech bubbles above their heads. Brett's mouth started to melt down his chin. His eyes swirled, dribbling down his face.

"Think we better take this outside," Cowboy said.

Brett left thirty dollars on the table, and they floated outside. They balanced along the curb like it was a high wire. Cowboy mentioned the giant cockroaches in the gutter wrestling each other. He counted them with his finger.

"And I don't mean like Madagascars or nothing," Cowboy said. "These fuckers are the size of possums. See 'em? *Right there.* Tearing into each other. If you think good thoughts, they won't bite you." He crouched with his arms out like he was landing. Rotated his head. "Hope they don't think we're crazy."

"It's Atlanta, man." Brett said, feeling very much like he was on top of a tower looking five hundred feet down. "This shit happens all the time."

"Why does shit turn out like this?" Cowboy said.

"How many did you take?"

"I mean, I'm a man of high doses. I can't be expected to boogie with just one or two Tic Tacs."

"Well," Brett was no longer on the same planet. "You get what you ask for. I can handle my shit."

"Doesn't matter what I'm taking, it always goes sour," Cowboy said. "Why is it like that? You open a portal, step into the gateway but all you see is Hell. Dismantle these outer layers and you wind up in Hell. Being scared is the best way I know of being healthy. Some crime writer said that."

"If you don't feel safe, why are you out here?"

"Hadn't seen you in a while, brother. Plus, I needed drugs. You gotta lay off these, you know what I mean? You gotta focus."

"Too late now," Brett said. "What do you do to take your mind off it?"

"Think about pussy a lot," Cowboy said. "But I don't get it up much these days. Gotta think about it to bring me back to life. Urges the lust for *something*. Gives me strength. Shatters cynicism. Maybe you should go back to school, Brett. Do some painting. Go back and practice the trombone."

"All right," Brett said. "Maybe. I pawned it, though. But I can always get it back. Hold on to something…"

They stood on the corner, ready to cross into the rest of the adventures awaiting them that night.

"I'll consider it," Cowboy said. He reached out for what looked like a swirling portal that had opened near the Krog Street Tunnel.

By morning, Cowboy had vanished, and Brett wondered if he'd been an illusion. He meandered the train tracks near Candler Park. He couldn't remember climbing over the fence, but he was in the train yard among old, hollowed warehouses where they sometimes filmed movies. It was deserted. Locomotives clicked and honked nearby. He followed the tracks southward, kicking gravel, fighting the urge to sit on the rails. Afraid of falling asleep on the tracks.

He heard distant voices, but the sun was too intense in his face to clearly see the approaching silhouettes.

"Cowboy?" He shaded his eyes.

There was a succession of kicks and punches to his face and head. They tumbled into him, getting in a few cheap shots, knocking him to the ground.

"The fuck you want?" Brett said.

Someone grabbed his collar and stood him up.

"Where's the money?" They wore black bandanas over their faces. Black men in urban combat fatigues. Strapped with guns but not flexing them.

"What the fuck," Brett said. "I have until the end of the month."

"Bobolink don't play."

"Hey, no need to get stupid," Brett said. "I'm good for it. Listen, I do the same job you boys do."

"*Boys?*" one of them said. "We ain't no boys."

"He always gotta send out a collection team for you," another said. "You been on a real shitty streak, ain't you?"

"Easy come, easy go, but I'm good for it." Brett said.

"Bobolink said you burned that bridge," their leader said. "You can't just run out on a tab like that, bruh. He gonna tell them to stop selling to you too."

"Don't matter," Brett said. "I stopped using."

"Final reminder, mu'fucka."

"Fuck, man. You can't do this to me. I work for Baron King."

"Maaaan, *no you don't*," one of them said. "That mu'fucka moved to Florida."

The main guy grabbed him and shook him.

"End of the week, five large," he said. "Meet us at the same bar you was at last night."

They bunched around him and pushed him to the ground. He dusted off and watched them walk away. The morning sun burned his face. He followed the tracks all the way to the subway station. With a grimace, he boarded the westbound, and let the train car's AC blast his face. He fell asleep and missed his station. Eventually he made it back to U4EaH and found his car where he'd left it. He was about to turn the key when he leaned his head back.

"Just five minutes," he said and slept eight hours behind the wheel of the car.

5

FLAMES

After the temple, Flames drove back to his house. In reality, his father's house, but the old man was already three years dead and buried. The house at least left him with chores and yardwork and that gave him purpose. Kept him busy now that work had slimmed to one job a month.

He went up the driveway, past the pool deck and slipped between the sliding door into the kitchen. He hadn't prepared a meal in a few days, but the kitchen was cluttered. Empty boxes of Domino's Pizza lay open on the island and stove, along with empty soda and beer cans.

He scrounged the pizza boxes but all that was left was crumbs.

"Thanks for saving me a slice." He scavenged anchovies and gelatinous cheese from the cardboard and then entered the living room. The temple lunch had already passed through him.

His niece sat in front of the TV while a Disney cartoon played. Eating her pizza crust-first. She waved without looking at him.

"Where's your mom?" Flames said.

What Flames couldn't see was that in the bathroom his sister Meghan was wiping her tears, and washing her mouth out, and spraying body mist behind her ears and her arms and hands. She came out and greeted him. By then he'd gotten cozy on the sectional couch.

"Sorry about the kitchen," Meghan said. "I just didn't feel like cooking. Gotta get ready for work soon. You're still okay watching her?"

"Sure," Flames said. "I'm tired as shit though. Might take a nap."

"That's fine. She's got all her cartoons with her. Should keep her busy for the afternoon. Oh, and her dad is here. He's sleeping on your bed."

Flames sprung to his feet. "He's what? Why the fuck is he even here?"

His niece stayed focused on the TV.

"I know," Meghan said. Her eyes diverted to the other room. In the doorway appeared a large man. He was shirtless and the top of his jeans were unbuttoned. His blond hair was cut close to his scalp. A patchwork of scars and tattoos covered his chest and back.

"Boomboom" Rooker, *not* a former boxer, but he was menacing, his body bearing witness to all the punches he'd ever rolled with. He stretched at the doorway and walked into the living room.

Meghan shut the TV off and told her daughter to go into her room.

"S'up, *Flaming Frankie*," Rooker said. His tenor was deep and guttural. He towered over Flames.

"Boomboom," Flames said. "You're not supposed to be here. You're not supposed to be anywhere near my sister. Court papers says so."

"Gotta see my kid, man."

"She was right there. Didn't look very excited to see you. In fact, she barely acknowledged you."

"Dude," Rooker said. "You weren't even here when I got here."

"I would have thrown your ass out, that's why."

"You don't know what the fuck you're talking about. You didn't see how excited she got when I came in."

"Well, you saw her," said Flames. "Get dressed and go. Please, don't start no shit."

"I ain't starting fucking shit!" Rooker said. "You started on me before even saying hello. Is that any way to treat family?"

Flames watched him cross the living room. He had a fresh scar on the right side of his head, about four inches above his ear. There was a long maroon line of dried blood.

"What the fuck happened to you?" Flames said.

"Ha. I'm glad you asked. Fucking around as usual. Last week was my birthday. Went out, ran into some old school punks I hadn't seen since high school. We got to acting stupid, taking all kinds of shit, drinking. I thought I would slide down the stairs at the train station and landed on my fucking head! They said it looked pretty bad, but I think they were just scared of all the blood. Next thing I knew I was throwing up all over the train tracks. I even shit my pants."

"I don't want to make an argument about this," Flames said. "I'm fucking tired."

"Dude, I'm sobering up. Let me at least smoke a cigarette before I go."

"Come on, man. You do this every single time. Don't yell, don't curse in front of Lizzie. Just fucking go."

"All right," Rooker said calmly. He went back into Flames' room and came out dressed. His boots were by the TV stand.

"You working now?" Flames said.

"Nah," said Rooker. "Got these off some bum. Imma go out by the pool and smoke."

Flames followed him outside.

"How about you?" Rooker said. He lit an unfiltered cigarette. "What kind of shit they got you doing now? You still putting in cabinets? I wanna get in on that."

"Not right now," Flames said. He clipped an unlit Newport between his lips. "But I'm always working."

"You ain't working now."

"Fuck you mean? *I'm always working.*"

"Whoa. Don't get mean. Ever since Freebird took off for Mexico, ain't much work to do from what I hear."

"Doesn't matter," Flames said. "The hustle continues, with or without him. Always some way to earn."

"You been reduced to hustling your butthole." Rooker laughed.

"Fuck you. You been to prison more than I have. You know about assholes more than I do."

"Heard something about a job happening this week. Heard anything? You got your ear to the street. The *gutter.*"

"I don't know shit, man." Flames said. "Not like I would tell you anyway. You've been banned by all the bosses and crews."

"Bosses? Ba ha, ha! What is this prohibition era Chicago? *Banned?* That hurts my feelings, man. How am I supposed to provide for my kid if I can't find a job?"

"You can't keep a job, motherfucker. That's the problem." Flames pinched the cigarette in his fingers, pointing at him. "And I saw the look on Meghan's face. You been giving her shit. I know."

"She's been giving me shit!" Rooker said. The neighbors could hear him now. "Hey, nobody called the cops on her when she hit me."

"Dude, there's no argument in that. Just get the fuck out. I'm not gonna say it again. I'll call the fucking cops."

"I'll fucking rat if you do! Don't think I won't tell them the shit I know."

"What shit do you know?" Flames said.

"Call the cops and find out, they'll drag me away and I'll never get a job and won't be able to pay child support."

"What the fuck are you talking about? You don't pay shit. *Ever.* Meghan's never received one fucking dime from you, motherfucker. Just get the fuck out."

"Fuck you, man. How can you do this to family?" He grabbed Flames and lifted him over his shoulders and slammed him on the concrete landing. Flames had helped his dad pour the concrete when he was 12. He shielded his fall with his elbows but had the life pushed out of him for those six seconds he couldn't breathe. He got back on his feet and spit.

"You're lucky I don't have my gun!" Flames yelled into his face.

"Is that supposed to scare me?" Rooker swung at him, but Flames ducked. Rooker swung around again and punched his ribs. Flames tackled him and pulled him down on the table and chairs where many a drunken night had been had playing cards and dominoes. Rooker got on top of him, hands around his throat. He looked over and Lizzie was watching them behind the sliding glass door. Rooker yelled into his face and left him there. He went inside the house and there was a lot more shouting. Flames remained flat on his back, struggling for air, searching for his cigarette, all the while little Lizzie was staring.

6

JOKERMAN

Chamblee is kind of the Chinatown in North Atlanta. Outside the city perimeter, isolated, and with so many varying groups of Asians that most businesses had signs in hangul, hanja or hangukmal.

Several Asian men in suits and sunglasses waited at the entrance of Barbang. When Jokerman arrived, one of them opened the door and directed him to a table to the left of the lounge.

"Only time white folk come here is to sing. Or buy drugs."

Barbang was dark and claustrophobic, neon pink and blue lights projecting from the ceiling. Row lights pulsated in various colors, rotating to the low music beat. Against the back wall was a well-dressed empty stage with various microphones plus monitors scrolling the lyrics to a Madonna song.

Pino sat at the head of the long table, lights flashing dark blue and hot pink across his face.

"That was a joke," he said. He was a small indeterminable Asian man with feathered black hair and wide fit-over sunglasses. His hand rested on the head of his cane. He looked straight on, never shifting his head, leading Jokerman to think he was blind. His wife Albina lay against him like a cat. She was a long-legged, white California hippie with pigtails and a long sundress. She made eyes at Jokerman as he approached. There was a small, silver briefcase resting on the table.

Pino craned his head at her, and she nodded and bowed, walking to the stage, and finding a song to destroy.

Jokerman folded his hands at his chest. No hello. No handshake. Pino pointed his hand at the briefcase but didn't look at him.

Jokerman's real name was Lorenzo McDaniel. He was ghostly pale and auricomous, with short, tight ginger curls. He had a long sheep-like face and a European nose. Black eyes sunken deeply into his face, made more wicked by the onyx contact lenses he wore.

He pulled a chair out at the side of the table where he stood.

"No, don't sit." Pino said. His bodyguard sat at Pino's side, filling in Sudoku squares. His eyes lifted toward Jokerman momentarily. Eyes said all they needed to. Jokerman stood back.

Silent stares.

Pino dressed casual. Pink guayabera and loose chinos with sandals. Jokerman acknowledged that his time away in Florida had informed his pastel attire.

Pino sipped hot tea and smacked his lips. Albina hit warbled, off-pitch notes from the stage, destroying "Like a Prayer".

"The newest stream is inside that case," Pino said. "Purple wanted a taste? There it go."

Jokerman acted coy and a little shy. "Mr. Pino, I'm honored to be part of this partnership."

Pino waved his hand, chuckling. Jokerman went to unlock the case with the pomposity of a gangster rapper (often the biggest poseurs out of all performers). Pino detected that when he'd walked in.

"No, don't open it," Pino said. "It's not for you."

Jokerman leaned back with the same pose, gauging the contents through its exterior.

"Kind of small," he said. "'Bout ten kilos."

"You see that just from looking?" the bodyguard said.

Jokerman shrugged. "Been at this game a minute, son."

"You've never been more incorrect, Mr. Jokerman," Pino said. "This is *Aquamarine*. Look like the shit at bottom of aquarium. Formula from Florida. We brought back chemist and he cook shit in basement here. Was running factory out of a trailer in Hudson. We cook it now. Took shortcut, but I confident we got it. We'll have more cooked up soon as we have more people in lab. Then we distribute. As you can guess with the other human trafficking shit Atlanta deal with, we running into various obstacles from customs. We're greasing those gears. That not your concern. The greatest job you ever have is handing over case to the man who ordered it, Purple Rain. Tell him we could not make it look purple as he requested."

"Consider it delivered," Jokerman said. "Not my first rodeo."

Pino remained quiet. Albina howled from the stage. Beams of neon pink and blue gave her a demonic glow.

"So, you sayin' you ready to roll with the big dogs down south now?" Jokerman said. He stared at Pino a while before realizing the man had no answer. There was no real answer. There was only the future he *foresaw*. "I mean, you know this is coke and H town, right?"

Pino nodded.

"You gonna need an army to jackhammer into the playing field, and penetrate this product," Jokerman said. "All that other shit out there is cheaper and easier to buy, and *classier*. The drug buffet in Atlanta is crowded with powder. Always has been. You wedging yourself into their playground, know what I'm saying? Without permission."

"Mr. Jokerman, I been in business longer than you were born," Pino said. "While *they* slept, we gave out samples. Like at grocery market. We also gave away cheap heroin sprinkled with a few secret herbs and spices. Fentanyl eliminating a lot of competition now. That our Trojan horse into market. We been in the mix for some time."

Jokerman took a back step with his mouth open. "Yo... *you* been stepping on shit with fent? That's messed up, man. Couple of my peeps pegged out on that shit like three weeks ago. They out here dying from shooting and snortin' fent so you can move new product?"

Pino nodded slowly. His hand tightened on the head of his cane. "When user fear inferior product, they go to the next *blue* thing."

Jokerman shook his head. "I know you're gonna say it's business and all that financial shit. But that's some cold bullshit. That fent outta control out there right now, chief."

"So, you do understand that it is business," Pino said. "Profits make you happy, yes? The poison deaths will taper out. When they do, aqua will already be in place. Everyone getting in on the street pharmaceutical business these days will want to distribute. Will happen very quickly. We getting head start now. Just like any other business. It's time we get out of Chinatown and bring it to housewives, white college kids, and busy fathers."

Jokerman stood still a long while.

Pino continued, "You want to level up in this kind of work, Mr. Jokerman, distance yourself from any empathy."

7

TOTAL BOGUS MAN

Friday night, South Atlanta.

"I know this place," Coco Dior said to Jokerman, crossing the mall parking lot together. Pickup trucks with their giant tires and glossy paint jobs parked while those in sports cars rolled up to the front of the building to the valet podium. Men and women in fancy clothes entered through the glass doors where the old Macy's used to be.

"I used to eat at the burger and wings place at the food court," Coco said. She was 23, Brazilian, looked about 16. If it was the other way around, Jokerman didn't want to know. He'd seen her ID and fake or not, it'd said she was 23. She was 5'3", white as he was but with strong African features white Brazilians were wont to exhibit. No plastic ass or tits. *All* natural, save for the curly extensions coiled around her real hair. She had a cherubic, celestial face and sparkling blue eyes. Succulent lips, deep cleavage, and thick legs in a tight yellow dress.

"Yup, same place," Jokerman said. He ignored her, walking several steps ahead. She grabbed his arm, but his response was

272

indifferent. Having met with Pino a few hours ago, he brought the briefcase with him. The tradeoff would occur later at the after-party.

They fast walked across the lot toward the entrance. Jokerman waved at cars that honked or stopped to chat. Hand over fist drug exchanges.

Jokerman glowed like a saint under the low humming parking lamps. His oversized white shirt fit like a short muumuu. Big square short pants came to his knees. Big white sneakers that looked like he was wearing toasters on his feet. Gold chains banging his chest when he walked. He was 5'5", all of 130lbs. Floating on air. Elated after talking to fans and friends alike. No high was like the high of being loved by the people.

"I'm vegan now, tho," Jokerman said to her.

"Mall food is straight trash," Coco said.

"We're not here to eat."

Coco smiled. Her face was glittery and gleeful.

"This is the runoffs," Jokerman said.

"You mean the *playoffs?*" said Coco.

"Whatever. I rank third. You best believe I'm moving up to number one, *tonight. Numbah juan!* Gotta start it up and then work it down. That's the name of the game. Final challenge is this dude, Sweathog. Bet. He top tier. This the game changer."

Greeters held the blackened doors open for them. The couple crossed a promenade decorated like a Valentine's Day parade. Fountains lit up with blue, red, and gold lights. Disco balls whirled above them. People dressed like prom night. Jokerman seemed to know everyone, from what Coco observed. At his side she was also a star attraction. The most beautiful woman in the room. Along the way to the arena, Jokerman sold drugs, shook hands, squeezed a few ladies, posed for photos flashing the peace sign. Coco let him have the spotlight for now. It was his night. His show.

The food court had been cleared of tables except at the center where a special high top was cordoned off behind red velvet ropes. There was a dance floor setup near a short stage. A DJ worked the ones and twos and people got down. Disco balls sprinkled the place with tiny lights. After a while the music stopped and then everybody circled a high-top table at the center. The matches began almost immediately.

Jokerman got them drinks and then pointed out Sweathog to her.

Coco whispered into his ear,

"That nigga outweighs you 3 to 1."

"Pssh, I got this," Jokerman said. "He's going to wear himself out. He's too stocky. He's swinging with too much weight. He'll fall over."

"You heard of physics?" she said.

"Bitch. Fuck you mean?"

"He has all that potential energy with his sheer weight alone. One swing…"

"Yeah, yeah, yeah," Jokerman said. "He's just big meat around tender bones. Size don't matter. They tell you that, but it don't. Watchoo know about this shit?"

Coco shrugged, unbothered. Sipped her cran and vodka and visually explored the crowd. The air was cloudy with chalk dust. So far it was big, bearded men who looked like champion weightlifters or wrestlers during these first matches. They all looked like clones of each other, off the same assembly line. The only thing setting them apart were their differing tattoos and ball caps and team jerseys.

"Beards help with the burn," Jokerman whispered to Coco. The crowd and music were at peak din.

Big Black went up against Asian Sensation. Bear Man and Pancho Villa followed. Matches came with their own set of cheers, jeers, and oohs, after the loud, open palm buffets.

"Why didn't you grow one?" Coco said.

Jokerman shrugged. "Beards intimidate my customers. I got a sweet face and don't wanna lose clients."

"Is Pino coming?"

"He's keeping a low profile right now. If he needs something, he'll send one of his boys. He's more into cockfighting, anyway."

"Slaps are way better," Coco said.

"He just doesn't give a shit. Purple Rain's coming to the after party, though."

Her eyes brightened even more.

"Aye, you see that guy over there?" Jokerman pointed. Coco saw a skinny white bearded man in a raggedy gray hoodie. Stoned, laughing within his circle of low-key thugs. "Beware Freaky Freddy. That's all I'm saying. His wife's lawyer or real estate agent. Maybe both. He comes down here for street-cred. He just like to slum it with real niggas is all. Straight perpetrator. A charlatan. Total bogus man."

"I seen him sell something to one of the bikini girls," Coco said.

"See, now, that cracker should know better. Fuck it. We'll settle that later. Pino wants to keep the peace right now until it's time to step up. I can't be lettin' dat cracker live rent free in the back of my mind."

A tall Asian woman in a glittery red dress towered over them with a clipboard.

"Formalities," she said to Jokerman.

He signed her paperwork and took out a mouthpiece from his back pocket. Then she vanished into the crowd.

"Imma ask her to come back with us after the championships," he said.

"Fuck you are," said Coco. "You leaving with me alone or we ain't hooking up."

"Think so?"

"Bet." She rolled her eyes and fluttered her lashes.

"Aight, we'll see who going home with the champ."

"Nigga, please. You forgot you gotta exchange that briefcase?"

"Damn, bitch, relax."

"Pino think he's just gonna let that shit hit like that? No consequences or war?"

"Fuck you know 'bout that?" Jokerman talked into her face. "S'long as Purple get it, we cool. Any war or disagreements, that's on *them*. I ain't no soldier. I'm a businessman. But why we even talking 'bout this shit now? Imma 'bout to win this. Have fun, baby girl. Get another cran-vodka or whatever shit you drink. I got a bottomless tab."

"I'm good," Coco said, looking a little less enchanted.

He went in for a kiss, but she only let him smooch her cheek.

"Everybody here to have a good time and watch some motherfuckers get slapped," he told her. "We can get railed later. In fact," he took out a small black capped phial and tapped a small white crumb on top of his hand and inhaled it. "Try some. It's not from our stash, so it's good stuff. Ain't no fent in it."

She obliged.

The spotlights changed colors, going from green to yellow to red. Another round of slap fights. So far, lots of dazed heads, black eyes, cauliflower ears, and busted lips and bloody noses. Someone had to be dragged away from the roped area. A big beast of a bearded man. Took four chaperones to drag him out. There was a thin blond woman with leather, studio-tanned skin and fake tits that stood over the beast man, fanning him as he was dragged off.

Coco and Jokerman watched 5 more rounds; 10 men total.

The last fight before Jokerman went seven rounds. Beasts chalked each other's faces with palms the size of hams. The harder the slap the louder the cheers. Penalties if slaps hit the head or below the ear. Necks were off limits.

It was a draw. Both players raised their hands and were walked off by the ref. They hugged it out and shook hands.

The crowd parted and Jokerman descended. Cheers and jeers accompanied his strut. Coco stopped right where the velvet rope was raised. She kept the suitcase between her ankles.

Jokerman reached the table and waved at the crowd. Once again, he looked ethereal under the lighting, his tattoos bright and animated. He glowed so white, encouraging the crowd to cheer louder.

At the opposite end another aisle opened, twice as wide. Sweathog made his way to the table. A stout, brute of a man. A shaved bear with a neck beard. About as short as Jokerman, but three times as wide. Thick, like a brick oven. His bald head looked like a weathered concrete ball.

Coco observed the gestures and chuckles of others behind the velvet ropes. They were betting against Jokerman, a known charlatan, a hipster. Money got passed around. Bets laid. A dwarf in a tuxedo walked around with fists full of cash. Here were sports spectators on one side, slumming bros wearing baseball caps, cheering, and spilling beers all over themselves. Old rich men and their young escorts, pimps and their lady workers, dealers, and tourists dressed for prom night.

The DJ pumped Parliament's "Flashlight" at top volume.

Jokerman and Sweathog faced each other across the small round table. Sweathog was just a kid. He blinked his eyes a lot but mostly he nodded his head and focused. They powdered their hands and shook. The referee was a short Mexican man with a white shirt and handlebar mustache. He disclosed the rules again and then stepped back. Jokerman won the coin toss. He cracked his neck and swung left to right. Rotated. Rocked. Once, twice, then swung his open palm into Sweathog's face. The bearded, corpulent man absorbed the impact under a cloud of chalk dust. He barely moved. Solid, like a stainless-steel refrigerator.

The crowd hooted and cheered. A lot of people laughed. The big guy nodded, lifting his arms to the crowd, gaining an even louder roar from them.

Jokerman smiled and waved at the crowd. For a moment they both competed for encouragement. Jokerman braced the table and locked himself down. He adjusted his mouthpiece and stared straight into Sweathog's eyes like he was indestructible. His sunken eyes leered like a demon gargoyle as he braced for impact.

Sweathog stretched his arm out as far as it would go, shook his hand, clenched his fist. His fingers were stubby sausages. He opened his hand back up and loosened it. He swung out and back, with a wide arc. Twice, wider. Farther. For the third swing back, he reached as far as he could. The crowd counted along with the ref. His arm came around like an aerial crane and landed with a *PLOK!*

The human wave rolled with a gasp.

Coco felt it. It pushed her back and she immediately choked on tears. The crowd felt it. The surrounding counties felt it.

Jokerman held the table while his body slowly convulsed. A trickle of blood dribbled from his bottom lip. His eyes twitched, eyelids fluttered. One of his black contact lenses had flown across the room, leaving a single crystal aquamarine eyeball exposed. He managed a smile while blood dribbled down his chin and white clothes. Eyes rolled to the back of his head.

Someone shouted,

"You got this, Jokerman!"

He dug into the right side of his mouth with his tongue and spit out a tooth that landed on the table and streaked toward Sweathog. The ref and the three people closest to him held him when he collapsed. Coco crossed the velvet rope, forgetting the briefcase. Jokerman died in their arms with his eyes open.

8

OWLS

They looked like owls under the pink streetlamp. Corner boys hovering the concrete island where Boulevard split. Lil B circled them on his razor scooter. Darnell held his arm around the post and swung around it like a stripper. Juicy was vigorously playing on his phone. They wore black hoodies, cargo shorts and Timberland boots.

"He ain't shit," Darnell said. "Purple don't scare me."

"Yup," Lil B said, circling around him. "Ay, yo, I see one." He scooted across the street and down the block. The oncoming car stopped and shut its lights off.

"Nigga better not fuck dis up," Darnell said, watching.

"Leave him alone," Juicy said without looking up from his game. "He been doing this only a week."

Less than a minute later, Lil B came around and handed Juicy a tightly folded $20. Juicy gave him a little square bag, no larger than a half-dollar coin. Lil B scooted back to the car and dropped off the bag, then followed as it drove past them slowly. It was hard to tell who was in the car, but they were watching hard. It rounded the corner of the park, and they didn't see it again.

"Yo, think we should move?" Darnell said.

"Nah, D," Juicy said. "They told us keep to here until they say so."

"We should get us a sofa or something to sit on," said Darnell. "This used to be G-Dollar's corner. Sacred grounds."

"I know who it belonged to, nigga. Is he here now? Nah. *Nigga dead.* Real dead. S'why we got it now. And tomorrow, who knows who got it?"

"You think Virgil could get it?" said Darnell.

"It's all territory, my nigga. You gotta swarm in once the opportunity present itself."

"I don't think he passed it through God."

"Maaaan, Godzilla ain't shit," Juicy said. "Don't need to pass shit by him. I mean, where he at? We out here, he somewhere else. Mufucka can suck my dick!"

"He gonna chop it off 'fore he suck it," Darnell laughed.

"Fuck that mufucka," Juicy said, back at his game. "We here. We here *now.* 'Less Godzilla say something, we in here, locked in place. Pretty soon, you'll have this corner. Then maybe we let Lil B handle something too."

"He only 10."

"Gotta start 'em young, my nigga." Juicy said. "I was 9 when I sold my first bag. Lookit me now."

Juicy was 15, Darnell 14. Shadows. Their shadows draped the sidewalk like owl silhouettes.

"Aye, Jokerman running for Purple now," Darnell whispered.

"That mixed dude?" Juicy said.

"He albino. Kind'a freaky looking. Got them deep, evil black eyes and pale, white face."

"So, he black or nah?" said Darnell.

"He mixed. So, he *both*. But something happen when he was born and he ain't got no pigment."

"What's that?" Lil B said, riding past.

"Nigga, it's yo' skin color. You know how you black as chocolate? Well, he white as a ghost but he *look* black."

"Oh," Darnell said.

Their concrete island was west of Vine City. Buildings across the street were boarded up. Wasn't anyone out in the park tonight.

"He ain't my boss," Juicy said. "He ain't out here working with us. Fuck his albino ass."

"Ha," said Darnell.

"Can we go to Casa del Fuego?" Lil B said on the way back. He spotted headlights at the corner, but the car kept moving.

"Them tacos nasty," Darnell said.

"That's 'cause they ain't got no real Mexicans working the kitchen," said Juicy. "'Cause they changed owners. I like the place where Head stay."

"Word," said Darnell. "They juss moving in where is cheap for 'dem to buy condos and shit, and then jack up everybody rent; they straight elbowing they asses in here, tryna take over *ALL* business."

"Yeah," Darnell said. "Next they's gonna be crackers opening up black barbershops and shit."

"I'm sayin'," Juicy looked up from his phone. Someone was coming up the street. "They gonna take these corners from us."

"I think we got a hit," Darnell said.

Lil B nodded and scootered up the block. Darnell and Juicy watched him go. He circled the car, then stopped to talk to the driver. He was there for more than a minute.

"Fuck he doin'?" Darnell and Juicy leaned out into the street to look.

Three quick pops went off and they saw the flash from inside the car. Protocol told them to run and then circle back to a meetup spot. They broke into a panicked run.

"Can't just leave lil man like that," said Juicy, running up the block with Darnell.

"Man, he dead." Darnell said. "Ain't nothing we can do about it."

The car sped up behind them. There was laughing and catcalling from inside it. Juicy and Darnell cut across the park. Jumped the short fence, then sprinted the ball court.

Pop. Pop. Juicy got it through the back of his head and neck. *Pop, pop!* Darnell turned to see his friend fall. He blinked and missed it but by then a bullet entered one of his eyes. The next one clipped his ear. Several covered his chest. He died under a post, bleeding into the grass.

9

SHARKS DON'T SLEEP

Flames was the first one Dead Johnny had picked up in the Olds.

"Search for the man bun, huh?" Flames said in the passenger seat after Dead Johnny explained where they were going. "Have you seen those corner boys? They get machine guns with their school supplies."

"We're bringing heat too," Dead Johnny said. "Mostly for show."

"This is dirty work, man. We're not 'enforcers' or whatever. That's what gangbangers are for. They get one look at us, and it won't matter how many guns we flash. We won't last the night, man. They're better armed than we are."

"Your time for refusing the job has expired," Dead Johnny told him. "You're on board now and I'm not taking you back home. Wanna pick up some coffee? We're gonna be out all night."

"What if I up and quit?"

"You'll lose all your future opportunities."

"Of working with you? I'm a free agent, bro," Flames said. "I'll go along with this for now. You know I usually work with professionals. I have status to maintain."

"Chuck said you'd say that," said Dead Johnny.

"About what?"

"Working with 'professionals'."

"Where's the lie?" said Flames.

"You're broke, man," Dead Johnny said. "Four-way split is a nice payoff."

Flames tilted his head until he heard his vertebrae pop. "All I'm saying is kids these days don't spook that easily."

"Last call, man," Dead Johnny offered.

"Whatever. I'll do it. Just give me a bazooka."

"When everybody's in the car I'll disperse with arms. Let's get coffee."

The Olds sailed west across the city.

"What happened to your face?" Dead Johnny asked him.

"Fucking sister." Flames said.

"You fucking your sister?"

"Ha ha. Fuck off, man. Her boy— her *baby daddy* did this. Fucking bastard. Ribs are sore too."

"Let's fix him when we're done with this, how's that?"

Flames looked over at him. "Yeah."

Atlanta potholes are like craters on the moon. Even the new developments, condos, and influx of white people couldn't cover up the wounds of the old city roads. Where there weren't gaping wounds in the street, there was a thick square of heavy steel covering it.

Clouds were low but there was no rain. Plenty of humidity though. They picked up Pike and then Brett. Pike was dressed in all black. Very tight, hipster black jeans, combat boots. Ball cap. Chains hanging from his pockets and belt loops. Neck brace and cane too. Brett wore a neat navy-blue blazer, jeans, loafers, and a fedora.

They rode two in the back, two in the front. The Olds afforded comfort even with its old cracked, faux-leather bench seats.

"Lookit this *douche*." Flames pointed back at Brett. "You just get out of church?"

Dead Johnny looked at Brett and then at Flames. They chuckled. Pike couldn't keep his laugh in.

"What?" Brett said. "Don't chuckle, Pike. I'll throw you down those stairs again."

"Don't be rude, bro," Pike said. He pushed back in the seat and stared out the window.

"You may wanna lose that hat, my man," Flames said.

"Old friend gave me this, fuck you," Brett said.

Afternoon traffic was slow and impatient. Dead Johnny took back streets that only brought him into thicker traffic.

"Fuck," he said.

"Let's walk," Flames said.

"Let's *die*," said Dead Johnny.

"You wanna get tacos after?"

"I'm craving donuts." Brett responded.

Dead Johnny said. "No telling what time we'll get back."

"Donut shop's going to be closed," Flames said. "So, it'll be late night tacos."

"Hell yeah," Brett said. "Tacos and tequila. "How about you, Pike?"

"Not hungry."

"But you will be. *Afterward.*"

"You don't know what I'll be later."

"Okay," Brett said. "But you'll always be a moody bitch."

"Listen," said Flames. "Tacos on me. Okay, ladies? Plug up your periods. No need to bitch at anybody. Sure you don't want, Johnny?"

Dead Johnny shook his head. "I don't eat after a job. I drink. And get high."

He then gave them a best-practice talk on how the caper should play out. Before it could all settle in, Flames looked at Brett.

"You look like shit," Flames said. "Rough night?"

"What kind of question is that?" Brett said.

"Well, since I talked shit about your outfit, I also have to mention your face. Just sayin'."

"Fuck off."

Flames giggled.

"You got AR's in the trunk?" said Pike.

"You kidding?" Flames said. "You got a permit for one?"

"Who needs permits?" Pike said. "Second Amendment, bro. Bill of Rights. Ever heard of them? *America.* That's what's up."

"You think those corner boys have permits?" Brett said.

"I didn't ask last time I bought crack," Flames said. "This guy's white. They're not going to just side with him."

"He's a talker," Dead Johnny said. "He's trying to build street-cred."

"You act like we're going to war," Brett said.

"I mean, both sides are heating up," Dead Johnny said. "Trust that we have the tools needed for the job."

Brett sat up. "You know where we're going?"

"I'm the driver, of course I know."

"Just making sure, since you ain't from around here."

"Lived here long enough to know."

"Yeah?" Brett said. "Did you know Crakula and 11th Street Pete?"

"Every city has a Crakula," Flames said.

"Doesn't matter," Dead Johnny said. "I know of them, didn't *know* them. Who the fuck wants to be associated with those characters? I work on my own terms."

He took a narrow street north on Memorial Ave., driving up the gauntlet of new construction and rows of half-built condos.

"Perfect name for this avenue," Flames said. "Just one long memorial for what it used to be."

"Don't kid yourself," Brett said. "They won't ever clean these gutters out. New paint on old shit ain't progress."

"White devil," Pike said. His gaze was lost out among the evolving construction.

"Green money," Brett said.

Pike agreed. "Still waiting to hear back about that construction job here, though."

"Me too," Brett said.

"Cement work is rough. But it's work," said Pike.

"I'm ready for it. I've had every shit job in this fucking city."

Flames, as if arriving late to the party, said, "Pike, why'd you say white devil? I mean, the mayor's black. She signed off on that shit."

"'Cause," Pike said, daydreaming out the window. "Is it going to be black folks living here? Doubt it. Just another group of whites pushing their way into a chocolate city, disenfranchising the natives."

"I don't know if pushing out drug dealers is a disservice, bro," Brett said.

Pike looked at him. "What?"

"Amirite?"

"You're absolutely *wrong,* motherfucker," Pike said. "Any angle you look at it it's all gentrification."

"Oh shit, here we go," said Flames.

"You're not even black!" Brett said.

"Don't have to be, bro," Pike said.

"Diversity goes a long way," said Dead Johnny. "Anybody can move merchandise. That's as Diverse-American as it gets."

"Vultures always see an opportunity," Pike said. "And swoop in."

"You calling white people vultures?" Flames said.

Dead Johnny cleared his throat. "Narcotics distribution is going corporate, gentlemen. Black, white, Asian, won't matter. In time, our jobs will be corporate too. Turns out these black corner boys will be the ones taking the brunt and losing out."

"Classic," Flames said. "Classic white-guilt talking now. Oldy but goody."

"Cheap labor," Pike said. "Most of those kids don't even know the value of what they're slinging. Or where it comes from, or what it does. Honestly? It doesn't fucking matter to them. I know because I was one of those boys not so long ago."

"Deep story, bro," Brett said. "But, fuck those corner boys. They bring down property values."

"Listen to this fucking guy," Flames said. "All of the sudden you're flipping houses? Who gives a shit? These punks would just as soon steal your fucking car and take your wallet."

"Hold on, man. I used to live in a nice area," Dead Johnny said. "And it wasn't poverty or drugs that brought it down, it was the yuppies who moved in and caused my rent to jack up. It's always been a thing. Yuppies always want to live closer to their drug dealers."

They couldn't help but laugh.

Pike shook his head. "Hey, I sell coke to yuppies."

"Of course, you do," Brett said. "You ever sell to the bun man?"

"We've all sold to the bun man," Flames said.

"True."

The car passed several corner boys on a concrete island hustling water bottles.

"I don't have change, otherwise..." Brett said.

"They're being taken advantage of," Pike said. "I see them pushing water, candy, even these college scams. No matter what it is, they're being exploited."

Dead Johnny said, "Not to get all Marxist and shit, but you know, we all enslave each other in some way."

"You the conscience of the group all of a sudden?" Brett said.

"No, that's Pike," Dead Johnny said.

Flames turned his head to him. "*No*, I'm the conscience, Dead Johnny is the balls, and Brett is obviously the *dick*."

Dead Johnny eyeballed Pike in the rearview. "Half of you are suddenly having a revelation of conscience. We agreed to this yesterday.

What the fuck's happened since then? If that's how you really feel about it, you can get off at the next fucking red light. I'll tell Chuck not to recommend you to anyone ever again because you suffer too much white-guilt. Pickings are slim these days, but don't go losing your local privileges, boys. Pike, I know you're in debt up to your tits and you need whatever cash you got coming in. Brett, you're haunted by everybody you ever bought a dime bag or eighth from. I'm not judging, god knows I owe some tabs, but I want you all in the fucking game with me or I want you the fuck out of my car. Decide now."

There was some brief harrumphing.

"Who told you all that?" Brett said.

"Chuck knows everything about everybody," Flames said. "And he talks a lot."

Dead Johnny passed a brown paper bag to Flames.

"Huh, you wanna huff?" Flames said.

Dead Johnny said, "I hereby anoint you, man-at-arms."

Flames looked inside the bag. "I get first dibs."

"I carry my own." Dead Johnny said. "Each of you take *one*."

"No shotguns?" Brett said.

Flames took out an oily and somewhat loose Colt .45 Blue 80. Pike got the Smith & Wesson Combat Magnum .357 4". Brett had his own Beretta 84 strapped to his ankle.

"Where'd you get these?" Flames said.

"Chuck has a trunk full of them," Dead Johnny said. "His father was a gun nut collector."

"Where's the extra ammo?"

"That's it, that's all of it. They're fully loaded. No one shoots a fucking thing unless I say so. Bun man won't see us coming."

"But those corner boys expect to get flexed on," Brett said. "They know the dangers of being out there, exposed. They *know* they're pawns. And they're loaded up."

"Listen to this guidance counselor over here," Flames said.

"If they live to be twenty, they consider themselves kings," Brett continued. "They think that they're fucking heroes out there. They don't hesitate to shoot first. And they *never* ask questions."

"Listen to all this white privilege talk about what is or isn't good for a pack of working black kids," Dead Johnny said. "We'll get our man, any means necessary. But I'm not shooting kids. First one to catch him can clip his bun off and keep it as a souvenir."

"I'm not white," Pike said.

"Excepting you, *Samoan.*"

"But it's correct to assume they're armed and ready to kill us if they see us coming," Brett said.

"And why shouldn't they be?" said Dead Johnny. "They have every right to protect themselves. More so than we do. They're out here risking their asses, without seeing the big picture because all they've ever known is inside their periphery. Shit, I was packing at age 13. The 11th Ward is fucking scary."

"We might kill a few of them if it comes to it," Brett said. "Think of the service we're doing the city of Atlanta."

There was a pause and a long sick stillness in the car as it drove.

"Where's bun man?" Flames asked Dead Johnny.

"Where's white junkie go to sell a loaded briefcase?" Dead Johnny said. "They'll think we're just four white boys out to score. *Ahem*, one *Samoan, three white boys*. Starting with Westview and into Oakland City. Then ride into the 11th. Like Marlow to Mr. Kurtz."

"This feels wrong," Brett said, rubbing his hands together nervously. "I have a feeling it's not just the briefcase. It's more than that. It's whatever distribution's been brokered. But it's bigger than that. Bigger than us, bigger than bun man, bigger than corner boys."

"I don't give a fuck about any of that, or them, or whatever," Dead Johnny said. "Whatever's in that case will get us paid. To hell with what comes after. We get ours now, worry about what moves in later."

They tensed up, rolling forward.

Pike spoke up. "One day, anarchy will sweep through here so fast and hard, our heads will be spinning so uncontrollably, we'll be decapitated."

Dead Johnny watched him in the rearview. "That's poetic," he said.

"Authorities and municipalities will dissolve after it's all been plundered," Pike said. "And all that'll remain will be these corner boys, robbing and maiming to maintain their square foot of territory. It begins now."

"The whites will burn it down first," Brett said. He rolled down the window and spit and then enjoyed the late afternoon air blowing his face.

"That's bleak." Flames looked back at the both of them.

"On god," Pike said. "It'll be."

10

INTERLOCUTOR

Driving into Mozley Park.

"Pretty sure I know them." Flames pointed at some men in the street. "That's Nelson, Rodney, and Isaiah. Used to watch Rodney play ball when he was in high school."

The car cruised.

"You bet on high school ball?" Brett said. "I lost a fortune on that shit."

"Kinda old to be working a corner," Dead Johnny said as they drove past. He made a right and slowed down.

"They're independents," Flames said.

"Won't last another season," Brett said.

Dead Johnny slowed the car to a stop and put it in reverse.

"Wait," Flames said nervously.

"Roll your window down," Dead Johnny said.

"What? Why?"

"You said you know them."

"These ain't corner boys," Flames said. "They're *captains*. Why would the three of them be huddled together in one corner?"

"Yeah, look like pit bosses," Dead Johnny said.

The Olds braked.

Flames straightened his shirt. Before he could say anything else, Nelson and Rodney came up to the car. Isaiah watched them from the sidewalk.

"Hey, meng," Rodney said. They dapped. "Whatchoo looking for?"

"We're looking for our buddy," Flames said. "He was high as fuck and wondered out of East Side."

"Yeah." Dead Johnny leaned over. "Bearded white dude, dirty hoodie."

Nelson and Rodney surveyed the car and passengers. They were dressed in slacks and collared shirts.

"Bearded white dude?" Nelson said. "That's half the white people in this city."

The two brothers looked at each other. They all laughed nervously.

Nelson said, "Yesterday, this white dude was tryna sell us a briefcase full of shit but it weren't his to sell. We ain't stupid."

"He a little cray," Flames said. "We don't want him to hurt himself."

The brothers looked at them suspiciously.

"Who gonna hurt 'em?" Rodney said.

"You never know," said Dead Johnny. "Wrong place, wrong time."

"Niggas don't fuck with crackers 'round here," Nelson said. "It just bring the heat down on us ferociously. Mayor don't 'preciate when white people die 'round here."

Flames nodded. Stroked his chin. "You know of any new shit dropping?"

"Nah," said Nelson. "But I know mufuckas dying from fent overdoses. Watch out what you snorting or shooting up."

Flames shot them the most honest look he could. "All right. Peace out."

Dead Johnny rolled off quickly.

"We should stay on them," Brett said. "Flex our guns. They're lying. I know they are. They know where he is. They're protecting him."

"We flex on them," Flames said. "And we'll wind up on the pavement covered in bullet holes."

The mood grew somber. They seemed strangers to each other in the car.

"There's a shift coming, I'm telling you." Brett scanned the neighborhood suspiciously. "I can feel it. It's inevitable. In the grand scheme, we're *all* gonna lose out."

"I'll just uproot and go someplace else," Dead Johnny said. "I'm a fucking nomad."

"City's getting hot," Brett said. "And I don't mean the weather. We should reconsider this search. Wait a while. Feel it out."

"Not an option," Dead Johnny said. "We sleep on this, we lose out. He was last seen a day ago, trying to sell it. Let's all regroup inside ourselves for a moment."

"Shit, I knew I should've gone to Florida for the week," Flames said. "But I'm broke."

"We should destroy it when we find him," Pike said. "Keep it off the streets. The buyers are the real culprits in all this. They're the real demand for supply."

"We're doing no such thing," Dead Johnny said. "We get a hold of it we wait to see who's offering a reward before we attempt to ditch it. And by that, I mean selling to the highest bidder. Flames, maybe you can broker that with those boys back there we talked to."

Dead Johnny gripped the steering wheel with both hands, watching the sidewalks and houses, driving slowly up and down various streets. Watching people, and in turn, being watched.

Flames rubbed his stomach like it was upset. "They won't touch it. They know who it belongs to. Purp don't play that."

Brett said, "Anybody spare a toke?"

"I got a joint I'm saving for laters," Flames said.

"No fucking around and getting high until we're done," Dead Johnny said. "I need everybody focused."

"The edge is getting pretty sharp," Brett said. "I need to soften it."

"You're welcome to put your mouth around the tailpipe of the Olds. That'll get you high as fuck real fast."

Brett scoffed, shaking his head.

"If they'd just legalized all of it," Pike said. "We wouldn't be here. Hookers, drugs, pimps: all should be legalized and protected by laws."

"Dude," Flames turned to him. "Your lamentation is suffocating me. Quit that shit right now."

Westview and College Town weren't what they used to be. Yuppies lined up for tacos to their left. There was a black motorcycle club to their immediate right. The neighborhood had an antiquated look. Like buildings seen in old photos from Watts or Harlem. Further up, new construction lined both sides, crawling over the neighborhoods like a skin-eating disease.

II

GODZILLA

Oakland City, Atlanta, was one of those neighborhoods where economic reclamation was attempted years back, but poverty and poor folks overwhelmed its good intentions. Especially when the local government signed those construction contracts only to line their pockets, in turn choking the community out, disenfranchising those at the bottom. In a matter of speaking.

Two blocks from the MARTA line, the old hotel down Milledge St. Built in 1971. Ten stories of gray bleakness that stuck out like a bruised thumb even in this blighted neighborhood. Dark mold shadowed the exterior walls where Hedera vines crawled like veins up the side of the building. Only the large *O* on the *Oakland Tower* neon sign worked. The block and building were both guarded by armed Hoodies. Governed by its own laws.

This wounded night had a hazy, humid quality after the rain. Everything was slick but dingy.

Third floor, to the west. Faced the junkyard and the shuttered Section 8 housing.

Most of the night Muscles leaned against the rail overlooking the busy parking lot below. Cars and pedestrians came and went, and only the regulars showed their faces around here more than once a day. When clients came through for merchandise, he used a secret knock. The inside doorman was Killah X. He opened the door and Muscles gave him the nod. Only one or two allowed inside the room at a time.

The air was dense with a marijuana smog, but the room also smelled like vinegar and chemicals. Smells that could never really been washed or disinfected away. Killah X kept a can of air freshener nearby but that only made the place smell like rancid salad dressing. There was a plastic patio chair against the wall to the left, a small round coffee table with a measuring scale on top beside it, and a bed against the wall. That was all the furniture in the room. No mirrors.

There was a husky man on the bed wearing a Godzilla balaclava. Only his fierce, wet eyes peered from the eye holes.

Killah X stood behind the customer just to make sure she wasn't going to snap and do something stupid. Killah X wore wide sun blockers, the kind used by the elderly. A black bandana covered the bottom of his face and a dew rag wrapped around his bald head.

Godzilla recognized the customer, but they weren't friends. Godzilla had business associates. *Clients*, not friends.

"Whatchoo up to, sis?" He said. "Been a minute."

The client was a well-dressed small woman. Thin as rails. Her arms were clean. Bootleg brand name purse, immaculate sneakers, and a short skirt over her tights. Fishbone tee-shirt. She strutted a certain charm and class.

"You know, got my late night *bizniz* to attend to," she said. "Peoples to meet. Tryna get my *place* where it need to be."

"Word," Godzilla said. "What's your fix?"

"Fuck me up, fam," she said. "The usual." She gave him a loose $20 and a $10. He measured a bump of heroin that looked like moldy cookie dough on the digital scale. He rolled it in plastic wrap and handed it to her.

"Can I fix here?" she said.

"This ain't no lounge, sis," Godzilla said.

"Aight." She tucked the lump into her pocket and bumped fists with him. Killah X let her out.

Outside, a quiet humid night in OC.

Ten minutes later another secret knock. Muscles stuck his head in when Killah X opened up.

"Say, God," Muscles said. "Crash wanna talk. Said it's urgent."

Godzilla was counting money. "She aight?"

"I don't know, she look shook as hell," Muscles said.

"She don't need no pass, nigga. Let her in." Godzilla tucked cash into a brown bag and put it behind him on the bed.

Crash had walked all the way from the desolate corners of the 11th Ward. She wore a pair of black denim coveralls and Timberland boots. Black dew rag on her head. All of her upper teeth were gold.

"Nigga, how you dress like that in this heat?" Godzilla said.

Her face drooped. Deep, dark eyes on the brink of tears. Angry tears that she wiped away.

"Nigga, don't you ever take that dirty sock off ya head?" she said.

"Is you high? This ain't no dirty sock. Why you rolling up in here looking all crazy?"

"First off, I ain't high," Crash said. "I walked from the Ward. Barely got out. Shit's fucked up right now. Nigga's creepin'. They pegging corner boys."

"You ain't shot back?" Godzilla said.

"How 'bout you show me respect like you do your other homeboys? They killed some of my slingers."

Godzilla paused a moment. The room was still. Like they were all sitting at the bottom of a swimming pool.

"Sit down," Godzilla told her.

"Nah, I'm good."

"You look shook. Wanna smoke? Need a bump?"

"Nigga, no."

"Well, go ahead, you got my attention. Yo, check wit' Muscles, see how long the line is."

Killah X nodded once and opened the door and told Muscles, "He said, they can wait."

"Talk," Godzilla said to her. "Speak. *Speak.*"

Crash roared. *"They shot at me! Purple's boys."*

"Purple ain't done shit," Godzilla said. "That's Stingy did you dirty like that. We got a truce with Purp."

"Shit just got worse at the 11th. They shot them boys in the park."

"*Gotdamn!*" Godzilla looked at Killah X. "Nigga, is she for real? How many?"

"Shit, I don't know," Killah X sounded equally surprised.

"Who got it?"

"Juicy, Darnell and some new boy, Lil B," Crash said.

Godzilla stood up and paced around the cramped space.

"Juicy was a sentinel," Crash said. "He was a tough lil nigga. Thought he was bulletproof."

"That was yo' brother?" Killah X told her.

"He was my cousin," she said.

"We lose any merchandise?" said Godzilla.

"Three boys," Crash said. "They had all their shit on them. They still had it on them when I found them. Police prolly still ain't got there yet."

Godzilla looked at Killah X as if for approval. There was a reason Crash was in the street and Killah was in the room. Killah X didn't know shit about shit.

"See what happens when I stay off the streets?" Godzilla said. "Was they Skullies?"

"Who else out there competing with us?" Crash said. "Nigga, that's what I'm tryna tell you! This might be the start of something. They not asking permission. They just moving in."

Godzilla considered it. "So, let them take that corner. They can keep that shit. They been creepin' on it for a while, but don't nobody wanna sling near the 11th no more. Shit, they's gonna be condos there next week it seem. They gonna run us out either way. Prolly want us to kill each other off."

"But you gonna let Purple Rain take our boys out like that?"

"We been at peace for a minute," Godzilla said. "Don't wanna be the one who break it."

"Nigga, our boys gettin' hit ain't war? Fuck you think? What, you gonna just let them walk in here and take over this tower? Whatchoo gonna do when we lined up for the execution?"

"Ain't gonna happen like that, sis," Killah X said.

"They just gonna keep creepin' and doing whatever the fuck they want?" Crash said.

"Is how they do, boo boo." Godzilla said. "Is how they always do. We gotta know our place. See this block where we at? That's not our piece of the pie. That's our whole cake. It ain't but a lil bit, but it's ours! Whatchoo spec me to do? We hit them back, what they gonna do? They just gonna bring attention to us here. Then come the police, then come detectives and drug agents, start sniffing around with they dogs. Issat whatchoo want?"

"God, we gotta act now. They gonna come evict us at gunpoint."

Godzilla, a man in a sweat suit with a somewhat frighteningly comical Japanese monster mask, nodded.

"Aight," he said. "But if you gonna hit, hit fast, hit hard. Ain't no mufucking prisoners in this war. This ain't but a quick action."

"Word," she said. She looked up at the ceiling as if in prayer.

"Yeah, you can ask for god's help," Godzilla said. "But he ain't coming for you. He abandoned us a long time ago."

"Taking some Hoodies with me," she said.

"Round up a dozen and go," Godzilla said. "How's that? You happy now?"

She nodded.

"All right," Godzilla said. "Killah, set that shit up. Get your boys."

"How 'bout that truce, chief?" Killah X said.

"They violated when they hit our boys," Crash said. "Miss me wit' that shit. Them niggas ain't never been loyal to it anyway."

"Like I said before," said Godzilla. "It was signed before our time."

"We need a new deal, chief." Crash stood and walked out. "Let me go remind them how we do it."

12

FRANKENSTEIN HEAD

"Yo Head, wait up!" Little Nickel let the door slam even though it pissed off his mother. She worked a third shift and daytime was sleep time. There was barely a front yard to cross onto the sidewalk. He paused, waited for her yell and when it didn't come, he cut a path through the empty lot across the street, trying to catch up with his brother.

Leon Sanford, aka Frankenstein Head, aka Head Sanford, stopped and waited.

"Mama said pick up some cigarettes for her. I see you going," Nickel said.

"Ain't coming back 'til later." Head shouted.

"You going now? Is early."

"Nigga, I gotta go to work. And I ain't heading to the store right now."

"Mama wanted smokes," Nickel said. "She gonna be mad she wake up and ain't got no smokes."

"So, *you* buy 'em."

"I'm eleven, son. You the one got hair on his chin."

Head sucked his teeth and walked. Nickel skipped behind him.

"Wait up." Nickel said.

"Keep up, nigga. I ain't in the mood for yo shit."

"Thought you was working Ackens St."

"I am," Head said. "I'm fynna get some food first. Gonna be a long afternoon tonight."

"Imma come and stand witchoo," Nickel said.

"Nigga, Imma be working. Go play your PlayStation."

"I already beat the game."

Up to the intersection, cut a left. Walk a block. Cross. The streets cratered with potholes. They hadn't installed steel plate covers yet. Even the Anglo side of Summerhill was wrecked like this. Cracked sidewalks buckled.

"I can't look after you all night," Head said. "I got to keep a watch out. You know what happens if you stay out late?"

"I'll be witchoo," said Nickel.

"Uh huh. Skulls gonna come 'round and pop a cap in yo' ass. That's what's gonna happen."

"They don't come down here!"

"Finish school, nigga." Head said.

"I already went today. You da one dropped out."

"'Cause I gotta job. Ain't ya got homework or something?"

"Head, listen," Nickel said. "I know it ain't hard whatchoo do. I wanna show dem I can do it too."

"They think you'll run off first time some shit go bad. Or that you'll run off and tell mama."

"But I don't wanna just stand there and sling all day and night. I know what your monetary gains are compared to what you sell. I wanna tap the source and reinvest."

"Reinvest? *Monetary gains?* Nigga, whatchoo know about that? You been listening to Steve Harvey again?"

"I know a hundy can make me a thou in a month." Nickel said.

"More like a week, Lil man. *If* you get lucky, it do. Who you gonna ask? Is already crowded up here with slingers and shit. More of us than the people buying. Shit don't even cost what it used to."

"Maybe I can talk to Godzilla himself."

Head stopped and looked at him and then started laughing. Hard laughing. Bent over and holding his belly laughing.

"Nigga, nobody talk to Godzilla," Head said. "Not even me. Why would you think that?"

"I know ain't no one fuck with him, but I wanna shoot my shot."

"You ain't got a dollar to your name, bruh. Fuck you think? A corner ain't no playground. You got competition, rogue niggas out to rob you and shit."

"You ever seen his face?" said Nickel.

"Ain't nobody ever seen it. I never even met him."

They arrived at a small strip plaza. Half of it was a package store, the other was a Chinese place that sold tacos and chicken wings. The parking lot was empty. The usual 'bos and baseheads that crowded the front entrance were absent this afternoon. The Salvadorian behind the glass looked up at them and nodded.

"Let me get six lemon pepper," Head said.

"Let me get some," Nickel said.

"You got money?"

"I'm waiting on my credit card to come in the mail."

Head laughed. "Maaaan, you ain't gettin' shit in the mail. Fuck you talkin 'bout?"

"Them offers always coming in the mail. They'll give one to anybody."

"True dat, but do you have money now?"

"I know how credit works. It's just paper moved around in place of real money."

The man behind the glass spoke into the tiny speaker box. *"Seven oh et."*

"Let me get a Dr. Pepper too." Head said.

"Eight feety," the Salvadorian said with a heavy accent.

Head put a five, and four single dollars into the money cup and the man pulled behind the glass.

Nickel moved to the left side of the exterior wall, leaning against the colorful mural of Outkast that had been airbrushed years ago. Head stood next to him once he got his food. They leaned, admiring, only in a way that they could, the end of the day and the sun sinking in the Atlanta skyline. Head ate all the wings by himself, tossing the bones on the pavement for future archeologists to uncover.

The sun hit Head's face and he glowed orange.

"How come you ain't a boss yet? Like a captain or somethin'?" Nickel said. He eyeballed one of the wings for the flesh Head had left uneaten.

"I'll move up when I do," Head said. "Can't really say."

"I seen other boys get bumped up real fast, been around less time than you."

Irritated, Head said, "Like who?"

"Buster D, Jamaikal Jones, Quovadis Thompson."

"Yeah, well, some o'dem niggas are dead too," Head said. "Life expectancy is short in this line of work, lil man. I ain't in no hurry. That answer why I ain't moved up? It'll come when it comes."

"You just a chump, is all." Nickel laughed.

"Nigga, Imma punch you, you keep up with dat bullshit."

"For real, though. Imma buy me an ice cream truck. That's where the deal is."

"You ain't old enough to drive."

"By the time I save up for it, I will be. They gonna know me. They gonna know they get a free ice cream cone with every purchase.

Whatever it's gonna be. Weed. Coke or heroin. They gonna know me for my free treats."

"Niggas who use don't get hungry," said Head.

"Oh, but they like sugar and ice cream, 'cause Atlanta gets hot as fuck."

The parking lot was mostly empty for the afternoon, with more white patrons than usual coming and going. Nickel studied them. Some brought their dogs. Some rode up on fancy bikes. One lady had on tight yoga pants and Nickel admired the curve of her ass.

They were about to head back at sunset when they heard tires screeching. Very quickly, a dusty looking Nissan Altima rolled up and parked crookedly in front of them. Nickel's mouth dropped open. Head looked nervous.

"That car is busted," Nickel said. Head took a long sip from his Dr. Pepper can.

"Yo, that's one of Purple Rain's boys," Head said.

"Who's that?"

"Shit. That's Savage. What he want here? Ain't supposed to cruise this block." Head looked at Savage straight on, finishing the last of the drink.

"Nigga need to upgrade his ride." Nickel chuckled.

Head leaned over and whispered, "Nigga, go on and get. This grown folks shit. *Git.*"

Nickel stiffened and ran into the package store next door.

Savage wore his black ballcap sideways. When he stepped out of the car, he zipped down his Adidas jacket, exposing multiple gold chains and his Glock, dangling from his waistband.

"Who invited you?" Head said.

"Nigga, I don't need no invite," Savage said. His fake smile exposed the line of gold teeth in his mouth. "We in this bitch."

"Ain't nothing here for you, nigga. I ain't got no gear with me."

"I ain't come here for your trash, my nigga. Purp missing some luggage. Says it got lost out here near the 11th."

"Nigga, there's dead luggage on every corner here. Just look in them dumpsters over there."

Savage grimaced. "You got a mouth on you, mufucka. You talking to a grown man."

"Nigga, *bye*. Ain't nothing here for you."

"They saw one of you lil jits running around with a suitcase."

Head chuckled. "Prolly 'cause niggas moving out this fucking place."

"It don't belong to them," Savage said. "Just tell me where the suitcase is and our transaction here is through."

"Ay, I ain't seen it, 'k?. I got work to do."

"What corner you working?" Savage said.

"Corner of Anderson and none-o-yo' got-damn business."

Savage stared.

"Imma have to teach you." He came at Head but Head drew a .38 snubby he'd tucked in front of his pants. He shot him twice in the chest. Savage pulled his Glock and shot back before collapsing. Head got one more good shot and fell on his side.

The sun kissed the horizon on this warm Atlanta day.

13

PEACHES & HERB

"Ay, yo, Peaches!" the man in the car called.

Peaches was 5'8", wore yellow high heels, tight faded jeans that scooped her ass up like two basketballs, and a tight blue tee-shirt. Her hair faded from a light brown to auburn, wild, and frizzy, corralled around the top of her head by a white headband. She smelled like black castor oil and cocoa butter. Her blue nail polish contrasted her light brown skin.

She popped bubblegum as she approached the chump calling out of his scrappy, smoking car.

"Ay, don't use my name like that," she said with immediate authority. "You don't know me like that, mufucka."

"Been coming to you here for years," the man in the car said. "Don't play that mess. I know you."

"Nah, nigga, you *don't* know me. You just think you do."

"Where your man 'Herb' at? *Damn*, girl. Look like you been going back for seconds on that cornbread. You slinging pussy too?"

"Mufucka, you want your ass beat before your afternoon nap?" She stepped back, crossed her arms. "You buying something or you want a quick trip to Grady?"

Standing by the lamp post was Shawn "Herb" Clinton staring right at him. He pulled up the front of his shirt to make sure the man in the car could see the butt of his .357.

"Oh, my bad." The man in the car laughed. He looked like he hadn't bathed or brushed his teeth or had a change of clothes in months. "Yeah, uh, listen, gimme two. I got a twenty."

"Twenty is now thirty, lil bitch," Peaches said.

"What? Come on, now. How's a man supposed to get his jollies?"

"Hassle fee right here, mufucka." Peaches smiled.

"Fuck you." The man dug in his pant pocket, pulling out a few crumbled bills. He balled them and tossed them out the window. "Kiss my ass."

Peaches squatted and picked up the money, ironing out each bill and checking for legitimacy.

"Kiss your ass?" she said. "How about you stick your face between my ass cheeks and inhale, mufucka?"

The man cackled. "'Bout you drink my piss out of my size 12 Chuck Taylors?"

Holding her middle finger up, she walked over to Herb with the crushed money. A moment later she was back at the car, throwing a tiny bag of cocaine which had been cooked down to ivory colored cookie crumbs. *Crack. Rock. Glass dreams. Bopper.* The man grabbed it greedily and cackled. He flipped her off, blew a raspberry and drove off.

"That mufucka gonna get shot next time he ride up here," Peaches said.

The power couple leaned against the pole, flexing B-boy/B-girl poses. Grew up on this corner. Not married but attached since the 8th grade. He was dressed sporty, like he was vacationing in Fort Lauderdale. Flowered yellow shirt, white shorts, green canvas shoes.

"*You* gonna do it?" Herb said.

"That nigga ain't worth it," Peaches said. "But he say the wrong thing to the wrong mufucka and guess what?"

"He do run his mouth a lil too much. Anybody else and they gonna show him what's what."

They were on an industrial block. She surveyed the street. No cars, few pedestrians. The old factory on the other side of the train tracks would be converted to condos soon enough.

"He ain't shit," Peaches said.

"He's our best customer." Herb stared her up and down, taking inventory on what he thought was all his. "Could *you* though, if you had to?"

Peaches put a hand at her hip. "What? Kill him? I don't know 'bout that, but you do know the number of niggas I've sent to the hospital…"

"I know. But, if it come down to it, would you be able to do a man if you had to? Like put a gun in his head and pull it?"

"Why? You been thinking about that?" she said. "Meditating with them thoughts? Going over it in your head?"

"I'm the arms in this partnership." Herb said and bowed his head.

"We equals in this shit, boo. Don't forget that. You know I carry a piece in my purse. You wanna be the arms in this, you keep telling yourself that. I got mine, and I'll keep it with mine."

He scratched his forehead. Wiped a bead of sweat away. All he had left to say was, "You looking good, boo. A real peach."

"I know," she said. She pulled away from the pole, her heels digging into the gravel and dirt. "No matter where I go, it follows me."

"What, dat ass?"

"All of *this*," she gestured to the neighborhood. "We're just two blocks away from enemy territory. We taking mad risks out here today."

"They can't touch us," Herb said. "There's a truce."

She faced him. "We been at this a few years now. Ain't it time we got our own squad?"

"We gotta squad. *You and me.* I'm the squad leader. And you my squad. Is about to change, though. We close to sitting down and talking, me and 'Zilla. We fynna get down and hash it out. And you know, when I rise, you rise. You gonna rise up like a queen by my side."

"Shit, if I'm a queen, I get my own kingdom. Ain't waiting on nobody."

"Don't be cold, baby. You know I love you." Herb looked down checking his shoes for dirt. Around his feet were phials of spent drugs littering the ground like excavated tribal curios.

"Hmm," Peaches said and stepped up on the sidewalk. Her balance was good, avoiding all the cracks and imperfections in the concrete. He went to her, putting his arms around her waist. She kept her eyes on the boulevard as his lips traced her neck. Her eyes kept to their territory, their kingdom, and it was all good.

They sold drugs until sunset, the sun sliding between two abandoned Spellman dorms. *Twin Towers* they called them like they were trying to give the city some sort of big city clout.

Not soon after, gun shots on the Boulevard, followed by yelling a few minutes after. The young boy rounded the corner, crying, breathing hard through his mouth. His clothes were dirty, and he was sweaty. They watched him turn on their block and run on the other side of the street.

"Lil man!" Peaches called out.

Nickel kept going.

Herb called, *"Hey, we ain't fucking witchoo, what's up?"*

Nickel stopped at the corner and looked at them. He'd been running since he'd escaped the package store. Hadn't even looked back on his brother, lying dead, surrounded by chicken bones. Head would have wanted him to keep running. Nickel had run east up to Lancer St., but it looked like the Hoodie Mob had Godzilla's corner boys surrounded. They'd brought baseball bats, but a few pointed guns too. He hadn't stuck around to see what they did to those boys, those boys who'd called him names and made fun of his entrepreneurial ideas. He'd heard the gunshots behind him as he ran.

Staying on the white side of Boulevard, he'd kept running, like naked prey. He wasn't associated directly with them boys, but they knew his brother was.

Two blocks south of Peaches and Herb, was the 11th St. tenements. Nickel considered the shortcut. Sun was all but gone. Late September and it darkened earlier.

He'd circled and then crossed Anderson, which crossed Georgia Ave., running a gauntlet past Pittsburgh's outer rim. The 47 bus honked and almost hit him. The Skulls took a shortcut and found him. They'd gone back for the Altima and pursued him.

Looking at Peaches and Herb now, Nickel thought of his mother again. The police would visit or call and inform her of her son's death, and she'd probably collapse with a stroke or heart attack. In that same thought he envisioned a cemetery and all his relatives around a hole in the ground.

All he had to do was circle back, hope the hoodies had left his street and then he could go home and tell mama himself. If he made it back.

But then he saw the Altima coming.

14

THE PLASTIC PEOPLE

Some people lead such straight lives after their habit you'd think they'd never had a needle in their arm or had ever woken up in their shit and vomit after passing out in an East Side gutter.

Sandra parked in front of a blue house in Cabbage Town, waiting on Katie. An expensive house, but Katie lived with four other roomies. Plus, mommy and daddy paid her rent. The steps to the house went up on a slant into some heavy shrubbery. Grass was overgrown with all sorts of weird art displayed in the yard. The neighborhood was all cobblestone

If she says, "Yass queen!" *one more time, I'm going to choke that bitch out.* Sandra felt a headache coming on. She checked her hair in the fold down mirror, testing her best smile. She winked and kissed herself then exhaled. The little white Kia Soul she drove was trashed with school papers, leaves and fast-food bags crumbled and piled on the floor in the back. White dog hair on everything.

Katie came down the steps and got in the car. At least they both smelled good. Sandra's hair was up in a bun, wearing maroon leggings and a leopard print leotard. Katie wore her shoulder length blond hair loose, down to her shoulders. Her yoga outfit was teal and pink, with a fuchsia tutu. She tossed her yoga mat on top of Sandra's and they were on their way.

"Um, we're picking up Bex." Sandra said at the stop sign. She squeezed her eyes shut, rubbed her forehead and shook her head.

"She's back from the dead?" Katie said.

"I guess... ugh. That girl. How's Trixie and her husband?"

"Girl, I can't even talk about it. I literally *cannot* talk about it. They're in so much trouble."

"Um, okay. Hope *she's* all right."

"She is. For now. Bale on the other hand, not so much. But I can't say."

"They just came in and scooped them up?"

"This city is lucky to be intact. Those protestors were going to burn it to the ground. Feds went in and raided all their shit. Locked their friends up too. God. Bale's in custody right now. That's all I can say. Honestly, I don't really know much else."

"Did they question her too?"

"Oh my god, yes, *and* they raided *all* their shit. Talked to neighbors, employers, ex-boyfriends. Short of sticking their fingers up her butt, they searched everywhere for anything. They detained her but let her go. *They* cut some sort of deal."

"I mean, they're not fucking around," Sandra said. "The city takes pride in all their history of non-violence and don't want their rep tainted by riots."

"Pretty sure they got ratted out," said Katie. "Also, it was more than just the protest. At least that's what I hear. Got him on conspiracy and charged him with *terrorism* because a bomb went off near them."

"But he's white," Sandra said. "They'll pin it on someone else in his group."

Katie chuckled. "White privilege is real, sis. I know."

"This city could certainly use a good burn. Clear all this bullshit out. I mean, you notice all the new construction creeping in? I'm thinking I'm going to buy one when they hit the market."

"For those prices?" Katie said. "Girl, I'll go half with you. How's Bex doing?"

"Girl..." Sandra gave her a sideways glance.

"Hot mess?"

"That doesn't even begin to explain it." Sandra shook her head.

Katie rolled her eyes. "It's been two years. Like, girl, *get over him!*"

Sandra agreed. "The poetry. The social media posts. She's fucking withering away. Looks like a bulimic Janis Joplin. She needs a good meal."

"Don't say that!" Katie said.

"Fuck it, she's my sister. It's still consuming her. She's just going to vanish into thin air if she doesn't get a meal soon."

"Thought she was in breakup hibernation."

"Girl, they been split for two years but she's still lamenting that abusive motherfucker. Now, she's just high all the time, never eats."

"I never eat," said Katie.

"Girl, stop."

"She's always been dark and gothy, so what's the difference?"

"Agreed," Sandra said. "But she tends to manifest such negativity, she's built a monster from her darkness. It consumes everything. Including her."

Bex lived just a mile away, close to the highway ramp near Old Fourth. The house was red brick. The lawn overgrown. Weird gnomes poking their colorful hats from the top of the grass. When they arrived, Sandra sent a text.

Bex came out in pigtails, denim shorts and torn stockings. She looked like a rag doll, eyes encircled with dark makeup, high cheekbones done up in rouge. Her face was a giant smile and she skipped toward the car smoking a long black joint, sticking out her tongue at them.

"S'up, bitches?" she said. She smelled of sandalwood, patchouli and weed.

"Hey, honey," Sandra said. "How you feelin'?"

"Like shit?" Bex chuckled. "You think you can run me down near the 11th?"

Sandra drove the car through narrow Atlanta traffic that was mostly a parking lot. When the car could move, it bounced over potholes.

"11th?" Sandra said. "Boo, that's all the way back that way."

"Tryna get me an eighth," Bex said.

Katie sat up excitedly. "I'm down. Shit, I'd rather snowblow than yoga."

"Girl," Bex said. "That shit *is* my yoga."

They cackled their secret laughter.

"You didn't even bring a mat, so I guess that's where we're going," Sandra said.

"Girls day out, *yay!*" Bex said. "Gotta go see my girl Peaches."

"Who?" Katie said. The mood in the car shifted to joviality. Even Sandra livened up. She'd worked eight days straight. She needed this break.

"That's my connect," Bex said. "She's a cute, hot black mama. My favorite slinger in the A."

"Can't she make housecalls?" said Sandra.

"Why?" Bex said. "I know where to find her. Go straight and then take the turn like you're going towards Bridge to Nowhere."

"Okay," Sandra said quietly.

"You guys wanna shneef it here, there or go back to my room? Ooorrrr the parking lot at the yoga place?"

"Whatever," Katie said. She took out her little psychedelic blown-glass pipe, lit the bowl and hit it. She passed it to Sandra who looked in the rearview and then held the steering wheel with her knees while scorching the bowl.

"We'll play it by ear," Sandra said and passed the pipe back.

"Ugh, how rude of me," Bex said. She pulled on her joint then presented it to them. Her fingers were long, the silver, red and blue nail polish chipped. "You can both hit on this bone, if you want. It's pure."

Katie locked eyes with her in the rearview, submerging in her sister's deeply buried sadness and melancholy. She grabbed the joint and took a long drag from it. When she eventually let out the smoke, she said,

"This thing's a cigar."

Sandra felt all the tension of the week release.

"I know." Bex laughed. "Rolled it this morning."

Katie felt it hit her frontal lobe almost immediately. It made her dizzy. *"Jesus."*

"Right?" Bex's eyes and cheeks disappeared behind her giant smile.

"I don't think I've ever driven here on purpose," Sandra said.

There were areas in the neighborhood that were rubble with no chance of a new fabrication, or even sympathy for the impoverished houses and the people who lived here. On the corner was a teal-colored bodega with black burglar bars. Broken, crumbling bus benches. Tents on the sidewalks, booted feet poking from under cardboard blankets or sleeping bags.

"The only reason to drive up here is to drive right the fuck out," Katie said, making sure her door was locked.

"Girl, I'm here for the shneef," Bex said. There was always a cackle at the end of her sentences.

"Hopefully those new condos come with their own dealers," Sandra said.

"Relax. If you're afraid, they're gonna know you're afraid."

"*They*? What, are we going to a zoo?"

Katie said, "Why can't you just have that shit delivered? Isn't that how your roommate gets it?"

"Girl, she pays way too much for her shit," Bex said. "I've known Peaches for a minute. She worked with me at the coffee shop. We'll be fine."

Hoodied youths stood around an empty lot, kicking cans, throwing rocks, or flexing their automatics as they drove past. Bandanas obscured their faces. Sandra maneuvered around their scooters parked far into the street. Hoodied eyes followed them. Sandra's Kia wasn't the fanciest car, was a few years old, but it still looked out of place amidst the impecunious neighborhood.

Loud music and loud marijuana from parked cars or houses.

"Smell that?" Bex giggled.

"All I smell is you," Sandra said.

"That's that real *real*," Bex said. She told her sister to turn on another street and they drove straight past overgrown lots and more gutted houses.

"Why do people let it get like this?" Katie said.

They had theories but no answers.

"We're almost there," Bex said. Her smile kept growing, joint dangling from her bottom lip.

Ahead were two figures in the distance. A man and a woman, the woman being taller than the man. They looked sporty and hip, right out of a fashion magazine.

"That's Peaches." Bex pointed.

The car stopped at their corner. Bex dug out her cash and poked her head out the window.

"Hey, girl." She said. "Wasup?"

Peaches was saying something to Herb and ignored the car with the white girls. She seemed to be lecturing something to him, leaning an elbow onto the light pole. After a minute, she acknowledged the car. Read all the faces. The stupid white girl in the back who looked like she was twelve with those pigtails.

"Wasup, home girl." Peaches approached. She placed one hand on the top of the car and leaned in.

"Nuttin'," Bex said. "Chillin' with ma girls. This is my sister, Sandra."

Peaches was permanently unassuming.

"Whatchoo looking for?" she said.

"Whatchoo got?" Bex said.

"I got rocks all day, 'less you want the usual."

"Yeah, that's what I want."

"Gimme sixty."

Bex handed her three folded $20's. Peaches came back with a baggie of something that she dropped into Bex's hand. Bex quickly tucked it inside her black bra.

"Bye, boo," she said. Peaches gave a half-hearted wave back from the pole.

"You're not going to check it?" Katie said.

"Nah, we down, she's cool," Bex said.

"Let's get the fuck out of here, ASAP."

Sandra sighed with relief and sped off.

"What'd she sell you?" Sandra said, looking in the rearview.

"Coke and some pills," Bex said. "Where we going? I mean, we can find a quiet spot and just roll."

Katie looked at Sandra with a smile. The car stopped at the corner of Adair Park, facing south. The vista was changing. Lawns trimmed. Signs against gentrification and eminent domain. There was less garbage in the gutters and sidewalks. There was a highway to the right and business park to the left. And another stadium ahead. More structures going up.

The occasional derelict ambulated in front of the car. The homeless were the patron saints of Atlanta.

"Holy shit." Bex pointed. "*That's Freaky Freddy!* What the fuck is he doing in this side of town?"

"Buying drugs," Katie said. "Why are we here? Why do white people come to this side of town?"

"I thought he went straight," Sandra said.

"Kind of," Bex said between them, playing with Katie's long hair. "Drive by slowly, I wanna say hi."

He was six feet tall, bearded. The bush of curls on his head was corralled behind a rainbow headband. Ragged sneakers, dirty tube socks and gray shorts that matched his gray hoodie.

Hobo or hipster?

He could have been one of a million white men in the city. He looked sweaty, moved sluggishly, like he was about to fall over. Moving slowly, eyes lit up. He looked very paranoid as they approached. He carried a small suitcase.

"He's married," Bex said. "Lives in East Side. His wife earns. Real estate agent. They have two kids."

"And here he is, high as fuck," Sandra said.

"Atlanta gonna Atlanta," Katie said. "Does he even have a job?"

"Does it look like it? Sommelier for Mad Dog 2020?" Sandra said. "What's with the briefcase?

"Guys, shush." Bex defended. "We used to room when we were in college."

"He's far from home," Katie said.

They pulled up beside him and slowed to a stop.

"Looks lost," Sandra said.

Freddy glanced at them through drowsy eyes. He recognized Bex and woke up. She waved and he smiled back.

"What are you chicks doing in these parts?" Freddy slurred. "Don't you know how dangerous this neighborhood is?"

"He needs a ride," Bex said.

"Not with us!" Katie said.

"Come on, Sandra," Bex said. "Maybe we can hang out at his place and get high."

"Until his wife gets home from work and spontaneously divorces him," Sandra said. "And what about his kids?"

"They're at a babysitter, I'm sure. If he doesn't get a ride, he's going to get hurt out here."

"Goddamn it," Sandra said. She signaled for Bex to open the back door.

"Fuck," said Katie. "Come on, we're not waiting all day."

"Thanks," Freddy drawled.

"Dude, what are you even on?" Bex laughed when he was all settled in the back among the clutter. He hadn't bathed and was sweaty but smelled of patchouli. He grinned and shrugged, holding tight to the briefcase like he was transporting a bomb.

Sandra drove north.

"How are your kids?" she said. "Your wife?"

"Oh, they're fine," Freddy said. "Their aunt watches them. I sometimes take them on a stroll when I walk the dog. Wife practically lives in her office these days. Somebody has to watch them. Where are we even going?"

"Driving you back to East Side," Sandra said.

"No, no, no. I was going to meet up with a friend of mine. He fynna trade me for *this.*" He tapped the briefcase. "Not too far from here. I'll be quick. I need something to perk me up. If you ladies want, we can find a place under a bridge and party down. You like to party down, right?"

"Where is this place?" Katie said.

"On the other side of the 11th," Freddy said. "We don't actually go into it. My dad owns the company that's going to demolish and rebuild it. Stingy's been hanging out, selling from inside. It's a cool place to chill. Nobody really there except a few of his crew."

"I'm not hanging out in skid row," Sandra said. "Not part of today's festivities. Sorry, not-sorry. I'll drop you kids off if you want, but I have places to be."

"I get it," Freddy said. "I mean, anything you want, Stingy can get it for you if you're looking to trip."

Bex giggled as he took her joint and stuck it to the bottom of his lip.

"What's in the case?" Katie said.

"Some shit called Aqua," he said. "I tried it, and the back of my head was like *BOOM!* Street value of this shit is like 500K or something!"

"Holy shit!" Bex said. "How'd you get a hold of this shit? Uh. You know what? Never mind. I don't think I want to know."

"Look," Sandra said. "I'll drop you off. Bex?"

"Yeah, that's cool." Bex said.

"Aw, y'all don't wanna come hang?" Freddy said. "Don't be like that. Come on and hang. We had a blast last time. Are you even living inside the perimeter if you ain't day-tripping?"

The building they came to was an old ballroom with a round porch and entryway, guarded by high columns. It was more Grecian in design than southern plantation. Built in the 1970's and seemed out of place. Grass was overgrown on all sides, and there were young black men wearing skiing vests, big baggy pants and bandanas around their necks standing around, smoking. Some wore skull balaclavas.

"Jesus," Katie said.

"It's chill," Freddy said. He kept the suitcase close to his chest.

"Cool," Bex said excitedly.

"It's chill. I know them. You scared of black people?"

Nobody responded.

Freddy stepped out onto the sidewalk like he'd arrived at his vacation destination. Bex was climbing out when a succession of gunshots sounded to their right. There was a whizz and the sound of glass pulverized. Freddy looked in the car and there was a giant hole in Katie's forehead. It never registered because it was so sudden and out of place.

The rest was a blur, if it even happened at all.

15

CHE GUEVARA IN BOLIVIA

That same day, within the fenced perimeter of the 11th, four sobbing black boys had been lined up against a crumbling, bullet-pocked wall. Their crying faces looked out at the rubble and scrap mounds and the overgrown forest as well as their executors.

The 11th Ward housing complex was a maze of long brick stockades, vacated for decades, awaiting their eventual and inevitable bulldozing. Roofs long gone, blown off, burned down, or crumbled.

Cracked walls covered in decades worth of spray-painted epistles and obscenities. Around it, a jungle of overgrown shrubbery had taken over.

Four black youths, hands tied behind their backs, not even given the decency of a blindfold or last request and prayer or blunt to smoke. Former Hoodie boys from Godzilla's tribe caught creeping, trying to access what Stingy had set up within this tenement maze. There'd been no accords declaring what methods to use during wartime because it was every man for himself and god against all.

Stingy sat out on the cracked basketball court in his frayed wingback throne, smoking a full-bent corn pipe clogged with weed. Green lightning-shaped sunglasses covered his stoned eyes. To his right was a row of hooded accomplices holding automatics. He whistled and one by one they stepped forward, pointing them at the four boys.

Sweat suits in various colors. No logos. The young men under them wrapped their faces in bandanas. AK-47s were bulky and tacky but reminded your enemy of past historical aggressions as seen on TV: The Vietcong, FRELIMO, Taliban. AK's were war machines made to shred a man to pieces.

Stingy waved them into their range positions, not too close together. Rifles clicked then raised. The boys against the wall pleaded and cried mercy. Stingy quietly gave the *ready, aim, fire!* command and they were quickly reduced to pieces of smoldering young boys. Except for the one kid who ran off and had to be chased and brought down by handgun.

Once the smoke settled, four hoodie boys dragged an old storage trunk and placed it in front of Stingy. One of them kicked at the lock, another shot it off. Everything was suddenly quiet and very still.

Another hoodie lifted the trunk lid open and slowly, Coco Noir's face surfaced. Her hair was clumped and bound; mud crusted. Her face was dirty, her lips white and dry. When they pulled her out, she stood barefooted, her dress slashed and torn.

"Dat's da bitch," Stingy said. "Baby girl, what happened to you? How'd you get ruint up like this? That albino nigga burnt you up, didn't he?"

She looked confused, feral. Her big blue eyes scanned her surroundings: heaps of trash, piles of abandoned cars, the shredded meat of young black boys at the foot of the wall. She was too exhausted, too dehydrated to speak or scream. Shivering, she stepped out of the trunk.

"Where'd you find that trunk?" Stingy asked one of the Skulls. A line of them to his right waited for orders.

"Took it from some white people lawn. They just left it there. That couch too." He pointed to the long sleeper couch behind Stingy.

Stingy shook his head. "White folks throw out all kind a stupid shit sometimes. For instance, lookit this young beauty here. Dating a baller ain't all glitter and glammer all the time, baby girl. I would apologize for the death of your mans, but more importantly, I need to know what happened to the merchandise he was bringing to Purple

Rain. You know, that lil briefcase? Goddamn. Imagine letting a nigga named Jokerman be the transporter for some new shit. Baby girl, who'd you sell it to?"

Quivering and holding herself she took a few steps forward.

"I ain't sell shit," Coco said. She swallowed hard and gave him an even harder look.

"I got boys out there killing other boys, looking for that thing," Stingy said. "Hoodie Boys bleeding out onna street 'cause people want this briefcase. Girl, don't do me like this."

"I lost it...after Joker died." Coco's voice was a deep rasp, echoing in the trash canyon. "I don't fucking know where it went!"

"Who else you fucking?" Stingy said.

Coco glanced at him angrily. She shook her head vigorously.

"Who'd you go with after that nigga died?"

"I-I went home," she said. "My heart was broken."

"A hoe ain't got no home."

"Your boys, they came and got me and..." she sobbed. "My head wasn't right after the fight. I forgot all about the briefcase. I was just holding it. Wasn't mine to protect."

"Well, the shit was missing when we got there, so where the fuck it go?"

Coco shook her head. "I swear, I don't..."

Stingy sucked his gold teeth. "Dang, that's a goddamn waste of a thick white girl. But I can't play witchoo right now, hoe. Get yo' ass on over there with them dead boys. You ain't gonna feel a thing."

Coco had trouble standing. One of the Skulls dragged her over by the pile of dead boys. She squirmed among the offal and steaming body parts. Stingy shook his head at her. One of the Skulls leaned in and told him,

"Why don't we try the *thing*."

Stingy turned and faced him. "Yeah!" He agreed and pointed an excited finger at him. He looked over at another of his minions who sat next to a wooden ordnance crate placed by a trash heap.

"They ain't ready for this," said Stingy. He waved at the Skull to bring over the crate and open it. Piece by piece the Skull took out a bipod, shell box and bullet belt.

"This mufucka came off the top of a humvie," the Skull said. He read inside the crate. "*MK43.*"

"Nigga, you know how to put that together?" Stingy said.

"Yeah, chief," the Skull said. "It's already built. Just gotta *assemble* it."

"You read the instructions?"

"Don't need to. There's pictures."

"Better for us, then." Stingy laughed. "Y'all niggas can't read no way."

Two Skulls carried the heavy machine gun and placed it in front of where Stingy sat.

"Go at it, chief." One Skull said.

"Aight." Stingy handed his pipe to his assistant, rubbed his hands on his pants and embraced the dusty machine gun. He tried to lift it, realized its weight, and then adjusted it. He panned as far left as he could. There was an old rotted wooden fence and gate that gave people from the street access to the 11th. He checked the scope, blew some of the dust off and squeezed the trigger.

Ten rounds burst and the recoil knocked him back. The MK fell on its side and his crowd stood around plugging their ears.

"Gotdamn!" Stingy said, clapping. "Shit! Line them up. Round me up some Hoodies and line them up!"

Coco pressed back as far against the wall as she could, already defeated.

"Fuck I say?" said Stingy.

The massacre had left a lot of the Skulls a little soft, leaning over and vomiting. They weren't aware that the human body could be turned inside out and raw like those boys had been. The way their insides exploded onto the dirt and grass and trash. The way their skulls collapsed under a thousand hammers strikes, arms severed, and legs chopped from under them.

"Goddamn," Stingy said. He turned his face and spit. "Keep that shit loaded. Let them pussy ass Hoodies come at us. See what they get."

He centered the machine gun at Coco.

"Y'all get the fuck out," Stingy said. "Get out there and bring me back my shit."

Skulls scrambled outside the fence. There was screaming coming from the street. White people screaming.

16

THE IDIOTS

"We been driving all afternoon, pretending to buy drugs," Flames said. He yawned and closed his eyes. "If I'm getting paid for this, I can keep doing it as long as you need me to."

"Gotta get the merch first," Dead Johnny said. He was monotone but focused.

Sundown Atlanta glittered like a tired Christmas tree right before it gets tossed to the curb. Midtown and Downtown were luminescent, but the inner urban areas stayed dim, haunted by low streetlamps and hobo fires.

"Fuck are we waiting for?" Brett said.

Dead Johnny's face remained solemn as he drove. He studied every corner carefully, checking anyone walking around who looked like they didn't belong. Much like three white men and one Samoan driving in an Olds 98. Collectively they watched for anyone with a suitcase

340

who wasn't a tourist. Flames' face looked troubled. Like he was about to cry. But that was his face. He bit his thumbnail and kept low in his seat.

Dim light posts made the streets glow pink. The 11th looked like a medieval hamlet left to crumble under an economic apocalypse.

"Reminds me of Baltimore," Brett said. "And not in the best way. Can't believe they haven't leveled all this."

"They need to nuke it out of existence," Flames said.

"Started out as a prison, then became low-income housing for blacks," Brett said. "Then the Olympics came and forced them out."

"I remember," said Pike.

The Olds snaked up the curvature of a narrow road. Dump road. Piles of tires, discarded sofas, bookshelves and a mound of toilets within the shrubbery and trees.

"If they see our faces, we're fucked," Brett said.

"They've already seen us, man." Flames said. "Word is out that a bunch of white boys are looking for a lost briefcase."

"Even if they have it, or him, they're not going to give it up easily," Brett said. "I mean, would you?"

"Shotguns would be great for this," Pike said.

Flames let out a nervous chuckle. "Or Tech-9's, Uzi's, whatever."

Dead Johnny stopped the car. The ten-foot fence surrounding of the 11th had a tall gate located northside. Chained and blocked off but opened enough to allow anyone to slip inside, low enough to climb over.

Flames ran to the gate. With headlights bright on him he yanked the chain, but it didn't give. He ran back to Johnny's side of the car.

"Uh, bolt cutters?" He said.

Dead Johnny popped the trunk and flipped his thumb back. Across the high beams, Flames ran holding long bolt cutters. He clipped the chain effortlessly, dragged the gate open, ran back to the trunk, shut it and got in the car. The Olds rolled over fallen tree branches, garbage, and scrap metal. Dead Johnny shut off the headlights and they sailed, nary a lamplight to guide them.

"Gentlemen, say a prayer... or four," Dead Johnny said. "*Armed with a burning patience, we shall enter the splendid Cities...*"

"Is that Jim Morrison?" Flames said.

Dead Johnny looked at him. "No, it's some guy name *Rambo*."

The car crept around the maze of brick tenements overgrown with vines, covered in graffiti. The boards had been pulled from all the broken windows to use as kindle. Furniture left behind by previous tenants had been pulled into the parking lots and burned. Electrical wiring, piping, siding, and roofing long gone.

To the northeast one of the tenements glowed.

"Where's that light coming from?" Flames pointed. Fire flickered behind the building, glowing orange. The light cast shadows and moving silhouettes to the other side.

"They look like dancing owls," Brett said. "With guns."

"We're rolling into a trap," Flames said. "We should head back."

Dead Johnny didn't speak. He drove slowly into what amounted to a smoldering netherworld.

"They do this once a month," Pike leaned close to the front seat, seeing what they were seeing. "Just a traditional fire."

"Natives are restless," Flames said.

No one said anything further.

17

SKULLS

While the sun was setting and Head lay dead in front of the taco place, a couple of Skulls had driven off with Savage's Altima. They chased Nickel down several streets as he'd cut and run between blocks. The car rounded the corner and skidded to a halt when they spotted him frozen with panic. All he could do was stand there and stare, pissing his pants.

Three of them, wearing skull masks jumped out of the Altima waving guns and shouting at him. They pointed their guns, surrounding him.

Shots came from behind them.

Peaches and Herb crossed toward them, both holding revolvers, giving the skulls the business from behind. Skulls had completely missed them. One of them turned and shot back. Herb had stepped in front of Peaches and got shot in his thigh. He'd never walk the same after that. Never play kickball again.

Peaches' war call echoed the block. She went in for the kill, shooting the Skull in the throat. He dropped his gun, both hands at his neck, bleeding between his knotted fingers. She stepped closer and shot his face. Nose and mouth collapsed into the void of his head. He collapsed among the other freshly killed Skulls.

Nickel watched, mouth agape.

"Move, muthafucka!" Peaches yelled and ran back to Herb. He squeezed his thigh, crying and yelling. Blood trailed behind him, puddling in the street. Nickel stepped over the dead Skulls, looking down at Herb.

"Call an ambulance!" Nickel said.

"*Hell, no!*" Herb objected.

"Nigga, take an ambulance or lose your leg," Peaches said, gun still hot in her hand.

Herb leaned back over the gutter, huffing, crying, and spitting. Blood trickled out between his fingers.

Peaches lifted him up and with Nickel's help they took him to the Altima, which was still running. Nickel sat up front with her as

Herb bled out in the backseat. She sped off, got as far as the next block when a gold Caprice t-boned them at the intersection. Two Skulls jumped out of the Caprice, shooting out the back window. Herb suddenly convulsed in his seat, bullets ripping into him. Peaches ducked down in her seat, low as she could. Nickel popped his door open and slipped out. Peaches followed him, bullets streaming past them. They ran along the fence enclosing the southern edge of the 11th. Skulls close behind. Peaches managed to shoot and wound one of them. Nickel ran ahead and found a loose opening at the bottom of the fence only he knew about. She helped him yank the fence upward and they slipped through, tumbling head-over-ass over each other, rolling down into the basin. They fumbled over old furniture and scrap metal along the way before they came to a stop at the trunk of a red cedar. She pushed him against the trunk and held him there. Gunshots popped around them. She put a finger at her lips to keep him silent. They waited. Above them on the street, tires squealed. They listened as the Caprice pulled away from the wreckage.

When they were gone, she said,

"Okay, little man, we have to wait it out."

Gunfire popped from the center of the 11th near the basketball courts. Atlanta always had nightly fireworks, but this sounded different. This sounded like combat.

"Guess, yo' man ain't make it," Nickel said.

They could barely see each other in the fading light. But he knew there were tears rolling down her face.

18

WHITE DEVIL

Before the smoking machine gun stood two white women, crying into each other's faces, holding one another like they were set to be thrown in a cauldron and cooked by local cannibals. In front of them was a white devil all strung out, hair scraggly. Man Bun. Freaky Freddy. One of the messiest, smelliest white men Stingy had ever met. Surrounding them was a circle of Skulls pointing guns.

"We try and try." Stingy sucked his teeth at them. "To keep these streets clean and safe. But when it rains, seems that a bunch of white trash always washes up into the 'hood. You folks came to the wrong pharmacy today."

Freaky Freddy stood twitchy but cool, chewing the remains of his fingernails. The group was sprinkled with blood, sparkling with small bits of Katie's brain.

"Like Willard to Kurtz..." Freddy mumbled.

Stingy looked at him. "What you say, cracker?"

"Look man, you are absolutely right," Freddy said. "We understand you were just cleaning up when we happened to arrive. But,

I'm here for business purposes. I don't give a shit about what goes on in here."

He lifted the silver briefcase, and someone snatched it and handed it to Stingy.

"See, I was bringing this to you to offer a trade," Freddy said.

"Trade?" Stingy laughed. "Mufucka, this belongs to *us.*"

"I mean, I'm tryna get me and my lady friends here fucked up, fam. We tryna roast and roll."

"Nigga, you ain't seen what's inside it? You stupider that you look, and you look like shit, *white devil.*"

"Now, that's kind of racist," Freaky Freddy said. "Don't you think, chief?"

"Freddy!" Sandra yelled. *"Shut the fuck up!"*

"Dang," Stingy said. He looked at his crew. "Ain't never heard a white woman scream like that. You nasty, girl. I can tell. Bring them over here to this couch."

Sandra and Bex held each other tightly.

Skulls obeyed.

Stingy opened the case, revealing a giant bag of what looked like aquarium aqua-scaping. Nothing glittery, just crystalline turquoise rocks.

"You been carrying these around and you ain't try one?" Stingy said, shaking his head.

"I mean, I sampled a few." Freddy giggled. "I ain't stupid, man. I know what don't belong to me and I knew there'd be a reward for returning it."

Stingy looked at him. "Ain't nobody say shit about a reward, you raggedy ass, rat cracker. Ain't never seen a dirtier, nastier, roguish rat. What make you think you deserve a reward?"

"You work for Purple Rain, right?"

"Don't mean shit," Stingy said. "You one of those, *I know the owner'* crackers?"

"I know my people."

"Ain't nobody here 'your people', *cracker.* You hipsters know exactly how to cash in on what's coming, don't you?"

"I knew it'd be worth something once I found it," Freddy said.

"You one roguish nigga," Stingy said. "Just took that case like it was yours."

"But I'm a smart *nigga,* 'cause I knew to return it to its owner."

"Gotdamn shame. You made me kill that thick white girl for nothing."

Freddy looked at the wall with the bullet holes, covered in human hamburger meat. Skulls were busy carrying away body parts, shoveling bloody remains. His expression was impartial, apathetic. They carried off the remains of a woman.

"I didn't take it from her, *per se,*" Freaky Freddy said. "But I took it when it was *abandoned.*"

Stingy didn't hear him. He pointed to the bloody mess.

"That could be you and your ladies there," he said. "You might just be a smart rat, you dumb ass cracker."

"You can keep your reward," Freddy said. "I just want a sit-down with the man himself, *Purple Rain*."

"Erbody do." Stingy laughed. "Don't mean it's gonna happen. Whatchoo think gonna happen?"

Before Freddy could answer, Skulls blasted boom boxes and brought out jugs of purple drink. Fires roasted in metal containers. They partied like it was the end of the world.

19

ALONE TOGETHER

Peaches wanted to light one up, but Herb had the stash, and he was dead in the Altima, up in the street.

"It's just two blocks separating these territories," Nickel said, pacing and kicking rocks in the basin. All dirt and trash down here. Decades of neglect had turned the lot into an illegal dumping ground. Along with slabs of concrete and crumbling cinderblocks, there were crushed washing machines, televisions, bisected cars, and broken furniture. "Niggas wanna kill each other over some old, cracked sidewalks and trash piles."

The metallic drone of cicadas clashed with the high-pitched siren of crickets. Peaches welcomed the deafening thrum. She sat beneath the cedar tree sobbing silently.

The street above was silent. Ambulance hadn't shown and no cops either. The 11th may as well have been walled in, isolated as it was from the rest of the city.

She wiped her sniffling nose with the back of her hand.

"It ain't the block, lil man," she said, following his pacing silhouette. "It's the habit. It's just business."

"You slinging too."

"I was. You?"

"Nah," Nickel said. "My brother Head was."

"I know Head. Started out about your age."

Nickel walked back to her. "You a beautiful lady. Why you slinging?"

"Been my life," she said. "What I look like got nothing to do with my business. My brothers was slingers. They gone. Jail. Dead. My man got me a good corner, now he gone."

Their eyes were bright in the darkness.

Nickel said, "I wanted to drive an ice cream truck and sling out the side. Don't care 'bout that no more. My brother's dead." His face looked troubled. Aged. "We gonna stay here all night? I'm hungry."

"Sorry 'bout Head, lil man."

Peaches' eyes had finally adjusted to darkness. She checked Herb's gun. Two shells left in it. Hers was empty but she had a six-round reloader in her purse. She dumped the empty shells and reloaded.

"You got guns," Nickel said. "We can just shoot our way out, *pow pow pow!*"

"Too many of them, lil man."

"Can I hold one?"

She closed the cylinder and held a gun in each hand. "You crazy, boy?"

He sat beside her when the coo-cooing began.

"Owls," he said.

"Them ain't owls," said Peaches. Though the shadows casted against the walls almost convinced her of them. Voices and screams carried from the other side of the building in front of them. Something tribal and ritualistic it sounded like.

"Restless niggas," she said. "Ain't even Saturday night. This might be the night they finally set fire to the 11th Ward and burn it to the ground."

20

BEX

Wood and trash burned inside the old steel drums, casting flames out of the courtyard where Stingy, Skulls, Freaky Freddy and the girls dawdled. They'd been at it all night, into dawn.

Sandra was catatonic in her corner of the ragged couch. Freddy sat beside her, oblivious to anything but his own vibes. Bex sat closest to Stingy, giggling, sticking her tongue out, even as Katie's body gathered flies over where the other bodies were laid. Sandra looked at her to understand her lack of response to their friend's death, but Bex was enjoying herself too much to notice. Her eyes and face were lit and enchanted. She been slipped something.

One of the Skulls came over and whispered something to Stingy.

Stingy announced,

"Pack this shit up and bug out."

His minions raised like cockroaches, carrying the MK43 off to the east of the courtyard. A dozen or more of them marched behind Stingy. Four of them carried his wingback throne for him. They came to a tall mound of gravel and scrap metal and camped there. The trash hill overlooked a field that opened like a runway. The city skyline could be seen from there. Lit like a birthday party for the elite.

Stingy arrived at the top of the hill with Bex proudly at his side. He had his arm around her, looking at her lovingly. Then more so at the MK43, which they'd propped up on a pile of bricks.

"We prepared for this very moment," Stingy said. Skulls surrounded him, made eerie by the way the fire lit up their skeleton masks.

Stingy said, "Hey, white girl, wanna give it a shot?"

Bex laughed. "Fuck yeah!"

He stood her behind the machine gun and held her arms. "Don't pull. *Squeeze* that mufucka."

She peeped through the scope at an oncoming car as it entered the basin. Its lights were off but distant lighting reflected the chromium trimming.

"This the biggest gun I ever shot!" she said, sticking her tongue out.

Sandra was among the rubble sobbing. Freddy stood behind Stingy and Bex, head buzzing, but not as much as Bex's head buzzed, with everything moving in slow motion with every round of artillery she let off.

Down in the field below, the Olds 98 swerved and sparked. Windshield shattered. Immediate blood spatter. The car u-turned and circled, squeaking, and limping along. It rounded some figure-of-eights and then stayed circling.

Skulls cheered and high-fived each other. There was a chorus of, *"Let me try!"* and *"I call next!"*

They'd all left their posts just to watch the white girl destroy the Olds.

Not far from where they cheered, there was motion on the sidelines. Behind mounds of debris, trees shook. Over the fence. Hoodies moving in the night. From the open slits in the perimeter fence, Crash and the Hoodie Mob had descended the scrapyard basin with Mac-10's, Tech-9's and Glocks sputtering.

Skulls formed a protective barrier around Stingy but started to fall almost immediately when the gunfire started up. Bex let the MK43 rip again, taking out at least half a dozen Hoodies before they reached the hilltop and slaughtered her. When she was later identified they found almost thirty rounds of lead inside her.

Freddy ran downhill like a wounded chicken before Hoodies came up behind him and tore him apart with their machine guns.

Skulls retreated downhill.

Stingy ran, losing his sunglasses. *"Yo, where my motherfucking briefcase? Where the other white girl at?"*

Skulls dropped all around him, bodies twisting and bursting with from gun flack. Hoodies came out of the dark, knocking them off like arcade ducks. Crash stormed through the rest of them with a pump shotgun.

Louder than fireworks. Stingy grabbed one of the Skulls to use as a shield, shooting blindly at all comers. He managed to shoot a few of his own crew before he ran through the trash maze, escaping out the back.

21

LAST EXIT

"Who's hit?" Dead Johnny finally asked. He stopped the car and looked at Pike, who was gushing blood from his shoulder and a large hole in his head. With his head twisted to the right, his flapping tongue seemed to be lapping at his shoulder. The door on his side was riddled with bullet holes.

The car finally wobbled to a stop. Dead Johnny looked on the passenger seat and Flames had balled up between the floor and seat. The back door opened, and Brett scrambled out and booked it.

"Later, dudes."

They never saw him again.

Dead Johnny yelled but gunfire muted him. Radiator hissed. The car tilted on two flat tires.

"If we die, they'll never find us in here." Flames cried.

"I ain't leaving my car here," said Dead Johnny. "Shit. I got hit. It's okay. Just got the tip of my boot."

"Lucky motherfucker. Without that briefcase, we're not getting paid. You owe me, you bastard."

"Fuck it. Send me an invoice. Let them kill each other for it." Dead Johnny limped out of the hissing car. He dragged Pike out of the back and onto the pavement and quickly got back in. He put the car in reverse and slowly drove backwards. When he was sure they were no longer a target, he sped up, wobbling on blown out tires, driving back through the gates, up the winding road and back to civilization. He drove as fast as the car allowed until it came to an abrupt stop a mile away.

"Don't push it man," Flames said. "It's dead."

"You might be right. You still want tacos?"

"I don't think so. I already shit my pants."

22

LAST CALL

Gunfire, louder than the 4th of July. The sky was smoky. The color of jade. Peaches had little time to react or respond. The gunfire was denser than before. Closer than before. Made their ears ring. Random bullets sparked off concrete close to where they were. Louder that downtown Bagdad during an American campaign.

She leaned against the tree, hugging Nickel to her body. She smelled his sweat, he smelled her fading perfume and powdery breasts.

A man came running out of nowhere, sweating, cursing, but gleefully laughing. He stopped and looked back at the warzone. He was huffing, hyperventilating. He spit and then vomited. And kept laughing.

"Fuck it," he said and fired his gun in the air, but it was empty.

"Pussy-ass bitch," Peaches said and stepped out of the shadow like she was part of the tree.

"Fuck you say?" Stingy rotated his head slowly and could swear in that last moment of being alive that he could see the bullet corkscrewing the air just before it entered the middle of his face.

Dawn.

Sun arrived early. Peaches and Nickel crawled up the incline, slid past the opening in the fence and were back on the street.

Someone else jumped through the fence hole onto the sidewalk behind them. A white woman smudged and in disarray. Peaches didn't hesitate to put two bullets in Sandra as she clutched the silver briefcase in both arms. Sandra fell to her side, still holding it.

Peaches pushed Nickel aside and grabbed the case. They looked around, listened for sirens, and crossed the street, heading east on Winton Terrace.

ABOUT THE AUTHORS

JEAN-PAUL L. GARNIER

is the owner of Space Cowboy Books bookstore and publishing house, producer of *Simultaneous Times Podcast* (2023 Laureate Award Winner, BSFA Finalist), and editor of the SFPA's *Star*Line* magazine. He is also the deputy editor-in-chief of *Worlds of IF* magazine & the soon to be relaunched *Galaxy* magazine. In 2024, he won the Laureate Award for Best Editor. He has written many books of poetry and science fiction. https://spacecowboybooks.com/

ALEX SLUSAR

is a writer of crime and neo-Western fiction. His work has previously appeared in *Grain, Saddlebag Dispatches, Starlite Pulp Review* and the anthology *Between Hell and Tombstone.* Hailing from the Canadian prairies, he is a member of the Saskatchewan Writers Guild and was selected for the SWG Mentorship Program in 2022. Apart from writing, Alex has worked in national politics and is a reserve Navy officer. He divides his time between Montreal, Quebec and Saskatoon, Saskatchewan.

MANNY TORRES

is an Atlanta, Georgia, transplant from Brooklyn, New York. His crime-noir books include *Dead Dogs, Father Was a Rat King, Perras Malas*, and *Cabrones Perros.* You can find his short stories in Starlite Pulp Review #3 and #4, and the anthologies *Bishop Rider Lives* and *Elegies in the Dust.* His new novel, *A*

Simmering Dissonance is a companion piece to *The Idiot Caper,* which is featured in this omnibus.

He enjoys painting, photography, watching films, the music of King Crimson, and looking after several cats. You can find him on Twitter @_MATorres_ and Instagram @_m.a.torres

BRIAN TOWNSLEY

is an award-winning writer, as well as a podaster, and the Executive Editor for Starlite Pulp. He is the author of the crime fiction books *A Trunk Full of Zeroes* and *Outlaw Ballads,* as well as three books of poetry. His short fiction has appeared in various publications, including *Mystery Tribune, Black Mask, Quarterly West, Frontier Tales, Connecticut Review,* and many others, and had a story make the distinguished list in *Best American Mystery Stories, 2019.* He is a graduate of the Professional Writing Program at USC and is also an alum of the mighty California Golden Bears. He and his wife share their time between the mountains and deserts of Southern California. www.starlitepulp.com

361

Also from Starlite Pulp:

Starlite Pulp Reviews #1-4

Praise for the Review:

"Pulp fiction in all its glory."

"An excellent first Review!"

"Starlite Pulp is the most exciting new publisher on the block."

Outlaw Ballads by Brian Townsley
A Sonny Haynes collection

Praise for *Outlaw Ballads*:

"Sonny Haynes deserves a seat at the bar next to Marlowe and Spade."

"Townsley takes readers on a film noir-style tour to the early '50's in Palm Springs, California, that bears little resemblance to the Los Angeles many of us know so well. The Sonny Haynes series acts as a mental time machine, and is worth every minute of the trip."

"Sonny Haynes did what other men boasted of."

Visit **Starlitepulp.com** for your pulp books, hoodies, tees, decals, submission guidelines, & so much more!